# TRAITOR TO THE BLOOD

The door slammed open and Pirs came striding in. There was a bloodstained bandage on his head and another on his arm. His face was so tight with rage that the bones seemed to be leaping against the skin. He nodded perfunctorily at his father, went bounding up the steps to the second table, nodding tightly at his wife, grabbed hold of Kulyari's arm and jerked her from the chair. Ignoring her protests, he took her up the short flight of stairs to the main dais, flung her to the floor in front of Angakirs. "I will not have this THING in my house. She called my moves to my enemy and I was brought near to death. She is traitor to the Blood."

Kulyari was so startled by all this that at first she could only grasp and struggle; she was frightened now. "No, no, lies, no," she cried; she pushed up onto her knees. "It's lies, all of it, I didn't . . . the Blood, no. . . ." Without trying to get up, she swung round and held out her arms toward Rintirry. "Tell them. . . ."

Rintirry shoved his chair back, came round the table.

Kulyari let her arms drop, her mouth widened into a triumphant smile.

He caught hold of her hair, jerked her head up and cut her throat. "Traitors die. That's what I say."

# JO CLAYTON
## in DAW Books:

A BAIT OF DREAMS
SHADOW OF THE WARMASTER

**SHADITH'S QUEST**
SHADOWPLAY
SHADOWSPEER
SHADOWKILL

**THE DIADEM SERIES**
DIADEM FROM THE STARS
LAMARCHOS
IRSUD
MAEVE
STAR HUNTERS
THE NOWHERE HUNT
GHOSTHUNT
THE SNARES OF IBEX
QUESTER'S ENDGAME

**THE DUEL OF SORCERY TRILOGY**
MOONGATHER
MOONSCATTER
CHANGER'S MOON

**THE SOUL DRINKER TRILOGY**
DRINKER OF SOULS
BLUE MAGIC
A GATHERING OF STONES

**THE SKEEN TRILOGY**
SKEEN'S LEAP
SKEEN'S RETURN
SKEEN'S SEARCH

# SHADOWKILL

## JO CLAYTON

**DAW BOOKS, INC.**
DONALD A. WOLLHEIM, FOUNDER
375 Hudson Street, New York, NY 10014

**ELIZABETH R. WOLLHEIM
SHEILA E. GILBERT
PUBLISHERS**

DAW Book Collectors No. 847.

First Printing, April 1991

1 2 3 4 5 6 7 8 9

DAW TRADEMARK REGISTERED
U.S. PAT OFF AND FOREIGN COUNTRIES
—MARCA REGISTRADA,
MECHO EN U.S.A.

PRINTED IN THE U.S.A.

# PROLOG

1

Shadith woke in the hold of a ship

She was lying on a pallet, canvas, something like that.

Naked. Half frozen.

Sometime before . . . while she was out . . . she'd been beaten . . . raped . . . brutally . . . she was torn, septic, she could feel the heat of the infections, the blood oozing from the wounds.

She lay in filth and stench, she hadn't been catheterized, just left where they threw her.

She'd been fed, watered, there were tubes taped to her face, running into her nose.

They wanted her alive, but broken.

They. Who?

Ginny?

She shifted position slightly, felt feces squishing under her.

When she had her stomach in order, she looked around.

Stasis pods, dozens of them, hundreds, all around her.

She *reached*.

The lifesparks in those pods were dim; most of them she couldn't recognize, but Rohant was there, nearest her. Azram. Tolmant. Nezrakam. Kinefray. Tejnar. Ginny.

Ginny?

She looked more closely at the strangers, picked up a faintly familiar ''smell,'' connected it to one of those clients she'd watched glide past her when she was in that corridor.

Ginny and his clients. Prisoners?

What's happening here?

Prisoners or passengers?

Ginny wouldn't tolerate stasistime. I know him. This isn't his ship. He wouldn't go anywhere on someone else's ship. I know him.

Prisoner. It has to be prisoner.

Who?

Never mind. Time for that later.

Her hands were fettered, but she had a little play in the filament that joined the cuffs.

Her feet were free.

She rolled off the pallet, used her feet to push it aside, then drew herself up so her hands were close to her nose.

She pulled the tubes free.

It was painful, sickening, but she got them out.

She used the water tube to wash herself.

It took a long time, but she managed to get her body reasonably clean.

She was cold, half frozen, the chill from the metal she lay on struck up through her flesh into her bones, but she was clean.

Using her feet, she got the pallet turned over, the bottom side was filthy and stained, but hospital hygienic compared to the mess she'd been lying in.

She clamped her teeth on the water tube, used her feet and knees to find the food drip and maneuver it into her mouth, then she slid the pallet over and stretched out on it. It was warmer and softer than the floor, not much but enough. She sucked on the food tube and began to feel almost human.

Kikun, she thought suddenly. I didn't *touch* him. Or Rose. Dead? Or what?

She went painstakingly around the hold once more, touching each of the lifesparks. They were all there, except Lissorn who was dead. Ginny was there. His clients. And this time she located Ajeri the Pilot. All there but Kikun. And Autumn Rose.

He slipped them.

Clever little lizard. Took Rose with him. I hope. Unless she's as dead as Lissorn.

He'll come after us, I know it. Yes.

All right.

They mean to break me any way they can.

Let them try.

2

She lay and *listened,* using the ears and eyes of spiders and other small vermin.

## 3

She lay and thought.

Slowly, carefully she began building *THE PLACE THAT COULD NOT BE TOUCHED*.

Slowly, carefully she withdrew HERSELF within *THE PLACE*, pulling memory and everything else vital to who she was inside the armor she'd built to protect herself from the interrogators that waited for her.

Mindwipe waited for her, where her memories would be evoked then unreeled and dissolved. A competent tech could strip a mind clean in a few hours, yet leave the organic machine intact, the basic intelligence unmarred—or mostly so—ready for reprogramming and resale.

*COME COME, SEE THE FINE BARGAIN. ONE FLESH MACHINE, FEMALE, FRESH FROM THE USED BODY SHOP.*

She hid from the Probe and dreamed another life for herself, leaving it for THEM to find.

*Yes, you creeps, you've got the body, but that's all you'll get. Break me, will you? You can try, then you watch your asses, they're mine.*

She set the wake-trigger, *(KIKUN: See Kikun and Know Again)* then she closed the last gap in the wall of *THE PLACE* and slept.

# CHASE:
# Autumn Rose and Kikun break free and start the long trek after the fiends who've taken their friends

1

A faint sting. Then PAIN!

Autumn Rose came swimming out of fog into a prickly awareness that she was in deep shit and there wasn't much she could do about it.

A hand dropped on her mouth.

Her eyes cleared and she saw Kikun's face, shining orange eyes ringed with white. He was in a panic, but controlling it.

He brought his head down near hers, whispered, "Can you walk?" Despite his caution the whisper hit the walls and the vaulted ceiling and came back to her as muted clicks and hollow oos, melding uncomfortably with the scrape of his boots, the clatter of something against metal.

Her face went hot and tight. She'd stunned her own foot trying to get a guard, it was such a stupid thing. . . . She didn't bother answering him, just concentrated on seeing if she could move her toes; her boots knocked against the hard floor covering, her pants leg brushed heavily over the thick black cloth of the robe she wore, the sounds multiplied by that goertafl'cht echo chamber, startling her, giving her an adrenal jolt that helped clear some of the fug from her head.

Right foot, fine. Left leg below the knee might as well be a block of wood. She bent her left knee, sighed with relief. As long as she had the knee, the rest didn't matter. She pushed his hand off her mouth. "Can't run races," she muttered at him, "but I can get it going. What. . . ."

"Not now." He straightened, stepped back, stumbled over the body of a dead guard, caught himself, shivering at the noises his feet made.

She rolled onto her knees, thrust her hand at him. "Help me."

8

He eased his shoulder under her arm and pushed up. Small-boned and shorter than Rose, with the racy leanness of a garden lizard, he didn't look as if he could lift an undersize cat, but she came off that floor so much faster than she expected, she nearly went over on her face.

He got her limping along as fast as she could manage and guided her through the guards' bodies, across the anteroom, and into the shiny tarted-up corridor beyond.

She helped as much as she could; what she'd seen before she went down was coming back to her, giving her cramps in her stomach and a powerful urge to get the hell out of there.

*Stun rifle held with deceptive casualness under his right arm (where he could get it up and working in half a breath) the merc strolled toward them. "Now, friends, you know better. The room's not ready yet, just turn yourself around and come back tomorrow."*

*Shadith yelled and shot him.*

*The Dyslaerors shot before her yell died out and the other mercs went down.*

*An alarm started yelping.*

*The instant Shadow yelled, Azram got his arms around one of the metal benches and charged the opening, getting there before the metal doors could slide shut; he dropped the bench on the slide tracks and went plunging through as the doors kept trying to shut, whining and slamming repeatedly at the bench. Shadow jumped the dead and went running after him. Lissorn went screaming past her, tearing off his cowl, clawing out of the robe. He'd forgotten everything but Ginny.*

*Autumn Rose swore and ran after him, went down as she tripped over a dead guard, stayed down as the rest of the Dyslaerors stepped over her.*

*Rohant roared his own rage as he got stuck in the gradually narrowing space between the doors as they beat at and crushed the bench between them. He freed himself and plunged inside.*

*Rose rolled onto her knees.*

*A hand grabbed her ankle.*

*She twisted around, shot along her leg, swore again as she hit her foot as well as the guard.*

*She pushed up, went limping to the door. She crawled over*

*the bench, swung herself inside, her leg dead from the knee down.*

*Lissorn was racing toward Ginny, stunner forgotten, claws out. He was only a few steps away, but the man wasn't moving; he stood watching unperturbed near the front rank of the pulochairs. It seemed to Autumn Rose he was more interested in the degree of his attacker's rage than in any danger to himself. Directing his own death? Ginny Seyirshi's last and best?*

*No.*

*He raised a hand.*

*Four cutters flashed from overlooks, hit Lissorn in midstride.*

*For an instant the Dyslaeror was a black core in the furnace where the beams met, then they winked out and there was nothing left, not even dust.*

*Rohant roared, his great voice filling that room. He lifted the stun pistol.*

*The other Dyslaerors spread in a broad arc, converging on Ginny.*

*Shadow stood at the edge of the bidfloor, staring at Ginny. He turned, nodded at her, started to lift a hand. . . .*

*Autumn Rose shivered, touched her head. . . .*

*A hand closed on her arm, small, warm. . . .*

*Pulled at her . . . no . . . she couldn't move. . . .*

*Oppression . . . her head, her head. . . .*

*Things moving slow . . . ly . . . slooow . . . ly. . . .*

*slooow . . . lyyy. . . .*

*Blackness. . . .*

*Nothing. . . .*

She remembered and understood. Null vibrator—they must have triggered it when they went charging in. Or Ginny had. . . .

Null-field. She bit her lip, her head wasn't working right, field must be operating still, on low power to keep the lid clamped down.

Kikun. The Null hadn't affected him. *Odd. What's happening? Who's doing this? Ginny? He went down, I saw him go down. That means diddly. He killed Lissorn. Why'd he kill Lissorn if. . . .*

The corridor was empty. She was surprised at first, then annoyed at herself. Kikun wouldn't be taking her along here

crippled up like she was in her head and leg if the way
wasn't clear. Clear for now, but not for long. . . . There
was a powerful urgency in him, he was almost carrying her.
*Shayss damn, my head's not working.* She couldn't seem to
concentrate on anything, mind skittering about hibbity dibb-
ity.

He hauled her out onto the gallery, dragged her a few feet
along it and pushed through ragged draperies into a room
thick with rat droppings and cobwebs and the kind of smell
you get down an alley on any skidder road.

"Egya cill'haiya, Rose. Missuk shai gavan cillahai'."

She stared at him, the syllables sliding off as if her brain
were waxed to a high gloss and impermeable. Slid off and
fell dead—echoes were paralyzed in here, like everything
else in this catafalque of a room.

He hissed and shook her. "Dyslaer," he breathed. "You
know it."

"Oh." She forced herself to concentrate. "Say again."
She stumbled over the Dyslaer words, repeated them. "Say
again."

"We have to have a ship, Rose. We have to get out of
here."

She rubbed at her head. The stench was hideous, every
breath gave her stomach spasms, and her knee was hurting
more by the minute. She shifted her stunned leg; moving
eased it a little. *Think, Rose, think.* "Shadow. . . ."

"She was too far in." His eyes glazed over. "I had to
leave her. If we're taken, there's no one to follow. . . ."

"Follow who?"

"Does it matter?"

She brushed at a bit of dusty cobweb clinging to her hand,
shuddered as she saw the desiccated corpses of half a dozen
spiders. She loathed spiders. "There're the Capture Ships
out beyond the Limit. We could call one in."

"No."

She heard the anguish in his voice and didn't press. "I'm
fogged, Kuna, I don't know . . . what's happening?"

"Don't you understand? I don't know. I don't know anything." His slitted nostrils fluttered, the muscles of his face
worked under the soft loose skin. "I'm following voices
. . . no . . . it's not . . . I'm not . . . listen to me. We have
to get out of here." The panic was beginning to break
through his control.

"Klar, 's klar, Kuna. Calm down. Let me see. . . ." She looked at her robe. It was filthy with dust and thick soft webs, but those would shake off well enough. The privacy fields in their cowls were gone—from the burns on her neck which were starting to hurt like bites from the devil, the Null must have shorted hers out when she went down.

They could pull the cowls forward and avoid lighted areas, it might be enough.

"You have your tools?" She shook her head. "Of course you have or you couldn't 've popped me awake. Any idea where the nearest shuttleport is? Vision or whatever, we'll run with it."

He dropped to a squat, closed his eyes, pressed his hands hard against them.

She went to the door, stood beside it listening. Heavy silence. Not even the scratch and scrabble of vermin. She could hear her own heart beating, could hear Kikun's too-rapid breathing. Then a sound like a door closing, a clang of metal against metal. Footsteps. Someone talking, word fragments, scattered, nothing she could make out.

A hand closed round her arm.

She started, swallowed a yelp.

"I see it," he whispered at her, the *see* hissing against her ear. She flinched, she didn't much like snakes. "Let's go," he said, pushed past the torn curtains, and scurried off along the gallery.

Rose grimaced, limped after him, catching up with him when he stopped at a gate into the pneumotube system. He reached for the caller.

She caught at his arm. "Wait," she said. "What about alarms?"

"If there are, there are." He pulled loose, tapped the square. "You want to walk a thousand kays?"

"Nothing closer?"

He made a small irritated hiss, but didn't say anything.

She tried a grin, small to match his hiss. "Be kind, Li'l Liz, and consider it the Null-effect."

2

Kikun took her on a twisting, roundabout route across the gutted worldship.

Between pneumotubes, he tugged her along faster and

faster, ignoring her protests, tossing her over his shoulder when her left knee threatened to fold on her, lifting her over nulled-out Holers lying where they fell when the vibrators went off, pushing her into murky stench-filled side ways when the sounds of men walking broke the eerie stillness.

She never saw them.

She had a feeling of soft secret doings all around her in the dust and decay, but she saw none of it, only the sprawled bodies of the Holers.

There were no alarms going off. Nothing.

"Whoever's doing this thinks he's bagged the place," she said aloud.

Kikun hissed again and she shut up. *All right, you're right, Li'l Liz. Shayss damn, I feel like I'm drunk and I didn't even have the fun of getting there.*

## ##

Kikun propped her against a wall. "Almost there, Rose. You wait here till I check it out," he whispered and glided rapidly away, vanishing into the murk of the dusty, long unused sideway.

She slid down until she was sitting on the crumbling mat, Kikun gone from her mind the moment he turned the corner. As the colored lighttubes painted a patchwork of bright transparent shadows on her and the newly oiled floor around her, she shook her head, trying to shake the fog out. It didn't work, just made her dizzy. She hauled up the robe, then her trouser leg and began massaging the muscles from knee to ankle. Riding in the cars had eased up on her knee some, but her leg wouldn't be right till she got time in an ottodoc. Her flesh felt like clay, cold and unresilient, as if it belonged to someone else. *Z' Toyff! Got to get out of here.*

"Rose . . ."

"Ah!" She scrambled onto her feet, struck out.

Kikun caught her arm, stopped her. "Rose!"

She looked up at him and remembered. "Shayss damn, Kuna, don't DO that to me."

"Sorry, Rose, I forgot."

She sputtered, the laugh startled out of her; it echoed back along the narrow curving corridor and made her angry at herself. Slips like that could get them all killed.

"It's all right, Rose. There's no one around to hear." He

pulled her onto her feet, got his shoulder under her arm.
"No guards, no nothing. Let's go, Op. Shuffle-shuffle."

## 

The lock's inner door gaped open, the cracks around it
clogged with ancient crud. Kikun lifted Autumn Rose over
the rim, helped her negotiate the crumpled flooring as they
moved toward a heavy metal plug with three tube caps lined
in a row across it. He hauled her to the one on the left end,
cycled it open, and tossed her in.

As she passed from the argrav field into the .00 something gravity of the tube, she lost traction, caught hold of a
tugline, and began hauling herself along the tube. Behind
her she heard the soft whine as the cap irised shut, then the
line jerked repeatedly as Kikun started after her.

## 

She eased into the pilot's seat with a sigh of relief, picked
her leg up and set it in place and with automatic skill locked
the crashweb about her. Having forgotten him again, she
twitched as Kikun slid into the co-seat. "One of these days
you'll give someone a heart attack, Kuna."

"Oh, no."

"You seeing any snags ahead?"

"Nothing focused. Be careful, but move as fast as you
can."

"Right."

## 

A red light flashed in front of her the instant she cut loose
from the tube. "Alarm," she said. "Somebody noticed."
She was working as she spoke, swinging the shuttle about,
sending it toward the gaping outer door of the lock. "Or
maybe it's automatic," she said. "With a little luck. . . ."

The port was near the top of the worldship where the
shuttles could jump in and out without getting tangled in
the web of tubes linking the central mass with the ring of
much smaller derelicts.

Autumn Rose booted the shuttle into a reckless arc over

that ring, came down to the central plane and darted for the skeletal marina that Ginny had provided for his bidders.

She circled the marina, put it between her and Koulsnak-ko's Hole, then pooted along behind the ships, looking them over for size and conformation, talking absently as she kept her eyes fixed on the scanner. "We want a small ship, one that doesn't take a big crew, two reasons, we couldn't handle a big 'un and a small crew's probably in the Hole, not lying about to make misery for us. And we should get one that can put down onplanet so we don't have to depend on landers, who knows where we'll end up. So, a small hot ship. None of these. No . . . no . . . ah! there's one that might do if we can't find . . . ah! Red light's gone out, don't know whether that's good or bad. Ah . . . ah . . . yes! Don't think we can do better than that one." She centered the small sleek yacht in the screen, enlarged the image. "What do you think, Kuna?"

He shivered. "Do it. Something's stepping on my shadow, Rose, breathing down my neck. Hurry."

"Right." Autumn Rose took the shuttle closer, nosed it around until it hung beside the yacht, lock nuzzling against lock. "Well, now it gets hard. Be helpful if I had one of Digby's trick boxes, but I don't, so we go with what we have. Let me see. . . ."

She began playing with the sensor pad, stopping occasionally to watch the screen. Nothing happened. She muttered to herself and went back to work.

Kikun closed his eyes, his face went slack, idiotic. After a minute his fingers began tapping a complex rhythm. And a moment after that he produced a singing drone—melody to go with the rhythm.

Rose swung around, stared at him, then swore and touched on the recorder.

His hand went still. For a moment it lay on the arm of the co-seat like a discarded bit of weed. Then he began again, went through the whole sequence a second time. He stopped the tapping and the droning, worked his fingers, opened his eyes. "That's it."

"What? Never mind. I know what it is. Aburr Uchitel's *Aubade*. I doubt there's a soul in settled space who hasn't had it played at him in some lift or another. Why?"

"It came to me."

"Oh. Shayss damn, we need the Singer . . . mm . . . maybe not. You know anything about music?"

"Dinhast. Nothing beyond."

"Oh. Well, let's see. . . ." She fed the recording into the shuttle's tiny brain, cast it at the ship.

Nothing happened.

"Shayss!" Clicking tongue against palate, she listened to the recording again. "If it's not the tune, maybe he's playing games with intervals. . . ." She went to work on the recording, running it through such permutations as the simple-minded shuttle brain would allow, matching the results against what she knew about key-psych and the parameters of amateur efforts along that line. She had a feeling it was amateur, any passkey twitched from such a collection of stale-isms as Uchitel's *Aubade* had to belong to a mind-set far removed from the life views of the math techs she knew, the ones who made a profession of locking things away.

She came up with a run that was so familiar it was almost comic. She tried it. *No. He's a hair smarter than that. Or she. Whichever. Shayss damn, I wish I had. . . .* She glanced at Kikun who lay inert, eyes staring at things she'd never see—and didn't particularly want to.

No help there. She pulled the possibles onto the screen, frowned at them, glanced at her ringchron. Time was passing. *Right. The complicated one. Fussy. Canon of a kind. Stupid kind. Goerta b'rite, let this work.* She cast the new recording at the ship and wiped the sweat off her face as the lock hummed open and an otto-docker caught hold of the tiny shuttle, eased it toward the gap.

"Wake up, Kuna my Liz, we're in."


3

Kikun drifted about the bridge, touching things, sniffing at them, occasionally standing with his eyes closed, swaying a little, humming softly under his breath.

Rose glanced up from the control pad she was studying, frowned at the screen. "Hey, look at this."

Something strange was emerging from the top of the worldship. A blob of glowing white fog wobbled out of the lock, separated from it, and floated pulsing and flickering above it. A black speck arced over the blob, cast a line at it, and began towing it toward the marina.

As it drew closer, she saw dark objects floating in the plasm. Bodies. Hundreds of them. ''Weird.''

Kikun ambled over, stood behind her, his hands on the back of her chair. ''Yes,'' he said. ''I see. What is it?''

''I don't know. Never saw anything like that. Never heard of it either.''

He leaned closer to her, she could feel his breath against her neck. 'Shadow's in there. Alive.''

''Oh.''

''We have to follow that.''

''Can you? On your own?''

''I don't know. For a while, maybe.'' He moved away. She swung the chair around, scowled at him.

He'd gone across the room and was sitting cross-legged on the carpet, his back against the wood-paneled wall. His eyes were closed, but he felt her watching and cracked them to look at her. ''Be ready,'' he said.

She snorted, turned back to the control bank.

Sweet ship, as nearly idiot-proof as anything she'd come across. The previous owner must have liked to pilot himself now and then, maybe when he was going places he didn't want people to know about. Like here.

She disengaged the tethers, walked the ship on pressors from its slot. With a wary eye on the blob, she eased the ship along behind the others tethered in that row until she was drifting at the sunside of the tieup, fingers crossed that the ship the tow wanted was down the other end.

*Yes. Yes. That big sucker. Z' Toyff, they came prepared for a hefty cargo. Whoever.*

Followed by two smaller ships, the large transport moved free of the marina, sucked in the blob as soon as it was clear, then the three ships hung together without moving or giving any sign of life for ten minutes, twenty, thirty. . . .

Abruptly they shot up, arcing high over the marina, heading for the sun.

*So what does one do now? Digby, Digby, wish I could call you. No. We'll play this out first, there's no time. No time. . . .*

Autumn Rose waited until they dropped out of sight, then went after them, hanging far enough back so they wouldn't spot her.

Kikun sang to himself. He'd found a clipboard somewhere and was slapping at it, drumming himself into the hunt trance, getting the Spirit Hound ready to go snuffling on the trail of the ships running ahead of them.

A flare behind them.

She read the monitors. Not the sun. Must be Koulsnakko's blowing. Bastards set it to go Nova. She shivered. *Goerta b'rite for Kuna's visions.*

The ships ahead hit the Limit and dropped into the insplit.

With Kikun's song and his drumming filling the bridge around her, she dropped after them.

# PRISONER 1:
# Ginny in chains

1

Two men came through double doors, walked toward a workstation on a dais; its screens were retracted, the sensor pads shrouded in plastic covers. Their footsteps echoed hollowly on the black and white squares of the marble floor.

It was an immense domed chamber and they were alone in it.

There were other workstations, smaller and less complex, ranked around the walls, over fifty stations, closed down now, hooded and silent, chairs empty. This was a holiday, a rest day for everyone but them.

The one with the manacles on his wrists and the leg irons was a little man with thinning gray-brown hair combed across a bald spot, a forgettable face and eyes like dead leaves. Ginbiryol Seyirshi, prisoner and not liking it—though he didn't let his anger surface. His hands hung at his sides, relaxed, loosely curled, as he stepped onto the dais and stood beside the lefthand seat, waiting with an appearance of mild interest for something to happen.

The other was an Omphalite, muffled in heavy black robes with a cowl shadowing his face. A big man, twice Ginny's size. There was arrogance in the set of his shoulders, in the boom of his distorted and deepened voice. He set a hand on Ginny's shoulder, pushed him down into the seat, and closed more fetters over his arms and legs.

##

The Omphalite settled himself before the operations console, brought a screen humming up and spreading before them, waved a gloved hand at the image that appeared when he tapped a sensor at the center of the board. "There she is, your . . . ah . . . nemesis."

19

The contempt and mockery in those words ate at Ginny, but he gave no outward sign of this.

A young woman with matte brown skin and hair a mass of bronze springs sat in a narrow cell staring into the lens. On one cheek she had an outline of a hawk acid-etched into her skin, an elegant brownline drawing. She looked tired and fearful, her eyes were red and still teary, though she'd stopped crying. She was twisting her hands together, repeating the same motions over and over.

It was almost three years since Ginny had first seen her; she'd looked about fourteen then. Despite the stresses and strains of the time since, she seemed hardly older though she had to be nineteen or twenty. Bone structure, he thought, and that baby skin. And playing the child. He didn't believe any of what he was seeing; he'd learned better. "Kill her."

The Omphalite snorted. "She's nothing," he said. "A front for that sauroid. A pawn. That creature was the real source of her so-called powers."

Ginny turned his head, stared a moment at the shadow under the cowl, the black jut of the voice distorter. You are a fool, he thought, but he didn't say it. He went back to gazing at the girl.

"No profit in killing a strong young thing like that," the Omphalite went on. "She's due for mindwiping tomorrow, then we'll put her into a labor levy and sell her services such as they are." He paused, contemplated the image. "We thought about training her as a courtesan, but she didn't catch the fancy of anyone here and she's not pretty enough to be worth the trouble. Strong back and clever hands, that's her forte. Just recently we acquired a contract labor company, Bolodo Neyuregg Ltd. It was forced out of business because a ring of Execs were caught dealing in outright slavery. Caught, hnh. Foolishness." He clasped his gloved hands over the solid curve of his belly. "We have reorganized the company and gotten it reinstated with Helvetia. It's proving a very profitable addition to our portfolio and a useful dump for products our Interrogators have finished with." Contempt crept back into his voice. "Since you're so nervous about that chocho, we'll flake her mindwipe for you. Watching her drool, you'll see you can forget about her and concentrate on your work." He touched another sensor and the scene shifted.

A Dyslaeror was prowling about a cell, his fury almost tangible. Rohant the Ciocan.

"Magnificent beast, isn't he." The Omphalite flashed images of other Dyslaerors onto the screen, ending with the dark glowering Tolmant. "Aren't they all. Along with the four we captured during the attack on Betalli, these are the first Dyslaera we've managed to lay our hands on. Interesting creatures. Dangerous. Which makes them all the more valuable. Rohant the Ciocan. He and his woman run Voallts Korlach, you know. We want that business. Very profitable. Excellent reputation. Access to places we haven't been able to touch, you understand." He grunted. "Stubborn beasts. We tried the probe on two of the younger ones. One of them's dead, the other might's well be. Vegetable. They seem to have some twists in their heads our savants haven't seen before. Perverse. One almost feels it's deliberate. Which reminds me, our chief Savant will be visiting you in a day or two, give him everything you know about the Dyslaera. Hnh. They'd make magnificent guards, very decorative and maybe even effective. Assassins perhaps. Think what we could charge for them if we could guarantee conditioning and control. We can start with these, but we'll have to have more of them. We need to know how to avoid stirring up that cohesiveness and bloody-mindedness they show when one of theirs is attacked. Or perhaps we could learn to transfer that loyalty to us. That'd be good." He tapped the sensor again.

"That's a tracer Op called Samhol Bohz, he's a native of Ekchua-TiHash, interesting world, I've sent a small expedition to see what we can pick up there. This obsession of yours, Seyirshi, it's proving immensely valuable to us. We acquired Bohz in that attack on Betalli; he was leading it. Works for something called Excavations Limited, the proprietor of which is one Digby no-last-name no-planet-of-origin. Digby. My chief Interrogator thinks the name's a pun, shows the way the blitsor's mind works, something he thought up when he started his business. Odd man, if you can call him a man these days. Tied to his kephalos with more fibers than a Paem bud to ve's parent. Stays in his nest, never goes out except by holo. Can't get at him. Which is the point, I suppose. He's beginning to be a nuisance, but we have to leave him be until we have more data. We're thinking of programming Bohz and sending him back to scavenge for us. Maybe, maybe not. Depends on what we can wring out of him here. Whatever, there's always the labor levy. One way or another, he'll make us a profit. We have expenses, you know, we can't afford to waste anything. Besides, recycling is a virtue, yes? Talking about profits. . . ."

He began pulling up images of the rest of the prisoners, commenting on each. Some were to be milked of everything they owned and killed. Those with positions of power in their home spheres would be given blackmail poisons, tailored parasites or other addictions, according to the assessment of the Savants and Interrogators, and sent home to work for Omphalos. A few would be sold to their competitors—through convoluted cutouts to keep Omphalos clean. These were stacked in stasis pods; they'd been kept unconscious so they wouldn't have any notion of who had collected them. "Except you, Seyirshi. If any of that lot came across you, say a year from now, I wouldn't give odds how long you'd last." He droned on until he reached the end of the images. "We should harvest several billions by the time we've finished with this. To say nothing of an exponential increase of influence in a number of sectors. A successful operation, wouldn't you say, Seyirshi?"

"Most commendable."

"Ah, yes. Now. One last thing. Certainly you would prefer to avoid the Probe. It's so easy to slip and apply just that little extra pressure that does so much damage." He tapped a sensor and retracted the wristcuffs that locked Ginny's arms to the chair. "So much simpler and safer if you give us the location, entry codes, and totals in your various accounts, then authorize the transfer of these funds as we direct."

Ginny Seyirshi turned to stare at him; then, without a word he began entering the data.

# DYSLAERA 1:
# Rohant

1

He lay on a hard cold cot in a room filled with white glare.

He was aware of everything, but felt nothing directly; no sensation, no emotion reached him through the fugue state the Dyslaera called nincs-othran which had wrapped around him the moment his body was seriously threatened.

**"STOP THE DRIP. NOW."**

Boss Questionman, he thought, cracking his whip over his crew. If he could have felt anything, it would have been a musty smugness. Dyslaera weren't so easy to tame as all that. We've done worse to each other than you can dream of, worm. You can kill me, but you will not bend me.

Touching him, here there places he could see places he couldn't see, sensors and probes, testing TESTING. . . .

**"READINGS THE SAME AS WITH THE OTHER DYSLAERORS, ADJUSTED FOR AGE AND PHYSICAL CONDITION. FUGUE STATE, SENSITIVITY TO INVASIVE TECHNIQUES ALMOST NONEXISTENT, NO PAIN RESPONSE, RESPONSE TO THE ADZTERPINE IS ANOMALOUS, EVEN IN TERMS OF THE REACTIONS OF THE OTHER DYSLAERORS. . . ."**

The voice went on, a dull monotone listing with little elaboration the tics and tocs of his body . . . when it stopped it was several moments before he realized the silence. And when he did, the silence was filled again with the booming voice.

**"HMM. EACH OF THEM SEEMS TO BE WIRED DIFFERENTLY. RIGHT. I WANT A SAMPLE SERIES FROM HIM AND THE OTHERS, YOU KNOW THE REGIMEN. ONE CAVEAT. THIS ONE HAS TO BE KEPT ALIVE AND INTACT. ORDER OF THE GRAND CHOM. WHO ALSO REQUIRES US TO CIRCUMVENT THAT FUGUE STATE BEFORE HE'S TOO OLD FOR ANANILES. I WANT THE SAMPLES**

23

**ANALYZED AND THE REPORT ON MY SCREEN IN
THREE DAYS.''**

2

He lay on the hard cold cot while techs worked over him,
faceless men in heavy silver bodysuits, their eyes obscured
behind magnaviewers, their hands shielded by the translucent film of silvaskin.

Nothing bothered him. He didn't care what they did, he
just wanted them to get done with it and let him go back to
planning his escape. nincs-othran protected him and at the
same time narrowed his focus drastically; everything he did,
every thought that flickered across his mind dealt with escape. He could wait with a terrible patience for the slightest
of openings and explode into action the moment it showed.
There was nothing yet. This lot were careless around him,
they weren't fighters, not any kind of combat types. If he
could get at them, they were dead and he was gone, but
their machines were sleepless and ubiquitous, not subject
to lapses of attention. If the crack came, it would
be in the interface between man and machine. It would come.
He waited.

# FISHING 1:
# Kikun and his gods

1

Spirit Hound put his head down and snuffled at the traces, but it was no good, the white threads issuing from the only ship left in view were dissolving like smoke blown by the wind. He struggled to run faster.

The ship faded, vanished.

Spirit Hound whimpered and whined and dug at the nothingness he ran on and through. He cast about, ran this way, ran that.

*Kikun!*

Hound heard the name, turned his head. The fine white threads that ran behind him were raveling, on the point of breaking and dissipating, leaving him stranded.

Kikun!

The name pulsed along the threads. Their white brightened, thickened. They twitched at him, tried to pull him back.

**KIKUN!**

The twitch was harder. Spirit Hound hesitated; he wanted to go forward, but there was no more forward to go into. He turned and ran back along the threads.

##

Kikun opened his eyes, stared blankly at the heart-shaped face hanging over him. Autumn Rose. He was weary, so weary it was almost too much effort to breathe.

''Kikun?'' She lifted his hand, let it fall. ''Goerta b'rite!''

She went away, came back with a cup of broth. Gathering him up, bracing him against her knee, she began feeding him the broth, sip by sip, slipping in an occasional bite of hipropaste.

When she was finished with that, she straightened his cramped arms and legs and tucked a pillow under his head,

25

then she went off again, came back with a mug of hot tea and a drinking tube. She set the mug beside his head, helped him with the tube. "You feel like talking?"

He sucked at the tea, let the cleansing warmth trickle through him as he considered the question. "Why did you call me back?"

"Didn't want you killing yourself."

"Just as well. I'd lost them. What's happening?"

"Right now, we're drifting—pointed the same way your last turn took us."

"Where are we?"

"The Callidara Pseudo-Cluster."

"What's that?"

"A very busy place. Nearly a thousand systems less than a light-year apart, two hundred of them inhabited, mostly colonized from other places, only ten of them have native pops. Kephalos tells me we have to go carefully. Sometimes the insplit round here is so busy its fabric shakes."

Kikun sucked at the tea, frowning. "That doesn't sound right. Omphalos wouldn't want close and inquisitive neighbors."

"Well, it's where you brought us. Omphalos?"

"Tlee!" He flattened his hands on the floor, tried to push up but his arms had no strength in them. "Help me up."

"No need to go rushing about. I have to purge the ship before we go near any of those worlds."

"Purge?"

"Pull her flags. We stole her, remember? I don't purge her, the first port we hit, zap, straight to jail."

"Ah. How long will that take?"

"I don't know. Depends on what system the PO used, previous owner, that is. Don't worry, I will get it. Digby sees that his Ops know a lot of things most powers say they shouldn't. You comfortable there, or would you rather go lie down in one of the staterooms?"

"I'll stay here."

"Right." She got to her feet. "First I find me a nice little planet with no people on it. One with air I can breathe so I can get the outside clean, too. Then I suppose I'd better call in and see what Digby has to say. Nothing much is going to be happening for a while, so you might as well get some sleep."

### 2

It was a nameless little world, a pretty world with nothing more than its looks to recommend it, the usual range of metals, no large deposits. No moons. There were a lot of lakes but no great, uninterrupted stretches of water. In an area with hundreds of other worlds much like it, it had been scanned a few times but mostly ignored. And it was close by—only a day off.

Autumn Rose set the ship down in the middle of a temperate long-grass prairie in the northern hemisphere, choosing a flat barren area near a large lake and one of the streams feeding into it.

Kikun wandered aimlessly about the ship as Autumn Rose settled to work. He stood behind her, watching her play with the kephalos until she swung around and snarled at him. "I loathe people looking over my shoulder. Haven't you got SOMETHING you can do?"

Kikun shrugged his narrow shoulders, ambled to the co-seat, turned on the scanners so he could look out over the land around the ship.

Tall grass stretched to the horizon, nodding in the wind, green and silver moire silk, fading to a washed-out blue in the distance. There were scattered interruptions of a darker, stiffer green where trees grew along a stream or deep in a wash. A few kilometers off, an immense herd of horned beasts grazed, leaving a strip of shorn land half a kay wide as they passed on. Overhead, a number of feathered fliers were black specks against the ice-blue of the sky.

Kikun was hatched on a tall-grass prairie much like this one, so much like it he might almost be looking across his sept's home range. He sat gazing at the scene and aching with a separation anguish he'd been too busy to feel since Lissorn rescued him from the stake and brought him away. Strange places, strange peoples, nothing to remind him until now.

"Kikun, do you mind. . . ." The image vanished, the screen went gray. "I need the kephalos' full attention for this." She scowled at the console, then at him. "It's going to take forever as it is. Barakaly Lak Dar, that's the PO of our chariot, he had a mind like a snake with hiccups. Why don't you take some lunch and a stunner and go for a walk or something?"

3

Kikun rode the lift to the ground and stepped onto patchy grass. The lightness of his body startled him. Autumn Rose hadn't warned him about the lower g. Moving was a little like walking in water without the resistance of water. A very peculiar feeling.

He held tightly to the rail of the lift and sucked in a long breath as he listened to the faint susurrus of the grass. That sound, ah that sound, it was an ache in the heart. A wound.

The morning sun was warm on his face, but the air was nippy; it smelled of pollen and grass, of fish and weed, mud and decay. Something dead a long way off added a faint pungency to the mix. It wasn't exactly his homesmell, but near enough to evoke a stream of memories.

He closed his eyes and let them flow over him, the good and the bad.

For the past three years he'd been caught up in Ginny Seyirshi's plots. No time to stop and think, no urge to let go and drown in memory.

Now there WAS time.

Too much time.

He panted and his fringed ears trembled, his eyes flooded with tear gel. He leaned against the railing, head down, remembering, remembering, remembering . . . until the spasm was finished, then he sighed and scrubbed away the gel.

After shrugging out of the backpack, he left it on the lift floor and walked cautiously across cream-colored sand to water blue as shattered sapphire.

He squatted beside the tender wavelets that lapped at the sand and scooped up a handful of the water. Lissorn would have scolded him until his ears rang: *one does not eat and drink promiscuously on strange worlds; bad things can happen to one's insides.* He smiled at the memory, tasted the water. It was fresh and cold, with a clean green flavor. He spread his fingers and let the rest of the liquid run away. There was a spiky weed growing a short way out in the lake. Balancing on one hand he stretched over, broke off a branch, sniffed at it, bit into it. Not much taste but a good crunchy texture. He squatted and chewed until all he had left was a wad of strings which he spat out. He scooped up more water, swished it around to clean his mouth, spat that out also.

He knew well enough what he was risking, but a certain recklessness drove him on, a recklessness that was his by godright and a plague on his comfort more than once.

He got to his feet, ran along the beach, restless, nervous, while the day got colder instead of warmer.

The wind rose. The sky was a pale pale blue, almost white, empty now except for a few, high rat-tails of cloud that merely emphasized the blankness of the blue.

His bare foot touched a length of driftwood bleached almost white by water, wind, and sun. Wood. He stared down at the section of branch for a long moment, then bent and picked it up. Yes. Fire. I'll build me a fire. Four fires. Fires to send a tocebai home. Yes.

Driven by a new urgency, he strode along the sand gathering pieces of wood small enough to carry. As soon as he had an armload, he took it to a long narrow spit where the feeder creek entered the lake, dumped it, and went back to hunt for more.

## 

When he had the wood he needed, he went into the prairie and gathered grasses.

## 

He settled on the sand and began smoothing and knotting the grasses into a sacred mat, his fingers twisting and pulling in a pattern so familiar he didn't have to think what he was doing. On DunyaDzi he would have whistled an ancient *sin-di* while he worked, the music gathering his forces and feeding power into the grass. Here, he was empty, there was no music in him and the grass felt dead in dead fingers. He went on knotting anyway.

Not so long ago, when Shadow had hinted for a reading—she wanted reassurance before they hit Koulsnakko's Hole and went for Ginny—he couldn't answer her, Gaagi wouldn't come. He told her he wasn't worried. It had happened before, his gods going off somewhere and leaving him to himself. They'd always come back.

This time felt different. Voices had come to him in the Hole, but they were chilly whispers as alien as this alien wind.

He was bereft. Yes. Good word. The right word. His gods were his tie to his home-earth and the personification of his several Talents. He needed those god images and they had to be REAL. Ghosts conjured by his imagination were worthless as guides.

He knotted and wove and wondered if he'd been too long away from DunyaDzi, if he'd worn his gods thin and finally to nothing at all. If that was true, he didn't know what he'd do, what he'd be. The thought frightened him.

He wove the ends into the mat, spread it on the sand, and went to stand at the lake's edge, watching the waves leap and sparkle in the wind. Nothing came to him. The water was alien, it rejected him. The sand beneath his feet rejected him, the wind would not speak to him.

## ##

He went back into the ship, collected food offerings, brought them to the mat.

Using the gathered driftwood, he built four small fires, east, west, north, south. He put the mat at the mid-point between them and sat on it, his shadow going out before him to touch the western fire.

He used the play of flames to ease himself into the god-trance where he could call them. Gaagi the Raven. Ellas-Xe the Lynx. Jadii-Gevas the Antelopedeer. Xumady the Otter. Spash'ats the Bear. Lael-Lenox, the Grandmother Ghost. 'Gemla, the Mask that was himself.

He called them urgently, his need for them in every syllable of those potent Names. Especially he called to Gaagi Raven-who-flies-before, Raven who had marked his path for him over and over since he was hatched. Raven who spoke with a clarity and brevity that could be more deceptive and more confusing than the deliberate smokiness of Lael-Lenox, the Grandmother who delighted in leading him her grandson into situations that made him scramble to stay alive, who always said: *See what you learned you wouldn't 've, Kiki. Listen to your Gramma and you'll never be sorry.* That wasn't true. It wasn't even close to true. Gramma's advice. It'd taught him how miserable he was when he was having his tail twisted by someone stronger or smarter than him. She told him that WAS the lesson, but he figured there were easier ways of learning it. Xumady scolded him each time he fell for her so-convincing arguments, but Otter wasn't much better; he was the comic grumbler, the joker who took nothing too seriously; he was also sneaky and murderous, with no limits to what he'd do to survive, what he'd tweak and trick Kikun into doing. Spash'ats was the dreamer, the ethicist, big and black and powerful, never seen quite clearly, the Bear who smacked Xumady down when Otter got too outrageous.

He called them and they came, but they were not the powerful mythic figures he saw most times, only cartoons, animation cells, translucent, flat, no force to them. They came and stared at him and were silent. One by one they retreated until only 'Gemla Mask was left, hanging before him, a silent summons to return home. *Not now,* he told Mask, speaking in the mind. *Not yet. You see. You see I need her. You see.*

Mask hung there, smoke wreathing about it, mingling with the white lines chalked across the black ground. It was silent, enigmatic, then it was gone. Recognizing the need.

Gaagi was there, suddenly returned, fluttering black wings, a male dinhast painted black, his head half-bird, half-dinhast, the webs between arms and legs glittering with black scales on the inside, black feathers on the outside. Transparent and cartoonish, but there.

Gaagi turned to show his backside and Kikun saw the threads spinning from him, delicate white threads, thin as Rose's head hairs, knotted and twisted, bunched into torturous tangles, going back and back until they touched a sphere floating in darkness. DunyaDzi. Immensely far away. Gaagi showing him that they'd come so far he was almost unraveled, reminding Kikun as Mask had reminded him that if he went much farther, stayed much longer away, he would rip himself loose from what nurtured him.

Gaagi turned again and pointed.

Kikun followed the finger and saw a patch of darkness, a pattern of stars spread across it, one of them redlighted— the target star. He stared until the pattern was burned into memory, along with whatever characteristics he could pick out of the image of each star and the sense he had of distances and directions. When he looked round again, the fires were down to red flickers over black coals and Gaagi was gone.

He had three griefs. Now one was gone from his heart. He had his gods again.

The second grief was lessened; he wasn't helpless any longer and Shadow was no longer wholly lost. In a little while Rose would have the ship ready and they'd go after her.

The third grief remained and there was no curing it. Lissorn was dead and gone. But there were services he could do for his friend, things he had to do.

Lissorn's tocebai—he'd left it to wander without direction. That was bad. The better and stronger the living, the more dangerous his ghost, the more harm it could do to the living. Lissorn's tocebai, his heartsoul, had to be summoned, prepared and guided to Hoz'zha-dayaka, the Garden of the Blessed. It was time. Now was the Proper Time.

Kikun rebuilt the fires, then settled himself on the sacred mat and *remembered* Lissorn:

> *the sun shining through a slit in heavy clouds turning Lissorn's short silky fur to molten gold . . .*
> *Lissorn's laughter as his tiny golden daughter came running to him, still uncertain on her stubby feet . . . as he tossed her into the air, caught her and ticked her under her chin . . . as he brought her to Kikun, saying* this is my friend, he's funny. . . .
> *Lissorn roaring into the circle of chanting daiviga Dawadai, alone, acting against training that said don't get involved with locals, armed only with a stunner and a knife. . . .*
> *That knife, ah that knife, it was a young sword that looked small in Lissorn's big hand, its blade red with firelight but not yet with blood. . . .*
> *Lissorn scattering the little daiviga males, tipping them onto their tailfeathers, destroying the Dawadai Circle. . . .*
> *Lissorn kicking the fogga bundles from under Kikun's feet, sparks flying like shooting stars. Roaring again as the daiva'vig gathered themselves against him, warbling their kill-chants, laying the daiva'vig out one by one until they broke and ran into the scrub. . . .*
> *Lissorn slashing Kikun loose and tossing him over his shoulder when he saw Kikun's swollen, broken feet, Lissorn running with him, irresistible and powerful. . . .*

Kikun went again to the lake's edge. This world's water would not speak to him, but it would clean him; that was

water's nature. He knelt in the water and yielded once more
to the flow of memory.

> *Lissorn facing off that mob with a red-lining stunner, the
> charge in it exhausted by the last daivig he'd flattened, the
> rest of them running from him just in time, all he had left
> was the knife. . . .*
> *Lissorn's body shaking as he laughed while he ran, taking a
> huge pleasure in what he'd done. . . .*
> *Lissorn in his father's arms, sobbing, his baby daughter
> dead, killed by Ginny's surrogates, torn apart by the bomb
> in the Korlach courtyard. . . .*
> *Lissorn running at Ginny, silent this time, caution forgotten
> in his rage. . . .*
> *Lissorn caught by four cutter beams, gone to ash in an in-
> stant. . . .*

Kikun knelt and gazed with glazed eyes out across the
lake until Lissorn stood solid and shining in his mind's
eye, then he stripped naked, waded out farther, knelt and
began scrubbing himself with handfuls of sand and singing the ritual chant. Except for the lightness of the lesser
gravity—which contributed strongly to the sense that he
was inside a dream—he might have been on the shore of
Plibajatsi Toh, the sacred lake in the middle of his home-
grass.

"Ah de an po ta ah," he chanted, ritual words, words so
ancient their meaning was a blur in the mind. "Hu ha apho
hae la ceh. E'mo boya can: O to encee eh."

He shifted to a song celebrating his friend:

> *"There came a man pace by pace across the grass*
> *He wore a lion face and lion eyes*
> *The sun caressed him*
> *As she watched him pass*
> *Lissorn*
> *The shining man."*

Kikun slid beneath the surface; his body was dense,
heavy, even here. The water would not hold him up unless
he swam hard and steadily. He undulated himself, washing
off the last grains of sand, then got to his feet and walked
out of the lake, singing as he walked.

*"There came a man bold and hot into the shadowsea*
*He wore a lion face and lion eyes*
*The shadows could not touch him*
*He put out his lion hand and lifted me*
*Lissorn*
*The shining man."*

The wind was sharp as knives, cutting to the bone. He ignored it. "Ah de an po ta ah," he chanted. "Hu ha a ho hae la ceh. E mo boya can: O tō encee eh."

He set out the food from the ship, fine small things the ottochef had made for him, fruits and meats and pastry, miniatures in small paper dishes. When he was finished, he ate a morsel from each dish, then folded them up and brought them to the west fire. He set them in the flames, sang as the white paper turned black and the pale blue-gray smoke also blackened with the burning food. He took two straight hard pieces of wood and sat again on the mat.

He struck them together, got a satisfyingly solid and musical tunk from them, then beat a rhythm from the wood. "Em canta na. He goh na ma khol," he chanted. "Ma gya a bat ta."

*We drink from different rivers now*
*O friend*
*Your heartsoul dances on a dry plateau*
*I am wet with life*
*There is nothing I can share with you*
*My friend*
*Your heartsoul is a lion*
*Dancing while it waits*
*Loudly your voice calls me to come*
*To show the way*
*You leap past the moon*
*You run among the stars*
*You rush to me crying out:*
*My feet will not cease running*
*Bring me rest*
*I hear you*
*My friend*
*I draw the labyrinth in the sand*
*The spiral of your life*
*My friend*

*Run the spiral, find rest in the center*
*I draw the double spiral to help you on your way*
*Mind your feet*
*My friend*
*Look neither to the right nor to the left*
*Go quickly and delight in what lies before you*
*Hoz'zha-dayaka lies before you*
*Garden of the Blessed*
*May Shizhehoyu Father of all bless you*
*My friend*
*Go quickly and do not keep remembering your brothers*
*Or your sisters*
*Do not keep remembering me*
*Go your way*
*My friend*

Kikun felt his spirit go out of him, Mask, his other self.

Mask danced in circles with Lissorn, a bit of ash wreathed in smoke. Lissorn ran beside him, golden lion, mane rippling, tail rippling. At first they ran the labyrinth together, then Lissorn drew ahead.

Mask slowed and slowed again; when Lissorn was gone, Mask melted into air and was also gone.

Kikun curled up on the fire-warmed mat and slept.

# DYSLAERA 2:
# Struggling to survive and get away

## 1

Azram wrinkled his nose. "Achcha, Fray. You stink."

Kinefray kicked at the door, yelled after the departing techs, "Bottoss! Jogin z'rafej!" He kicked the door again, shambled over, and dropped onto the plank bed beside his cousin. "What's happening?"

Azram looked round the cell, scratched a claw through the scabby moss growing on the stone. "Gunk keeps growing."

"Haven't had you out?"

"Torture by boredom, that's what it is. What'd z'rafej do to you this time?"

"Samples of every liquid I've got in my body. I've got more holes in my hide than a sandsponge. Rest and stress." He yawned, stretched. "Wonder how come z'rafej they keep us together? I managed to get a word with . . . oh, ssst!"

"What?"

"Those bottoss z'rafej, they shit ticks every place we go."

Azram extruded his claws, clicked them against the chains holding the bed to the wall. "Yeh? So what's the prob, Fray? Anything you going to tell me, z'rafej already saw."

"Oh. Yeh. Well, I got a word with Tolmant, z'rafej had him in for some the same tests I was getting, so he said I was the first of us he'd seen since the Hole, so I was just wondering, how come z'rafej keeping us together?"

"Don't know. Don't care. Any idea where we are or who's got us?"

"Na. They wear those masks and stuff and they make sure we don't get a look outside. None of us."

"You and Tolmant had y'self quite a chat."

"Yah. Set-up, you think?"

"It's all a set-up here."

"Yah." Kinefray jumped to his feet, began prowling restlessly about. "Back and forth, all the time the same way. Nothing. Just walls. Stupid stone walls. Then the lab. Tube lights, cages, stress booths, tables. Like what we do, only this time it's for people, not animals.''

Azram scratched at the stubble on his chin. "Animals," he said. "That's it, then. Getting ready to put the collar on us. Got to know the beast before you can control it. Or use it. Or hunt it.''

## ##

Savant 1 entered a note into his data pad. "One forgets they're intelligent, with all that hair and claws.''

Savant 2 stopped and looked over his shoulder at the two young Dyslaera. "Intelligent? It's debatable.''

Savant 1 snorted. "Less so than yours, if that's the way you interpret evidence.''

"Ooooh-oooh, who got out on the wrong side today? You want a cup of kaff?''

"Maybe later, after I get through all these damn reports. What do those techs think we are, memory machines?''

"The boy said it, I'll give him that. Got to know the beast before you can control it.''

# PRISONER 2:
## Ginny bows his head and plots revenge

1

Another room. Ripely elaborate. Designed to be disturbing.

It was a long thin rectangle with a door in one of the narrow ends and a semicircular dais at the other with five throne chairs on the platform.

A guard in gray led Ginbiryol Seyirshi in and ordered him to stand within a black circle inlaid in the white stone of the floor with a double spiral black on white inside it. The floor was translucent, lit from beneath. The only other illumination was a cone of white light shining onto that circled spiral from a single spotlamp dropped from the high dome.

Black basalt walls were carved over every inch in deep relief, nude bodies winding in and out across it, none of them larger than a man's thumb—here an orgy, there a harrowing of hell, in another place skeletons in a dance of death or crawling like maggots over heap on heap of skulls.

Crawling.

As Ginny shuffled in beside his escort, he found the walls lumpy and unpleasant; as he got farther into the room and saw them more clearly, the tiny writhing figures made him feel itchy, as if his own skin were crawling and pustulous. It didn't help that he himself was unclean. After he'd done what they wanted, the Omphalites had shoved him into a filthy fetid box and left him there for five days. Left him to contemplate his helplessness and their power.

Logic said he should be rewarded for compliance and encouraged to continue his cooperation. They were using arbitrariness and illogic as a method of breaking him to harness. It was stupid. If they did manage to reduce him to a puppet, they'd destroy what made him valuable to them. He had found it easier and more effective to select his tools to fit the task. He might manipulate their weaknesses and strengths to make them do what he wanted, but he didn't

try to alter them. The failure with the girl was no mark
against this system. He understood that failure now. It came
from a lack of preparation. He had seized on what seemed
like the Lady's gift without giving himself time to study the
girl and get to know her. Ignorance had defeated him. He
would not let that happen again.

His jumpsuit was creased and stained, though he had
managed to keep from soiling it with his wastes. Lice and
other small-lives crawled through his hair and in the crev-
ices of his body—he was convinced they were deliberately
introduced into his stinkbox to help erode his self-esteem.
He ached all over from the unnatural positions he'd had to
maintain, he was dizzy from hunger and shaking from weariness, but he had control over himself still and he meant to
do whatever he must to stay alive.

He stood on the spiral and waited for one of the five to
speak to him. His shoulders were rounded, his eyes watery
and blinking in that blinding light; wisps of his thin brown
hair stood up in spikes, a dull halo about his smudgy little
face.

The five men sitting on the throne chairs were bulky in
their heavy robes, their faces lost in the shadow of their
cowls. Their black-gloved fingers were weighted with massive silver rings, one or two on each finger and two on the
thumbs; the gems in those rings were the only touches of
color in the whole room, shimmering red, green, and blue
with every movement of the hands.

The man in the center leaned forward. "Ginbiryol Seyirshi," he said, voice distorted and amplified. "I am the Gran
Chom of Mimishay."

Seyirshi said nothing, just hunched his shoulders a bit
more and bowed his head.

"You will be pleased to hear that we wish you to continue
your work. Within certain bounds, of course. Omphalos will
choose your targets and control your sales. You will be given
considerable creative freedom, but your budgets and meth-
ods must be approved by this council." The Omphalite
stopped, waited for a response.

Seyirshi stared at the floor. Rage shook him, but he took
care not to show it. When he had control of his voice and
veins, he said, "What are my options?"

The Chom touched fingertip to fingertip. "You have none,
unless you consider death . . . hah! . . . a viable option."

A soft chuckle, turned sinister by the distorter; Seyirshi stiffened his face. What stupid, pretentious nonsense, he thought. I could do better with nine-tenths of my brain shut down.

"To speak frankly, Seyirshi, you have too much potential for us to kill you outright, but you're also much too dangerous to turn loose. You have an obsessive vindictiveness that overwhelms your reason and leads you to do things no sane man would contemplate. That flaw in your makeup has cost you your freedom and your wealth; don't let it cost you your life. You, we won't drop into a labor levy. You can work for us or we'll turn you into fishbait."

"If I am to do a halfway adequate job, I need my ship and my Pilot."

"Sorry, can't do that. Your ship was destroyed when the Hole went Nova. Your pilot happened to be aboard at the time. Unfortunate, but there it is. We will provide what support you need—transport, technicians, equipment." He shrugged, drawing a muted rasp from his robe as fold rubbed on fold.

Seyirshi shivered. He didn't want to, but he couldn't help it. His energy levels were low and this was something he hadn't expected. Talk about stupid! For a moment he didn't believe them. It was braindead to waste so wantonly the rich lodes of information in his kephalos, to say nothing of Ajeri and her skills and her memory. It was doubly humiliating to be brought so low by such men as this.

He thought again and knew it was true. His ship was gone. Why else would they question him about his accounts? He had done a little test on them, given them less than half and nothing about Ta'hai Tolla where he had his Xanadu and his complete records and a considerable horde of portable wealth. They took the truncated report as truth and the whole truth. One look in his kephalos by a halfway competent decoder would have made a liar of him.

The ship, yes. Ajeri, no. She was in the Hole when Omphalos took it, nowhere near the ship. She might be dead, but if she was, they killed her here.

His stomach knotted, but he was cold, cold and calm. *Watch them. Note their weaknesses. Study them like you have studied your target worlds.*

Already he had a growing list of soft spots. They prioritized wrongly, put self-service above all else including the

projects most important to them. They were willfully blind
to the realities of emotional response. Threat, coercion,
pain, these things contained their own rot; short term they
seemed to work, in the end they failed. Blind spot. How
many times had he used that blind mind-set to crack a world
apart? Sooner or later, he would crack the House of Omphalos. The sooner the better. And this business with the
Dyslaerors. Tchah! They saw claws and teeth and told
themselves here were beasts not men; Dyslaera history and
culture meant nothing to them. Blind spot. They worked
from abstractions born out of theory developed more from
what they desired than from careful and detailed observation. Theory and their desires told them that threats would
drive him. HIM. Ginbiryol Seyirshi. Blind, oh, blind!

From the moment he achieved self-awareness, there was
one thing Ginny had refused to permit. NO ONE gave him
orders. Several times he had been where he was now, a
prisoner with no options. He had fought free and destroyed
utterly those who had attempted to control him. These fat-
heads thought so long as he could keep making his flakes,
he would let them give the orders, set the goals. They
thought he did the productions solely for the money they
brought him. They did not see that he would fight to the
death before he would let them pollute his vision, before he
would wear the bridle they had fashioned for him. Blind,
blind, blind.

The Chom set a thumb ring into a socket on the arm of
his chair and a screen rose in front of the wall to Ginny's
left. A twist of the ring and a world was suddenly there,
turning against a thick background of stars.

"Bol Mutiar," the Omphalite said. "On the edge of the
Callidara Pseudo-Cluster. There are two small moons, you
can't see them now, they're on the far side. No bigger than
asteroids, not good for much but spy platforms. Warm water
world. Very little land area, mostly small islands and island
chains. Low in metals. No shells or pearls. Jungle. Rain
forests. The wood's low grade, spongy, not worth bothering
with. Savant Tetrayd, continue."

The Omphalite at the left end of the arc took up the tale.
"Bol Mutiar was found and settled by a bunch of rabbity
Cousins in the first Diaspora. And promptly lost again when
the settlers went back to pre-stone savagery. Found in this
century by a drug prospector who came across it when she

was nosing through the Cluster fringes. She hacked about some, found a few bulbs she thought could lead to something, nothing important, nothing to interest the Pharmaceuticals. And she got out alive, which is more than most the others did, the ones that came after her.'' He settled into a morose silence as the Chom fiddled with the sensor board and the image shifted to a fat yellow tuber with a tangle of vine growing from the top.

"Savant Tierce," the Chom said.

The next man over started talking. "Doesn't look like much, does it? The locals call it Tung Akar. It apparently grows everywhere, equator to arctic. The Pandai—that's what they call themselves, they eat it at least once a day throughout the year. It has . . . aaah . . . changed them. One outcome of that change was the fact that bringing that plant offworld cost us fifty lives." He sat back, laced his gloved fingers across his middle.

Ginny blinked at the image, interested despite his preoccupations. "Why bother?"

The Chom spoke. "Something very odd has happened on Bol Mutiar. Involving that tuber. According to a researcher on University who acquired one of those tubers somehow, it has mutagens laced through it along with some complex organics that match nothing he's seen before. In the millennium since the world was first settled, that plant has reshaped a ragtag bunch of scourings from a dozen different races and cultures into genetic homogeneity. It's a low-tech world and likely to stay that way, no continents, just a lot of islands and island chains, you saw that. No flight. Waterships are powered by wind and sail. Everything they own is handmade, no factories, no machines, no printing presses. But. . . ." He paused for effect, then said slowly, impressively, "Ideas, even information, diffuse throughout ALL the islands in less than a month. Remember, the only way to get ideas or information from island to island is by written message or mouth to ear. This is not telepathy, that's been investigated; not a wiggle on any of the most sensitive detects available to a University scholar. Which brings up the second aspect of interest to us. The scholar I'm talking about made this world his project and has spent thirty some years studying the people and the rest of it; he had no trouble from the locals or the livestock. On the other hand. . . ." He touched the sensor panel again and images began to pulse and shift, flashes of squat brown people, of white sand and blue water, of sailing canoes and fish with hyper-developed fins, of plants and beasts and birds.

"Savant Deuce."

The Omphalite at the right end of the arc leaned forward. "We obtained a viewing of his reports and we determined to send a team in. There were amazing possibilities, I'm sure you can see a number of them without half trying. The team leader was one of our best propagandists. He had a light hand, a quick and clever mind, he had operated on a score of worlds without missing a beat. He put down on one of the larger islands and opened communications with the locals. Six days later he was dead. Everyone on the team was dead except the lander pilot and he was so shaky he had the devil of a time getting the bodies offworld. And he breathed his last the minute the lander was securely docked."

"Savant Prime."

Except for the direction of the sound and the different body postures, there was so little difference between the men Seyirshi had a hard time understanding why the Chom bothered to introduce the speakers. The voice distorters smothered individual tones and even to some degree different rhythms—or the Omphalites made a practice of suppressing such differences when talking to outsiders. Ginny noted all this and set it aside for later consideration. At the moment it seemed neither a weakness nor a strength, merely a peculiarity of this aggregation of individuals.

"Naturally the ship's crew sealed the bodies into an isolation chamber," Savant Prime said. "Then they brought them back here. Our best researchers found nothing organically wrong with the men, only a slightly lower than usual residue of chemical and electrical energy." He fell silent, turned his head toward the Chom.

Images on the screen:

> bodies and more bodies. There is no blood, nothing but the emptiness of the flesh to show that these men are very dead indeed.

"We were annoyed," the Chom said. "We sent a larger force, filtors."

*An island rushes toward them as the POV shifts rapidly downward, a cloud of dust, smoke, tongues of fire, chaotic snaps of death and destruction.*

"They set up a security dome, filtered the air, didn't go outside unarmored. They erased the Pandai on that island except for a few saved out to be questioned. These they kept in a sterile Cell sealed off from everything, them included. You know the procedures."

*Half a dozen bewildered Pandai—four square brown men, two women, one young and pretty enough in a chunky way, one an old hag with snag teeth and coarse white hair and everything drooping. At first they seem confused and uncertain, then terrified, then they huddle together, pressing against each other.*

"The locals were dead in less than an hour. They just sat down, closed their eyes, and died. The filtors cremated them, burned out the Cell. More Pandai showed up. Didn't do anything, just squatted in a circle staring at the dome."

*Men with heads shaved and blue markings on their faces. The POV sweeps around the circle, hesitating a little at each so each impassive face is clearly visible.*
*Someone from the dome begins shooting. Five Pandai fall over. The rifle explodes in the hands of the shooter. Five new Pandai take the places of the dead.*

"The filtors started dying. The shields went down. Instruments and weapons had their charges drained without warning. Or the weapons exploded, killing anyone who happened to be about. The dome was rotting about the filtors. They were rotting, too. Team leader gathered his men and got offworld; just barely got off. He wanted to drop a hellburner on the place, but the ship's captain shoved him and the remnant of his force into isolation. Later the captain had to put them all in restraints, then drop them into stasis pods when they continued to deteriorate physically and mentally. They were all dead when time came to remove them. Again with nothing to show why."

*POV moves from pod to pod, showing bloated, rot-blackened corpses.*

"Whoever can control that force . . . mp! I leave to your imagination the possibilities. Unfortunately there seems to be no way to exploit the Pandai without losing men and materiel. We want you to devise a way we can handle them and their weapon. Turn them around so we can live down there and take control of that world."

## 2

They put Ginbiryol Seyirshi in an austere cell that was a combination office and apartment and gave him a novice to run errands.

"Just let me know what you need. Send him," a wave of his hand at the young Omphalite, "for me if there's any difficulty," the Chom told him. "I'm sure you understand the limits on what you'll get. You can have as much freedom as is prudent. Outside of that, name it and most likely you can have it."

## ##

"We collected the researcher from University as soon as we became interested in Bol Mutiar," the Chom said. "And all his records. You'll find them here." He tapped the bezel of a thumb ring against the canister of flakes he'd placed on the workstation desk. "No, you can't talk to him. There was a regrettable accident with the probe and we had to dispose of him. I put a treat in there for your spare time." The distorter did little to hide the smirk in his voice.

Ginny ignored it. A pinprick. A nothing. His eye was fixed elsewhere.

"While the girl was in the hold," the Chom said, "we kept her under observation, a mosaic from those flakes is in the can, labeled as such, along with the record of her interrogation and the mindwiping session. Enjoy, my little friend."

## 

Ginbiryol Seyirshi settled to a brood over the flake player and the canister.

He had no intention of going anywhere near Bol Mutiar, all he wanted was access to a ship, but he went carefully through the data the Omphalites provided, made copious notes. They were watching him, they *knew* they'd broken him, bought him. He could feel the watchers preening themselves and despising him; he wanted to keep that complacency pristine.

Bol Mutiar. A dull planet. If he had been looking for a target world for one of his productions, he would have dismissed this place. It was monochrome, no individuals, only nodules on an invisible root system, no drama, no passion. Just rot. And there was nothing aesthetically satisfying about rot.


## 

Ten days later, when he finished the notes, he had found nothing to change his mind.

He leaned back, contented with what he had done. Not enough data in their files. They would have to send him out, send him with his tools. Yes. Nineteen days through the insplit. It was not much, but if he could not get control of the ship in that time with that much materiel at hand, he deserved whatever this lot threw at him.

His contentment soured as he watched Mutiar hanging against the spray of stars. What Omphalos was forcing on him was a wretched perversion of his art. When he destroyed worlds or societies, he was simply taking them to their ends in an act of creation that made those ends more profoundly important, more coherent and meaningful. What he did had nothing to do with control or oppression. No. He set free. He sanctified. There was a purity in death, there was none in tyranny.

Yes. Omphalos had given him the subject of his next production, but it was not the one they thought.

It was a delightful irony. Savior of the Universe. The Deathmaster Dancing to the Rescue of Life. He smiled, pleased with the wordplay.

He thought about Shadith. He wanted her in this. He

needed her. She was a focus of destructive forces, a vortex that tore apart whatever she knocked against. Yes. He knew her now, he could pull her strings and twist her dance of destruction to his profit. The Dance of Rot and Nihilation.

He looked through the flakes, ignored the mindwiping session, he wasn't interested in that, found the one that recorded her interrogation and slipped it into the player.

## ##

He stared, astounded.

It was a lie from start to finish.

He played it again, matching her statements with his memory of things she had said and done, things he had seen in the EYEs he had focused on her.

A logical, coherent, convincing LIE. Even her body language lied. She played the terrified child better than she had with him. He looked closer. Yes. Because she was not playing. She BELIEVED and that belief was so strong it colored everything that happened. She fooled the Interrogators and she fooled the probe because she had fooled herself. Formidable.

He played the flake a third time, trying to see how she did it, stopping it again and again to examine face and body. He saw nothing. Somehow, without the help of psych-machines or drugs, she had constructed another personality with another history and sealed off everything of the old. Formidable indeed.

He replaced that flake with the first of the mosaic flakes and watched the snippets recorded there from her time in the ship's hold.

The fools had left her conscious for at least a month. They had made her sick and filthy and they had ground her helplessness into her—as they had done with him—meaning to make her an easier victim. And as they had done with him, they had completely misread her.

He watched Shadith come awake, watched her struggle to clean herself and fight off cold, fear, sickness.

She lay blank-faced after that, staring at nothing.

He knew what she was doing, by bitter experience he knew. She was mind-riding, using ship's vermin to hunt out everything she could discover about her captors. She was listening to crewmen and Captain, sucking in data and storing it against future use.

And she was planning.

What the Omphalites saw as near catatonia, he recognized as the intense activity of a brain he had learned to respect.

He tapped his tongue against his teeth when he saw her face change suddenly. Her mouth dropped open, her eyes rolled back in her head. She was concentrating so intently, she looked idiotic. She is doing it, he thought, she is doing it right in front of me.

Her face changed again, slackening as if the energy had drained out of her.

She stopped caring for herself.

Two days later she went deeply unconscious.

Alarm bells rang.

The Omphalites scooped her up, ran her though the ottodoc and dropped her in stasis for the rest of the trip.

He sighed and removed the flake. She must have included a trigger to resurface the hidden memories when the danger was past. He spent a few moments wondering what the trigger was, then let it go. It was not important.

He went through the interrogation sequences one last time, spectator to a superlative performance. Such a deadly dangerous child. And Omphalos has no notion of it. None at all.

Find her. Yes. Trigger that memory. Yes. Set her at Omphalos. Yesssss. And kill her when it's over, before she kills me. Yes.

They are dropping her into contract labor. Where?

They already think I am warped about her. Let them think it; keep picking at them, make them so tired of my agitations they tell me what I need to know.

He ejected that flake and began sketching possible avenues of attack on the Pandai of Bol Mutiar. He was smiling as he worked.

# MIRALYS/DIGBY 1

1

Miralys prowled about while Digby floated languorously in his bubble pretending to be exhausted by her energy. He was in a puckish mood and the room reflected this. Every time she turned around, the place had changed on her so she was threading her way through prickly columns of colored light or tripping over a newly materialized piece of furniture or a plant in a pot, or something so esoteric it was only marginally recognizable.

The third time that she bruised her shin, she hissed, laid her ears back, and stood glaring around until she found what she thought was a chair. She kicked at it, scuffing the toe of her boot. Solid. But when she lowered herself to the seat, the chair melted under her, dropping her into a sprawl on the floor. She growled, straightened herself up, folded her legs, and sat where she was; it was safer that way, he wasn't likely to melt the floor under her. "Why don't you grow up, fool!"

He chuckled, the pickups taking the breathy sound and playing it around the room. "You're beautiful when you're angry, Toerfeles."

She snorted, then smiled reluctantly. "All right, so I feel a bit better now. What's this about, Digby? You didn't ask me here to pat my shoulder and listen to my sorrows."

"Two pieces of information. Not much in themselves, either of them, but suggestive." With exaggerated grace he swung round in his bubble until he was sitting cross-legged like Miralys. "One of my Ops . . ." his black eyes sparked with laughter, "a character named Woensdag, one of Frittagga's more successful offspring, if you accent the OFF," his lids drooped again and he sighed, "by some odd coincidences which I won't bother describing, happened across one of Seyirshi's customers," he looked blank a moment, listening to voices inside his head, "a type called Olom

49

Myndigget. We're reasonably sure he was at Koulsnakko's for the auction. He's home now. Curiously unsinged for someone who's been through a Nova burn. Woensdag couldn't hang about, but I've sent another Op in, see what she can find out. Considering the ships that left before the burn and the reappearance of Myndigget, I'd say there was a possibility at least that Rohant and the others are still alive.''

Miralys closed her eyes, rocked on her buttocks, her breathing harsh as she fought for control. She wanted her Ciocan back, she wanted that passionately, compulsively, she'd spend every cent Voallts Korlach had to get him back, but she wasn't a fool or reckless, there had to be a real chance; this wasn't it. Not enough. ''What's the second thing?'' she said.

''Someone's been sniffing around me. I know the sniffers, but I don't know who hired them or why. I'm working on that. Any unusual interest in Korlach?''

''I don't know.'' She rubbed at her eyes, drew her hand hard over her headfur. Her petal ears were pricked high, her spine was straight and taut. ''I don't know. I've been . . . distracted.'' She extruded her claws, stared down at her fingers. ''The attacks on us have stopped. Last one was two months ago. Seyirshi wouldn't have called off his dogs, not unless he was made to or dead.''

''Right. I'll send an Op across to look around. Rizga, I think, yes, she's been out of therapy for a month and getting itchy.''

''Rizga. She was the one with Hannys and her team? On Louat 4, right?''

''Right.''

''Good.'' Miralys got to her feet. ''Hannys will be pleased. We'll see what there's to see, hmm, I'll give it a week, right?''

''Right.''

Digby closed his eyes and watched her stride out, vigor back and purpose in the forward set of her ears; he followed her until she'd left the building, then let his visualization drift. He liked Miralys and had grieved to see her so poorly. That was changed now. Much better. His mouth twitched, his eyelids fluttered as he shifted his attention and plunged deep into his ties, doing his own devious investigations through the city networks and the planetaries.

# SHADITH IN SHADOWS:
## No memory and a new name

1

Stench.

Unclean bodies packed in a small, bare, room with icy breezes wandering everywhere.

Where?

What am I doing here?

Who am I?

Who AM I?

WHO am I?

She curled up, knees against chest, thumb in mouth, eyes squeezed shut.

Her head hurt.

*Who am I who who am I who am I who. . . .*

Women were talking beside her, around her, women and girls.

She was afraid of hearing what she didn't want to hear and tried not to listen, but she heard them anyway. Their voices were like the odors of their bodies, inescapable.

*Where is this place. . . .*
*What. . . .*
*Girna or something like. . . .*
*Aghirnamirr. . . .*
*So you so smart so what you doin here. . . .*
*So what's it like, this Aghawatsis. . . .*
*Cold as Hoobi's Hell, that's what. . . .*
*Diggin in the dirt, that's what. . . .*
*Field work. . . .*
*What'd ye think, frega, you'd be sitting round sucking tit? Didn't they tell you unskilled, what you think unskilled mean? Grubbin, that's what.*
*No choice. . . .*
*Yeh. . . .*
*No choice at all?*

*You sign up? You did?*
*(Laughter, harsh and bitter.)*

A hand on her shoulder. "You all right, child? If you can, you should be getting up, the vendage it'll be starting any minute now."

She took the thumb from her mouth, opened her eyes.

A big, solid woman with warm brown eyes and a friendly smile was bending over her.

"Vendage?" she said and was startled by her own voice—she'd forgotten what she sounded like. A singer's voice, she thought. *Who am I?* She closed her eyes again, but didn't resist as the woman took her hands and hauled her up.

"Hey, you want honesty, I should've said meat market. Us, child. The locals they look us over and choose who gets which."

Head throbbing, stomach queasy, she clung to the warm strong hand. She heard what the woman was saying, but it was hard to understand how the words applied to her. She shivered.

"Hai hai, not used to frigger travel? Get you in the gut, don't it. Scramble what brains you got. Yes, luv, yes, just you hang on to Tinoopa a minute or two, the fuzz will clear out y' head now you on you feet. You want to be looking perky and full of it at the vendage. Yes. You want to be first pick. First pick gen'rally get the best jobs. Being so young, I expect this you virgin contract."

She thought that over. "I don't know. . . ."

"A weel a weel, that don't matter. You just listen to Tinoopa, she been round and back and round again. Think you can walk now? Let's go wash your face. Move you foot. That's it. Now the other foot. One and two and one and two and here we are."

The water was cool on her face, the dizziness retreated.

The sink was clean, white, the towels and washcloths hanging there were clean with a faint sweet smell. They were old and threadbare, but clean. This surprised her, though she couldn't think why. Why should she expect filth? Then she remembered the smell she woke up to. The smell that was coming off her as well as wafting past her. How long since we had water for bathing? Why? One more *why* to add to the list forming up in her mind.

She held her arms out and submitted passively to the scrubcloth and the cold water.

Somewhere there were answers. I must have know them once. What happened?

The panic was still there, but distanter somehow. Maybe it was having someone take care of her. Like a mother. Do I have a mother? Do I have friends? She shook her head, impatient with herself. She wanted to DO something, but there was nothing in her head or outside it to get a hold on. Except Tinoopa. Irritating. Letting other people do for her irritated her. Must be something from before, something that survived whatever or whoever it was took her memories from her.

The room they were in was as clean as the sink, scrubbed until the walls and the floor were silky white with the stoning they'd gotten. It was a crude structure, thrown together from rough-hewn planks cut green so there were cracks where they'd split or warped apart. Harsh sunlight and a cold dry wind was coming through those cracks, the wind eddying about the prisoners.

Why did she think of them and herself as prisoners?

She shivered.

"I s'pose they figure anyone who gets sick in here isn't worth putting to work." Tinoopa wrung the scrubcloth out, draped it over a bar, pulled loose a towel, and began rubbing her dry. "You be careful round the local men," she said, "some of these types go for anything with a hole in it. One good thing, you're not pretty." She chuckled, pushed the hair off the face she was drying. "Don't worry 'bout that, luv. Pretty fades fast. Cool head does you better. Hmm. My name, the whole thing, Tinoopa juhFeyn of Fuyo-Geeyur on Shimmaroh." She hung up the towel and inspected her handiwork. "You starting to look like you maybe gonna live. Convict," she added cheerfully, "me, I mean. Thief. Good at it, too, though you couldn't tell it from what you seeing now. Luck took a walk on me, cop stuck his fat nose where he had no business being and caught me wrong place wrong time. They give me the choosing between life in a Shimmaroh jail or ten years contract labor and don't show my face again. A weel a weel, seeing what those jails are like, wasn't much of a choice. Done five years already, five to go. Miss my kids." She wiped her hands along her sides, looked round the crowded room. "Haven't had a word from them. A weel a weel, no way they could find me. Six girls and a boy. Talk about spoiled, that lad. Still, My Jao's fond of his ol' mum and. . . ." Her comfortable flow of chat cut off and her brown eyes twinkled shrewdly. "Well, he wouldn't thank me for running on about him. What's your name, child?"

She'd been listening with pleasure, but that question hit her like a brick in the face. She crumpled and started crying. "I don't know," she got out. "I can't remember anything. I don't know. . . ."

Tinoopa caught hold of her face, long strong fingers on one side, long strong thumb on the other. She turned the face to the light, pushed back the thick springy hair at the temples, flipping aside longer hair to expose patches of new growth where her head had been shaved. "Mindwipe. 'S no wonder you such a mess. Now I do ask myself what you been up to, luv. You don't look old enough to be that dangerous . . . well, never you mind, don't matter what it was, you just start looking ahead." She let go and stepped back. "You going to need a name. You let me give you one?"

"Please."

Tinoopa set her hands on her hips and chewed on her lip. "Elegant bit of work on your face. Left cheek, yes, that's right," Tinoopa nodded as she reached up, drew her fingers across her cheek, "etched into the skin, looks like. Must 've hurt like hell, but who did it is one real artist. Hawk, hmm. Can't call you hawk, you not big enough. Kizra, that's a little 'un where I come from. What they call sparrowhawk in interlingue. Kizra. You like that?"

"Yes. Thank you. I'll be Kizra."

"All right, come over here, Kizra, let me do something about that hair. Looks like you got knots in it been there for years." Talking all the time, she nudged Kizra to a corner of the room, took a piece of comb from a pocket in her coverall and began working on what was left of Kizra's tight-curled hair.

# DYSLAERA 3:
# Exercise and illusion

Azram stepped from the dark tunnel, stood blinking.

It was an open pen, maybe twenty meters on the short sides, thirty-five or forty on the long ones, tall thin watchtowers with bulbous tops growing from the outer two corners. The walls were at least three stories high, covered on the inside with ceramic so slick even the dust wouldn't cling, pale green, ugly green, an insult to the eyes.

"Vomit," Kinefray said and pushed past him. "Eestee, Azri, look at that." He started running across the gritty cement.

In the endwall to the north there was a spigot about waist high. It was dripping into a skim of scummy water in the shallow sump beneath it.

They stripped and scrubbed each other. Cold water on a cold day—at first they were shivering, then their blood was steaming; they splashed water at each other, started chasing each other, bouncing off the wall, wrestling. . . .

The door slammed open. Tolmant stumbled out.

Azram saw him, pushed Kinefray off and sat up, staring.

Tolmant seemed disoriented. His eyes were wild, his ears tight to his head. A line of drool crawled from the corner of his mouth.

Nezrakan came from the tunnel, caught hold of his uncle, eased him across the pen, and got him seated with his back against the wall, his knees up. He moved Tolmant's arms onto his knees, brought his head down so it rested on his forearm.

He touched his fingertips a moment on the gray-sprinkled fur between his uncle's ears, then he straightened, crossed to Azram and Kinefray. "How you two doing?"

Kinefray scratched at the stubble on his chin. "I'm full of holes and Azri's bored to stone." He pointed with his mouth at Tolmant. "What's. . . ."

Nezrakan started to answer, was interrupted by a shriek of rage. He wheeled, started running.

Tejnor screamed again, swung round and started back into the tunnel.

Cables whipped from the wall, caught him by the legs and torso and slammed him against the ceramic.

An augmented voice boomed from one of the towers: ''Don't move, you.'' A pellet ricocheted from the concrete near Nezrakan's foot. ''Next one moves an ear 'll get it shot off.''

One of the novice wards who escorted them about came from the tunnel, still trying to pull his robe to some kind of order. Tejnor had clawed him good when he broke loose after he'd gotten a look at Tolmant. He undid the belt to his robe, straightened it out, slapped it a few times against the concrete. The belt was six leather straps, all of them studded with burrs of steel.

He proceeded to beat the shit out of Tejnor.


##

''Interesting. Close call there. If the ward had kept up the whipping about two seconds more, they'd have been on him, shot or not.'' Savant 2 sniffed. ''You ever smell one of them when he's angry or frightened? B'sheeeh!''

Savant 1 sent the cursor to the opening sequences, began replaying the events. ''There's that reflex again: you hit my kin, you hit me. If we can isolate and do the right alterations on the triggers, we just might be able to convert that loyalty to us. . . .''

# SHADITH IN SHADOWS 2

1

The shed door opened.

Light blew in, cold blue-white light that broke the murky twilight inside, wiped it out, making everything clear, pristine. It even seemed to submerge the smells of sweat and stale urine issuing from the women.

Eyes tearing at the sudden brightness, Kizra followed close behind Tinoopa as the big woman marched out, then scurried around and walked beside her, glancing repeatedly and surreptitiously up at her.

Like all the women, Kizra included, Tinoopa wore a grubby gray coverall. It didn't flatter her wide-shouldered, big-hipped body. She had beautiful skin, soft and smooth, a dark amber; her black hair was thick and coarse; she wore it in heavy braids wound about her head. She had a handsome strong face, bold cheekbones and a decided chin, heavy dark brows over eyes that Kizra had seen friendly and laughing. They went stony when the door opened. Kizra found herself believing that this was not only the motherly creature who'd tended her, but a practiced and successful predator.

##

The women were herded along an alley between massive stone and timber buildings and into a large pen where a number of other women were already waiting, about a hundred of them.

She stayed close to Tinoopa, clinging to her as the only certainty in a world that kept dissolving on her. She tried to be casual about it. The depth of her need frightened her. She couldn't give in to it. That was another thing that came popping out of what she couldn't remember; there was something inside her that said however frightened you are, however needy, hide it. Don't let THEM see you whimper.

The beaten dirt floor was packed hard as rock by generations of feet . . . how many labor cadres had walked through here to what end? The walls were three meters tall, made of planks like the walls of the hut with cracks and knotholes and warped places; the wind came through in much the same way. No color anywhere, nothing but gray. The unpainted wood was weathered to a soft dull gray. The fine clay soil was a grayish tan. The women were all in gray. And fair, with light-colored hair from ash blonde to dirt brown. All but one.

That one had hair so furiously red it seemed to pull in the meager sunlight and burn with it. Red hair . . . Kizra tried to see her face, but the woman had her back turned . . . red hair . . . red. . . . She looked away, angry and disturbed because there were things in her head she couldn't get at. . . .

There were other, more obvious problems about the look of the women in here. She frowned at her hands. Brown hands, darker than the dirt she was standing on. Dark as Tinoopa. She looked from them to the pale pink women all around her—and was suddenly afraid.

## ##

A walkway with a three-bar railing ran along the top of the west wall with doors opening onto it from the building behind. A man came from one of those doors. He stood looking down at them a moment, then away over their heads, his nostrils flaring. The wind blew his hair sideways, long hair, straight and fine, so blond it was almost white. He wore black wool and black leather and carried a heavy pellet rifle cradled in the crook of his arm.

He shifted the rifle, banged the butt against the top rail and began talking, raising his voice so he could be heard above the whine of the wind. "Irrkuyon of the Families of Aghirnamirr will be coming here to look at you. They will select from you." He fumbled at his belt, held up a short metal rod.

The name of it popped into Kizra's head: laser marker. *Language. I've forgotten everything else, why do I remember words?*

He thumbed it on, moved it about; a round red circle flicked from woman to woman. "When you are chosen thus," he dropped the marker, touched a woman's arm with the dot, "move here." The dot swept to the door they'd come through. "When the door opens, go out. A guard will take you to the holding room."

He went away again.

A few minutes later a woman came out the same door. She was tall and lean with prominent cheekbones and a large mouth. Her hair was drawn tightly back from her face and covered by a wide band of black cloth; the little that was visible was as pale as the man's. Her brows were almost white and her skin was colorless. She wore a heavy gray jacket fitted close to her body and a long, full gray skirt. She was visibly pregnant, five months or six, and her face was pinched, stern. Her hands were bare, large hands, strong hands. She gripped the rail tensely as her light eyes moved over the women in the pen.

Kizra *read* her anger and her dislike for this business, felt also the grinding weariness that she was struggling against. After a minute she realized what she was doing and was startled by it. A Talent? she thought. Yes. Is that why. . . .

The man returned, stood beside the woman. He gave her the marker and waited.

Her mouth tightened, but she said nothing. She lifted the rod, flicked it on.

The red dot landed on Tinoopa's arm.

For a moment Tinoopa didn't move. The man stirred impatiently, scowled at her. Tinoopa sighed, patted Kizra's shoulder and walked toward the door, her head high, her shoulders straight, light as a dancer despite her size.

Kizra folded her arms across her breasts, trying to hug reality to her as she felt it start to trickle away.

Then the red dot landed on her arm, breaking over a crease in her sleeve. With a relief that nearly turned her legs to jelly, she hurried after Tinoopa.

## ##

The big woman grinned, held out her hand as Kizra came into the waiting room. "Thought so. Anyone that'd pick me, she'd pick you. Noticed the rest, huh? They pretty much of a type, yes? Easy to figure the sort of nakaweeks settled

this world, huh. Minute I saw ol' whitehair up there I had
me a baaad feeling, maybe Shimmaroh's jail would've been
better. A weel a weel, there's no going back.''

2

When the Irrkuy woman had her quota, a set of guards
herded the chosen women from the holding room into a
dusty mudbrick courtyard with a scant layer of gravel over
brittle hardpan. White dust stirred and fell back with each
twist of the sluggish breeze and filmed every surface in the
place. Near the massive gate there were three vehicles
parked in echelon—two landrovers and a huge boxtruck.
The rovers were heavily armored and one was top-heavy
with what amounted to a gun-station on its roof. All three
had pneumatic tires made from some polymer that had come
out a mottled purple fortunately grayed down by the omni-
present dust.

Kizra stared at them in surprise, she hadn't expected to
see wheeled vehicles—and gulped as the thought finished
forming itself. And seized hold of it eagerly and nearly cried
out when it slipped away from her. It was a fragment from
the past which had been scraped out of her, but only a fragment, a dislocated bit with no connections she could trace.
Her eyes stung, but with fierce determination she refused to
cry.

The guards herded them to the back of the boxtruck and
sent them up two cleated planks into the dust-filled cavity.

There were cartons and bales packed around the sides
with a thick layer of straw laid down in the middle, a strip
of canvas laid over the straw. Up near the front a pallid light
struggled through the grayish-white crud that covered two
small windows. They were double-paned with wire mesh
embedded in the thick glass, one window starred about a
small hole.

Tinoopa stood with her hands on her hips, the rest of the
women eddying around her as they hunted out places to sit.
She ignored them and continued her leisurely inspection. She
saw the hole in the glass and snorted. ''Looka that, Kiz.''
She snapped thumb against finger, pointed at the window.
''Pellet. This thing been through the wars for sure and that's
where we going, right back into it. Huh.'' She looked over
her shoulder. The guards were standing around the back of

the truck, talking in low tones. "A weel a weel, they don't look much worried." She shrugged, strode to a section of canvas next to a bulging cloth-wrapped bale, dropped easily down. "Come on, Kiz, no use gawking about, pick you a place." She got her back comfortable and settled herself to sleep.

Kizra heard her breathing slow and deepen and she envied her. She crossed her arms on her knees, leaned on them, and stared past the other women at the pallid scene out the back end of the truck.

A thin, small woman went poking about the edge of the straw. "Blankets. Whatcha know, could be this's better'n we think." Her voice came out a basso bellow. "Eeda, have one." She tossed a folded blanket to another woman who might have been her twin but probably wasn't, then she started tossing blankets to anyone agile enough to catch one.

Kizra snagged one of them, shook it out and tossed it over Tinoopa, plucked another out of the air and wrapped it around her own shoulders; she drew her legs up, pulled the blanket over them.

The guards stopped talking.

The pregnant woman walked past, moving with an angry impatience despite the fatigue and pain in her face. She made a quick gesture and passed out of sight.

The guards closed the back flaps and chunked in the lockpins. The box was suddenly stuffy and full of smells from the women and the goods sealed in with them.

Tinoopa snored.

Kizra gritted her teeth. Her coverall was too short in the body and cut into her whenever she moved and the armholes were in the wrong place and chafed at her skin. Helpful as Tinoopa had been, her easy acceptance of this situation was almost as irritating as the miserable coverall.

There was a muted roar, rough as an old wino clearing his throat. The box began to shudder. The roar smoothed out a little, there was a grinding sound and the truck lurched forward. Wherever they were going, they were on their way.

Kizra slipped into a panic. The uncertainty of her future and the unknowability of her past merged into a black hole that dropped over her, choking her. She started breathing faster; her body shook.

The woman next to her patted her hand. "No so bad," she said in interlingue spiced with a small lilt and a slurring

of the sibilants. "Hard work and bad food . . ." she
shrugged. "So so, you healt'y, you live okay." She squealed
as the truck jounced over a deep pothole and threw her hard
against Kizra. When the vehicle returned to its usual sway
and lurch, she resettled herself and went on talking as if
nothing had happened. "Me, Bertem, these . . ." she waved
her hand at the two women huddling close to her, "my
cusinas, Luacha 'n Sabato." The three of them were very
much alike, with light brown hair cut short and waxed into
spikes, cheerful monkey faces, tiny agile three-fingered
hands. "Don' worry, chickee, we been at this awhile, we
know. What we call you?"

"Kizra."

The skinny woman was sitting across from them, her legs
drawn up, her arms draped loosely over bony knees. She
leaned forward and grinned at Kizra. "That's right, Kiz,"
she said. "Me, I'm Jassy, that's m' sister Eeda. Our ma and
gramma was Contract, too. We been 'cross the Known and
back, an't lost nothin but time. Your first?"

"She don't know," Tinoopa said. "Some gleek mindwiped her and dumped her."

Kizra started, then clamped her mouth shut, annoyed at
Tinoopa for going off on her that way and the minute she
woke up, broadcasting Kizra's business to everyone.

"Mindwipe, yeeh-hah!" Jassy's eyes opened wide and
she stared at Kizra with increased respect, though she asked
no more questions. "Bert's got it," she said, "you don't
wanna worry, kid. I don't say it's somethin you'd choose
had you your druthers, but you gen'ly get clothes and mostly
enough food."

Beside her, Eeda nodded vigorously. Already it was obvious she did everything vigorously except talk; could be
all those years with Jassy had suppressed the urge to words.

Kizra found her silence more comforting than her sister's
vehemence.

Eeda grinned at her, then pulled the blanket up round her
shoulders and settled herself to sleep.

When Kizra looked around, Tinoopa was gone again and
the rest of the women were either talking quietly and privately or dozing.

She was still angry, but the panic was gone. She wriggled
around, tugged at the coverall until she was as comfortable
as she could get, then she settled into a simmering resent-

ment, its targets Tinoopa and the pregnant woman who'd more or less bought them, but most of all the person who'd stolen her life from her. All right, she'd survive. She'd not only survive, but she'd find the bastard and wring the reasons out of him—or her, and with them her history. Panic fluttered again as she realized the difficulties ahead of her, but she let anger burn it out, anger and determination. She closed her eyes and slept.

### 3

The lurching, the rattles, the bone-jarring vibration went on and on, bad roads and almost no springing. Tinoopa slept through all of it, adjusting to the bumps with an automatic ease.

Kizra didn't. Despite her determination, the stale dusty air, the constant and punishing vibration and the pain from the binding seams of the coverall brought her out of her first heavy sleep and kept her dipping in and out of a nightmare-ridden doze until she couldn't stand that any more and stayed awake.

She glared at Tinoopa. People who were too adept at adapting themselves to circumstances got annoying very fast.

Jassy was awake and talking. "Eh, Eeda, y' getta look at what Missus was wearing? Homespun or I'm a three leg kumis. Dewi Baik, y' know what *that* means. An' looka this truck. No ottolooms where we goin." The skinny little woman's voice rumbled loud enough to drown the other women talking together and the three girls giggling in a corner near the back.

"Eh-ya, Jass," her sister shrilled back at her. "But's better'n hoein rocks."

"Betcha we do that, too, huh. Evathin, Eed. Wan' it, y' make it. Djauk! 'Tis worse'n Overbite."

" 'N Overbite were worse'n Kacsa Kypsa."

" 'N Kacsa Kypsa were worse'n Maoustie."

They stopped their chant and giggled, then dropped into silence, bored with games they must have played over and over again.

Kizra stared into the dusty twilight and brooded over the bits and fragments she was dredging from her ravaged memory. She got feelings about things and those feelings had to

come out of past experience. The experience was no longer
*there,* but it'd left something like a ghost behind. And she
knew things. She knew what a world was and that she'd
come from another one than this. She could recognize and
name a truck, a pellet rifle, all kinds of things. She knew
about pregnancy and contract labor, and . . . gods knew
what else. It was confusing and hope-giving, because there
was the implicit promise that more and more would come
back to her, though she knew enough about mindwipe to
understand that absolutely shouldn't happen. But then something must have gone at least a little wrong in the process
because she shouldn't have known anything at all about
mindwipe.


                              4

The truck slowed, turned onto an even worse road; clouds
of dust came up around them.
    The sound of the tires changed. The dust fell away. They
were on stone.
    The truck stopped.
    When the back flaps clashed open, the sun glared in; it
was low in the west, maybe an hour from setting. The guards
standing in the gap were dark pillars with melting outlines.
    One of them banged against the side of the truck. "Out,"
he bellowed. "Night stop." He banged some more and kept
on yelling. "Houp houp houp, out you napanapas. On your
feet. Shithouse round back, got a hole waiting for your dirty
asses."
    A limber stick slapped against his arm.
    He yelped and swung around.
    "The Matja Allina does not permit." It was a rough,
ruined voice, but pleasant despite that, calm and mild. The
speaker was a long lean man with a badly scarred face.
    "What you on at?"
    "Go home, Knarkin, you and your cadre. We are all the
guard that Matja Allina alka Pepiyadad needs."
    The guard glowered up at him, hating his need to bend
his neck. Standing in the opening at the back of the truck,
Kizra cringed as the man's spite and petty fury came blasting at her. "Wasn't you hired us, P'murr, was the Artwa."
    "Then you can go lick his boots until your time is up,
tirghe. You leave now, you can make the aynti lpirra before

midnight. This aynti is hired to the Matja exclusive. Your choice. Under a bush or lpirra.''

The guard glanced around. He had his four, but there were at least a dozen men standing relaxed and casual between him and the main house. Three of them started for the truck. He shrugged, hitched up his pants and walked off, his men trailing after him.

His long thick plaits slapping against his back, scarface P'murr swung around, waiting for his men before he spoke. These were very different from the city guards; except for P'murr they were a stockier, hardier breed; only one of them was blond, the rest were a mixed lot of browns and brunets. They wore thick gray homespun trousers stuffed into heavy handmade boots and elaborately smocked shirts. They all carried pellet rifles, ammunition in crossed bandoliers, handguns in holsters on leather belts.

Kizra and the locals stared at each other a moment, then P'murr brushed loose hair from his eyes and smiled at her. "Come on out," he said, "we'll be spending the night here."

## ##

When the women were standing in a shivery clot beside the truck, he held up a hand. "One thing you need to know right now, nights are dangerous, there are walkers in the dark who'd cut your throat for a pair of boots. This is the only warning I'm going to give you, do what you want about it. For washing and like that, there are facilities around the back. Ilip here, he'll show you." He dropped a hand on the young blond's shoulder. "Do what he tells you. Supper in half an hour."

## 5

They were finishing a meal of stew and crusty bread when P'murr came into the barracks room where Ilip had brought them.

"Any of you know aught about birthing?"

Tinoopa looked up. "I do. She comin early?"

"You will address the Irrkuy as Matja Allina, chapa. No, it is only a little over five months, but it is a boy and boys come hard on women here. Anyone else? No? Come with me.''

Tinoopa pulled Kizra up with her. ''Might need another pair of hands,'' she said. ''All right?''

He jerked his thumb at the door, then went out.


## ##


Matja Allina was sweating, in pain, listening with barely concealed impatience to a long-necked stringed instrument being tortured by a delicately pretty blonde girl sitting on a stool beside the bed.

Tinoopa pushed past P'murr and strode across the room. ''Shut up that noise,'' she told the girl. ''Enough to turn a cat sick. Make yourself useful, scat to the kitchen and have them boil some water, eh? For hot bottles. You got them?''

The girl gaped at her, too startled to say anything.

Tinoopa snorted. ''If you don't know what I'm talking about, get some empty bottles, fill 'em and cork 'em and wrap 'em in towels and get 'em up here like five minutes ago. And have the cook heat up some broth. If the Matja don't need it, cook can drink it herself.''

Before the girl could get out any of the words crowding in her throat, Matja Allina lifted a weary hand. ''Do it, Kulyari. Please.''

When Kulyari had flounced out the room, Tinoopa bent over Matja Allina, touched and prodded her, took her pulse, inspected her eyes and her fingernails, talking all the time in a comfortable flow, asking questions, hardly waiting for the answers—as if she knew them before they came.

''. . . should be examinin your head, comin on a trek like this, 'specially since you've lost 'em before. You have, haven't you, lost 'em this late before?''

''It is woman's lot,'' Matja Allina said. Her words came out with the patness of a lesson long learned, but there was nothing pat or submissive about her face or the rigid set of her body.

Kizra went as pale as the Matja and sweated with her as another spasm of pain seized her.

Tinoopa was feeling nothing but placid interest and cool calculation and the handmaids—there was nothing in them but a pale sympathy. They all seemed opaque, stone figures, while she and the Matja were filled with light, red light, shining pain.

She moved closer to the bed, drawn against her will deeper into that flood of pain.

Matja Allina's eyes opened wide. They were beautiful eyes, an odd, pale blue-green only slightly darker than polished aquamarine, exotic in her stern lean face. She stretched out her hand and Kizra took it, smiling uncertainly. If this is a two-way link. . . . She thought: *peace, calm, accept.*

Quiet flowed like cool water through her arm and into Matja Allina, her stiffness and her anger washing away on that flood. Though Kizra couldn't do anything about the pain, the Matja found it easier to bear now.

Tinoopa looked from one to the other. "A weel a weel, I'd say the trouble's over this while. Where's that silly girl with the water? And the soup. Have you eaten, Matja Allina?"

The woman smiled a little, moved her head from side to side. "I didn't think I could keep anything down. Better to go hungry than start something I couldn't stop."

"True enough." Tinoopa clicked her tongue. "Send someone for that ooba-onk or she'll take all night. What you need now is warming inside and out."

"Yes." Allina turned her head on the pillow, freed her hand gently and beckoned to a short, stocky middle-aged woman standing in the shadows by the door. "Aghilo, you go. See that the soup and the water bottles are brought immediately." After the woman had bobbed a curtsy and left, Allina folded her hands over the bulge in her middle and looked up at Tinoopa. "She's a fosterling, Kulyari, youngest daughter of my brother-by-law Utilas ampa Cagharadad. If you don't know the practice, chapa . . . what is your name?"

"Tinoopa, Matja Allina."

Kizra waited for her to add the rest of it, but Tinoopa said nothing more.

*Right. Lesson for the lesser folk, don't irritate your betters with more than they need to know.*

She moved as inconspicuously as she could manage over to the bed table, finishing up with her back against the wall;

she had a feeling this wasn't a great time to attract attention; besides, she wanted a closer look at the instrument lying on the bedtable. Her fingers itched to get at it.

"If you don't know the practice, chapa Tinoopa, it's a game of lessening your responsibilities by passing them off to your kin. And you, child, who are you?"

Well, that didn't work. "Kizra, Matja Allina." Nervously she ran her fingers along the dark polished wood of the musical instrument, touched the strings with her nails. The wood seemed to caress her fingers, comfort her.

"How did you learn to ease like that?"

"I don't know, Matja Allina. I have no memories before I woke this morning."

"I see. May your life be happier here, Kizra Shaman. You touch that arranga as if your fingers remember it though your mind may not. No, no, don't move away. Try it, see what you can do. I have a fondness for music." Her mouth twisted. "Though you might not think so from what you heard when you walked in. Sit there." She pointed at the stool where the blonde girl had been sitting.

Kizra lifted the arranga, held it as she remembered Kulyari holding it. Tentatively she touched the strings, sounding each of them. Yes. Her hands did remember. She closed her eyes, let her fingers walk through a simple tune that quickly grew more complex. Forgetting weariness and fear, she let the music come out of her—until the door banged open, there was a hiss of rage, and Kulyari snatched the arranga from her.

Matja Allina clicked her tongue; her face twisted with anger, then smoothed to a calm mask. "Alka Cagharadad, come here."

Clutching the arranga to her breasts, the girl went to the bed and stood beside it, sulky and unreceptive.

"Does the arranga belong to you or to me, alka Cagharadad?"

"To the Arring Pirs, Matja Allina." Kulyari looked smug, her pale blue eyes were hard as stones. "A woman owns nothing but her virtue."

She hates her, Kizra thought, startled. REALLY hates her.

"Put it on the bedstand, alka Cagharadad."

Lips compressed in a straight line, Kulyari laid the arranga on the stand. "Don't expect me to touch it again if that dirt smears her filth on it."

"That is as it is. Go to bed, alka Cagharadad."

When she was gone, Matja Allina sighed. "Watch your back, young Kizra; she'll sink her fangs in you if she can. She's tried it with me," a quick smile, rueful, self-deprecating, meant to reduce the force in her words to a proper femininity, "and lost a tooth in the process." She closed her eyes, sighed wearily, "But she grew it back. So, be careful, Kizra Shaman." She moved restlessly as Tinoopa drew the covers back, took the flannel-covered stone bottles from Aghilo, and began placing them where the heat would do the most good.

"I have to have this baby," Matja Allina said; she was talking as much to herself as to them. "I HAVE to. He MUST live."

Aghilo murmured soothing syllables at her, helped her to sit up and tucked pillows behind her.

"I have two daughters now, but no sons. If this boy dies. . . ." She sighed again, closed her eyes, let Aghilo begin spooning the savory brown broth into her. Between mouthfuls she said, "Play for me some more, please. You were a musician once and will be again, Kizra Shaman. Play."

6

The convoy moved steadily along a narrow black-topped road, an armored six-wheeled landrover at point with a gatlin fixed to the top and the heavy shields laid flat for the moment to cut wind drag. P'murr and his guards were in this car with a sentry up top under a tarpaulin, long-glasses sweeping the rolling brushland around them.

The second armored landrover followed; it was a bedroom on wheels, air-conditioned and marginally more comfortable than the other vehicles. Matja Allina rode here, protected from the worst of the jolts by a gimbled bed, plagued mostly by boredom, which Kulyari exacerbated by her sulks and snits. Aghilo and her handmaids were silent women, they had nothing to say (at least, nothing they wanted Kulyari to hear), so they said nothing.

The boxtruck was the last of the vehicles, it rumbled along with numbing steadiness. The women inside slept as they could, the urge to talk dulled by fatigue and the difficulty of making themselves heard above the motor.

Kizra knew them all now, their names, the worlds they came from. Why some of them were here. That some wouldn't talk about why they were here.

Jassy chattered endlessly, Eeda nodded, laughed, added a word here and there. They were third generation contract labor and knew half a dozen worlds from the ground down and told Kizra interminable tales about them whenever she looked halfway receptive.

Bertem, Luacha, Sabato. They were convicts like Tinoopa, with wild stories about the places they'd been and the scams they'd pulled. Kizra was skeptical, but she enjoyed the stories anyway. They were facile in half a dozen langues and impossibly deft with their tiny three-fingered hands.

Tictoc, Evalee, and Dorrit were cousins from Connafallen, fourteen, fifteen, and sixteen—they'd signed up to get away from neighborhood wars and bride fairs, figuring anything was better than that. So far it was, ah yes it was, or so they told anyone who'd listen.

Anitra was small and so extravagantly fair she was nearly translucent, silent as the ghost she resembled, expressionless.

Beba Mahl was short, stubby, with faded brown eyes that blinked continually and teared in bright light. Another silent one, she hadn't uttered a word the whole trip, just sat in the corner by the backflaps looking grim—she was from a forest world and seminocturnal, most comfortable in halflight like that in the truck.

Zhya Arru took the other corner, curled herself up and slept with a determination that Kizra found depressing; she was another blonde, a streaky one with freckles and limber as a snake.

Lyousa va Vogl had braids long enough to sit on and square, busy hands; she sat playing with strings, knotting them into a bag of sorts, doing it for her joy in the complex pattern of bumps rather than the completed object. Kizra watched her with amazement—the woman's fingers went so fast and so surely it was wonderful to see—and she felt a nudging at her mind as if the knots brought out a memory ghost.

Ommla, Jhapuki, Fraji, Rafiki—friends or cousins or lovers, they sang and chatted in their rapid staccato langue, played finger games and laughèd a lot and paid almost no attention to anyone else, four tiny women with the palest of gray-brown hair like ancient dead leaves. Beast handlers, Tinoopa said. She'd come across them before, not this particular tetrad, but their kind. Nomads from a hot dry world called Jinasu.

Ekkurrekah and Yerryayin were tall and bony, with mops of hair like year-old straw—as slow in speech as they were fast in hand, picking flies from the air with a casual ease that amused Tinoopa and amazed Kizra who'd been after a pest buzzing about her eyelashes. She kept slapping her own face without appreciable effect on the fly. Ekkurrekah and Yerryayin were amiable creatures without much to say for themselves. The calluses on their big hands spoke their history for them.

Tamburra the Kiv'kerrinite was the one with hair like burnished copper which she wore twisted into a complex knot on top of her head; she had green eyes, the color deep and clear, cream velvet skin, slowly eroding under the grind of the dust and the thin dry air. She was a woman at the noon of her beauty and so obviously in the wrong place that Kizra ached to ask her what she was doing in this lot. She didn't ask. Tamburra's innate dignity and self-containment made questions seem an intrusion and after the woman came awake screaming on the third night of the trip, Kizra decided she really didn't want to know.

Tsipor pa Prool was a listener. Secretive. Kizra shivered when she caught Tsipor looking at her. She wasn't sure why, there was nothing but a mild interest radiating from the woman, but it was rather like being watched by a snake.

Vuodee and Vassikka were twin dumplings, plump fair gigglers, a year or two older than the Connafallen cousins. Ordinary girls, neither intelligent nor gifted, just surplus. They giggled together and chattered in an incomprehensible argot but had little to say to anyone else, flushing red and fidgeting if they were directly addressed.

Day after day, same faces, same voices.

They were ground into her like the dust that never settled.

# DYSLAERA 4:
# Vivisection

SCENE: Operating theater; the captive Dyslaera as audience in two lines of cages raised head-high above the floor; techs in masks, white robes, white gloves, working at stations about the room, some waiting, some already collecting information from sensors sealed to shaved areas on the heads and bodies of the captives.

The older captives are in the cages on the wall opposite the single entrance.

Rohant: Though his nincs-othran has been drug-diminished, he is detached, sitting like a lump; his health seems good, his bodyfur is sleek, his mane thick and springy.

Tolmant: His body is spasming in withdrawal from the massive courses of drugging that have wiped away everything but rage, hunger, and a struggling, distorted lust. His personality is gone, his memories, his capacity to learn, to respond to anything outside his skin.

Nezrakan: His hair is falling out in clumps, his bodyfur is almost gone; what is left is gray or white, it looks brittle, as if it would break off if you touched it.

Ossoran: He is cool, calm; like Rohant he seems sleek, almost untouched, though there are subtle signs that his appearance is misleading. He is sharing the cage with his closest friend.

Feyvorn: He is also healthy, vigorous. Both of them move with a hesitant awkwardness, as if they are holding themselves so tightly in check that every move must be visualized before it is made.

In the cage on the opposite wall, the young Dyslaerors glance repeatedly at their elders, look quickly away, each time more disturbed by what they are seeing.

Tejnor: His body has been shaved clean to facilitate healing; he is still plastered with spray bandages from the beating in the pen. He sits hunched over on the floor of his cage. Now and then he lifts his head, but he avoids looking at his teacher/master Tolmant.

Azram: He is brooding, miserable, though he has not been touched by the techs. He shares his cage with

Kinefray: His head is shaved bare, a metal cap has been bonded to the skin. The bodyfur is gone from his forearms and lower legs, metal strips are bonded to the skin. Otherwise, he looks vigorous, healthy.

## ##

The heavy double doors whooshed open.

Two lines of techs came in, their white robes brushing about their silvaskin-sealed feet, a table rolling between them, young Veschant clamped naked on it.

Outputs flared at the workstations as the sensors on the other Dyslaera transmitted their reactions as they saw the boy for the first time. Except Tolmant. He didn't seem to know what was happening.

Veschant's eyes were closed. His chest rose and fell steadily. In the harsh light from the overhead, his bodyfur was sleek, glowing, and he was even a little pudgy, though Dyslaerors seldom acquired much bodyfat.

The techs bustled about, setting up an instrument tray, inserting tubes and electrodes about Veschant's body, shaving patches of his fur, sealing sensors in place.

Protected by the remnants of the nincs-othran that the techs had tempered in him, using what they'd battered from Tolmant, nearly destroying him in the process, Rohant watched and wondered distantly why they hadn't done all this preparation before they brought Veschant in.

The techs settled in at their stations, the operator stripped off his gloves, held out his silvaskin-sealed hand for the cutter.

"We will begin with the legs," he said and made the first incision.

Veschant's eyes snapped open and he screamed.

The clamps held him immobile and the operator continued slicing away the skin, baring muscle and sinew.

## ##

Savant 1 (speaking to notepad):
That veggie wasn't quite the waste we thought he'd be. Tech Kadda's notion for recycling him has paid off. NOTE: enter commendation, arrange for a day at Black House as a reward. We have collected readings from the other Dyslaera, especially the older ones. It seems that the kin-bond of theirs grows stronger with age. SUGGESTION: Acquire some cubs, see what happens if they are reared in isolation. Also, if possible, acquire gravid females and remove the infants as soon as they are viable.

# SHADITH IN SHADOWS 3

1

After the fifth stop there were no more ayntis. P'murr passed out water bottles and warned the Contract women that it was all they'd get for the day so they'd better make it last.

The land was beige under a pale yellowish sky, the tag end of winter sucking the color away.

It was as empty as it was colorless, except for dark specks soaring too high above them to be identified when they pulled up for rest and meals. Jassy pointed them out with macabre zest; she was sure they were vultures, she'd seen that sort of thing before. She and her sister Eeda produced a series of revolting stories about the habits of vultures on other worlds they'd favored with their presence—until Tinoopa made them stop because several of the younger ones were sweating and turning green.

It was dark inside the box, there were only those two small windows to light the space and both of them were gray with ancient muck. Outside, the tires on the two landrovers and the truck threw up fluff-tails of white from the dun-colored earth, fine floury dust that crept through the most minute of cracks to powder the women and everything inside. Air came from outside through filtered vents, bringing with it the pungent smells of the countryside; it was cold dry air that leached moisture from their noses and mouths, cracked their lips and made them bleed.

The convoy stopped twice a day. The women in the labor cadre were given bits of coarse dun paper and sent into the Brush to do what they had to and warned not to linger. Four armed guards went with them, more armed guards lay flat on the truck's roof, each facing a different direction and the rest took turns watching over the Matja Allina. This and the loneliness of the land spooked even Tinoopa. She hurried into the truck as soon as she'd eaten and relieved herself;

the others scrambled in with her, giving a collective sigh of relief as the back panels clanged shut.

Kizra was frightened every moment she was outside. She hated that, so she hated this place for doing it to her and she cursed the Matja Allina for bringing her here; most of all she raged against the Unknown who'd stolen her memories and discarded her like garbage.

## ##

Though she was uncomfortable there and increasingly ambivalent in her attitude toward the Matja Allina, wanting to dislike her, unable to dislike her, Kizra had to spend part of each day in the landrover amusing her. With Kulyari glaring at her, then turning her back on her, she knelt beside the Matja's bed playing the arranga.

When Matja Allina felt strong enough, she whistled tunes for Kizra, sang the words once Kizra had the tune right, teaching them to Kizra and smiling with pleasure when Kizra sang back to her. She enjoyed the teaching; it was something to do to make the hours pass, difficult hours for Allina since the landrover was only a degree more comfortable than the truck and she was worn out by the jolting and the boredom.

Most days Tinoopa was there, too, spinning tall tales when the Matja was too tired to sing, tales about Shimmaroh real and mythical.

Kizra watched this and listened, enjoying the stories and absorbing the lesson. Tinoopa had her charm going full blast; she wasn't missing a beat as she contrived to make herself valuable. It was an education in how to deal with power when you've got none yourself.

## 2

Kizra heard a flurry of sharp cracks, a rattle against the landrover's sides, one of the windows starred but didn't break; the pellet that hit it went whining off. She stopped playing. "Wha. . . . "

Matja Allina's lips tightened to a thin line. "Tumaks," she said and motioned for Kizra to keep playing. "Nothing to worry you. We're well protected."

Tinoopa sat cross-legged, her back against the sidewall—

the one away from the main thrust of the attack. "What are tumaks?" she said. "Better we know so we can help against them."

Matja Allina sighed. "Tumaks are hired fighters. Before you ask, no, I don't know who did the hiring. Procagharadad Family is in Kirtaa with several other Families at this moment. It could be any of them." Before Tinoopa could ask, she laughed and went on. "Yes, yes, Kirtaa. Private war. Mostly an exchange of snipings. It's juvenile nonsense and . . . be quiet, Kulyari, I don't care to hear you rant . . . and desperately wasteful, but that's the way things happen here." The landrover picked up speed and the jolting increased exponentially. Matja Allina ignored the difficulty, spoke around the major jounces. "There's . . . nothing much you can . . . do, chapa Tinoopa . . . just learn to . . . find shelter quickly . . . when the shooting starts. Ungh! No, no, I'm all right. That was a bad one, wasn't it." She lay pallid, sweating and breathing hard, silent for several breaths, then took up where she'd left off. "You'll have to watch for Brushies, too, the organized tribes don't bother us . . ." she paused as the landrover slowed, settled to a more sedate progress. "There, that's over for the moment . . . but there are always outcasts ready with a knife or poison dart, so you should stay behind the Kuysstead walls. Ah yes, there were no natives on this world, the Brushies are either Contracts who left before term or the land-tied who untied their knots." She smiled again, shook her head. "Not a good life, chapa, no way a good life. You'll be far better off staying with us."

## ##

Day after day the truck roared on. Matja Allina's face got puffy and bruised, her eyes were feverish with unabated fatigue. When she wasn't spinning wild tales, Tinoopa massaged and bathed the Matja, Aghilo held her and fed her; Kizra sang to her, eased her tensions, helped her sleep. Ignored and resenting it, Kulyari settled to a spite-filled seethe.

Day after day. . . .

3

On the fifteenth day the truck passed through the gates of
the stockade about the main buildings of Ghanar Rinta, the
Landhold that Arring Pirs ampa Cagharadad and Matja Allina alka Pepiyadad were wringing meter by meter from the
stony wilderness.

# FISHING 2:
# A strike

1

Kikun drifted onto the bridge, stood at the back watching the screen which was labyrinthine with windows inserted into windows, windows sluggishly moving, vanishing, appearing again as Autumn Rose worked over a broad sensor pad. A section cleared in front of her. There was a series of flickers across the face of the screen, the windows crawled furiously about, some changing size and shape, some vanishing altogether to be replaced by others.

When the activity stabilized, Rose settled back in the chair, scanned the results. She sighed, moved her shoulders, shook her arms.

Kikun scratched among the loose folds of skin under his jaw. "About finished?"

She looked around. "Another hour, maybe. Or two. Unless you've had a brainstorm you want to talk about."

"Noooo, but I might have a place to go once we're ready to go somewhere." He nodded at the screen. "I see you've got your fingers up to your elbows in that thing. Could you free up some starcharts and a Looksee?"

"For how long?"

He lifted a hand, twiddled his fingers, let the hand drop.

"Hmm." She called up a status report, frowned over it for a moment. "I can cut the auxcom loose for about twenty minutes, if that'll do any good. Give you access to the chart files and . . . hmm . . . a search-line. I'll have to block you out of the main kephalos, you know." Her fine blonde hair was soaked with sweat, plastered against her skull; she pushed at it impatiently. "Otherwise we could get tangled in there and spend the rest of our lives squatting on this nice but boring world." Her eyes were blue as the sky outside and about as warm; she was still immersed in her puzzle and not all that interested in what he was up to. "Um. You've worked Charts before? Good. This is pretty much

79

an idiot-proof setup. Not that I'm saying you're an idiot, Kuna," she added hastily. "Just that Chart functions tend to be standard and Barakaly Lak Dar installed the usual. Right, you know where the auxcom is? Good. So go, Kuna. Don't waste your time, huh? Hit the beeper when you're ready."

2

CONFIGURATION NOT FOUND

The words blinked at him from the dark screen. Kikun scowled at them. He'd fed in the characteristics of each of the stars, their approximate distance apart. At least the Chart hadn't humiliated him with the INSUFFICIENT DATA message. Wait. There was a note running at the bottom. *See HELP.* Yes, I seem to need help. He touched the sensor.

Question: POV?

What? Oh. He'd forgot. Default POV was the ship's current position. Gaagi wouldn't be looking from this world, he'd be looking from DunyaDzi. The center of his—my—being.

He knew the coordinates of his home sun, Lissorn had made sure of that. In case of trouble, Lissorn said. Capture teams don't lead the safest of lives. If anything happens, he said, I want you to be able to go home. If ANYTHING happens. People change, you know, he said, get jealous of proprietary information which is what those coordinates are. Just remember them, Kuna. That way you're free of everyone, even us, and you can go when you need to.

Kikun pressed his hands hard against his eyes. He had given Lissorn's tocebai rest, but not himself. What Mask and Gaagi had shown him, he was feeling in his bones. He was alone, his connections to home and kin so tenuous they were close to breaking. He didn't know what would happen to him if they did, he didn't want to find out.

He wiped away the tear gel, scrubbed his hands on his trousers. No time for this now.

He entered DunyaDzi's coordinates as POV and managed a smile when a familiar configuration of white dots filled the screen. He redlighted the star he wanted, saved the coordinates when they appeared, and signaled Rose that he was finished.

The screen went gray.

He lay back in the chair and closed his eyes. Metal room.
Angular. Precise. He felt like an intruder here, on suffer-
ance as it were. The curves and bulges of living flesh didn't
belong in this place—at least, not his curves and bulges.

He'd never been alone in a barebones metal room like this.
Lissorn's ship . . . He sighed.

Lissorn's ship had its angles softened by the processes of
living and the Dyslaera love for hot, bright, primitive color.
Paint and fabrics, carvings and hand-knotted rugs, plants
everywhere. Noisy places, those ships, to the eye, ear and
nose. Mixed crews, loosely organized, occasionally squab-
bling. Full of life.

He didn't feel any life here—though that might come from
what he knew about the owner. A man who could enjoy one
of Ginny's productions must put death and pain into everything he touched. Or a numbness so profound that . . .
that. . . . He had no words to describe that nullity, that absence of . . . of everything. Maybe Shadow could make a
song that would name the void and tame it. Shadow wasn't
here. He shivered and went back to the bridge. He hadn't
found all that much warmth in Autumn Rose, but at least
she was alive and friendly.


### 3

Autumn Rose frowned at the screen. "Well, I'll give you
this, the location fits. That star is just off the line we were
on when you lost the trace."

Kikun frowned. "In the Cluster?"

"No. There's a rift, then this system." She touched in a
code and a system schematic appeared, along with a short
addendum.

STAR: IKSALGUN:        gal. cat. MLG372-199-34
PLANETS:
            inhabited:   YONG'M (8)
                         ARUMDA'M (9)
                         KOCHIL'M (10)
                other:   seven burnt-to-bedrock spheres
                         (1–7) kept that way by
                         frequent sunflares, three gas
                         giants (11–13), four large
                         iceballs (14–17)

"The world called Arumda'm has the best climate, the biggest population," she said slowly. "I imagine it's the one we want." She yawned, sipped at the tea she had left from the supper she'd dialed when she finished the purging. "There's this, too, Kuna. Record shows Lak Dar's been there several times." Her mouth twisted. "He seems to be a type who needs to know every crack before he steps on it, so he's got enough stuff in file to write an encyclopedia about the place. Clutter, most of it. Well, going through it will be something to do while we're splitting there."

Kikun inspected the schematic, then the index window. "I see." He brooded a moment, ears twitching restlessly. "You said you were going to call Digby."

"I put the call out." There were shadows under her eyes like smudges of ink and the bones of her face seemed about to come through the skin. "He should be clicking in within the hour."

"What are you going to say?"

"What is there to say?"

"If he calls you home?"

"I go. What do you expect, Kuna? What can I do on my own? Look, I'm sorry, but that's it."

He gazed at her until she twitched her shoulders and turned away, angry at herself and at him, then he went to the backwall and sat on the silken carpet, waiting for the call.

4

Digby's face filled the center cell, broad and brown with black eyes in nests of smile lines. "Nice to know you're alive, Autumn Rose."

"Li'l Liz there," she swung away from the screen, waved her hand at Kikun who was still squatting by the backwall, swung back, "he's the one that did it. Listen, Dig. This is where we are now. . . ." She sketched out everything that had happened since the debacle at Koulsnakko's Hole, ended with the star system Kikun had dredged up. "So. We have the ship, it's clean, plenty of fuel, we've got a thread we can pull on . . . or not. Up to you, Dig. Do I go with it?"

"Hmm." For several minutes he communed with his ties, his face a lumpy mask, the life that informed the flesh gone,

then he blinked and looked at her with grave approval.
"How's your rat supply?"

"Ten racked, two gone."

"Should be enough. You're on a roll, Rose. No point in
wasting the impetus. Hmm. While you're splitting, get down
every detail you can remember and rat it to me. So Lissorn's
dead."

"Ash. Saw it."

"Too bad, another blow to Miralys. And you think the
Ciocan's alive?"

"I don't know. Kikun says he's one of the prisoners taken
from the Hole."

"Hmm. From what I've heard, his record's good on that
kind of thing."

"Uh-hmm."

"Omphalos."

"Kikun again. I can't confirm."

"Right. Leave that to me and go with what you've got.
Use the rats to keep me up on what you're finding."

"Will do. Anything else?"

"Not at the moment. Except . . . discretion, Rose. If you
find the lode, don't spook the guards. You can get a bit
brisk, luv.'

"I hear you, Dig. Better watch the Dyslaera if you don't
want brisk."

"I'll deal with that when it comes up. Take care, Rose."
The screen went dark.

Autumn Rose pushed at her hair and sighed. "Brisk,
huh!" She twisted her head around, gave him a tight smile.
"There you have it, Kuna. Ticket to ride. You know, you're
a useful being to have about, Li'l Liz. We'd be nowhere
without you." She straightened, cleared the screen and began entering flight data. "While I'm doing this, why don't
you pick out a stateroom and get settled. It's not a long way
from here to Arumda'm, but we'll be moving slower than
usual because of the traffic in the Cluster."

He got to his feet, went to stand at her shoulder. "How
long?"

"Anything from two weeks to a month, depending, I'll
let you know later. Right?"

"Right."

5

*A useful being to have about.* Kikun turned on his side, drew his legs up. The bed shifted gently under him, adapting to the changing weights and arrangement of his body. *Useful being.* Shadith worried about using him. Rose was more practical. And less attached.

His gods were shadows, his friends were dead or gone. He was empty, a skin stretched over a void.

He couldn't go home, not yet awhile.

The daiviga K'tawal . . . Lissorn called her a subqueen which was close enough . . . who governed the Grass had put a price on his head and the Dawadai priests would haul him to the nearest stake and torch him the minute they got their hands on him.

How long was it?

Only five years? That was standard years.

Dunya years were longer. A little. He didn't know how much.

Say five years.

That was close enough.

Five years. The K'tawal Ilafur wouldn't have lost a feather in that short stretch, let alone her memory of the dinhast who'd hung up caricatures of her on every corner of Ootlakil.

Even without that, he couldn't go home, not really home. His sept had cast him out, he was a non-being among the Dinhastoi. That was always the fate of the Clowngod's avatar, according to the songs.

Clowngod was uncomfortable company.

A sport of nature fitting nowhere.

A singleton rogue in a people of triads and triad multiples.

A god who didn't believe in gods, at least, not for worshiping, more for trading with or getting round.

A breaker of laws, disrespecter of persons, rebel and iconoclast, bad enemy and worse friend.

Personification of Change in a world more comfortable with day after day of the same thing, no matter how miserable that might be, where nearly everyone was frightened of the turmoil and chaos that change invaribly brought.

Avatar. He was the avatar for this generation. He'd been given no choice about that. If the proposition had been put to his formless soul before it was seeded into his fetal body, he would have rejected it indignantly.

He tried rejecting it later. He shared the dinhast mind-set that was much like the Dyslaera mind-set when it came to kin and kind. He NEEDED friends and family.

It was no good. He was what he was.

He suffered because he couldn't make dinhast life fit him or make himself over to fit it.

The alien friends he'd found helped fill the emptiness. He'd invested first in Lissorn, then in Rohant and Shadith. Friendship wasn't enough, but it helped.

Lissorn was dead.

Rohant was gone.

Shadith was gone.

Shadith. He lay wondering what had happened to her. Was she alive or dead? Surely the Omphalites wouldn't go to the trouble to capture her just to kill her?

Shadow girl, don't do anything foolish. We're coming for you. You must know we're coming. Hang on. Wait. Wait. . . .

He sighed and slept.

# SHADITH (Kizra) ON THE FARM

## 1

Kizra jumped down. Her knees went and she would have fallen if Tinoopa hadn't caught her.

"Long day," the big woman said absently. She was watching the man standing before large double doors at the top of a wide flight of s-curved steps. He was a tall, lean man, a gold and bronze man; he shone like a hero in a stained glass window. The bronze coal lamps at the upper corners of that door turned his fine blond hair into a shimmering halo about his lined face, sank his eyes into glinting shadow.

He came down the stairs, crossed to the landrover where Aghilo and the handmaids were helping Matja Allina down the folding steps. There was an urgency in him that filled the whole of the irregular courtyard, melding with the urgency in the woman. Their greeting was a simple touching of fingertips, eye meeting eye, the woman bowing to the man, the man lifting her. It looked formal, but the formality was on the surface. Beneath. . . .

The force of the feeling that lay beneath those heraldic surfaces woke an ache in the emptiness where Kizra's memory had been. Her eyes prickled, but she refused to cry, just turned away to inspect what lay around her.

The court was paved with squares of dusty blue-gray stone webbed with cracks. The court walls and the walls of the Great House were sod and cement. Short stiff grass grew on the sod like patches of coarse fur. Coal lamps smaller and less elaborate than the two giants by the house door were scattered about those walls, throwing inky shadows into deep-set doorways and arched window openings. Beyond the broad court and the House, towers like snag teeth stood black against the crimson of the setting sun, towers everywhere, round and square, fat and thin, with flattop roofs or conical caps. There was construction in every direction she

looked, scaffolding, upper stories half complete. The smell
of the sod was pungent as the heat leached out of it, mixing
with the smells of people standing quietly in shadows.
Hordes, it seemed to her, of small fair people waiting in
shadow for the signal to move, to talk.

The other women in the labor cadre stood beside her, a
ragged group lingering by the only thing they knew, the
truck. The youngest and newest to Contracts (Tictoc, Evalee, Dorrit, Vuodee, and Vassikka) were looking eagerly
about, poking each other, whispering and giggling. The rest
stood silent, waiting for someone to tell them where to go,
what to do.

Tinoopa watched the Matja and the Arring meet, then
nudged Kizra away from the others. She turned her shoulder
to the landrover, set her hands on her hips, and gave what
she could see in the growing dark a good lookover. "Quite
a place," she said. She'd pitched her voice to carry.

"Uuuuh HUH!" Kizra said. "Considering how many rifles it took to get us here, lovely walls." She stretched,
groaned. "I would KILL for a hot bath." She, too, let her
voice carry, made a song of the words, a song to remind
Matja Allina how much ease they'd given her during that
miserable journey. She snatched furtive looks at Allina as
the woman stepped away from her Arring and raised her
hands in a ritual greeting to her household, then spoke quietly to Aghilo, pointing as she did so at Tinoopa and Kizra.

"Hey, it worked," Kizra murmured.

"Maybe," Tinoopa said. "Maybe she meant to all
along." The Shimmarohi tapped Kizra on the shoulder, a
habit she had before she dropped into aphorism disguised
as advice. "Good intent is a fine thing, but you don't chance
you life on it, Kiz. Rules say they have to pay us, treat us
right. Yeh. Tell you this and you remember it. Rules mean
shit-all out here. Forget everything else, but remember
that."

"If I'm allowed."

"A weel a weel, that's not like to happen twice, luv. Not
here, anyway."

Leaning heavily on her Arring's arm, Matja Allina went
up the stairs and into the house.

Aghilo took Tinoopa and Kizra in behind them.

The rest of the women were lined up and marched into
the women's quarters in one of the side wings.

2

The second floor hall was lit by rank on rank of torchieres
with dozens of wax candles impaled on spikes, candles with
glass chimneys over them to keep off the drafts that wandered throughout the House despite its thick earthen walls.
The herbal perfume from the oils in the wax drifted on the
drafts, riding atop the heavy stink of the hot wax. Tinoopa
and Kizra sat on an inadequately padded bench outside the
door to the Matja's suite.

## ##

"No electricity," Kizra said after a lengthy and fidgety
silence. "Candles, shooh!"

Tinoopa chuckled, a warm rough sound that rubbed
against Kizra like a blanket. "You," she said. "You don't
know what bad is." She thumped Kizra's shoulder; it was
lay-down-the-law-time again. "Listen, luv, from now on,
no comments. I know people like this pair. They can be
generous, but it's on their own terms. You show 'em you
think you have rights, you threaten 'em. They get mean.
Happens every time." She frowned at Kizra. "Don't com-
plain. And be ready with that little extra bit of service. If
you're valuable, you're treated better. We made a good start.
But it's only a start. It's a rough world, this'n, looks to me
like someone could get killed round here."

Kizra yawned, thrust her hands into the side pockets of
her coverall. "All right. Look, there's something been
itching at me. How come I still know stuff . . . things like
about laser markers and different worlds and . . . well
. . . I mean . . . stuff? Doesn't mindwipe get rid of all
that?"

Tinoopa twisted around, raised her brows. "We're all
talking local, aren't we? How? Think about it."

"Oh." Kizra rubbed her shoulder against one of the
knobs on the seat back. "Oh, yeh."

Tinoopa chuckled again. "Yeh. Easy when you think
about it, huh?" She straightened around, folded her arms
across her breasts, and dropped into a doze.

## ##

Kizra yawned and yawned. She was exhausted. And bored. And if something didn't happen soon, she was going to go to sleep in spite of the knobs on this damn bench. She fidgeted some more, wiggled her toes, scratched at her head (wondering with irritation if she'd picked up visitors from the scabby places she'd been sleeping in recently), sucked at her teeth . . .

. . . until Tinoopa lost hold of her temper and slapped at her head (slapped lightly, but hard enough to get her attention). "Act your age, nit. You driving me buggy."

"Age?" Kizra fit the tips of her fingers together, tapped them against each other one by one, forefingers first. "What age?"

"Hmp. Just sit still, will you?"

"I sit still, I go to sleep. How much longer we stuck here?"

"Until. Now be quiet."

Kizra subsided. Till now she'd been frightened, groping for she didn't know what. Coming up here, though, just a minute ago, something had happened to her. Like a boot in the behind. Between one breath and the next, she relaxed all over; it was as if she'd shed centuries of worry and just sort of settled into her body, letting it do its thing. Or maybe she was just so tired, she didn't have enough energy left to stay scared.

There was a kind of freedom, now she thought about it, in having no history to set its claws in her. She didn't know who and what she was, so she could make herself up as she went. Well, not quite free. Tinoopa was there to tell her things, poke her when she needed to notice something. Talking about poke, why did they put knobs on this furtzen bench just where they were sure to poke the sitter in the ass . . . hmm . . . funny how the oil in that wax made little balls of fog about the flames, then went eeling up out of the chimneys. . . .

Tinoopa drove her thumb hard into Kizra's ribs, muttered, "On your feet, nit. Look sharp, will you?"

Kizra was up and smoothing her coverall before she was awake enough to be aware of what was happening.

Aghilo touched her arm. "Come," she said. "They want you." She nodded at Tinoopa. "Both of you."

3

The rooms were rich with dark wood, warm red-brown wood with umber streaks in it, polished until it glowed with soul.

They crossed a short hall with closets, a kind of ante-room, and stepped into a sitting room with a soft, silky blue-green rug on the floor, backless benches instead of chairs, piles of cushions covered in rich damasks, in striped cloths and embroideries. Heavy drapes fell in gleaming folds over two windows opening to the north. On tall stands flanking the windows there were flowers in cloisonne vases (Kizra pulled that word out of memory, startling herself—it didn't seem likely a Labor Contractor would include it on his langua-tape. Who was she that she knew things like cloisonne? She started tensing up again, then told herself forget it, doesn't matter, isn't worth a sneeze). It was a warm, cluttered, cozy room, filled with flickering shadow from the candle lamps in brackets on the walls.

She took an incautious step and slipped on the silky pile, waved her arms to regain her balance without kicking over one of the little tables with their litter of bijouterie.

Tinoopa caught her, steadied her. "Watch your feet, luv."

"It's like walking on ice," she muttered. Her boots were worn and old, the soles smooth as ice. She lifted her feet and put them down with exaggerated care and thought about those boots. She hadn't before, they were just there, she took them off at night and put them on in the morning and that was that. They were like cloisonne, not something a Contractor would have provided; they must have come from the time she'd lost. Later, later, she told herself. You can think about it later. Keep your mind on what you're doing. Tinoopa might be sleep-inducing on the subject, but she's right.

The next room was a bedroom, larger than the sitting room, less cluttered. The bed was carved and fluted and draped with pale blue gauze tied up with pale blue silk ribbons. Matja Allina lay beneath a blue silk pouf with crisp white pillows tucked behind her. Her blonde hair hung straight over her shoulders; it'd been brushed till it shone. Her hands lay limp on the starched white sheet folded over the top of the pouf. All this delicate, delicious fuss did not become her; it made her look gaunt and drained.

Arring Pirs stood beside her, frowning a little; he wasn't happy with this business or with them.

Matja Allina managed a weary smile. "I commend these women to your notice, Mi-arring. The elder is Tinoopa, the other Kizra. They have given me ease and enjoyment where I expected none."

Arring Pirs bowed. "I am obliged, chapa." His voice was deep and slow, a perfect voice for a stained glass hero.

Kizra glanced at Tinoopa, bobbed a quick curtsy a second after the Shimmarohi finished hers.

There was a touch of amusement in Matja Allina's shadowed face; her eyes opened a hair wider. "Yes," she said. "I hadn't expected such a fortunate dip in the pool, but I mean to use it now that it's shown its head." She spoke slowly, her voice dragging. Arring Pirs bent over her, whispered urgently. She touched his face, shook her head. "Now," she said. "I want them established in place before I come downstairs tomorrow. You'll do that for me?"

He kissed her fingertips, straightened up. "I will do it, Mi-matja."

She closed her eyes a moment, then turned to him again. "Help me shift a little, I've got an ache building."

When she was more comfortable, she said, "Aghilo, come here." She clasped the little woman's hand. "Listen, my dear, no one can or will take your place with me. Do you understand that?"

Aghilo nodded.

Matja Allina settled back on the pillows. "Yes. Young Kizra there is a gifted musician, Mi-arring. Is that not so, child?"

Kizra stared at her hands. "That's for others to say, Matja Allina."

"Well, I do say it." She paused, closed her eyes. "Your music was a joy to me, child. I wish you to play for me each night, it relaxes me and gives me rest. Tinoopa."

"Matja Allina."

"Yes. You're a strong and capable woman; I don't ask what brought you here, though I suspect someone found you entirely too capable. I need people I can trust," she smiled up at Aghilo, squeezed her hand, "more people. There are too many about who don't want this baby born alive. I dare trust neither doctor nor midwife. Anyone could be bought or coerced or work against me for the pleasure of it, people

being what they are. If you and Kizra give me complete
loyalty and intelligent service for the next year, help me
birth the boy alive and see that he stays alive, I will have
your Contracts voided and I will do my best to send you
offworld anywhere you wish to go, with a stake to keep you
while you look about for work. Not a large stake,'' she
added cautiously. "We're cash poor, our wealth is the land
and what grows on it. Mi-arring, do you second me in this?
Let it be said.''

"Mi-matja, your will is mine in this. If you're sure. . . .''

"Yes. Besides, what choice have we?''

"Very little.'' He shook his head, his gilt hair shimmering in the half-light. "Jirrilscadad dropped by last week
while you were gone. He brought his two youngest daughters.'' There was a dry distaste in his voice. "I had to sit
through string plucking and coos and blushes and giggling
until my hide itched. Once the boy is born, though. . . .''
He bent and touched her hair, forgetting for the moment
everyone else in the room.

Matja Allina sighed, turned from the two beside her to
the two at the foot of the bed. "Well?'' she said.

Tinoopa snorted. "Need you ask?''

"Yes. I do need.''

Tinoopa bowed her head, spread her arms and spoke
with more care and formality than she usually bothered
with. "I agree to serve you with mind and body in whole-
hearted loyalty for the term of one year in return for the
voiding of the Labor Contract and your good will for the
rest of it.''

"I see you have some understanding of the dangers involved. Good. Kizra?''

"I agree. Same as Tinoopa.''

Matja Allina relaxed, closed her eyes, the bruises under
them and the fatigue lines on her face more pronounced than
ever.

Arring Pirs tapped Aghilo's shoulder, pointed at the door.

As if she could see through closed eyelids, Matja Allina
said, "No. One last bit. The chapa Tinoopa is to have full
authority as sub-Housekeeper. Let Polyapo keep the title
Ulyinik. . . .'' She stopped, turned to them at the foot of
the bed. "That means Mistress of the House. But don't confuse that with Mistress of the Kuysstead. I am the Matja.''
She coughed, waited while Aghilo bent with a warm, damp

towel and wiped her face. "Leave her the Name, Mi-arring, but nothing more. Make that very clear to her and everyone else. I'm tired to death of her sniping and incompetence. Establish the chapa Kizra as my personal companion and servant, under no one's orders but mine. Make that clear also. Especially to Kulyari who has already shown her spite. Will you see to this for me, Mi-arring?"

"With pleasure, Mi-matja."

Kizra caught a grim satisfaction in the words. Obviously Pirs was not all that fond of his niece.

"Um, Aghilo love, see that they have clothing and supplies suitable to their status. And rooms in this wing. And see that Kizra has the arranga with her at all times from now on." She opened her eyes. "Meals and a hot bath for each. I believe I heard someone saying she'd KILL for a hot bath."

4

The room on the third floor was long and narrow, with pegs in a white plaster wall instead of closets and paneling. There was a narrow bed with a coverlet white as the walls, loosely woven in an intricate pattern, pretty in the candlelight that picked out the texture and emphasized the pattern and turned the whiteness pearly.

Kizra pulled the door shut behind her, edged around the bed and set the candle on the table. She sat on the bed with her slippered feet hanging beside the boots flopped on the floor next to her wadded-up coverall. She didn't care if she ever saw that coverall again; it was stiff and stinky with old sweat and clogged with white dust—and her chafed places were still burning from the fifteen days she'd worn the thing. Remembered wearing it anyway. She thought about kicking it out the door but was too relaxed and drowsy from the bath to want to move.

She sucked in a long breath, let it out. She was clean. She smelled good. The candle gave the room a warm welcoming glow. It smelled good, too; it was one of the fancy ones from the Matja's supply. Aghilo told her to enjoy it while she had it; the next one she got would be tallow and not nearly so nice.

She pinched the candle out, took the robe off and got into bed, shivering a little as her warm body hit the cold sheets.

She had on a blousy nightshirt, very soft and flowing, but it didn't help at all with the cold. She wriggled around until she was comfortable, then shut her eyes and arranged her mind for sleep. . . .

Moonlight streamed through the narrow window beside the narrow bed, white and chill and far too bright. Moonlight. It was eerie. Things looked different. She pulled her hand from under the covers, stretched it out to intersect that slant of moonshine. The color was leached from her skin; the fingers seemed bonier, they trailed light like smoke.

She wiggled her fingers and watched the shadows play inside the beam, then pulled her hand back into the dusk where it took on an ordinary dark solidity.

Sleep, sleep. She flopped over, the nightshirt twisting about her body, pulling tight against her neck. She humped herself about, tugging at the cloth, smoothing wrinkles that felt like ridges under her.

The inside of her knee itched. She twisted around and down, scratched and sighed. The itch moved to the middle of her back. She chased it as high as she could reach, shuddered all over, kicked the covers off, and rolled out of bed.

Scratching at her arm, she padded to the window and stood frowning out at a strange colorless landscape, at roofs with pantiles like humpy scales, at a wall two stories high and wide enough to drive the landrover on, with merlons along the outer edge and towers black against a sky hot with stars, so many stars even the huge yellow-gray moon couldn't blot them out—a full moon rising into a cloudless sky, limned against it a pair of strange mountains, black silhouettes like pointy breasts with hardened nipples.

And a river like a streamer of silver silk, splitting around the Kuysstead. Moat, she thought. Gods. Tumaks? Brushies? Those what they're this spooky about? I wonder what they look like. All we saw was empty land. Empty land the guards were watching like it could hatch trouble any instant. Did, too. She shivered as she remembered the shooting.

North and west for fifteen days, looong days, had to be at least two thousand kays from where they'd started. Thirty days of misery for Matja Allina, coming and going. And for what? For us. Twenty-six women. If that was the measure of her desperation . . . ay-yai!

Matja Allina, is she crazy? Thinking up enemies for her baby? Or is it real? Will she do what she promised? Can she? He backed her, but maybe he's just humoring her. He doesn't like us much; that was so thick in the air I could sink my teeth in it. He said he'd back her promise with his. He meant it, I think. Now. That doesn't say anything about later. When the time comes. He might and he might not. If she's crazy . . . paranoid . . . then what she said, it's just words and we're stuck for the duration. Ten years. Gods, I hope not. I don't like it here. I don't like having to kiss up to a bunch of. . . . Hmm. Does that say something about what kind of person I was before?

She leaned on the windowsill and contemplated her reactions since she woke in that miserable hut. Up and down, elated, depressed, angry, excited. And tired. Sometimes she felt a hundred years old, sometimes about six. Sometimes she felt in charge of herself, sometimes she felt utterly helpless, though mostly she was somewhere in between. Like now. And right now she was so tired she ached, but her eyes simply wouldn't stay closed and her body was giving her the fidgets of hell.

She blinked, startled. A small red dot bloomed high on one of the black mountains. A fire. It flickered at her, vanished as if a wall had been put in front of it, reappeared, vanished, reappeared. Then was gone altogether.

It's a piece with everything else. Conspiracies to suppress a fetus. Things in the brush that need to be shot at, not just shot at but machine-gunned. Signals from a mountainside, aimed at . . . who? Someone in here? What did that mean?

She yawned, suddenly so heavy-eyed that she wasn't sure she could make the bed before she melted in a puddle of sleep. Another turn in . . . in the fog. Wasn't it fog for everyone, who could read the future? Not me. Not anyone. . . . She stumbled the few steps to the bed, fell onto it and wriggled awkwardly about until she'd got the covers where they should be, over her—not under. She wriggled a last time, like a cat kneading a pillow, getting it right. Then she dropped into the abyss.

If she dreamed, she didn't know it.

# DYSLAERA 5:
# Training trials

Savant 1 (speaking into note pad):
Removed cap and restrainers from subject 3F (native name:
   Kinefray) . . . using CPF24sub2 as a reinforcer . . . subject continues docile, emotional reaction damped down
   . . . under orders, cut the hand off subject 7T (native
   name: Tolmant), showed no reaction to subject's protests
   or struggles . . . satisfactory contrast to earlier reactions
   to this subject.
RECOMMENDATION: Continue this regimen for another
   month without reinforcement other than the CPF. Important to know how permanent this change is. If temporary,
   important to know how long the treatment lasts.

## ##

*IMAGE: Kinefray sits in the cell like a lump; Azram is talking
and talking at him, agitated, crying as he tries to reach his
cousin. He shakes Kinefray, slaps him, then retreats to the
far side of the cell and sits there, suffering.*

## ##

Savant 1 (speaking into note pad):
Subject 3Tj (native name: Tejnor) . . . youngest of the
subjects . . . perhaps the most intractable, despite his
youth . . . which might be considered to contradict trends
suggested by previous data . . . probably an anomaly due
to individual differences within the species . . . the subject sample is, unfortunately, too small for anything more
reliable than a hint. . . .

NOTE: recommend immediate attempts to enlarge the sample.

Have broken through the trance state repeatedly . . . made it impossible for 3Tj to retreat from attack, while maintaining intelligence levels and some degree of free will . . . have managed also to breach the strong ties between this apprentice and his master, subject 7T (native name: Tolmant) . . . to the point that he was willing to participate in a pain-inducing session with 7T as subject . . . during this session he proved so enthusiastic that 7T was accidentally killed . . . no great loss, the subject was badly mutilated at the time . . .

NOTE: Tech 1 Rivas has suggested the killing stroke was deliberate, not accident; 3Tj was questioned under probe, results inconclusive—the drugs present in his system hinder analysis of his reactions.

TENTATIVE CONCLUSION: Rivas is mistaken. If 3Tj were still feeling the pull of the kin-bond, he could not harm 7T; if he were not, he'd have no reason to harm 7T.

RECOMMENDATION: Continue testing, gradually decreasing dosage. Necessary to determine the holdover strength of the regimen, how much of the change is permanent, how much transitory, what is the overall effect on intelligence and agility.

##

*IMAGE: Tejnor lying on his cell bed, curled into a fetal knot, his body twitching at long intervals, his head cradled in the curve of his arms.*

# SHADITH (Kizra) ON THE FARM 2

1

Morning.

When the housemaid knocked at her door, Kizra groaned and crawled out of bed.

Aghilo had given her leather sandals to wear with the long gray skirt, the smocked shirt with the narrow scarf for a belt. She thought about wearing them, but something made her pick up the old boots and hold them and sit gazing at them. Her link with the past. She slid her feet into them, laughed a little as nothing happened. No epiphany. No magic rebirth. Not today anyway. She went downstairs, feeling vulnerable and tentative till she came up with Tinoopa and smelled the meat frying and the new baked bread waiting for them.

## ##

". . . says auntee Akitha caught ol' Tinkkar playin fumblefinger with young Impanni, you coulda heard the noise in the next aynti over. . . ."

". . . you see that redhead?"

"Gonna be trouble with that one."

"Taljee even sniff in that direction, he gonna. . . ."

". . . Jarrin says the young 'un she some kinda witch, she got healin hands or somethin . . ."

"Talking about witches, that Kulyari, she was in some kinda snit, made my life even more a misery than usual. She. . . ."

The chattering housemaids seated about the long table fell

abruptly silent as Tinoopa and Kizra stepped through the arch into the servant hall off the kitchen's south end.

Cook had the armchair at the head of the table, a big woman, with massive arms and breasts like pillows. She didn't say anything, just sat waiting for the newcomers to greet her; she reigned here and wanted no doubt of that in their minds.

With Kizra a nervous shadow in her wake, Tinoopa swept in, stopped beside Cook, held out her hand. "I greet you, Kuriya Kuma chal. May your shadow never grow smaller."

"That's as it may be." Kuma chal touched the hand. "Aghilo chal tells me it's you'll be doing the ordering and such from now on, what is it, that fancy word? liaison, that's it. Liaison between us 'n the Ulyinik Polyapo. Eh so?"

"I have become . . . um, shall we say acquainted with the Ulyinik." Tinoopa put what was impolitic to say aloud in the dry tone of her voice, the quick lift of a brow. "I shall study to make life easier all round." She bowed her head. "With your help, Kuriya Kuma chal, since I'm new to this place and don't know the sweet ways, the clever ways to get done what has to be done."

Kuma chal contemplated her for a moment, then she nodded her large head. "Yes. Jilipa, fetch a chair for the chapa Tinoopa, set it here," she patted the table beside her. "And you, girl, yes, you, the little one, don't hang about like an addled mouse, you too skinny as it is, sit down, eat eat."

## 

The morning was cool and damp with dew. In the distance Kizra could hear the blatting of some kind of beast, a fussy, irritated sound. She could hear men's voices mixing with the blats; she couldn't make out the words, but she thought that they were swearing. Probably at those beasts, sounded like the kind of misborn creatures who stubbornly and perversely refused to do what they were supposed to do.

*And how do I know that? Gods, I wish . . . I wish the wipe had took all the way, then I wouldn't have these ghosts . . . no, I don't, no. . . .*

She could hear squeals and loud whinnies. She could hear a rhythmic thudding, with a second thudding just off the beat, she could hear singing that wove around that thudding. She could hear birds twittering, insect buzzes, a thousand small sounds that blended into a sense of peaceful purpose, a pleasant background hum for a bright sunny morning at Winter's End.

Matja Allina stood on the steps pulling on her gloves and letting Aghilo tuck shawls about her to keep her warm.

Her daughters were there, a short distance from their mother, Ingva the older, thirteen, almost as tall as her mother and thin. An austerely pretty child, with the promise of beauty later on, intelligence sparkling in violet-blue eyes, spirit in the set of her body, the alertness of her face as she looked about. There was a wildness in her that burned through the patina of control. Kizra thought she looked like a deer about to start running, not because it was afraid but from the sheer joy of stretching its muscles.

Three years younger than her sister, Ylapura was shyer and less appealing, a wispy child with a worried little face. She had her mother's eyes, pale shining aquamarines set in sooty lashes, but she lacked her mother's vigor, maybe her intelligence.

The Jili (tutor) Arluja stood behind them, a thin gray woman with a tired, too-intelligent face.

Kulyari was there, too, hanging about the edge of things, looking very pretty, her hair braided and wired into intricate whorls, her skin milk white and rose pink; her mouth was a soft rose and her eyes a dark blue; they glared hate when she glanced at Kizra and a sullen dislike when she looked at Allina, a dislike that melted into demure shyness whenever Pirs was around.

Polyapo was there, Tinoopa beside her; the Ulyinik was a sour woman, full of vague resentments, but she'd pasted a simpering smile on her face in honor of the occasion.

Kizra couldn't understand why Allina kept these two around, what constrained her. It wasn't Pirs' doing, he was indifferent to both women, barely noticed them. He was indifferent to everyone but Allina and his children.

Leaning heavily on Aghilo's arm, Matja Allina walked down the stairs and across the courtyard to the long table where her female overseers waited with the new women lined up behind them.

2

After she was settled in the cushioned armchair, Matja
Allina set a roll of papers on the table in front of her, flattened them, and held them down with two bits of slate set
there for the purpose. From where she stood just behind the
Matja, Kizra could see a list of names with a brief notation
beside each. Anitra, Beba Mahl, Eeda, Ekkurrekah. . . .

Matja Allina pulled out the second page, let it roll up
beside the stone weight. "Nunnikura chal Weavemistress,"
she called out, and waited until a heavy middle-aged woman
with thick gray braids came to the far side of the table. "I
have seven for you, one with some pre-existent skills, the
others trainable." She looked beyond Nunnikura chal at the
labor cadre. "The chapa whose names I call, you will go
with the Weavemistress. She will show you where you will
sleep, equip you with clothing and other necessities, and
put you to work. Lyousa va Vogl. Sabato. Bertem. Luacha.
Tictoc. Evalee. Dorrit."

Matja Allina waited patiently until that was sorted out,
then called, "Intoyo chal Dyemistress."

Kizra clasped her hands over the arranga case hanging
from its shoulderstrap and withdrew her attention. Tinoopa
had been heavily into aphoristic advice after they left the
breakfast table.

*It's all very well,* the big woman said, *being backed by
the local bosses, but I have to make that backing stick.*

*I got that Polyapo soothed down,* Tinoopa said. *It was
easy, some butter and a sweet or two, mostly a sympathetic
ear and agreeing with her vision of herself. She thinks because she's Irrkuyon born and bred the rest of the world
should flatten themselves at her feet and say yes'm and no'm
and do everything she says 'cause it's her that says it. Stupid woman. Just as well, though, Kiz. If she weren't blind
and an idiot and pretty well loathed by everyone who knows
her, I wouldn't have this cushy job.*

*Vindictive bitch, that Kulyari,* Tinoopa said. *She's going
to make my life a hell, yours, too, unless. . . . Hmm. I
wonder what they consider unforgivable around these parts.*

Kizra shivered at the memory of that predatory look in
Tinoopa's eyes. Allina was right. The Shimmaroi must have
found Tinoopa far too formidable to want her anywhere near
their world.

She was impressed when she found out about the mind-wipe. . . . Funny thing to be impressed by. I suppose it was because I somehow scared someone enough he had to wipe me out like that.

Mindwipe. Things keep leaking over from somewhere . . . last night she'd dreamed . . . most nights she dreamed . . . things . . . that she couldn't quite remember when she woke . . . except the feelings. And the day ghosts . . . ideas and images that slid into her head and out again before she could catch hold of them. . . .

## ##

"Ingalina chal Beastmistress."

A thin wiry woman came forward, tanned leathery skin, sun-bleached blonde hair cut short.

Matja Allina took the last of the rolled up sheets, passed it across to the Beastmistress. "Ommla. Jhapuki. Fraji. Ra-fiki. Zhya Arru. Tsipor pa Prool. Go with the Beastmistress and do what she tells you." She settled back into the cushions, accepted a cup of hot broth from Aghilo. "That ends that," she said. "Ulyinik Polyapo, come here, please."

She continued to sip at the broth as Polyapo waited across the table from her. Finally she set the mug down. "The supplies I brought from Nirtajai have been stored and inventoried?"

"It is being done, Matja Allina."

Kizra blinked. That's a lie, she thought. She glanced at Allina, decided the woman knew perfectly well that her Ulyinik hadn't stirred herself, that the supplies could have sat out and rotted for all Polyapo cared about them.

"Good. I will expect a plan and a listing, a full accounting by sundown. I'm sure that will be plenty of time since you are already working at it. However, I would appreciate your personal involvement in this inventory since you'll need to know exactly what you have to work with during the following months. Chapa Tinoopa will assist you in this and in anything else that will ease your labors. Amurra's Blessing, Ulyinik Polyapo."

"Blessed be Amurra, Matja Allina." Polyapo creaked stiffly through the ritual bow, then went sweeping off with Tinoopa following placidly behind.

Aghilo brought out the flask of broth, touched the mug,

but Matja Allina shook her head. "No more, thank you.
Aghilo chal, your arm, please."

### 3

The dye vats were in a large open shed in a secondary
court west of the main court. There were lengths of cloth
drying on lines shaded by thatch roofs, hanks of yarn draped
over pegs, and vast steaming tubs of color with women
walking on narrow ledges about them, stirring the cloth or
yarn or tufts of wool with long wooden paddles, their hair
protected by kerchiefs from the steam, their faces smudged,
dark colorings under every fingernail. Blackened with coal
dust and red with the heat, young girls tended the fires under the vats, fetched coal from bins built into the yardwall.
Others rushed about with fleeces, fresh yarn, rolls of cloth.
It was a busy, noisy place, women talking, laughing, the
girls singing, chattering, all of that despite the hard heavy
work they were doing.

Matja Allina inspected everything, the stores of ground
colorings and other supplies, the work done while she was
gone, looking for quality and quantity. Then she settled onto
the leather seat of a folding stool. "Uri, Gintji, little chals,
little songbirds, come and sing for me. Teach young Kizra
here some homesongs."

Uri was a small pink and white child, with hands dyed a
dozen colors and frizzy blonde hair escaping from short
plaits. Gintji was longer and thinner, with less color in her
face and more in her hair. They curtsied solemnly, con-
ferred in whispers, faces flushed, blue eyes skittish. Then
they turned and stood holding hands, singing in sweet true
voices, small voices that fit the moment and the song.

*"The sun rises,"* Uri sang.   *"The sun sets,"* Gintji sang.
*"Mayra spins the red*   *"Hirmnal tends his sheep.*
*threads.*   *The moon sets.*
*The moon rises.*   *Hirmnal shears his sheep.*
*Mayra spins the white*
*threads.*
   *"Sun and moon, moon and sun,"* they sang together.
*Love waxes, love wanes*
*Day turns to night, night to day.*
*A young man grows old*

*A girl bears and rears*
*Sun and Moon, moon and sun*
*Love waxes, love wanes.*

| *"The sun rises.* | *"The sun sets.* |
| *Mayra weaves her bride* | *Hirmnal fattens his* |
| *cloth. . . .* | *sheep. . . .* |

Kizra picked up the tune, began playing her own thread
to the song; the girls were startled and stumbled over a word
or two, and then were back on track and finished with a
flourish.

## ##

As Uri and Gintji retreated among their friends, Kizra
kept on playing, sliding into another tune that seemed to
drip from her hands, a strongly accented upbeat thing that
had the women clapping and stamping before she'd played
a dozen phrases.

Matja Allina let the play go on for about five more minutes, then she nodded to Aghilo, got to her feet and went
out, leaving a buzz of talk behind.

Kizra felt the women's eyes on her as she went out, sensed
speculation and some resentment, with a few spikes of outright dislike. Favor, she thought, they don't like a new-
comer landing such a cushy job. They liked my music well
enough. Not me. No, not me. She bit on her lip, tried to
tell herself *bunch of backwater provincials, don't mean a
hiccup to me. I'm out of here first chance I get. . . .*

## ##

Weavers, embroiderers and fancyworkers, clerks, me-
chanics, turners and joiners, leatherworkers, herbalists,
blenders, oil pressers and gardeners, field workers, millers
(in the watermill on the riverside, the air white with flour
and gritty with bran), herders in from the field, beast ten-
ders in the home paddocks, the sick and wounded in the
infirmary, pregnant women, prisoners serving out drunk-
time, or recovering from the lash given for assault and other
offenses, they visited them all, Matja Allina had a word with
one or two, then Kizra played and learned songs while Matja
Allina rested, drank more broth.

Allina rested, but she never stopped; weariness grayed over her emotions, but she didn't show any of that; she listened, smiled, saw everything and moved on.

## ##

After several hours of this, Kizra began to worry. Getting out of the mess she was in depended on that baby and the mother's exhaustion couldn't be good for it. She dropped back until she was walking beside Aghilo. "Is it really needed, all this?" she whispered urgently. "The Matja is too tired now. She shouldn't let herself get that tired."

Aghilo patted her arm. "Yes," she murmured. "I know. Don't say anything." She flicked the fingers of her left hand at Kulyari's back. "That one." She shrugged. "Give her a crack to pry at and she'll have the Matja out before . . . tchah! Once the Matja has seen everyone, she'll rest. She can't miss anyone out. There are jealousies. . . ."

"I see."

"She's a blessing to us all, you don't know." Aghilo shook her head. "You just don't know, child. It's why the Irrkuyon hate her so much, even her own Family. She makes them look . . . ah . . . like what they are. She shames them. You keep your eyes open, you'll understand. Now hush, there's nothing you can do but sing your songs and play your music and make the day brighter for her and for us. She knows what she has to do. She'll rest when it's time. Go, go, I've talked too long. . . ."

# DYSLAERA 6:
## Spree

The gym was a long oval with three tiers of seats along one side where the spectators could look down on the games being played out on one section or another of the springy floor.

Nine Savants formally dressed in cowl, mask, black robe and gloves sat in the lowest of the tiers, a waist-high wall the only barrier between them and the floor. Behind them there were two score techs in their formal whites. Behind these stood a dozen wards in cowls, black leather, and stainless studs; six had heavy-duty stunners, six held dart tubes armed with exploding missiles.

Down on the mat, facing the Savants, Ossoran and Feyvorn stood naked, arms dangling loosely by their sides. Ossoran's fur was rexed and sprinkled with gray; it shimmered in the light with each breath he took. Feyvorn was a red Dyslaeror, he shone like liquid copper. They were heavily muscled, and despite everything the techs had done to them, they were in magnificent physical condition. Savants and techs murmured with pleasure. The guards stood imperceptibly straighter.

Savant 1 leaned forward, spoke. "Look up, Dyslaera."

A black cylinder emerged from the ceiling fifty meters up, the cable it was attached to lengthening slowly as it paid from an unseen drum. It stopped when it was about five meters from the mat.

The cylinder dissolved, revealing a Dyslaerin in a cage. She was very young, terrified, furious—and in season. Her claws had been removed, her fingers shortened by a joint; she was biting at the bars, wrenching at them, trying with everything she had to bend them just enough to let her limber body through.

Savant 1 watched the Dyslaerors, smiling with satisfaction. "A contest," he said. "You will fight each other for

106

her. The victor will be allowed one month free of tests and the services of the female. One of you must die. If both are alive at the end of the time we will set, she dies. If you refuse to fight, she will be artificially inseminated and as soon as the cub is born, she will be vivisected like that youth you saw a short while ago. Questions?''

Ossoran stared at Feyvorn. Feyvorn nodded.

"How long?" Ossoran said.

"Thirty minutes."

"We will fight."

## ##

They circled around each other, feinting, retreating, moving so fast they'd finished one set and were on to something else before the watchers fully realized what had happened.

This went on for several minutes, then they ran full out at each other. Feyvorn hit Ossoran's hands, shoulders, bounded upward and caught at the bars of the cage; he twisted his body round, got his footclaws hooked over the base, surged up. He reached through the cage and tore out the girl's throat.

As soon as Feyvorn was airborne, Ossoran ran at the wall, vaulted it and began mauling everyone he could reach, using his teeth and claws on his hands and feet.

## ##

Savant 4 (speaking to notepad):

. . . bloody debacle. Savants 1 and 2 are dead. Savant 3 has been sent to the meat farm with massive injuries including one arm torn from his body. Three techs were also killed or injured. Two of the guards panicked. Unfortunately, they were armed with the dart tubes. They killed the subjects, but also blew away several techs and Savants 8 and 9.

OBSERVATIONS: (1) the techs on duty at the data stations are to be commended, recommendation: honor bonuses for each.

(2) Preliminary analysis of readings indicates a reluctance to accept control from external sources that is far more powerful even than the kin-bond.

NOTE: We have a weakness that must be held in mind at all times when dealing with these Dyslaera. Their claws and fur lead us to think of them as beasts and this induces us to discount their intelligence. That is dangerous. On looking over the flakes of this disastrous event, I have noted that the plan was set and agreed upon in that first glance they shared. Without having to consult, they noted the best points of attack to achieve their goals, devised their plan, and set it in motion.

RECOMMENDATION: I must add my voice to that of Savant 1 in the course that he suggested: Acquire Dyslaera cubs, preferably before weaning. Also gravid females. These last should be kept comatose and their cubs surgically removed at term. If we can tame these creatures, they will be servants without peer, highly intelligent and physically magnificent.

# SHADITH (Kizra) ON THE FARM 3

1

Dinner over, her duties finally done, Matja Allina lay on her side, pillows tucked about her to help with the weight of the baby, hot water bottles spread around her, warming the aches out of her as the hot milk had warmed her inside. She was drowsing happily, sighing with pleasure as Tinoopa kneaded her back and shoulders; now and then she sang a few words to the music of the arranga.

Her grasp on the notes was sometimes shaky. She frowned when she was off, looked irritably at Kizra as if the arranga's tuning were off, not her voice.

Kizra got the message; she played to minimize the clashes, mushing the accompaniment, shifting her fingering to follow the wanderings of the Matja's voice. Crawl, Shadow, crawl, she sang under her breath. Her fingers faltered as she realized what her mindvoice had said. Shadow. Who . . . what . . . was Shadow? She gripped her lower lip between her teeth and forced a brittle calm over her nerves.

Ingva and Yla were sitting on the floor in a corner, a low table between them, playing a complicated game of cards but not absorbed in it. Kizra saw them looking repeatedly at their mother. She could feel their anxiety. Confined in the room, they were confronted with her fragility and their inability to do anything about it.

The muted comfortable sounds of the Kuysstead shutting down for the evening came through the open casement; the sunset glittered crimson off the diamond-shaped panes; high overhead a hunting raptor screamed and stooped, then swooped away with its prey dangling from its talons. The wind was rising and a few clouds drifted past, high clouds pink and gold with the sunset.

## ##

Pirs came in. He waved Tinoopa away, settled on the stool beside the bed and drew his fingertips along Allina's bare arm. Kizra continued to play quietly though her fingers shook with the impact of what lay under that gentle restrained gesture.

After a minute Allina caught his hand, sniffed at it. She didn't say anything, just looked at him.

"Raid on the South Pasture," he said. "Not Brushies. Tumaks. A dozen of them. It got hot there for a while, but we drove them off. Karr and Ritmin were hurt, flesh wounds, nothing to worry about. We chased the ones left alive past the boundmarks, they had a rover hidden away, got to it before we could get close enough. We let it go, no chance of catching up with them on horses. Too much chance of ambush."

"So close to the house. How they dare. . . . Damage?"

"Slaughtered a herd of woollies, tried to fire the brush, but it's not dry enough yet. Karr thinks they're townbred, their landcraft was more notable by its absence."

"Fire."

"Yes. That was a mistake. I saw a Brushie watching and a pair of l'borrghas. I don't think we'll have more trouble with fires, Lina aklina. I don't think the tumaks will have time to strike a match if they try it again. Just to make sure, though, I'm going into the Brush tomorrow for a limalima with Chul-Gop."

"It's not necessary."

"I think it is, Mi-matja. You know Chul-Gop, he won't lose his head."

"If he kills you. . . ."

"He hasn't before, Lina mi'klien."

"Tell no one. I'm not worried about the Brushies. Well, not much. It's your kin that . . . brother Mingas drools in his beard when he thinks of this Kuyyot. And Rintirry. . . ." She caught his hand, held tight to it. "I'd burn the Kuysstead and kill myself before I let Rintirry lay one finger on it or me."

In their corner, the two girls had gone very quiet.

Aghilo crossed her arms and hugged herself, her face blank.

Tinoopa stood in a shadowy corner, brooding over this new turn.

Kizra kept playing the same song over and over, the sound like water flowing, unobtrusive, gentling.

Pirs stood. "It's time you slept, Mi-matja. Aghilo, cousin, take the girls and . . . wait. Come here, Ingva, Yla." When they were standing before him, he touched each head, lightly, a small caress. "Say nothing of what you heard tonight, you hear, my lirrilirris?"

Yla blinked. "Not even to the Jili Arluja, Papay?"

"Particularly not to the Jili Arluja. Even if she asks, hmm? It's for her protection, Yla-lirri, what she doesn't know she can't be expected to tell."

"I won't, Papay. I won't tell anyone."

"Ingva."

The girl looked fierce. "I won't, Papay; it's none of their business." She stroked her hand along his arm, took his hand. "You will see us soon's you come back, huh, Papay?"

He laughed, tapped her on the nose. "The very minute. Now go get your baths and go to bed."

"Papay?"

"Ingva?"

"Take me with you. I won't keep you back, I ride better than Wurro even, I do. You talk to the old 'uns, I'll talk to the young 'uns. Babeyla and Tink and the rest. They're as good as the old 'uns at looking out for strangers."

"Not this time, lirri. It's a good idea, but now's not the time. I tell you what. We'll do it in a week or so, when I see how things are going to jump. All right?"

Ingva gave a brisk quick nod, then took her sister's hand and went out.

Tinoopa curtsied, said, "Arring Pirs, be sure we shan't speak of this even to each other." She hauled Kizra to her feet and hustled her out.

2

Pirs rode from the Kuysstead an hour before dawn.

Kizra woke sweating and moaning from a nightmare whose details evaporated before she got her eyes open. She flung the covers back and went to the window where she saw him on the ferry, his uncovered head shining silver-gilt

in the starlight. The rider beside him was long and lean, with
plaits bumping against his back, blond, too, but duller, like
rope braided from last season's straw. P'murr the Loyal.
Blood brother, as close to Pirs as chal ever got to Irrkuyon.

They rode the big Blacks, Pirs' prize horses, skittish
beasts, snorting and sidling, hooves noisy on the floor-
boards of the ferry, the sounds that they made as loud in
the clean stillness of the predawn as if she were standing
beside them; she could hear almost as clearly the put-put of
the winch motor and the creaking of the windlass.

She watched them ride off the ferry and vanish into the
predawn gloom, moving toward the leftward of the two
mountains, the one called Patja Mount.

*Well. Good luck to him.*

She shivered and started to turn from the window.
Something flickered. On the wall near the mill.
She pushed the window open farther and leaned out.
Someone was running along the wall. Fair hair and skirts.
The way it moved, young. Accustomed to that Talent of hers
by now, content to view it as the equivalent of her ear for
music, she *read* the figure, nodded.

*Kulyari. Up to something.*

She could smell it—spite, triumph, and a furiously busy
mind.

*What is it? What could she do, that little rat?*

Kulyari flitted along the wall like someone set her tail on
fire.

*Coming inside fast as she can scoot. How? Somewhere on
the ground floor, no other way in. All right, let's get down
there and see what we see.*

She kicked her slippers off, threw the robe around her
shoulders, and went running out.

### 3

Kizra leaned over the gallery rail, peering down at the
Great Hall. Shadows and emptiness. No movement. Nothing. She *read* the runner again.

The garden, that was it, Kulyari was coming down into
the Family Garden. She stopped, then she was moving
again. She stopped again, stayed still. Doing something.
Very busy. Sense of vindictive satisfaction. She was talking
to someone. Talking? Who?

Using her *reach* as a dowsing rod, Kizra ran down the
stairs and through the smudgy darkness, until she was
touching the south wall of the Great Hall. One hand on the
wall, her bare feet silent on the elaborate parquet, she
ghosted along, getting closer and closer to the girl—until
she was standing outside a massive door.

She leaned against the door and tried to hear what Kulyari
was saying. The wood was too thick. She chewed at her lip,
nodded, eased the latch up, and opened the door a crack.
She saw a bluish-white light flickering, a ghost light hardly
brighter than the shadows.

*Com. Must be battery powered. I didn't think. . . . Don't
be stupider than you have to, Kiz, this far out, of course
they had to have a com.*

"... before dawn, I told you, less than thirty minutes
ago." Kulyari stopped talking, listened to a muted mutter.
Kizra thought it was a man's voice, but she couldn't be sure,
and she hadn't a clue what the words were.

"No. No one saw me. They're all asleep."

Mutter mutter.

"Two of them. On the Blacks, with a pack mule."

Mutter mutter.

"P'murr."

Mutter mutter.

"Northeast. Toward Patja Mount."

Kizra didn't have to hear any more. Aghilo, she thought.
And right now.

4

Kizra tapped at Aghilo's door, tapped again, swore under her breath. Come on, woman. Come on!

Aghilo opened the door. "Chapa! What are you doing down here? And dressed like that?"

"Let me in," Kizra whispered. "She's coming up the stairs, I can hear her feet."

"Who?"

"Kulyari."

"All right." Aghilo stepped back so Kizra could come in. "What are you talking about?"

Kizra stood by the door listening. "On second thought, you'd better go see that it's her out there. I've a feeling my word isn't worth much when it comes to the Irrkuyon."

Aghilo pressed her mouth shut. She nodded. "True. Wait here. Leave the door open if you wish." She snatched up a robe, flung it around her shoulders, and went out.

5

"Visiting a lover?" Aghilo's voice was peppered with scorn. "Shameless one, out of your bedroom this late."

"Get lost, old woman. Keep your mouth shut or I'll have you whipped for impertinence. And don't think I can't do it." Kulyari laughed. "I don't have to explain anything to Garaddy's bastard." She swept off, laughing again.

Aghilo came back. She pulled the door shut, sighed. "You have your witness."

"She's putting it on. Under that arrogance, she's scared."

"Oh, really. What IS this about?"

"I woke up a little while ago, nightmare I think, but I don't remember. Anyway, I was looking out the window and saw Arring Pirs crossing on the ferry. Someone else was watching; once Pirs and P'murr were across, she took off. It was Kulyari. She came down in the Family Garden and got into a room there, I don't know what the room was, but there's a com in it. I cracked the door and heard her talking to someone on the com. She was telling him, I think it was a man, about Pirs, where he looked to be going, who was with him, you know, everything he didn't want to get out."

"Ah." Aghilo stripped the tie off her long plait, began pulling the strands apart.

"Is there any way we can make her tell who it was she was talking to?"

Aghilo moved to her dressing table, began brushing her hair, her strokes full of nervous energy. "No," she said. "The only one who could touch her is Pirs."

"Matja Allina?"

"No. No. You don't understand the way things are here." She dropped the brush and twisted her long hair into a knot atop her head, began shoving in hairpins, each darting movement of her hand emphasizing a phrase of what she was saying. "She's the heir's daughter. Utilas. He sent her here for fostering—once he saw what Pirs and Allina were making of this place. For fostering and to make trouble. Get rid of Allina. Be there to marry Pirs."

"He's her uncle, almost like seducing her father. I. . . ."

"No, I told you, you don't understand." Aghilo slapped in the last pin, got to her feet. "It's done here often enough. Usually the second wife, if the first dies or has to be put aside." She took off her robe, threw it on the bed, moved about, collecting underclothing, a skirt and shirt, talking as she moved. "The Families don't want conflicting alliances and it conserves the wealth. She's here to marry him if she can manage it. Viper. Him or his successor if she gets him killed."

"Since her father's the heir. . . ."

Aghilo pulled a folding screen out from the wall, went behind it and began dressing. "No. He's got enough on his hands with the old property. It'll be Mingas or Rintirry gets this if Pirs is killed."

"The baby doesn't count?"

"Who's to speak for him? Matja Allina? Don't be silly. If Pirs is killed, the baby's nothing. Boy babies die so easily on this world." She came from behind the screen looking quietly neat and lowered herself to a stool at the foot of the bed. "Go get dressed, chapa. You shouldn't be down here like that." She thrust her feet into her sandals, bent, and began working on the buckles. "Meet me. Ten minutes. You hear?" She gave a soft little grunt as she switched feet. "When I tell you to speak, you say just what you told me. And nothing," she looked up, "nothing about what's to do. The Matja will say. She knows the situation. Don't even hint what you're thinking. You don't understand. She has enough trouble without having to deal with you. Go on. Get.''

### 6

Matja Allina was tired and red-eyed. She sat in the only armchair in her bedroom, wrapped in a fleecy white robe with a blue-green silk lining. Tinoopa knelt at her feet, massaging them with a scented cream, working the toes, the muscles of her calves, humming a placid soothing three-note tune. The smell of the cream was strong in the room, a sweetness with an acrid underbite.

"After Aghilo challenged her," Kizra finished, "Kulyari went sweeping off in a snit."

"So," the Matja said. "Our precautions were useless. Hmm. Aghilo, I saw Wuraj in the infirmary yesterday, didn't I?"

"Yes. He'd tangled with a young l'borrgha and had clawmarks here and there. Bone-deep some of them. Otherwise he wouldn't have bothered to come in."

Matja Allina closed her eyes, rubbed at the vertical lines between her brows. "He didn't look bad. . . ."

"Well, he should probably rest at least a week."

"Bring him to me. If he can't go, he'll know who's best to send."

"Matja . . ." Aghilo said tentatively, raising her hands in protest.

"I know, I know. I don't mean here." She dragged her hand across her mouth. "I wish . . . no . . . impossible . . . everyone knows everything that happens. Bring him to the entrance hall. I'll be down immediately." She cut off Aghilo's protest. "It has to be me, my friend. You know that. Get Gilli chal and Ghineeli chal, they're loyal, I'm sure of it. Put them to watching Kulyari and Polyapo. I wish . . . no." Once again she closed her eyes. "Tinoopa, thank you, that was lovely. I want you to help me dress and get downstairs as quickly as we can manage. The sooner it's done . . ." she pushed at her hair, "the sooner I can rest."

7

Wuraj was a small wiry man with coarse gray hair in a braid that reached past his belt. He braided his beard to match; it hung in two tails down his front. His eyes were a light yellow-brown, narrow, set in a weave of wrinkles. One arm was heavily bandaged. Three ragged scabs raked down the side of his face.

Matja Allina frowned. "I'm sorry, Wuraj, I hadn't realized how bad it was."

He looked scorn and didn't bother answering.

"You're sure?" Matja Allina said.

"Ya."

"What will you need?"

"Name a the Mirp they headin for. The roans Arring keeps in south paddock, rifles, ammo packs. For me 'n them. They wouldna take any but sidearms they goin to meet Brushies. Bag a taffys for the Brushies. Might need sweet'nin up. Red cloth fer presents. Ah . . . and I want the Jinasu, you don't mind. Nut'n else I can think of right now."

"You'll have it." Matja Allina put her hand in her sleeve, brought out a small white card with a seal on it in red wax. She held it out to him. "If anyone questions you, show this."

He nodded, tucked the card in a belt pouch.

"Bring the roans to the Kitchen Gate and wait there for the Jinasu and the rest of it." She held out her hand. "Bring him back whole, Wuraj mi-chal. For all our sakes."

She watched him out, then turned to the others. "Tinoopa, go wake Cook, get a bag of taffys from her and trek supplies. Do you know anything about packsaddles?"

"No, Matja Allina. I've lived in cities all my life."

"Cook will show you. Go quickly. Everything I've promised you depends on him, do you understand?"

"Oh, yes, I do surely understand, oh, Matja." Tinoopa dipped a curtsy and went out, moving at a fast trot.

"Aghilo, more running about for you. Wake Ingalina chal Beastmistress, have her send the Jinasu to the kitchen equipped for a trek. Do that first, then send someone for a bolt of cloth, red cloth, make sure they know it has to be red, doesn't matter who you send, just someone who'll do it fast. Who you can trust to do it fast. Here." She twisted a key off the ring at her belt. "Take this. When you get back, lock up the Arring's study. I wish I'd thought of it before, that's the one key Polyapo doesn't have, Amurra be blessed. Or Kulyari. Then go wake Loujary chal and Wayak chal, I need them to carry me up to the armory, I don't want to have to climb those stairs. And fetch Kulas chal, good old Kulas, if there's any chalman I can trust, it's him. I want him standing guard while I open the armory, I need him to take charge of the ammunition packs and the rifles and bring them down to Wuraj. . . . " She grunted, crossed her arms and bent over them. "No . . . ah! no, Hilo, don't worry," she gasped. "It's not labor, just. . . ."

Kizra dropped to her knees, pressed her hands against the active bulge of the baby, sent *calm, ease, reassurance,* felt the spasms relax under her palms.

Matja Allina straightened. Absently, she patted Kizra's shoulder as she turned to Aghilo. "Go," she said impatiently. "The sooner Wuraj is on his way, the sooner Pirs will be safe."

## 8

Kizra leaned out her window, watched Wuraj on the ferry, riding one horse, leading another with a small pack on its back. The four tiny Jinasu were there with him, brown ghosts nearly impossible to pick out of the dark.

So many things she didn't understand about this place.

A man could send his daughter to his brother's house and expect her to . . . well . . . seduce his brother.

That same daughter could plot her uncle's murder and rejoice in what she considered her cleverness.

I thought it was craziness when Allina fussed about the danger to her baby and herself. Now. . . .

When Wuraj was across, she turned away, pulled on her boots, and went down to breakfast.

## 9

After lunch Matja Allina went to bed and stayed there, leaving Tinoopa and Aghilo to keep order and continue the work of the Kuysstead.

Kizra was forced to sit with her in the darkened bedroom, playing the arranga for her, singing now and then the songs she'd picked up yesterday and on the trip here. She was pleased that her memory was so good despite what someone had done to her head. It was reassuring.

The day crept along.

Now and then, when Matja Allina let her stop playing for a while, she pushed the drapes back and looked out one of the sitting room windows, watching the chal and chapa move about the court below, chattering knots of girls, gossiping older women, busy, laughing, serious, none of them stuck away in a suffering eddy like this one where she was. She envied them. She was bored. More than anything she was bored.

Tinoopa crossed the court, heading for the storage yard, a covey of chattering maids trailing behind her. She looked vigorous and contented; even this far off, Kizra read a bursting energy; the woman was enjoying her fight for authority, using her cleverness and experience to get what she wanted.

Some time later Tamburra the Kiv'kerrinite walked from the herb drying rooms and headed for the entrance to the women's living quarters. She glanced up at the face of the House as she walked by, saw Kizra watching her, and then looked quickly away. Kizra scratched the inside of her elbow and wondered again what it was brought that woman to this place.

Matja Allina called her back into the bedroom. "Play that thing you did for dinner last night." Her voice was fretful, her face was flushed, there was a shallow vertical pain-line between her brows.

"This one, Matja Allina?" She let the easy undemanding song drip from her fingers. Boring. Boring. All of it. Stifling. Gods, I want to . . . I want. . . . She didn't know what she wanted, except it wasn't this.

"You're frowning. What are you thinking?" Matja Allina's eyes caught what little light there was, seemed to glow. "Kizra Shaman, do you know something about Pirs? What is it? Tell me. You have to tell me."

"No, Matja Allina. Of course not, how could I? I was just . . . just thinking."

"About what? What worries you?"

Kizra blinked at her. Not even my own mind belongs to me, she thought mutinously. What to say . . . what? Ah. "Kulyari," she said. "I was thinking about how disappointed she's going to be when the Arring walks in. What

a snit she's going to throw." She moved her shoulders.
"That wasn't what bothered me, it's what she's going to do
next. After the Arring walks in."

"Walks in. Yes. So we must hope." Allina closed her
eyes, the brief spurt of energy draining from her.

"Matja, ah. . . ."

"What is it?"

"Aghilo didn't want me to bother you, but. . . . Is there
ANY way you can find out who Kulyari was talking to?"

"Little chapa, it's all right." The Matja's feverish intensity faded to a drowsy musing. "It's no bother because I
don't need to ask. I know who she was calling. Rintirry.
My loving brother-by-law. Dear Rintirry who is so very fond
of his brother he tried to rape me as soon as he saw Pirs
wanted me." She clicked her tongue. "Hai, Kizra, you listen so deeply it's easy to say far too much. Pirs doesn't
know about that. No one knows. I broke the bastard's nose
for him and he went away. Please. If you say anything it
will make more trouble than you can possibly understand."

"All right."

Matja Allina closed her eyes. "Go find Gilli chal, will
you, please. Then come back and tell me what Kulyari's doing."

## 10

Kizra knelt beside the bed, her hands folded in her lap.
"Kulyari slept until just after the noon gong. She went into
the garden and pulled heads off flowers there until Polyapo
looked out, saw what she was doing, and scolded her back
inside. Then Kulyari hung around the Great Hall. When she
thought no one was around, she tried to get into the Arring's
study. Gilli chal says she had a screaming snit when she
found out it was locked. She's back in her room now, trying
on clothes, changing her hair, driving the maids till they're
ready to bang her on the head and stand the consequences.
That's it."

"Polyapo. Do you think she's involved in this?"

"If I had to guess, no. There's no tension in her. And
she's not . . . um. . . ." Kizra sneaked a glance at Allina
to see how far she dared go.

Matja Allina narrowed her eyes to slits, her mouth
twitched. "And she's not intelligent enough to hide it."

"Well, yes." Kizra got to her feet. "It's time you should eat something, Matja Allina. You know what Tinoopa said, small meals but frequent. Do you want me to ring the kitchen?"

"No. I don't want much. A cup of broth and a roll will do."

"Just a minute, then." Kizra crossed to the fireplace, took the lid off the brazier, and set on the covered pot of broth. She put a fresh roll in a small dutch oven, then leaned against the bricks of the chimney while she waited for the food to heat.

"Chapa Kizra, come here, help me to sit up. Bring the extra pillows, will you?"

## 11

Time passed.

Matja Allina drowsed.

Kizra went back to watching what was happening in the court below. To wondering what her dreams meant. To speculating if she and Tinoopa would get what Allina promised them. To yearning for release from this tedium. It always came back to that. She loathed being shut away from what was happening. It was as bad as being in jail, at least according to Bertem's tales. Or Tinoopa's. Boredom and being jerked about by anyone that had the power to jerk.

*And even if I ran, where do I run to? I don't know who I am or where I belong. I don't KNOW anything. How can I DO anything. . . .*

## 12

The day ended finally.

That night Kizra sweated through more nightmares, worse than any night before this. She remembered bits each time she woke:

*giant spiders with intelligent eyes and orange pompoms where their ears would be if spiders had ears, relentless, implacable, she shuddered with horror when she saw them. . . .*

*crashing in a small fast ship, going down and down and nothing she could do about it, dying, all the pain and emptiness of dying. . . .*
*women dancing, thin, etiolate, all bone and skin and huge dark eyes, eerily unexpectedly lovely creatures that brought with them the anguish of loss (she knew why in the dream but couldn't remember later). . . .*
*a red-haired woman weeping for a lost child, a grief Kizra shared as if it were her own (she knew her in the dream, knew her like a sister, a deeply loved sister, but when she woke, there was only the face and the hair, the long fine red hair). . . .*
*two cats died and a man cried out in anguish and rage, a lion man, she shared that anguish till the dream faded. . . .*

Nightmare followed nightmare until she dropped into a hard-fisted sleep that left her as tired when she struggled out of bed as she was before she lay down.

### 13

Matja Allina's estate office on the ground floor was small and intimate with a bow window looking out into the Family Garden. She sat in a cushioned armchair drawn up to a swaylegged table, her hands were folded on the table, and she was listening to a dispute over the distribution of cloth.

Polyapo stood beside the door, despising everyone in the room for allowing the dispute to happen.

Sitting on a low bench in the bow window, half-hidden behind a carved and pierced screen of some dark rich local wood, Kizra watched the Ulyinik's long nose twitch and thought:

*if it were up to her, everyone involved in this would be whipped until they knew their place and left to go without cloth until they were naked and properly grateful for anything they were given.*

"The promise, Matja Allina. The Daughter's Promise. I want the bolt for Lahirra's wedding. Blue cloth, fine blue, not just ordinary tirrk. For all girls when they wed, by your word, O Matja."

The Weavemistress snorted. "And you got it, Luwlu chal, on Winterstart, you signed for it and carted it off and you know it."

"Can I help it if N'gwaral gets hisself clawed by some filthy l'borrgha and dies two months later leaving my Lahirra a sorrowing widow? What's a mother to do? Ignore her child once she's wed and let everything after go as it goes? The promise is made, when a daughter weds, cloth for her dowry. So Lahirra is going to wed with N'trurr next week. So she's due another bolt."

Aghilo slipped through the door and stood beside Polyapo, looking agitated. Kizra rubbed at her chin. I wonder what's up.

Matja Allina's eyes flicked to Aghilo, then she returned to her absorption in the speeches of the two women.

"Huh," the Weavemistress said, "the way the girl goes through husbands, she should open a clothing store. Lahirra has her dower, all she has to do is carry it down two doors when she moves in with N'trurr. And take better care of this one so he doesn't die on her."

"Hard, hard, you're so hard, Nunnikura chal, how's my little girl to blame, she didn't send her man out there to get chewed up." She burst out sobbing and keening, producing more noise than tears.

Matja Allina knocked gently against the table. "Quiet, Luwlu chal. Answer me a question or two, if you please. No, Nunnikura chal, you can speak later if you so desire."

Luwlu sniffed, wiped her nose on her sleeve, dipped a curtsey and waited.

"Luwlu chal, how much of the first bolt remains?"

The woman looked sullen, but she didn't dare protest. "About half," she said after a long silence while she was pretending to remember, "Matja Allina."

"It is certainly no fault of Lahirra that her first husband met with an angry l'borrgha and if the time between her weddings were somewhat longer, there would be no question about providing a second dower bolt. Nunnikura, you will measure the length remaining of the first dower bolt and complete it so Lahirra goes to her second wedding with the same gift she had at the first. And, given the tragic circumstances that make the second wedding necessary, you will also add a length of wedding cloth, fine green for the twice married bride, and a length of lace for her wedding shift from my own stores. Do you consent, Nunnikura chal? Do you consent, Luwlu chal?''

Nunnikura Weavemistress compressed her mouth in a straight line; she didn't approve, but she wasn't about to say so. She nodded, dipped through a perfunctory curtsy.

Luwlu chal had a discontented look, but she, too, nodded and curtsied her acceptance.

"Then let it be done, Nunnikura chal, and done within the hour. I thank you for your courtesy, y-chala. Amurra Bless.''

"Blessed be," Nunnikura said. She glared at Luwlu chal who hastily added her *Blessed be*, then both left the room.

"What is it, Aghilo? You have something to tell me?'' Matja Allina's voice was cool, but there was more than a little fear behind the mask.

Aghilo glanced at Polyapo, unwilling to give her message in the presence of the older woman.

Matja Allina sat back in the chair, dropped her hands on the arms where they were hidden from the other two women. "Ulyinik Polyapo, you will help me greatly if you would see how many supplicants remain outside and have one of the girls you trained so well make a list of names and when possible a short summary of each complaint. Will you do this for me, please? Good. Amurra Bless.''

"Blessed be Amurra.'' Polyapo resented furiously being pushed out like this and given what she considered a make-work task, but she knew also that her place here hung by a thread and that thread was the Matja's good will. So she went.

As soon as the door clicked shut, Matja Allina brought her hands up, clutched at the table's edge. "Pirs? There's word?''

"No, Allina, it's early yet. This is almost as bad.'' She looked down at her hands, touched the ring of keys at her belt. "I was in the Family Garden, setting up the screens for your tea. I heard glass breaking. It was Kulyari, she was trying to get into the study. I had her taken back to her room, there was a cut on her wrist, I used that as an excuse. Loujary was with me, you know, to shift the screens. He had to be rough with her.''

"I understand. If she complains, I'll back you. Go on.''

"Yes. Well. I saw the summons light blinking on the com; I expect Kulyari did, too, and that's why she tried to break in. Anyway, I thought it was someone calling her and it might help if I saw who it was. But it wasn't for her, it was Tribbi. You remember my half sister, the one who keeps Aynti Tingger? Yes, well, she kept trying to get us, but with the door locked there was no one to answer the com. She wanted to warn us. Your father-by-law, the Artwa Arring Cagharadad flew in yesterday with his bodyguards and bed-warmer and Rintirry. He stayed there overnight, left this morning. He'll be here sometime before sundown.''

Matja Allina looked down at her hands. They were shaking. She flattened them on the table. There was no color at all in her face. "How very convenient," she said. "That Rintirry's here when the news comes about Pirs. How very, very convenient."

She sat silent a moment, staring at nothing.

"Before sundown. Well." She forced herself upright. "I doubt there's a chance Pirs will be back tonight, even if Wuraj comes up with him and nothing's happened." She lifted a hand, let it fall, a curious halfhearted gesture as if she were too weary to finish what she'd started. "Aghilo, find Tinoopa quickly; warn her about this descent on us. As soon as you've done that, go see Cook, you know what we'll want. We're not supposed to know he's coming, but we'd better cater to his tastes as closely as we can. The suppli-cants. It's nearly teatime, anyway. Tell Polyapo to send them away as soon as the list is finished. Um . . . you know which servants to put with the Artwa. No maids. He'll have to make do with the bedwarmer he'll bring with him. Um. As soon as the skimmer's down, send word round to the women that Rintirry's come. No girl between eight and fourteen is to show her face or anything else as long as he's here. They know him, but I want to make sure. Warn Ti-noopa about him, tell her if Polyapo tries to send a girl to serve any of that party, she should take care it doesn't hap-pen; she can use any means she needs to, I'll back her. Warn her to stay as inconspicuous as possible. For her own sake. Let Polyapo do the greeting and appear to give the orders. Tell her my father-by-law can't abide dark faces. He'd have her whipped on the slightest suspicion of inso-lence. That she's breathing and on her feet would be enough. Be as frank with her as you think useful, I won't ask what you say to her. So. Anything more? Good. Go, luv, quickly.

She watched Aghilo scurry out, then she scrubbed her hand across her mouth. "Kizra, come here."

Kizra brought the arranga with her, lifted it to play, but let it fall when Matja Allina shook her head.

"I have to say to you what I told Aghilo to say to Tinoopa. Stay in the background as much as you can. I won't be able to hide you, not with Kulyari making mischief. She knows the Artwa's . . ." She twisted her face in a brief fastidious grimace. "I said he can't abide dark faces. That's not the whole truth, child. He won't have them around him—except in his bed. And the more reluctant they are, the better. In his eyes, this isn't rape because they are beasts and beasts are put on this world to use as one pleases. But don't worry, child, you'll be safe enough." She rested her hand on the bulge of her son. "Pregnant women are indulged, especially when they carry sons; if I have a fancy to keep you with me, he can't demand you. And Rintirry has to keep his hands to himself, be thankful for that. Unless he can catch you alone somewhere. After they're settled in, I want you to sleep in my sitting room. Never leave me when you're out of it. I don't want trouble, not now. Ay-Amurra if only Pirs were here. . . ."

She sighed, shifted among the pillows, then grunted as pain seized hold of her.

Kizra hurried around the table, set her hands on Allina's neck and did again what she'd done before, transferred calm and relaxation so that the tension in the woman untied itself and flowed away and took with it the pain. She stepped back. "Do you want me to call the men to take you upstairs? You know you'll need all the strength you have once the Artwa comes."

"No. I'm not going upstairs, not yet. It's lovely outside. We'll have tea in the garden as I planned." Matja Allina touched her face, looked at the damp on her fingertips from the sweat that was beading her brow. "Yes. Get the lists from Polyapo as soon as they're finished, you can read them to me later."

14

It was warm in the garden; the high mud walls kept the worst of the wind off, the late afternoon sun was still high and bright enough to flush the perfume from the flowers and draw shimmers of heat off the pond; the fountains glittered and murmured, jiltis and flying jejantis hummed and skritched, the new green leaves on the trees whispered together, the flowering plums shed pale pink and white petals that landed on the grass and stirred again as Ingva and Yla played with their cats and chased each other in endless games of tag and catch.

Matja Allina was stretched in a lounge chair, sipping at a cup of broth when she remembered to, drowsing in the sun, listening to her children play and to the flowing music of the arranga. A maid was massaging her feet, the screens Aghilo had set about her captured the sunlight and the warmth while the sorrowing willow beside her provided enough shade to ease her eyes. Tinoopa was handling the House, there was nothing she could do to avert the trouble coming at them, so she set aside her troubles and let herself enjoy the afternoon.

Kizra was bored.

She hated that nothing music she was tinkling from the arranga, she hated the bugs crawling on her arms, miggas and tarynas and a dozen other kinds of pest, she hated the willow pollen getting in her eyes and up her nose, not quite making her sneeze. And she was cold. She was in deep shadow, close beside the trunk of the willow. No sun for her. And if she stopped playing to slap at the bugs or scratch, she got a fratchetty complaint from the Matja. There was one blessing in all this, she didn't have to think . . . she was getting tired of questions and ghosts and wondering. . . .

A small gray-green lizard ran up the trunk; she caught the movement from the corner of her eye, but didn't really see what it was until he was almost nose to nose with her. She stared at him and he stared back, loose gray-green skin, tiny orange eyes. . . .

Shock jolted through her. She dropped the arranga, cried out.

The lizard ran away and she fainted.

## 

She was out only a moment, opened her eyes to find the girls bending anxiously over her.

"What is it? What happened?" Ingva clutched at her arm, shook it. "Why did you do that?"

Kizra blinked, winced at the pain in her head. She'd hit a knotty root when she went down. Moving stiffly, she sat up. "A lizard," she said. Her voice was hoarse; saying the word sent more shocks through her. "It scared me."

"Lizard." Ingva got to her feet. "Lizard won't hurt you," she flung over her shoulder, "Ylie, come on, let the ol' fraidycat lay there, I got the mocsoc, come see come see. . . ."

Stomach cramping, black spots with tailed halos swimming dizzily in front of her, Kizra pushed up onto her knees. She didn't understand what was happening to her, she could feel the Matja's anger, the children's scorn, the indifference of the housemaids standing like plants in the background—she could feel out beyond them the life in the compound, busy busy life. . . . Everything enormously brighter, stronger, hammering at her. . . . As if some sort of filter had been peeled from her brain. . . .

It was too much.

She knelt hunched over, clutching at herself, nearly out of control . . . too much . . . too much. . . .

Matja Allina called her servingmaids to her. With the girls' help, she sat up. "Jili Arluga," she said. "Take the girls inside, please. Be quiet, Ingva. You and your sister do what you're told. I don't want argument from you, daughter."

She sat silent as the subdued girls trailed out after their tutor, followed by their serving maids, then she passed a hand across her face. "Chapa Kizra, get yourself together and come here." Her voice snapped with irritation and impatience. "And think about what you're going to tell me. I don't want stupid stories about lizards, you hear me?"

"Yes." Kizra forced the word out as she groped about for the arranga. When she found it, she wrapped her hand in the carrystrap and got shakily to her feet.

She moved from the shadow of the willow withes and stopped at the foot of the lounge chair.

"Well?"

"I don't know. What I said was true, Matja Allina. A lizard ran up the tree and frightened me. I don't know why it did, something in my head, I suppose." Another shudder passed along her body.

"I see." With her maids' help, Matja Allina swung her legs off the lounge and struggled to her feet. "I'll need you to play for dinner this evening. Will you be able to?"

"Yes, of course." Kizra spoke quickly, but her voice was still shaking and there was an icy knot in her stomach.

"Not of course." Old disciplines kicking in—Kizra was one of her charges and due a certain level of consideration—Matja Allina suppressed her irritation. "You need rest." She frowned at Kizra, eyes moving from the beading of sweat on Kizra's face to the tight clutch of her hands on the arranga. "I think . . . yes. I will authorize a hot bath for you. Soak a while, rest in your room. I'll want you with me an hour before dinner so we can lay out the program. You'll stay in your room until I send for you?"

"Yes. Of course." Kizra curtsied, stepped aside to let Allina walk heavily past.

There was a coppery taste in her mouth, the taste of groveling.

*Gods. Shadow, you're a worm. . . . Shadow?*

She shivered again, slipped the arranga's carrystrap over her shoulder, and went inside.

# DYSLAERA 7:
# Blood magic

Azram paced from the ventilation grate to the door-grid, turned and went back, back and forth, back and forth, glancing each time at Kinefray sitting on one of the plank beds.

Kinefray's ears moved restlessly, his eyes blinked, a muscle at the corner of his mouth twitched erratically. Two hours ago he'd walked into the cell, sat down; he hadn't said a word since.

Azram sighed, stopped in front of his cousin. "Fray."

Kinefray's eyes glazed over. He stared past Azram with no further reaction.

Azram extruded the claws on his right hand, touched the tips to the side of Kinefray's face, running in a shallow arc from the corner of his eye to his jaw just below his mouth. "Fray, listen to me."

Kinefray moved slightly, retreating from the prick of the claws. After a minute, he blinked, hissed a threat.

Azram stepped back, scowled as Kinefray's face went empty again. "Oh, Fray," he said, all his grief in those two words. "I don't know what to do."

## ##

Savant 4 (speaking to notepad):
It begins to look like we've managed to break the very close kin-bond between this subject 3F (native name: Kinefray) and the control subject 3A (native name: Azram) . . . unfortunately this seems to require large and frequently repeated doses of CPF24sub2 combined with Levastrayin and trace quantities of the ananile called Dragon's Blood . . . the result does not justify the expense for anything but purposes of research . . . the rapid me-

tabolizing of these drugs by this species complicates the
study . . . in addition, there seems a slow deterioration
in the physical well-being that we have so far been unable
to check, especially when this is combined with the ef-
fluents of rage . . . see the reports of subject 3Tj (native
name: Tejnor) . . .
NOTE: Final report on 3Tj submitted at this point to the
panel of Savants. 3Tj dead of massive cerebral accident
during forcible administration of a new drug series. See
Flake DDY-37 for details of incident and autopsy.

## ##

Azram rolled up his left sleeve, working with meticulous
care, getting the folds smooth and even. He cut a deep
scratch in his forearm, watched the blood ooze out. Holding
his arm level, he got up, crossed to Kinefray's side of the
cell, and dropped beside him.

Kinefray's ears twitched as the blood smell reached him,
but he didn't look around, just stared at the dusty gray
floor.

Azram watched the dark red liquid round into beads on
his fur. When he thought there was enough of it, he wiped
his hand across it; in a continuation of the same motion, he
smeared the blood across his cousin's face.

Kinefray screamed, lunged up, and leaped at Azram.

Azram ducked away, circled him, batting at the hands
reaching for him, claws out. He kept his claws carefully
sheathed; at first he was afraid, but his reaction time was
unimpeded by drugging, so he was much faster and stronger
than his cousin.

Kinefray snarled, slashed at him—but seemed to realize
finally that there was no threat here, seemed to realize finally that this was only Patti-Paw. Confused and uncertain,
he retracted his claws.

Azram darted in, caught him about the torso, and muscled him to the cell floor.

In minutes they were play-fighting, wrestling vigorously,
even enjoying themselves. . . .

Savant 4 (speaking to notepad):

ADDENDUM: By application of several primal forces—blood smell, anger, strenuous physical activity, subject 3A (native name: Azram) has managed to reestablish the kin-bond and to a considerable degree negate the effect of the drugs and the conditioning.

RECOMMENDATION: Considering the expense, the loss of subject material and the ineffectiveness of the drug treatments, this series of experiments should be brought to an end. We should concentrate on more efficient ways of acquiring information. We will also need more subjects for experiment. Though the acquisition of that young female lost with subjects 70s (native name: Ossoran) and 7Fy (native name: Feyvorn) cost us a number of agents and proved useless in the end, I believe we should attempt to acquire more females. It might also be useful to build up a stock of pre-pubescent males. The one thing we must do is locate additional sources of Dyslaera. Spotchals is becoming difficult about our presence there; according to reports from our assets in the records department, this is due to the continuing agitation of one Digby of Excavations Ltd and one Miralys, Toerfeles of family Voallts and Director of Company Voallts Korlatch. The abduction of that female has stirred even the most lethargic of the Spotchallix authorities to action.

NOTE: Our security seems suspect. It is as yet uncertain whether the Toerfeles Miralys knows who took her people; however the suggestion is that Digby has discovered what happened at Koulsnakko's Hole. How? This is a question that MUST be answered.

# SHADITH (Kizra) ON THE FARM 4

1

The skimmer landed in the main Court, pulverizing a number of the paving stones, taking up most of the open space. On the side facing the House, a ramp unfolded. As soon as it was down and stable, the Artwa Arring Angakirs Cagharadad came marching out and stood before the stairs like the earth was his but beneath his notice. Rintirry lounged behind him, looking bored and beautiful.

Perched in the opening behind the oriel window above the Great Doors, Kizra watched Rintirry look around and decided Allina had splendid judgment when it came to men.

He straightened suddenly, his eyes fixed on something across the Court.

Kizra pressed her face against the glass, swore under her breath. Tamburra the Kiv'kerrinite was standing in a patch of sunlight that turned her hair to fire, emphasized the translucence of her skin, the perfection of bone and body. Posing for him.

*Gods. That's trouble, that is.*

The Artwa was a tall lean man with an abundance of coarse white hair and a vigorous white mustache. His face was bright red, his skin rough as a rutted road. He glared at the silent facade and twitched his long nose.

Everything was stilled, waiting.

The great doors opened and Matja Allina came out, leaning on Aghilo's arm, Polyapo and Kulyari a half-step behind her. She stood quiet a moment at the top of the stairs, looking down at the Artwa. A flutter of her fingers summoned Polyapo to her side. With both women helping her, she came down to greet him.

She stopped five paces away from him, placed her palms together, bowed her head, then let Polyapo and Aghilo lower

133

her to her knees. While they prostrated themselves before
the Artwa, Matja Allina rounded her back, brought her
hands up, palm to palm, pressed her thumbs against her
brow and waited to be acknowledged.

The old man spoke. "Matja."

"Ghanar Rinta is honored," Matja Allina chanted in the
tonal version of the local langue, a formal singsong that her
voice made into music, "Artwa Arring Angakirs Procagharadad. Amurra Bless thee and thine. This House and all in
it are thine. What is thy pleasure, Artwa Arring?"

In the cloudless pale blue sky a single raptor glided in
wide circles over the Kuysstead and precisely on cue gave
its wild, eerie call, then went swooping off after something
Kizra couldn't see. She pressed her hand over her mouth to
stifle the giggles that threatened to burst out of her (nervous
giggles—though the scene had gone comical on her, there
was still a soupcon of fear in it).

"Get up, get up, girl," the Artwa said, a heavy geniality
in his loud voice. "I'm an easy man, you know. These formalities. . . ." He waved a hand, then scowled. "Where's
my son? Got his nose stuck in a book somewhere? Or is he
so grand these days he can't come to welcome his old father?"

With Polyapo and Aghilo boosting her, Matja Allina got
to her feet. "Artwa Arring Angakirs, there was a raid on
one of the outer pastures. Arring Pirs has gone with guide
and guard to look into the matter. If he had known you were
coming, Sar, of course he would have postponed his departure long enough to greet you. If you will enter your House,
Sar? I have set the servants readying the Honor Suite for
you and your household. Will you take some wine and cakes
and rest yourself a while?"

He nodded graciously and strode past her, half-running
up the steps, then striding into the House.

Rintirry strolled after him. He reached with languid grace
toward Matja Allina as if he intended to draw his hand
across her belly. She didn't lift a hand to stop him, simply
looked at him with calm contempt.

Rintirry laughed at the Matja; it was meant to be a taunt-
ing laugh, but it didn't quite come off. He waggled his fingers at her and went sauntering up the steps.

Kizra ran her fingers through her hair, hurried back to her
room.

2

There were two tables at the end of the Great Hall, the high table where the men sat and the lower one for the women. The high table was in a large curtained alcove raised a good two meters off the floor. The candles in the torchieres flickered in the drafts that wandered through the hall, waking shimmers in the damascened cloth-of-gold tiedrapes and a deeper sheen in the green velvet folds behind the gold. The rug was the color of fresh blood, the table a dark tight-grained wood, the dinnerware silver with gold wire laid into it in a series of interlocking double spirals. The wine in the crystal goblets was oxblood and there were yellow and white and blue flowers in oxblood vases.

Artwa Angakirs wore viridian and gold, a heavy gold chain about his neck set with emeralds, turquoise and chrysoprase, rings on all his fingers with more emeralds in them. Green and gold were the family colors and much of the Family wealth came from the emeralds found on Caghar Rinta, the gold in its streams and hills. And the pockets of turquoise that kept turning up. In the flickering candlelight he was magnificent, an old king: stupid as a rock, vain and selfish, but an impressive presence when presence was all you needed.

Rintirry lounged beside the Artwa in a smaller chair, dressed in a gold-crusted crimson velvet tunic with wide oversleeves trimmed in white fur. They fell back to show the black sleeves of his undertunic, a silky knit that hugged his muscular forearms. His only jewel was a single earring, a black opal teardrop hanging like dark fire from his left ear. The candlelight played games with his bright hair and gave an illusion of strength to a face that was a sculptor's dream.

Kizra sat in shadows on the second level, concealed from the tables by a carved, pierced screen, six panels of polished wood, hinged together and zigging across the small stage. She was playing musical wallpaper again, waiting for the dinner to start.

The double doors opened and Matja Allina walked into the light as onto a stage, a queen to more than match the power of the old king waiting on the dais, tall and slender, graceful despite the heaviness of the child. She wore a dress of royal blue damask, high waisted and full in the skirt, not hiding her pregnancy but diminishing it. Her hair was braided into a regal knot, with a chain of aquamarines and silver twisted through the silver-gilt plaits. A wide necklace of beaten silver and aquamarines filled in the scoop neck of the dress, the pale greenish blue of the stones almost a match for her eyes. The sleeves of the dress were narrow, fitting close to her arms with wide wristlets of aquamarines and silver made to match the necklace and the heavy earrings. She wasn't pretty like Kulyari following very much in her shadow, not beautiful either with her wide full mouth and angular bones.

> *In a room full of women, you'd look at her first, and if you looked away, you'd come back to her. A sharp and ironic intelligence, vigorous moral force, tightly controlled passion like a perfume, invisible but potent.*

Angakirs was leaning forward, his weight on his forearms, his body tense. He was watching Allina intently, a glitter in his eyes, hating her and wanting her with about equal intensity.

Behind her screen, Kizra used one arm to wipe the sweat off her face while she kept the tinkle tune going with her other hand. If they got through this night without disaster, she was going to be very much surprised.

After a quick lift of his head when he heard the doors open, Rintirry lounged gracelessly in his chair and stared at his plate, doing his best to ignore the women. Hate as strong as the Artwa's came off him like smoke. Hate and desire.

> He tried to rape me at my betrothal feast, *that's what the Matja said. I thought she was um exaggerating, but I sure as hell believe her now.*

Matja Allina crossed the hall and came up the stairs without help, the other women trailing after her, mostly unnoticed.

Kulyari glanced repeatedly at Rintirry, but he was so busy pretending to ignore the Matja he didn't have time for her. When she realized this, her smile lost its glow, her movements were angular with rage.

For the first time, Kizra felt some sympathy for her. These

last few years couldn't have been easy. There was Angakirs blaming Allina for alienating Pirs, his favorite before the marriage, and seeing her as a failure as a wife since all her sons had been stillborn. There was Utilas the heir, jealous of Pirs and willing to do anything that would injure him (as long as he could do it without his fingers showing). There was Mingas the third son; an old suitor gone sour, he wanted to see Allina reduced to poor relation and presumably available for seduction. And there was Rintirry the youngest who wanted anything he could get his hands on whatever he had to do to get it. All of them urging her, tempting her, sending her here to Ghanar Rinta to seduce her uncle and get rid of Allina. It must have taken her less than a day to discover how hopeless that was. Take an ambitious and shrewd girl, put her where ambition was thwarted and shrewdness was useless, no wonder she wanted Pirs dead and Allina dispossessed. And now it was obvious that Rintirry had no eyes for her, only for the Matja.

Matja Allina bowed, then let Aghilo help her into her chair. She lifted the silver bell beside her plate, rang it, and the meal began, male servants sweeping in with platters of meat and all the rest of it.

Kizra laid the wallpaper noddling to rest and began the program that Allina had laid out for her.

He likes the old epics, the Matja said. You've learned something of the *Gharadion,* you'll begin with that; it doesn't matter that you don't know the words, you wouldn't sing it anyway, he wouldn't stand for a woman singing that or anything else, not at dinner. As soon as the first serving is finished, I'll send Impajin around to you, he'll do the singing. Hmm. And Paynto, he's fair with a flute, knows all the old songs. After the *Gharadion,* he'll take the lead, you can improvise around him, give some depth to the music; he's pedestrian at best. He's loyal, though, and he's got the ear if not the talent. He'll be happy enough to have you there, distribute the blame if any; the praise will come to him, not you, he knows that.

The meal went on with murmurs and the clink of silver against silver, the sounds of glass and china, Paynto's flute and Kizra on the arranga blending and moving apart and Impajin's rough tenor louder than both. The candles flickered, the colors shimmered, shifting light and shadow picked out texture and sheen; it was like a brocade print,

gorgeous and rare. And spoiled for Kizra by the constant
undercurrents of hate and fear, anger and disgust.

*Tinkle toot, let's get this thing over with.*


3

The door slammed open and Pirs came striding in. There
was a bloodstained bandage on his head and another on his
arm. His face was so tight with rage that the bones seemed
to be leaping against the skin. He nodded perfunctorily at
his father, went bounding up the steps to the second table,
nodding tightly at his wife, grabbed hold of Kulyari's arm
and jerked her from the chair. Ignoring her protests, he took
her up the short flight of stairs to the main dais, flung her
to the floor in front of Angakirs. "I will not have this
THING in my house. She called my moves to my enemy
and I was brought near to death. She is traitor to the Blood."

Kulyari was so startled by all this that at first she could
only gasp and struggle; she was frightened now. "No no,
lies, no," she cried; she pushed up onto her knees. "It's
lies, all of it, I didn't . . . the Blood, no. . . ." Without
trying to get up, she swung round and held out her arms
toward Rintirry. "Tell them. . . ."

Rintirry shoved his chair back, came round the table.

Kulyari let her arms drop, her mouth widened into a triumphant smile.

He caught hold of her hair, jerked her head up, and cut
her throat. "Traitors die. That's what I say."

# DYSLAERA 8:
# News from home is better than a kick in the pants

INTERROGATION
  NOTE: Drugs used instead of probe because subject
  7R (native name: Rohant, Ciocan of clan Voallts)
  tests in the dangerous zone re: probability of probe
  damage. Unusual configuration of energy zone. Tech
  1 refused to guarantee results if probe is not used.
  Claims since subject has not been fully broken from
  the fugue state, drug trance cannot be established
  properly and mechanical/electrical responses cannot
  be calibrated to a satisfactory degree of precision.
  FURTHER NOTE: Tech 1 is showing signs of
  deviance. Investigate.
TECH 1: Subject is prepared.
SAVANT 4: Tell me your name.
SUBJECT: Rohant vohv Voallts, Ciocan of Family
  Voallts, Gazgaort of Company Voallts Korlatch of
  Spotch-Helspar.
SAVANT 4: Who are we?
SUBJECT: I don't know.
SAVANT 4 (to Tech 1): Well?
TECH 1: Given the limitations. . . .
SAVANT 4: Yes, yes, we've been through that.
TECH 1: I like to have things clear. I would say he's
  probably lying.
SAVANT 4: Ciocan, you heard?
SUBJECT: Yes.
SAVANT 4: Look to your right; you can turn your head
  sufficiently to see the bench by the right wall. Do you
  see it?
SUBJECT: Yes.
SAVANT 4: What else do you see?
SUBJECT: Someone lying on the bench, his face is to the
  wall, but it looks like Tejnor.
SAVANT 4: Yes. He is drugged at present, but can be

revived if we need him. If you lie, we will remove
parts of him. We won't let him die, he's valuable test
material, but we won't waste painkillers on him. Do
you understand?

SUBJECT: Yes.

SAVANT 4: Who are we?

SUBJECT: Omphalos.

SAVANT 4: How do you know that?

SUBJECT: I saw Omphalites at Koulsnakko's, I see you.
The robes are not the same, the smell is the same.

SAVANT 4: Is that last metaphorical or physical?

SUBJECT: Both. Please yourself how you explain the
metaphorical part. The physical? You and four others of
your kind—they're not here now—you walked past me
at the Hole. I have an excellent memory for sensory
data.

SAVANT 4: I didn't see you.

SUBJECT: Considering the nature of my activities, that
shouldn't be surprising. We took care to keep out of the
way.

SAVANT 4: You had no prior knowledge of our presence
and our plans?

SUBJECT: No. We were there for Ginbiryol Seyirshi.

SAVANT 4: I see. Your Toerfeles was quite possibly
warned about us. How would you explain that?

TECH 1 (interrupting): There was a very strong surge of
emotion at that statement, Savant. You are giving him
information he didn't have before, information that
excites and pleases him.

SAVANT 4: Yes, yes. Ciocan, answer the question.
OBSERVER'S COMMENT: In the following
answer, note how subject 7R takes extreme care with
word choice. Observe the readings appended, see
how he manages to keep his statements in the neutral
realm while providing as little useful information as
possible.

SUBJECT: I can't know . . . uuuh . . . absolutely . . .
but you can have my conjectures. Seyirshi attacked
Voallts Korlatch viciously during the past year, we
were bombed and murdered by his agents, forced into
defending ourselves in any way we could. Necessarily
this made us sensitive to all unexplained inquiries and
intrusions. You made me watch the incident with

Ossoran and Feyvorn, I saw the girl, I knew her. You got her from Voallts. Your agents must have left traces behind. Voallts always defends itself from any attack and the best defense involves knowing the attacker.

SAVANT 4 (to Tech 1): Well?

TECH 1: He's not lying. Maybe hedging a little, but not lying.

SAVANT 4: By what other means would your Toerfeles learn of us?

SUBJECT: Digby, Excavations Limited. It's what we pay him for. Don't bother asking me what his sources are. Digby presents results. How he got them is his business and he's not about to disclose it to outsiders.

SAVANT 4: Well?

TECH 1: Not lying. Being careful not to lie.

SAVANT 4: Do you, Voallts Security, your Toerfeles, or Digby have sources within Omphalos?

SUBJECT: No. Digby, I can't know for sure, but I don't think so. I'd like to say yes and see you sweat, but it wouldn't be the truth.

TECH 1: Not lying, not hedging.

SAVANT 4: Good. Name and locate settlements of Dyslaera other than the Voallts Compound on Spotchals.

SUBJECT: No.

SAVANT 4: We will peel the boy inch by inch in front of you.

SUBJECT: (SILENCE)

TECH 1: Reading steady. Truth. He will not speak to save subject 3Tj.

SAVANT 4: It's futile, Ciocan. Such things are public knowledge. It may cost us say a year to find them, but we will.

SUBJECT: (SILENCE)

SAVANT 4: Very well, that's enough for today. Take him out. Put him on a three-day water fast. After that, we'll see.

## 

Rohant stretched out on his plank bed, closed his eyes. He'd tiptoed round the truth and got away with it. Shadow was out there somewhere. Her and Kikun. It had to be them.

Somehow. Miralys was well. The fear was gone, that sick emptiness that'd been rotting at his guts since he'd seen young Kalaksi in that cage. Miralys was well and tending to business.

And I'd better be, he thought. Shadow. I don't have her gift, but maybe something like it. . . .

He remembered what happened between her and him when she mindrode Sassa. Two-way flow there. Maybe . . . we never thought it was possible, the Tie, yes, the blood-bond with the tiebeast, but mindriding. . . . I don't know. Well, it's time to start thinking the impossible. I certainly haven't anything better to do these next few days.

# FISHING IN A SMALLER SEA:
## Kikun and Autumn Rose troll for the one who knows

1

Kikun came yawning onto the bridge and stood a moment blinking at the woman in the pilot's chair. Autumn Rose was wearing dull brownish-purple trousers and an acid green tunic. And she'd dyed her hair an ashy brown, her skin olive-tan.

Clicking his tongue and shaking his head, he sauntered over to her. "Rose, you're a sight for sore eyes and if they weren't sore before they'd be now."

She chuckled. "Camouflage, Kuna. You have yours, this's mine."

"Tlee!" Scratching at the skin folds under his chin, he frowned at the green and blue and brown and streaky white of the world taking up most of the screen. "So tell me about that."

Rose grimaced, a twist of her wide mouth, a quick wrinkling of her long nose. "Well, I have an idea or two. Look." She played a moment with the sensor pad, talking while she worked. "Barakaly came here about once a year." She clicked her tongue. "The man was a cretin, you know. He had the best blocks available installed in his kephalos, then he goes and keeps his list of keys in this idiot antique desk in his quarters. Took me all of fifteen seconds to find the secret drawer he put his faith in, once I had time to look around the place. I mean, there it was. . . ." she paused, frowned at the screen where a map was developing in one cell, with images clustered about it of buildings and individuals and a sidebar slowly filling with data; she made some changes, then went on, "this old . . . um . . . THING just sitting there begging me to go poking about in it. I found porno flakes and a bunch of crecards in different names and . . . ah well, never mind . . . anyway, there was this notebook with all you need to know to uncrunch his codes, so I've been going through his personal records. Not

143

a nice man, Barakaly Lak Dar. Chatty though, I mean looks to me like he got kicks from telling about the things he pulled, business and personal junk. Not a nice man. Oh, no.''

Kikun lay back in the chair and let his eyes droop nearly closed, absorbing what she was saying through skin as well as ears, tone of voice and behind-emotion, everything she was saying through intonation as well as words. Thinking was for him a physical process, sensual more than rational.

''You say it's Omphalos responsible for this. Maybe yea, maybe nay, but one thing's sure, Barakaly doesn't know from Omphalos, not a word even in his twistiest files and if you'd 've seen what he's got there, you'd know he must 've put EVERYthing in. He's been to Arumda'm lots of times, though. Seems there's a Black House there that provides victims to order,'' she coughed, grimaced again. ''All I can say is, it's no wonder he was one of Ginny's clients. Anyway, it's a mess of a world. Every island its own nation and there are a furtzen lot of islands, haeds they're called.'' She grinned. ''You'd think with that many heads around, they'd have a little wisdom thrust on them, but not so, my friend, not so. The place is full of tiny wars, whenever some local vaarlord gets an itch for someone else's land, he whips up a war and tries to take it. It's worst in the south, there's more land there, more big islands, sub-continents I suppose you'd call them. Haemundas to the Rummers. Don't look at me like that, Kuna. That's what they say when they're talking about each other—according to Barakaly, though I admit he's not a source I'd trust about anything sensitive. We'll just have to wait and see. Anyway, where was I? Ah, good thing that's in the north.'' She pointed to the city map. ''The biggest city they have. Tos Tous. The Landing Field's there and it's a Freecity, lots of strangers coming in and out. Offworlders too, freetraders and types like Barakaly in for the . . . um . . . amenities. I've dug out the names of some contacts he had who might be useful. They set up his stays at the Black House and other little pleasures. Seems to me, those are the types who'd have the information we need to get at . . . well, call it Omphalos. What I think is, we go in, look over the ground, go after these contacts, take them, question them and. . . .'' She shrugged. ''That's as far as I can go now. What happens after that depends on what we find out. Probably we scat for home and Digby and

Miralys. We'll need a small army if Shadow and the others are here. If they aren't, well, we better go add our ignorance to the rest and see what we can do about it.''

He blinked at her. "Question?"

"Nothing bloody, luv. Even for Digby, I don't do torture. But I picked better than I knew when I took this 'un. Barakaly has himself a nice little selection of head softeners. Drugs, luv. Our targets, they'll sing like baby birds when some of that stuff hits the blood."

As she started fiddling some more with the sensor pad, there was a familiar rustle of feathers, a scratch of feet. Kikun turned his head and stared into the corner beyond Autumn Rose. Gaagi was there, his armwings folded tight against his sides, his golden eyes wide and staring. Grandmother Ghost was half behind him, bent over, peering around the wings, snorting repeatedly because she was allergic to feathers. She winked at him, but didn't say anything—for which he was profoundly grateful; every time she opened her mouth, she dropped him in trouble so deep he thought he'd never see day. Gaagi spread his arms wide, caught Grandmother in the face with a feathered membrane and left her sputtering with annoyance. He began signing, his supple fingers moving so fast that Kikun had difficulty following him.

*Journey of many days, many sorrows, hurt and hunger, tedium and terror. It finishes here, yes, it finishes here, but not this journey nor the next. Come home, Nayol Hanee, come home, O Ta'anikay, or die here and know the Dinhastoi do die with you.*

Rubbing at her nose, Grandmother Ghost pushed past Gaagi, who faded into a black film, then was gone. She shoved her little bulldog face at Kikun, waggled her crooked forefinger at him. Her voice was a mosquito whine in his mind's ear.

*Aya aya, get you home or I be a fly on your backside biting. Get you that girl and leave off this interfering in foreign hashendilis, you got your own to worry over. Hah! I give you till you finish this'n, then you won't know what sleep is you hang off any longer. Hah! Ya!*

And she was gone.

Kikun sighed. None of that was any help. If that was all his gods and ghosts could do for him. . . . Tlee! when Grandmother got mad, she had a bite like a borer fly, he rubbed his shoulder, grimacing at the memory. That wasn't the only place she'd got him, either.

"Messages?" Autumn Rose sounded irritated.

"What? Oh, No, nothing to do with this." That wasn't quite true, but he didn't intend to spend his time explaining Grandmother. Or Gaagi either. "Rose, something's occurred to me. What are you going to do with the ship?"

"If you'd been listening to me. . . ."

"Sorry."

She snorted. "Really. What I was saying is, I don't want to leave her parked in orbit. This is a free trader's market which means basically that anything left lying around unguarded is fair game. Bunch of pirates, even the best of 'em. Not putting them down, you understand, I'd probably do the same, given the chance. What I'm saying, a sweet ship like this without a watch on board is gone. Even without you to clue 'em, Kuna, the average trader round here would get past security not even breathing hard. And I don't want to put her down at the Landing Field. Too many noses around wondering what your business is. And too expensive. Anything's too expensive. Except for my crecard, I'm about broke and Barakaly doesn't carry cash, at least, I didn't find any. They're used to traders slipping in, doing their business and scooting; no one's going to pay much attention to us. I've picked a place to stash the ship. See that isthmus? No settlers and close enough to where we have to go."

2

The air was fresh and sweet. They'd come down through a rainstorm into a mountain dawn and when Kikun emerged and looked around, crystal drops clung everywhere, picking up the sunrise, glittering red and gold and brilliant white. The local life was already recovering from the intrusion; there were grunts and whistles and a sudden soar of melody. Then the pattern repeated with changes.

He rode the lift down and walked into the middle of the meadow, absorbing shape and color, sound and smell, relaxing into this new world. The reprocessed air on the ship was clean and properly humidified, even faintly perfumed with touches of leaf and flower—choice air, one might say, pampered air. Despite this, it smelled of metal to him, as artificial as Ginny's arm. He breathed deeply and his soul expanded.

They'd landed on the narrow isthmus that was the spine connecting the north and south nodes of Haemunda Chajiari, a sparsely populated area because the land was mostly vertical and stony, interrupted with steep narrow fjords where cliffs dropped a hundred meters straight down into the ocean water; the isthmus could support trees, grasses and small mammals, but a man would starve to death.

Kikun chanted under his breath, apologizing to the local life for the shock of the landing. Eyes watched from the treetops and the brush, looked up at him from the grass. Not much fear here, because no one came, just an ordinary wariness.

He settled his backpack more comfortably, leaned against a tree stump, and waited.

The lift hummed again. He turned. Autumn Rose was coming down with her pack leaning against her leg and two miniskips like hobbyhorses resting by her feet.

"Help me, Kuna," she said when the lift reached the ground. "I want to run west with the edge of dark and we'll miss it if we don't start soon."

He hauled his emskip onto the grass, shaking the icy dew over his feet and over its metal surfaces, then stood back, watched the lift rise, fold itself in until the skin of the skip was sealed tight once more.

"West by north," Rose said. She touched on the effect, swung into the saddle. "Set the tonc at two seven four corrected. Got it? Good. Let's go."

3

They reached the Tola Hills above Tos Tous with dawn pinking the sky ahead of them, landed the emskips on a brushy ledge with a good ten meters of weathered stone rising above them and a drop over the lip of fifty meters straight down. Once the emskips were wrapped in a camouflaged groundcloth, it would take some hard looking to spot them; besides, as Rose said, who in their right mind would look there.

Despite the awkward weight of the pack, Kikun climbed the crumbly stone face like his looksake garden lizard going up a wall; Rose followed more slowly, grumbling all the way. She didn't like heights, she wasn't going to have any skin left on her front or her hands, besides she was freezing and starved. There had to be a better way, Z' Toyff, there had to be. She reached up, Kikun caught her hand and helped her onto the flat above the cliff.

Tos Tous rambled around the curve of a wide lovely bay; the city was a quilt of many colors all of them gray or brown, thousands of small buildings gathered in haphazard clusters. No street—if they were streets, not merely gaps between adjacent buildings—went straight for more than a few meters.

"Lovely place. Anthill someone stepped on, squashed all to hell and gone." Autumn Rose unfolded the map she'd had the kephalos print up for them, looked from it to the city below. "That's the part we want." She pointed. "There, near the middle of the curve where most of the wharves and warehouses are. Um. We'll be going through the main market—if we're lucky enough and this is market day, you should be able to collect quite a lot of coin. Do the best you can, Kuna, we need the cash." She chuckled, nudged him with her elbow. "You should be about the best pickpocket alive with that Talent of yours." She sobered. "I can use my crecard in emergencies, but I'd rather not. I don't know who or what's watching readouts round here."

Kikun sighed. "That's the third time you've said that, Rose. I heard, I heard."

"Nerves, Kuna. Always get 'em when I'm about to jump in something I don't know anything about." She frowned over her shoulder at the eastern horizon where the tip of the sun was poking up, a brilliant vermilion blob of light. "Twenty kays we have to walk. At least that. Well, better safe than sorry. Come on, Li'l Liz, let's go."

4

They reached the Tos Tous Highroad as a line of plodding
bullocks walked past two by two, pulling carts piled high
with raw leather and leather goods, the smell lingering long
after they rounded the bend ahead.

There was a young boy on the back of each left lead
bullock, whistling and tapping now and again at the withers
of the pair, stirring them back to a brisk walk when they
threatened to slow to immobility. These boys wore heavy
bullhide trousers, bright wool tunics slit fore and aft, and
long knitted scarves wrapped around their necks, the ends
fluttering along the bullock's sides. They turned to stare at
Rose (not at Kikun; of course, they didn't notice him) from
large dark eyes in small brown faces, their straight black
hair blowing in the wind.

A man and woman sat on a bench inside the last of the
carts, he was stocky and bald and wrapped in a heavy overcoat; he gave Rose a single shrewd glance, dismissed her,
and went back to watching his carts. The woman wore an
identical overcoat but added a shawl over abundant black
hair twisted into a high knot. She didn't bother looking at
Autumn Rose; her eyes were fixed on the back of the bullock boy, she was frowning at him, spitting words at the
man beside her.

Ten minutes later a line of heavily laden flats hitched together and pulled by a motorized tractor came rumbling
along the road, slowed to a sudden crawl as the tractor
reached the last of the carts and couldn't go round because
there was a caravan of large hairy beasts plodding north
along the highway, heading for the Landing Field.

Autumn Rose ran at the last of the flats, pulled herself
onto the bed. It rocked under her and the hitch clanked
loudly. The flats rode on a single wheel and tilted at a heavy
thought. She waited, erect on her knees, until she was reasonably sure the trader hadn't noticed he'd acquired a pas-
senger, then she settled between two bales, leaned against
a third, and sighed with relief as she stretched her feet out.

She started, made an exasperated spitting sound as Kikun
plopped down beside her and stayed present in a way he
hadn't been for the past several miles. "One of these days
I'm going to think I'm dreaming you, Li'l Liz, and go not
so quietly crazy."

5

An hour later the flats slowed again, crawling through scrapshacks and garbage dumps on the rim of the city. The dumps had a number of sluggishly burning fires producing a nose-numbing, eye-biting smoke that drifted in a bluish-yellow clots across the road. People crawled like dung-beetles over the discarded paper, rags and other junk, half obscured by the smoke clouds, grimly silent in their searches.

Kikun fidgeted nervously, his fingers moving in complex patterns Rose suspected might be counterspells or something similar. Finally he slapped his hand on the bale beside him. "Let's go, Rose. Now."

"Why not."

They slid down and strolled along behind the flats, coughing as smoke blew over them, keeping apart from the other walkers, most of whom were scavengers going to or coming from their particular mounds of refuse.

The string of flats swerved to the side of the road. A small horde of men came from a blocky building, surrounding the flats, while their leader waved a clipboard in the face of the trader driving the tractor.

"You are being cleared for three flats," he said. "You are having six. That is going to cost you, Tusuk."

"You are needing to read that thing again," the trader roared at him. "Six wheel it is saying. Is not saying nothing about flats. You are needing to count 'em, fool. Six wheel."

"Huh." The guard brought the clipboard closer to his nose, scowled at the papers on it. "Wheel is meaning flat."

"Wheel is meaning wheel." Tusuk pounded his fist in his palm. "You are needing to count 'em," he insisted. "Six wheel. I am having already paid the padj. Six wheel, sixty peras." He waved a paper heavy with purple wax in the guard's face. "Paid paid paid!"

Kikun nudged her. "Come on, come on, Rose. It's all very interesting, but we've got things to do." He pinched her arm lightly. "I'm ratchetting up the effect. See you later."

6

The houses were stone on the first floor with narrow slits instead of windows. The second floors (and the rare third floors) were wood with loopholed shutters over grilled windows. About half of these windows were closed tight, even through it was nearly an hour after noon. These were wary secret houses, ready to close up at too bold a touch.

The city had no walls. According to the ship's kephalos, despite the wars that seem to be the natural state of things and constant raiding from wandering bands of pirates (marauders whose only bases were huge junks that moved from island to island within loosely defined territories), even villages had no walls. Walls involve a communal mind-set. Walls are meant to protect groups and need many hands to build and staff. It takes much less cooperation to build individual structures and arrange them so that the overlap provides mutual defense (hence the angular semi-streets). Also this world had been intermittently rediscovered by free traders and was a good market for what weapons the traders were willing to sell. Jump harnesses and pellet guns with exploding missiles made walls irrelevant. It was more efficient to provide covering fire. That's only a contributing factor, kephalos said. If there were none of these weapons around, it would be the same thing. These people simply have no love for walls. They like mobility. Walls shut in as well as keep out.

She ambled along through hordes of children playing in these semi-streets, round games and ball games and complicated versions of tag, games she remembered from her own childhood, though she'd spent more time watching than playing, shut away from the street children by the walls of the Chateau where her mother lived and worked. She thrust her hands in her pockets and slowed yet more, enjoying the clamor and confusion.


## 

As she rounded one of the sharper angles, she nearly stepped into a group of four guards (dark green with crimson slashes and black leather accents) beating a ragged man with their long whippy canes, all five of them silent except for grunts and squeals. One of the guards straightened,

glared at her. Hastily, she cut out into the street and walked
on by—like the rest of the locals getting out of there as fast
as she could. It was a warning, a timely one, reminding her
to stop gawking and get to business.

## ##

As she passed from the semi-slums near the outskirts, the
traffic got thicker. Women with bales of cloth and fancy-
work balanced on their heads (she admired and briefly envied the beauty of their walking, the music of their voices.
They wore what looked to be long rectangles of patterned
cloth wrapped in complicated folds about their bodies, batik
prints with a silky sheen, some local fiber, no doubt. If I
have time and some spare cash, I should get me some lengths
of that, it looks like it feels wonderful against the skin).
Men leaning forward and plodding along under backframes
loaded with tubers and gourds, sacks of flour and other sta-
ples. Handcarts and flats of the two-wheeled variety with
small noisy tractors pulling them.

## ##

She went round another angle and saw a clot of angry,
shouting, arm-waving locals and three guards trying to shift
them away from an accident. A tractor without its flats being raced along the thruway by a gang of boys had crashed
into a handcart loaded with local chicken-types. There were
feathers everywhere, blood, squawking birds, locals trying
to get at the boys, the guards pissed off at everyone. A
different set of guards. These had dark crimson uniforms
with green strips angled down the front. One of them lost
his patience entirely, aimed his pellet rifle at the ground and
blew a hell of a hole in the dirt.

The crowd scattered and the boys on the tractor ran off.

The only one left was the hapless soul with the handcart.
The guards hit him a few licks and went off, leaving him to
right his cart, repack it, and trundle it around the new hole
in the middle of the road.

## ##

Laughter and a satiric run on a stringed instrument of some kind.

Rose looked around.

A street musician was standing in a doorway, swaying, a lutelike instrument cradled in his arms. His face was flushed and he looked more than a little drunk. After a moment he began to sing, improvising a comic account of the accident, describing the guards, the careless boys, and the hapless would-be trader in scurrilous terms, picturing them as capering ludicrously about the hole in the road which he invested with enormous significance, mostly sexual and wholly comical. He had a crowd in moments; laughing and clapping with him, they threw coppers at the case open at his feet. Then someone yelled, someone else took the lute from the singer and bustled him away and again the street was empty—until a squad of guards came marching around an angle.

Behind them the Vaarlord of this Kehvar (quarter, ward, neighborhood) lolled on the seat of a groundcar, his gorgeousness exhibited behind pelletproof glass as he looked over his subjects. He was a big man, with a seamed, scarred face. He didn't loll well. Cultural things, she thought, idleness as an attribute of greatness. No, as a loller, he was an abject failure. There was too much animal vigor in the man; his eyes moved over the houses and the people, over her as one of the people, with hard possessiveness. His hair might be gilded, his mustache and goatee stiff as gold wire, his face enameled white, his lips carmine, but none of that mattered. She watched him pass and shivered. Head down, Rose, she told herself. It's survival time.

Quiet went down the street with him, the people around her going still as he passed, prey beasts in the presence of a lion, praying he wasn't hungry.

One of the guards following him looked at her, interest sparking in his eyes. He kept walking, but he turned his head to watch her as he went along.

As casually as she could manage, Rose turned down one of the semi-streets that crossed this one, moved swiftly through several angles, ran into a swarm of beggar children, turned again to get away from them, nearly ran into two guards at the boundary between two Kehvars engaged in a

bracing match that was clearly on the verge of breaking into
a shooting war. The locals were smarter or faster than her,
they'd gone for cover. She backed off as quickly and quietly
as she could, ducked down another of the winding ways and
made her way back to the main trafficflow.

## ##

Street noises grew louder and less distinct, voices of the
child beggars and the street singers blending with drums
and pipes and lutes. There were more guards out. New ones
like wasps, dark yellow tunics with black vee stripes down
the front and back. Kephalos had said it would be so, each
Vaarlord hired his own guards. There was a HighVaar over
the whole city, but he ruled more by consent than coercion.
He was a convenience, a court of last resort, the keeper of
the peace; he was the only one who could force the Vaarlords to keep to their boundaries, but he didn't meddle inside those boundaries.

Which meant she'd better keep her eyes wide open and
stop dreaming her way through these streets. Come on,
Rose, you know the score. Get a move on, the sooner you're
under a roof the better.

# 7

The market was five acres of dust and noise. Several free
traders were down onplanet looking for this and that, trading what they had for as much as they could get, a complex
system of barter that both sides played out full-voiced and
passionately, games both sides enjoyed to the max. Spice
dealers and flower women, dealers in rare oils and essences,
these turned the air into a soup of smells. There were cloth-
sellers and leather dealers, used clothes men, lampsellers,
knife women, pot women, chandlers and cosmetics dealers,
dealers in everything imaginable. Jugglers and jongleurs
plied their varied trades with varying success. Painters and
sculptors and a local brand of artists who produced a complex combination of both with a touch of performance
thrown in, these had their stands and their rivalries. A max-
imum of confusion and stimulus. Rose sighed with pleasure
and plunged into the middle of it.

8

"Tuluat the Tukkaree, that is being me, buying and selling, selling and buying, come by, come and see, treasures
for the trading, come by, come and see." Tuluat stopped
his chant, leaned across the table toward Autumn Rose, big
dark eyes warm and confiding. "And what can I be doing
for you, Jonjabaey, lovely Jaba'i?"

Autumn Rose smiled guilelessly back, newly browned
eyes warm and trusting, the warmth as genuine as his.
"Why, Fentu Tuluat, perhaps you can. I have a few trinkets
. . ." she sighed, "that have sad memories attached. I hate
to lose them, but a break is a break and time heals wounds.
Perhaps you'd like to look at them?"

"The blessing of the Tanadewa, time and its healing."
Tuluat shook out a square of black velvet, smoothed it on
the table in front of him. "Do be letting me see."

Autumn Rose took her gleanings from the ship and set
them with slow care onto the cloth, a ring with a starstone
(slightly chipped), an antique chronometer in a nicked and
battered gold case, a fingerstone of Tongjok jadeite in the
form of a smiling fat frogga, an Escalari earbob its dangles
carved from hardalwood and set with fossil amber, and half
a dozen similar small but valuable items. When she finished, the serious bargaining began.

9

Autumn Rose weighed the coins in her left hand, shook
her head and ran them through the portable assayer she'd
found in Barakaly's antique desk. She clicked her tongue.
"Short, Tuluat. Lovely striking, but there's too much base
metal in the gold. I think another ema and two silvers, what
are they, ah, peras will make up the difference."

He shrugged, grinned and handed the coins over without
protest. "Now if you are liking to sell that little gadget, I
am offering . . . hmm . . . a nice sum, say . . . hmm . . .
300 emas."

"No no, I don't think so." She tucked the assayer back
in her belt pouch, flickered her fingers at him. "You've made
enough from me today."

He shrugged again, laughed. "So so, I will be having it
within the week anyway and cheaper at that. Unless you

prove more alert than I am thinking, Jonjabaey, lovely
Jaba'i.'' He turned away, flung out his hands, ''Tuluat the
Tukkaree, that is being me, buying and selling, selling and
buying, come and see, come and see, treasures for the trading, come and see, come and see.''


                            10

  ''You are being a free trader, Jonja?''
  Rose started, cursed under her breath. The guard had
come out of nowhere, was suddenly pacing beside her; he
wasn't one of those in the market, he had a combination of
green with purple diamonds and black slashes that was eye-
blinding and surprised her because she couldn't imagine him
fading into shadow, no way. Tuluat just might be right, I'm
not into this yet. ''No,'' she said, ''just a traveler.''
  ''Where do you be heading?''
  Uh oh, she thought. I hope this isn't what it looks like.
''Just ambling around, seeing what there is to see,'' she
said. Mistake, she thought, I shouldn't 've answered in the
first place. I don't know. I don't know. One thing I do know,
I don't like the smell coming off him.
  ''There is not being much worth looking at round here.
Better you are letting me show you a place I am knowing.''
  Right, she thought, just come alonga you, huh? No way,
skinkhead. She didn't say anything, just kept walking, looking straight ahead. If she couldn't handle this jerk, she
should've stayed away. Best if she could just lose him some
way.
  A long file of women came walking toward her, baskets
on their heads; they were laughing and talking, walking with
willow grace. Beyond them there were several handcarts
and a tractor pulling a line of flats trundling along at a crawl
beside the carts. Other flats and handcarts and oxcarts were
coming from behind her. When the women got close
enough, if she broke away suddenly, cut around them, didn't
get run over by a tractor, with a reasonable amount of luck
she could get lost before the guard made up his mind what
he was going to do. She risked a glance at him, stopped
walking, her mouth hanging open.
  The guard was sinking to his knees, folding down with a
surprised look melting from his face. A small gray-green

figure in a gray-green shipsuit had him by the elbows and was easing him down so that he didn't bounce.

She looked at him and remembered. Z' Toyff! Kikun.

He hissed at her, flickered his long fingers impatiently, gesturing at her to get on, let him deal with this.

Right, Li'l Liz.

She swung round and strolled off, the incident immediately wiped from her mind along with Kikun.

## ##

She moved through a double dogleg, found herself in the kind of place she hadn't seen before, a green space, grass and trees and a small fountain in the middle and behind that a graceful columned structure that was the antithesis of every other building in the city, open and airy, white marble with insets of colored stones in repeating patterns like those in the cloth the women wore. Three women were dancing on the grass, three women drummers squatted beside the fountain, along with a flute player and a woman crouched over an angular stringed instrument, plucking at it with a metal pick like a teardrop. A ninth woman sat cross-legged beside the walkway, murmuring blessings as passersby dropped coins in the wooden bowl in front of her. When Rose got close enough, she saw that the woman was blind. There were terrible scars on her face and one hand was mutilated, three quarters cut away, with only the little finger and a stub of thumb remaining.

The blind woman lifted her head as Rose walked past. "I am smelling blood," she cried out. "I am smelling danger. A demon is walking among us."

Embarrassed and annoyed, Rose walked faster, muttering to herself. Very impolite. Commenting on visitors to their faces. What about a little friendly hypocrisy, haah? She walked quickly on, constrained to a steady pace because she didn't want to look like she was running, though she would have run if anyone had done more than stare at her. Everyone around stared at her. Blind bitch, what right had she got, saying things like that. You want demons, lady, look closer to home, haah!

A few doglegs on she stopped, sniffed. Sea air all right, where . . . ah! that way. Now, Rose, find a place you can go to ground. Then we'll see, we'll see. . . .

11

Autumn Rose stood on the walkway and examined the
house. Another white card in another brass and glass case.

```
┌─────────────────────────────────────────────────┐
│                                                   │
│                     ROOMS                         │
│             TWENTY KURIES THE NIGHT               │
│               ONE PERA THE WEEK                   │
│                                                   │
└─────────────────────────────────────────────────┘
```

The Rumach was as shabby as the rest she'd looked at so
far, with worn, weathered shakes on the upper floors and
salt stains on the shutters, but there was a vigorous vine
growing about the door with trumpet-shaped crimson
blooms nodding in the brisk wind off the water behind her,
water glittering between two warehouses on the far side of
a space that was more like a street than any she'd seen in
this place, its form dictated by the water's edge one line of
buildings away.

She considered the Rumach. The flowers were nice, the
touch of color appealed to her, it was the first she'd seen on
the outside of any house. She curled her toes inside her
boots. There was a burning on her heel where a blister had
burst, she knew it had, she could feel skin moving with each
step. Goerta b'rite, if this Rumacha is marginally less a sleaze
than the other oof'narcs I've talked to so far, this'll do.

She climbed the short flight of stairs, tugged at the stag-
hoof that served both as bellpull and signifier.

The woman who opened the door was tall and lean, with
a cloud of tightly curled white hair and a face carved from
dark chocolate. Offworlder and female. Rose sighed with
relief. "I'd like one of those rooms you're advertising," she
said, "I'll be here several weeks."

12

Rose shut and locked the door, tossed the key on the bed,
shrugged out of the backpack and dropped it on the floor
next to a large overstuffed chair with a blue throw on it sewn
from the silky cloth she'd seen in the clothing of many of
the women. She yawned, threw herself into the chair and
sat a moment running her hands along and along the padded
arms, relishing the cling and slide of the brilliantly colored

material. Then she bent, jerked off her boots, tossed them aside and scrubbed her feet back and forth on the rug, braided from more of that cloth, green and red and purple and bright blue. The room was shabby and well used, but clean and comfortable and pleasant on the eyes, furnished by someone who had a love for color and the strength of personality to force order out of exuberance.

There was a saggy double bed with crisp white sheets and a pile of quilts. A table beside the bed with a lamp and a blotter and stylus, a ladderback chair pushed in under it. Next to the table was the room's only window, deeply recessed with a cushioned window seat built atop a chest. Kikun was sitting there, nested among the pillows.

Rose gasped, blinked. "Hello, Li'l Liz," she said finally. "Um . . . can't you fix it so you don't do this to me every time? I could drop dead with a heart attack."

The folds of skin on Kikun's face shook with silent laughter.

Rose unlatched her belt, pulled it from around her, tossed it on the bed with the key. "I picked up ten emas, two hundred peras and a handful of kuries for the junk I brought off the ship. How much did you get?"

"I haven't counted it yet. Let's see." He dumped his sac on the cushion, began arranging the coins. "Hmm. One hundred coppers to one silver, one hundred silvers to one gold, right?"

"What kephalos set the assayer to."

He swept the coins back into the sac, announced the total. "Fifty emas, three hundred peras and about a hundred kuries. And a handful of offworld coins, no telling what they're worth, I don't recognize any of them."

She yawned. "Z' Toyff, I'm tired. Hungry, too, but I don't feel like moving."

"Trailfood in your pack."

"I know. I'll dig it out in a moment. Kuna, you going to be all right here? This doesn't look to be a good world for outsiders and you're more outside than most."

He shrugged. "I'll get along."

"Well, take care, I'd rather have a disappearing dinhast than a decaying corpse." She yawned a third time. "I think I'll get some sleep. It's been a long day. Tomorrow's soon enough to begin winnowing out our targets." She groaned, pushed onto her feet. "You want the right side or the left?"

"Huh?"

"The bed, Kuna. What'd you think I meant? There's one of it and two of us. Which reminds me, I'll have to get a key cut for you tomorrow, I don't think I'd better ask the Rumacha for an extra. So, which is it, right or left?"

"I don't like walls. Let me have the outside."

"Good enough." She stretched, groaned again, shook herself and started breaking open the fastening on her shirt. "If you wake first, Kuna, shove me out. I'm so tired I could easy sleep till next week, but the sooner we start looking, the sooner we'll know. . . . ."

# SHADITH (Kizra) IN THE HALFLIGHT

1

A blood halitus sweet and musty spread through the room as the Irrkuyon on the dais stood without moving, a tableau that held until Rintirry dropped the knife on Kulyari's body and strolled to the end of the table. He flung himself into his chair, poured a dollop of wine into his glass, and gulped it down.

Matja Allina exchanged a quick look with Arring Pirs, got to her feet. She signaled the women at her table to follow her, then went sweeping from the room.

Behind the screen Kizra clutched at the arranga and wondered what she should do. Danger was as thick in that huge room as the blood-stink off the body. She wanted out of that place now, no! ten minutes ago.

Fragment by fragment, since the encounter that afternoon with that signifier lizard, she was reassembling her past and with that past regaining an acerbic view of

> MEMORY:
> She turned a corner, found herself in the middle of a kidnapping.
> Before she had time to re-act, one of the men had an arm wrapped around her and a slicer against her temple. "Move and you're dead," he whispered. His breath was hot on her ear, she was pressed hard against him; he wasn't much taller or wider than she was, but she kept thinking of steel traps and sword blades and other hard and lethal things. Lethal, yeh. He wanted to kill her so badly she could smell it like body odor.

power and the powerful, a view underlined by what had just happened, a lesson of what would happen to her if she followed her natural tendencies in this world.

161

MEMORY:
The door whooshed closed
behind him, expanding as it
moved to fill the whole
space of the opening as if it
erased itself to underline
the futility of trying to escape the cell. Hands
clasped behind her, Shadith
scowled at the seamless
wall. ''Mashak! Dafta!
Your soul smells like dog-
shit.'' When she was
trapped in the diadem she
was essentially immortal.
She'd abandoned all that
when she had Aleytys de-
cant her into this body.
I must have been out of my
alleged mind.
That struck her as funny
and she giggled, but the
spurt of humor was quickly
gone. Time meant more
now. The idea of wasting
her counted hours in a hole
like this one with nothing
to see, nothing to do, made
her wild.
She closed her eyes and
*reached,* searching for
other eyes, single or compound, large or small, anything she could look
through. Somewhere,
somehow, he must have left
a crack he could worry at
until it was big enough to
let her crawl out of this.

A small dark maidservant
slipped like a shadowmouse
from the curtains behind the
screen and touched her on
the shoulder. Ghineeli chal.
When Kizra started to speak,
Ghineeli touched a forefinger to her lips. Then she
beckoned urgently, pointed
at the curtains.

MEMORY:
She came painfully awake,
looked up into the liquid
copper eyes of the sauroid
captive. She was lying on a
floor somewhere and he
was kneeling beside her.
She wasn't tracking too
well, whatever Ginny used
to put her out seemed to
have pushed the slow-
button in her head. She
rubbed at her eyes, groped
around with numb hands.

Kizra followed her out
into the kitchen hall. ''What
. . .'' she whispered.
Ghineeli shook her head,
then went scooting along the
hall to the swinging doors at
the far end. She pushed open
the lefthand door, stood
holding it until Kizra was
through, then she eased the
door shut with no more noise
than a faint whoosh. She
touched Kizra's arm. ''The
Matja said go to her rooms.
Now. By the serving stairs.''

She took her hand away and left, slipping shadowmouse through the wide service door into the kitchen quarters.

Kizra clicked her tongue. Matja Allina. She wasn't sure how far she trusted the Matja. The woman would serve her own first and drop overboard anyone or anything that threatened them, promises or no promises, good will or ill. Still, there was no one else right now who even looked like offering protection, so what could she do?

Moving as swiftly and silently as she could manage, cursing under her breath when an awkward turn made her bump the arranga against the white plastered dirt wall, she went up the back stairs. Her nerves were stretched tauter than the arranga's strings.

Turn and turn, then out on the second floor, scurry along the service corridor, push out into the main hall after listening nervously and hearing only the hiss of candles burning, after peering out and seeing only shadows dancing in the drafts.

> MEMORY:
> She scowled at the black figures seated by the fire, two of them standing, and shivered involuntarily as she heard the two on their feet arguing on and on. . . .
> It was about her and the others, she knew that, it was like an auction in a way, as if they were agents bidding for the contents of the cage. . . .
> She thrust two fingers into her boot, smiled as she touched the hideout's hilt. Braincrystal knife, limber as a Company Exec's morals. Hold it wrong and it would whip back on you and slice your hand off. Rohant dropped to a squat beside her. His eyes shown red like bits stolen from the fire. "Soon," he said. She nodded. "Soon."

Stand before the Matja's door and wonder: *should I knock or not? If I don't knock, how does anyone know I'm out here?*

## ##

The door opened. Aghilo took her wrist and tugged her inside, an urgent, fearful pull on her arm.

Matja Allina looked up, nodded, then let her head fall

MEMORY:
She extended her reach, sweeping through wide arcs, finally touched a big-eyed moth hunting gnats along the dark stream.
She went swooping through the night with the prowling moth, in and out among the trees, soaring on muffled wings that read the air currents so exquisitely they beat just once or twice a minute, only speeding up when she rushed down on a swarm of prey insects.
A sudden burst of heat drew her, heat radiating away from the cooling engines of a grounded flit, an open flier capable of lifting a score of passengers. The moth played in the thermals like a child dancing in wave-froth, forgetting her hunger in the exuberance of her tiny joy.

back, her eyelids droop closed again. She said nothing. Her daughters were crouched at her feet. They didn't know what was happening, but they'd sensed danger and were pale and tense. Ingva was looking fierce again.

Candles were burning in here also; the current that fed the bedroom lamps had been diverted into the Honor Suite.

Hot wax and fear. The stink of both filled the room.

Aghilo dropped her arm and went back to the chair where she'd been sitting.

Tinoopa was already here, sitting cross-legged on the floor in the lefthand corner of the room where she had a view of the door but was inconspicuous behind the chair where Polyapo sat.

The titular Housekeeper looked older by half a century than she'd been at the start of the meal. Though Polyapo was Irrkuyon by birth, she was also female and a poor relation without any protection but her relatives' good will. And when relatives fought, if she guessed wrong about who'd win, if she went too far with the wrong loyalties, she'd be one of the first to perish. She wasn't an intelligent woman, but instinct told her that this situation could go in any of half a dozen directions, most of them deadly, that she could do nothing to influence the outcome. Nothing but sit here and pray to whatever gods a preybeast had that the powerful and the angry wouldn't notice her.

The Jili Arluja was in more or less the same situation, but she was in less danger, being without ambition. She was

MEMORY:
Stripped to his dry rough hide, Kikun strolled away from the cluster of buildings and walked along the ruts to the wharf. Shadith looked at him, found herself looking away, forgetting him, looking back, startled each time she saw him. His hands were empty, he had no weapon, nothing visible anyway. She looked away again, forgetting him again as she heard yells of anger and disgust, then a rattle of shots from the largest of the crumbling warehouses.
Shadith lifted the stunner, waited.
In the boat, Kikun slid behind the driver; as the kana jerked away, the sauroid took his helmeted head into an enveloping embrace, twisted sharply. With a continuation of the neck whip, Kikun flipped the local into the river on the shore side, used a boathook to shove the body under the wharf where it got hung up among the rotting piles.

content to be here and teach the girls as long as they needed her, what happened after that she was also content to leave to the good will of the Matja. Any dreams she had, time had leached out of her. She was sitting quietly beside the girls, touching them now and then, a gentle encouragement and comforting. Especially Yla. As Kizra crossed to Tinoopa, Yla gasped suddenly, turned and pressed her face against Arluja's knees. The tutor sighed, stroked the girl's hair.

Kizra dropped beside Tinoopa.

The woman touched her arm in greeting but said nothing. Like the Jili, she knew when to keep her head down.

The women sat and waited. No one spoke.

The curtains were pulled back from the windows and moonlight streamed in to fight with the candles. Shadows flickered over the faces of the women and the silent girls.

Clouds were blowing in, rapidly thickening and there was a dampness in the wind that howled around the towers, rattled the diamond panes and crept through the cracks; it promised a storm before the night was over.

Matja Allina opened her eyes and sat up. "Kizra." She cleared her throat. "Play. Something light. Quiet." She closed her eyes and sank back.

MEMORY:
Shadith inspected the fingernail she'd glued on to replace the broken one, then swept her hand along the harp strings.
*Happiness came by me again*
(clap your hands, oh yes oh yes)
*Yesterday*
(clap your hands, my dears)
*He wouldn't stay*
*I wrapped him in my arms*
*Displayed my charms*
*Like smoke he slipped away*
She played a lively tune, brought them onto their feet swaying and clapping a counterrhythm.
*Sorrow came by me again*
(clap your hands, o softly softly)
*And stayed a while*
(clap your hands, my dears)
*To caress and beguile*
*Bittersweet*
*Is better neat*
*And tastier*
*Than honey*
*I would not let him go*
*But he faded so—*
*Like smoke he blew away.*

Kizra rested the arranga on her knees, tested the strings, then went with meticulous care through the complex process of tuning though she could see that the jagged disconnected sounds were setting the women's teeth on edge.

When she finished, she thought a moment, then let her fingers walk the strings in a simple tune that slipped without thought from dreamtime, maybe from her past. It was a happy tune with a tinkly, spritely lilt to it. There were words, but not in the Irrkuyon langue. She played the tune and played with the words; translation was useless, but maybe she could. . . . Yes. Section by section. She smiled, a dreamy inward smile. It wouldn't be elegant, her rendition, but maybe amusing. Considering the situation. Why not. "Step easy, Stepchild," she sang. . . .

*Step easy, Stepchild*
*Watch where you walkin*
*It's wolfdays, Stepchild*
*Bourghies in your garden*

Humming along with the tune her fingers were elaborating, she considered the second section.

*Stoop swiftly, Gyrfalcon*
*Your Eyases are shriekin*
*It's catdays, Gyrfalcon*
*Pussy on the pantiles*

Kizra stopped singing and whistled softly along with the arranga. Yla was leaning against the Jili's knee, tearstreaks drying on her face. She was good at whistling and proud of it; she tapped her fingers a moment to catch the rhythm, then whistled with Kizra, the sound flowing like water from her, flute song melting into the more abrupt arranga tones.

*Step easy, Stepchild*
*Wasps are in your willows*
*It's rage days, Stepchild*
*Stingers pricking wild*

*Go grimly, Grimalkin*
*Your kittens cry for dinner*
*It's hunger days, Grimalkin*
*Famine in the straw*

MEMORY:
The air shook and the brightening day turned suddenly dark as a vast blanket of sleds filled the sky over them, flying low enough to brush the fronds of the lower trees.
Cutter beams slashed through the foliage, churned the mud, boiled the water around them, bracketing them, missing them again and again. She was splattered by mud thrown up by the bombs, metal fragments went whining through the sides of both boats; one ripped across her arm, another clipped a tuft of hair above her ear.

Ingva couldn't whistle, but there was a tradition of nonsense syllables in the Irrkuy women's culture; she caught up the rhythm and blended her voice with Yla's whistle. "Ba ba vay ba lay la vah," she sang. . . .

The song went on and on, blending the Stepchild's story with the beasts around her/him, some verses translating more successfully than others, some more surreal, some more pedestrian, but it did the job the Matja wanted, took their minds off the danger stewing below them.

2

The door to the bedroom opened and Arring Pirs came through it into the sitting room. He stopped beside the couch where Matja Allina was sitting. "He's settled in," he said, touched Allina's head, fingers sliding gently over her smoothed hair. "He called Utilas and told him. Ut won't be coming."

Allina caught his hand, held it against her face. "At least there's that. I don't think I could bear it, watching Utilas and Rintirry stalking around each other like a pair of randy tomcats."

"Randy," he said. He dropped to the couch beside her. "Yes. Rintirry. His blood's up. You know what that means. You've warned our women to stay inside and bar their doors?"

"And if he kicks the door in? What are they supposed to do then?" Matja Allina's control was slipping. "What could WE do? Slap his wrist and say Bad Boy?" There was rage in her voice. "He doesn't care whom he uses. You know that. Even our daughters aren't safe. And the Artwa would support him. You know that. Do something, Pirs. I don't care what it means, I won't have ANY of our people . . ." Her mouth worked. "Used. I won't."

"And if the Artwa calls the mortgage?"

"Let him try. He can't afford an inside Kirtaa to add to his other wars. And if he's foolish enough to go ahead with it, I'd rather go into the Brush. I swear it, Pirs. I will go into the Brush before I turn my head and sacrifice a baby to Rintirry's lust."

He took her hand, kissed her fingers one by one. "Yes, sweet warrior, mi-Matjali, yes." He set her hand down. "I put P'murr on guard at his door with orders to make sure he stays where he belongs. He'll enjoy doing it, mi-killi. He's tired," the laugh lines deepened about his blue eyes, "he lost the tip to his ear and has a butt-burn from a pellet out of a tumak's rifle. He's quite annoyed at Rintirry." He bent, touched Ingva's cheek and ruffled Yla's hair. "You sleep in your Mama's bed this night, lirrilirris."

"Mama?"

"She will be in with me, Ingvalli. You and Yla and the Jili will be all alone." He straightened. "Jili Arluja, take them in now, please."

He watched them out, then turned to Polyapo. "Ulyinik, you are welcome to a pallet here as long as this situation lasts, but if you prefer to return to your own quarters, I think you will be safe enough."

Polyapo got slowly to her feet. She bowed perfunctorily and left without a word.

Pirs waited until Aghilo was back from barring the door after the titular Housekeeper, then turned with grave formality to Tinoopa and Kizra. Kizra could feel his unease with them; he was a better man than his father, but he was also a product of his culture; what was in his bones and blood fought the pale overgrowth from his mind. He was honest enough to realize this and recognize the roots of his distaste for them, but he still felt it—and showed it in his dealings with them.

MEMORY:
Shadith felt her power come on her, nothing but the intensity of the belief before and behind her. Kikun squeezed down that force and funneled it into her.
The feedback built and built until the air clanged like metal.
She began to shape . . . digging deep within herself . . . laying hold on the power offered her . . . crafting out of memory and instinct . . . out of the people's belief . . . she SHAPED the THREE and sent THEM dancing over the crowd . . . made them sing with the voice of the throng. . . .

"It would be best," he said looking past Tinoopa at the wall, then forcing himself to look directly at her, "if you would spend the night here. Things being as they are, you would probably be safe enough in your rooms, but . . ." he shrugged, then turned his eyes on Kizra. "I owe you my life, child." There was a shade more warmth in his voice; he touched the bandage on his head, then the one on his arm. "It was close there for a while. Without the warning and the weapons, I might easily be resting in some l'borrgha's belly. I thank you."

Kizra bowed her head, said nothing.

"Yes," he said. He closed his eyes a moment, then stirred himself and finished what he'd determined to say. "And you, chapa Tinoopa, you have made the Matja's life infinitely more pleasant even in the short time you have been here. I have said nothing before now. For this lack I ask your favor." He turned abruptly, took the hands the Matja held out to him, and pulled her to her feet.

At the bedroom door, he looked over his shoulder. "Aghilo, if the chapai decide to stay here, take care of them, please. We know how surely we may rely on you."

### 3

Aghilo went out without waiting to ask if they meant to stay.

MEMORY:
A redheaded woman came riding through the Cicipi Gate, sitting in an arslibre howda mounted on the arching back of an immense and ugly warbot like the worse possible cross between a spider and a lobster.
Two more paced alongside and a third followed behind. They shot gouts of steam through spiracles along their sides, opening a path for themselves through the surging throng of pilgrims, walked with ominous sinuous agility through the steam clouds. "Eh, Shadow, Dea ex machina reporting for duty." "Eh, Aleytys." Shadith closed her eyes, opened them again as she remembered. "You better machinate some more or this world is going to go BOOM."

"Backwater worlds," Tinoopa said. She stood, stretched, looked around the room. "It's the floor for us, dust headaches and an aching back. Ah, well. Could be worse. You could easy have been the goat, Kiz. Hung out for that oogaluk to gnaw on."

Kizra wrinkled her nose. Lecture time. Tinoopa was going sententious again. She was getting tired of being instructed, especially as her memory drained back. She loosed the strings on the arranga, set it on a table and moved to a chair.

Tinoopa rubbed at her arms and frowned at one of the windows. A raindrop splatted against the glass, then another and another. "We haven't seen a strong storm yet, not the kind they call a kwangkular. Sound of that wind says this might be it. Too bad. Lasts a good week they say. No flying in that weather. Those two oogaluks might be stuck here for days. You've been shut up with the Matja most of the time, you don't hear what the chal are saying. It's only a matter of time, they're saying. Pirs is better than most Irrkuyon, but he won't stand up to his father, he never has except maybe when he courted the Matja. They're taking bets how long he'll last.'' She glanced at the door, stopped talking.

MEMORY:

Arel the smuggler got to his feet. He was a small dark man with a bony sardonic face, fans of fine wrinkles about the outer corners of his eyes and his mouth. His long dark hair was pulled through a filigreed silver clasp at the nape of his neck and hung halfway down his back.

"What am I doing here?"

"You can bypass Goyo Security, get a lander down and off again unnoticed?"

"Oh, Shadow Shadow, you need to ask that? It's my business."

"I need a back door. Just in case."

"Operating against one of the families, aren't you?" His brow shot up.

She didn't answer, figuring it was none of his business. "You owe me danger money, then; those Goyo are tricky bastards.

Aghilo came in, two maidservants following her with bedding and rolled up pallets. She waved Tinoopa and Kizra aside to give the girls room to make up the beds. "I'm going back to my room for the night. The door out there, chapa Tinoopa, you lock and bar it when we're gone." She twisted a key from the chatelaine on her belt, tossed it to Tinoopa. "I'll knock and call out my name in the morning when it's time for you to be up. Be very sure who's out there, chapa Tinoopa, before you open the door. Use the peep to see if I'm alone. Do you hear me?"

"I hear, Aghilo chal."

4

She died again in her dreams. Plunged down and down through fire and pain and crashed.

She woke sweating.

Tinoopa was getting up, smoothing her hair out of her face, shaking out her nightgown.

Someone was pounding on the outer door.

What. . . . Kizra scrubbed at her eyes. There was a terrible urgency in that knocking, though it wasn't as noisy as she'd first thought when it crashed into her dream. She kicked off the blankets, rolled from the pallet, and got to her feet. Lifting the front of her borrowed nightgown so she wouldn't step on it and fall on her face, she followed Tinoopa into the anteroom.

The knocking continued; she could feel the desperation, the fear and anger in the woman on the other side of the door. Aghilo. What was happening?

After a quick look through the peep, Tinoopa turned the key, slapped the bar up, and tugged the door open.

Aghilo stumbled inside. Her face was drained of color, her mouth was working. She put out her hand, flattened it against the wall, and stood leaning into her braced arm while she caught her breath and stifled her panic.

After a moment she straightened, looked quickly from Tinoopa to Kizra. "You'd better get dressed," she said. "There's trouble." She started past Tinoopa, but the Shimmarohi caught her arm.

"What happened?"

"Contract woman. She killed Rintirry, hung herself. I have to wake the Arring."

"Wait, wait, just a minute. It's barely light now, you've got plenty of time before the Artwa goes nova. Sit down." Using her size and her grip on Aghilo's arm, she maneuvered the smaller woman to one of the benches and muscled her down. Then she stood with feet apart, hands on her hips. "How'd you find out?"

MEMORY:
The room was as stale and sordid as she'd expected; she felt a little sick when she saw it. She closed her eyes and told herself it didn't matter. But it did. Arel put his hands on her shoulders. He was exactly her height, his mouth on a level with hers. She focused on that mouth, not daring to meet his eyes.

"Give me a minute, Luv." Whistling softly, he tossed

Kizra collected Tinoopa's clothes, brought them to her, then started pulling on her own clothing. When she was dressed, she dropped to the rug behind Tinoopa, where she could watch Aghilo but be more or less out of sight.

Aghilo twisted her hands around and around each other as she was dressing. The sight of the Shimmarohi shaking out the nightgown and starting to fold it seemed to reassure her and she began talking. "Well, first thing I knew, Loujary chal was beating at the filthy bedding into a closet, brought out clean sheets. He made the bed with an expertise that had her smiling; he caught her at it and his whole body laughed. For a moment she couldn't breathe.

He took an incense burner from his shoulder bag, filled and lit it. The scent of pines drifted to her, cool and clean. He brought out a pair of thick green candles, lit them and turned off the light.

The room was filled with flickering shadow, touched with magic. The outside world with its threats and dangers was banished for the moment.

"Come here," he said.

my door, he'd gone into the Honor Suite to clear up and make sure things were right for when they woke, you know, warm the towels, pick up whatever was thrown about, kind of things they'd expect to have done and get . . ." she grimaced, "get cranky about if it isn't. Anyway, P'murr let him in, said it'd been a quiet night, Rintirry hadn't given him any trouble. Loujary said they talked some before he went in, this and that, he didn't go into what they said except what I told you. Soon as he was inside, he twisted the rheostat way down and turned the lights on and went around picking up, getting things ready, you know. He looked in at the Artwa. Old man was sleeping. Snoring. He went in, picked up there, folded, set out. You know. Artwa didn't stir, just kept snoring. He went in Rintirry's bedroom." She shuddered. "I couldn't believe him, I had to go see." She pressed her hand across her mouth, closed her eyes briefly, then forced them open. "I can't forget. . . ."

Tinoopa took her shoulders, shook her a little. "No time for that now. Listen, I need to know what it means for us. Chapa and chal, what do we have to do to protect ourselves?"

Aghilo squeezed her hands together, moving one over the other endlessly, the soft sound of skin on skin filling the tense silence. "Amurra bless, I've never seen worse, even . . ." she shook her head while her hands kept moving. "She cut his throat, that was first, I suppose. It had to be, that's where the blood was . . . you could smell the blood all over the suite, I don't see how Loujary didn't, I suppose the door was shut then, shut it in . . . cut his head completely off and set it on the pillow, the eyes were open, it

was like he was looking at you. And she cut him . . . ah
. . . cut it off and put it in his hand like he was . . . ah . . .
and she cut open his chest and took his heart out and put it
down there where . . . ah . . . and the skin on the arms and
legs, it was gone . . . ah . . . except for his hands and feet,
it was like he was wearing gloves and slippers and . . . ah
. . . she'd cut the skin she got in strips and braided it into
a rope . . . ah . . . it must have taken her most of the night
. . . ah . . . and when she was finished, she used that rope
to hang herself . . . ah . . . from one of the bed posts, it's
a big bed, like the Matja's, you've seen hers, carved like
that, with posts holding curtains . . . it's the drafts, come
winter, it's hard to heat the rooms, we don't have that much
fuel . . . ah . . . there's coal in the mountains, but we've
just started getting it out . . . she was naked, red hair hanging down to her waist, no blood at all, she'd washed it off,
in the bathroom, bloody water and she'd oiled her body,
smelled like . . . ah . . . I had to look . . . see everything. . . .''

"Who?"

"The one called Tamburra, tall, red-haired. Strange
woman. The Matja assigned her to the Herbmistress, she
worked in the distillery.''

"How did she get in? Wasn't P'murr supposed to stop
that kind of thing?''

"I asked him. She didn't go past him, I suppose she must
have been inside already when the Arring set him there.''

Tinoopa scowled. "I don't know her. . . .''

Kizra scratched at her nose. "She was the one who had
nightmares every night. On the trip here.''

Tinoopa looked around and down. "What?''

"You must have heard her screaming. Woke everyone up
several times. Didn't explain except it was nightmares.''

"Got her. Yeh. The beauty. All she had to do was be
where the man could see her, he'd work out the rest of it.
Probably told her to go in and wait for him, keep quiet about
it. He knew what the Arring thought of him?''

"It wasn't any secret.'' Aghilo was settling into lethargy,
as if by telling all this she was passing it on to Tinoopa,
making it Tinoopa's responsibility. "Us? Nothing we can
do. Artwa might want P'murr skinned, he's head guard. The
Arring won't let that happen. P'murr's loyal; you can't buy
what he gives. If the woman hadn't hanged herself, if she'd

run, there be trouble. She's dead. That should finish it. I don't know. You understand, anything could happen . . . Artwa doesn't need a reason, it's his right, we're his by law, chal and chapa, too. He can do anything to us he wants, all we have is the Arring and Amurra only knows how far he'll go to protect us."

"Right." Tinoopa twisted round to look down at Kizra. "Kiz, get the sitting room cleared, I'm going to see what I can do with the maids and houseservants." She straightened. "Aghilo, you'd better go on in and let the Arring know what happened. Tell him we'll be ready for anything he wants us to do even if it's just keep out of the way." She hauled Aghilo to her feet. "Just tell him what you saw. He'll know better than us what he has to do. He knows his father. You all right?"

"Better." Aghilo smiled, shook herself, went soberly out of the anteroom.

"Kiz," Tinoopa murmured, "I hope this turns out better than I think it's going to."

Kizra shrugged. "We stick with the Matja, I don't see we have any other choice."

"And hope she can put some starch in the Arring's spine. I'd better get moving. You take care, Kiz." She looked like she was about to start one of her lectures, then she glanced over her shoulder at the door. "No time for talking. I mean it, child, keep your head down."

# DYSLAERA 9:
## Lizard magic

Rohant sat in the Pen absorbing the sun; it was good to be out again. And eating again. He'd always been astonished how easy it was for other Cousins to fast for days on end without serious damage to their bodies. Digby said hunger goes away; you forget about it. You shake a little, get dizzy, but you forget about eating.

He smoothed his thumbclaw along his mustache. Dyslaera weren't like that. He was not at all like that; he went cold and weak and his mind started shutting down.

There was a flicker of something down by the sump.

Lazily, not much interested, he turned his head, saw a small gray sauroid perched alertly on the rim of the sump. He smiled. It made think of Kikun. Li'l Liz.

The lizard(?) spun, its long thin tail snapped out, the prehensile end whipped round a large flier that was circling down for a drink and slammed it hard against the concrete floor of the pen. It sat up on its haunches, took the insect in its hands and turned it to expose the soft underside. With absurd small relish, it began biting fastidiously at its prey.

*Interesting. Wonder what they call it here? It had an almost Dyslaer facility with those tiny hands. Tie with that? Why not.*

Rohant let his eyes droop closed and considered the creature, tried to sense it with the faculty he'd used before he could speak. Male and female, Dyslaera were born with the Talent to link with certain beasts, to tie into their nervous systems, to vibrate in tune with their feeling lives. It wasn't nearly as broad-ranged and apparently indiscriminate as Shadith's ability to mindride, but there were possibilities. . . .

It took time to build the Tie, time to understand the beast,

176

to relate what was sensed to realtime acts and reactions. Time . . . lots of time . . . he'd had Sassa from the egg, carried that egg against his body, warming it, becoming slowly aware of the creature inside. He'd relinquished the egg just before it hatched to allow the hatchling to imprint properly on his own kind, took him back as eyas, kept him always near, sleeping in the same room, trained him, was trained by him, an intensifying give and take until the Tie was complete. Months and months, more than a year.

It was much the same with the mutated panthers Magimeez and Nagifog; he didn't want to think of them, their death still screamed in his head, their terror and rage and pain.

He thought instead of the not-lizard.

A name. What should I call you, little liz? Miji. Yes. Nimble Fingers, abbreviated because the whole would be too long. Miji. I can't take a year to get to know you, Miji, all I've got is an hour or so, but maybe we can hurry it up some. The sun is warm today. Very bright. Just a few clouds. A shadow of a cloud is passing over you, Miji, do you feel the difference in the warmth? Aaah. Yes. Astonishing. It seems rubbing against Shadow opened some doors in my head. Opened them a crack, anyway. Shadow . . . no, Rohant, get your mind on what you're doing. Do you have any curiosity in you, Miji? You're not wholly a reptile, are you? Native to this world? Life in the process of evolving? The change altered or cut short by us intruders? Do you feel me . . . aaah. . . .

Miji the not-lizard lifted his frilly head, stared at Rohant. His eyes were large for his head, black as jet beads, lively eyes, bright with the curiosity Rohant wanted to find in him.

Miji, Miji, come and see. He formed the words in his mind and tried to project the welcoming warmth generated around them.

Miji shivered, ran a few steps toward him, retreated.

Time passed unnoticed.

Slowly, warily, Miji got closer and closer, finally close enough to sniff at Rohant's fingers.

Rohant didn't move.

Miji panicked, skittered back about a meter, sat on his haunches, and contemplated the Dyslaeror.

Rohant's ears quivered. He heard the sound of footsteps in the tunnel; the walkers were several minutes off still, but he knew them. His warders come to take him back to his cell. For the first time he looked directly at the not-lizard. "Go," he said aloud. He slapped his hand several times against the concrete, hoping Miji would understand the warning. It was a common one among the reptiloids of Dysstrael his homeworld.

Miji chirked (the first sound he'd made), slapped the spatulate tip of his tail against the concrete, then went scooting away, darting down the outflow pipe at the bottom of the sump basin.

A moment later the grill clanged open and the five masked wards assigned to him came stomping out.

## ##

Savant 4 (speaking to notepad):
A rather amusing incident. The Capture Specialist playing his tricks on a common sakali. Appears the subject is suffering from boredom.
QUESTION: Except for samples of body fluids and brain tissue and drugs to suppress the fugue state, the Ciocan has been left undisturbed by orders of the Council. The failure of all attempts to control adult Dyslaerors cannot, of course, be counted a waste of time; negative results are often as valuable as positives. However, work with the remnant of the sample has reached the point where further experiments will not be worth the expense. The council must agree that it is time to start collecting infants and gravid females and dispose of this lot.
SUGGESTION: Ransom one or more of them to Voallts Korlatch, alive but Wiped. If ransom is refused, then dispatch them to Black House so we can recoup some of our expenses. They are too dangerous to keep.

# SHADITH (Kizra) IN THE HALFLIGHT 2

## 1

Shadith prowled about her room, going round the bed and back again in the narrow floorspace left for her to move in, window to door, door to left wall, back again.

*Memory. Funny thing. Still can't remember how I did it . . . or why . . . set up this forgetting. . . .*

She shuddered as another image intruded. . . .

*Cut his throat? Skinned him? Hung herself on the rope she braided from his skin? Gaaah! Don't think about that. Memory. Lizard. I set up the trigger to trip the next time I saw Kikun and got it tripped by a six-inch garden lizard. That's a giggle. My mind's more creative than I thought. Just as well, Kikun's a*

MEMORY:
She sang.
Wordless sounds filled with joy, pain, desire, fear. . . .
In a half dream, deeply relaxed, she sang to her sisters, her six dead sisters, the Weavers of Shay-alin. . . .
*They rose from the mirror tiles, slender and angular, black and silver similitudes of Naya, Zayalla, Annethi, Itsaya, Tallit and Sullan, spinning threads from themselves to shape the images of Goyo dreams. . . .*
She sang the ancient croon that mated with that dance and filled the spaces this alien voice she'd claimed could not reach with the pure flowing tones of the harp. . . .
Her sisters danced HER joy, celebrating her love with her, commiserating with her on its ephemeral nature, helping her to rejoice in what it was and re-

179

*long way off, dead maybe. No. Li'l Liz is too slippery for that. . . .*
*I hope.*
*All right, all right, now's not the time, but I've got to get out of here. Stop leaning. Drifting. I know a lot now, my name, friends' names. If I can get a call out, someone will come. Call. . . .*
*That means getting to that city, what was it? Nirtajai. That's not so easy.*
*Won't get easier if I sit around and do nothing. Drifting. Can't do that any more.*

*frain from unreal expectations. . . .*
*She sang laughter as she saw Itsaya wink at her, saw Naya smile and clap her slender hands, saw Zaya shake her hips and grin over her shoulder, as she saw each of her dead sisters show their pleasure. . . .*
*She rode that surging wild wave, a hair away from disaster always, out of control . . . rode it with a mastery she'd never reached before and might not again. . . .*

*I'm safe here and comfortable.*
*Comfort's an illusion and nobody's safe.*
*Do it now. Now. Start working at it, anyway. There's lots I can do to get ready. . . .*

She paced, the movement cooling her rage and impatience, planning how to get back to the port city and win access to a skipcom so she could call someone to come get her. In essence it was the same problem she'd had on Kiskai, but there she'd had Rohant and Kikun to help. And Asteplikota. And mobility. She wasn't stuck off to hell and gone with the only transport available walking around on four legs.

She stopped at the window and scowled down at what she could see of the main court and the skimmer that mostly filled it. It was a gray and gloomy day with scattered spatters of raindrops pattering against the walls and the skimmer's dome.

*Stow away? No.*
*He'd have thought of that, the Artwa would.*
*This kind of society, no way the Irrkuyon would trust their precious persons to unsecured transport.*

MEMORY:
Kikun caught up a tree
branch, knocked out the
last fragments of glass in
one of the windows,
climbed through it. Shadith
climbed through after him.
The wind snatched at her
skirts, threatened to whip
her off the narrow, heavily-
carved ledge. The stone
around her had an eerie lu-
minosity, faint but enough
to give her the outlines of
the building, the walls and
towers. . . .
She reached the end,
clutched at the stone and
waited for lightning; the
tree was jerking desperately
about, creaking groaning; a
section of branch tore
loose, came flying by her
and slammed into the win-
dow beside her, then went
clattering away along the
wall.
Flash.
She jumped, landed
sprawled across the limb,
clutched at it as it bucked
under her. She steadied
herself and crawled cau-
tiously inward, cursing as
her dress snagged on a broken branch. She tore free
and struggled on. . . .

*Kitchi-kooing round the Artwa?*
*Since he had a thing for dark*
*girls? No.*

The thought made her
want to vomit.
And it wouldn't work.
He wouldn't take her with
him—not back to his home
ground where people would
see what he was fucking.
She smiled. It was com-
forting that inclination
matched with circumstance.
Not that she'd have done it
anyway. She wasn't backed
into a corner here and there
are some things that corrupt
so deeply that whatever advantage they give is de-
stroyed in the doing.

*There has to be some way. At*
*least 2000 kays. Fifteen days*
*travel across land I don't know.*
*Fifteen days in a truck, not on*
*horseback. We were attacked*
*twice on the way here, fol-*
*lowed, sniped at and we had a*
*dozen guards, armored trucks*
*and a gatlin. I need allies.*
*Brushies . . . I wonder . . . Ti-*
*noopa . . . I don't think so.*
*City woman.*
*Couldn't sit a horse three days*
*let alone the thirty or forty days*
*it'd take.*
*Maybe longer. Don't know if I*
*can. Who. . . . Damn, it looked*
*like a good thing having the*

*Matja favor me . . . made life easier . . . would have been better*
*if I was down with the rest . . . stuck up here, isolated as much*
*as if I were in purdah . . . damn . . . have to get out more . . .*

MEMORY:
The pod was on the launcher, a shadowy black seed. She crawled into the flightspace, stretched out on the pad and eased herself into its hollows, fitting her skin against the sensors.
A moment later she felt the hard sharp kick of the launcher.
Her vision cleared. She could see the *Cillasheg* floating half a kilometer away, could see all round herself. She shifted her vision out and out until she could see the asteroids, frost in the darkness, white and black glitter in the light of the dim, distant sun, shifted down again until her vision was confined to an area the width of her wings at full deployment. She snapped the wings out full, gossamer fields like shadows in glass. The lightwinds filled them, pushed her outward. She gathered speed for the turn, feeling the sunmoth come alive under her as she drank the winds and rode them out and out.
She laughed and groaned, making love to the winds, laughed again and swung round, tilting her wings, slipping the winds, tacking

*talk the Matja into giving me a break. . . .*
*I have to get out of here . . . somehow . . . get to Nirtajai . . . find a skipcom . . . like on Kiskai . . . wonder how they're getting on with their reforms, if they've got the world they wanted or if it's falling apart in their hands . . . Miowee's probably back to singing in the streets if things went like most rebellions . . . Aste back in the swamps . . . well, that's their business. . . .*

She heard noises below and leaned out the window. Something was happening in the court, but she couldn't see anything from here. She pulled back in and ran for the door.

### 2

There was no one at the oriel window, though it was one of the better outlooks in the House.
She climbed into the round hole, pressed her face against the colored glass.
Pirs stood at the top of the steps, ignoring the splatters of rain that came every few minutes. He was standing very erect, his head up. He wasn't saying anything.
The Artwa stood on the same step, a double arms'

right, tacking left, sweeping toward the sun, on and on, faster and faster, time compressing to nothing. Her blood was wine, her body sang, on and on. . . .

length apart from his second son. The old man was seething, the younger one deeply disturbed, but there was no grief in either of them. At least none for Rintirry.

Pirs was miserable, but that had more to do with his father's rejection than the loss of a brother.

*Give him his due. Half brother. And one trying to kill him. Not the sort you mourned.*

The big doors boomed open. Loujary and Wayak came out and moved carefully down the steps, carrying a litter with Rintirry's body on it, wrapped in heavy white damask. Shadith relaxed; she'd expected a lot more trouble than this, infected with Tinoopa's gloom, probably. And the weepy gloom of the day, as if the skies wept for the double death. She sniffed, fancies with no touch of reality, even old Cagharadad wasn't grieving. She grimaced.

MEMORY:
Lissorn was racing toward Ginny, stunner forgotten, claws out.
Ginny raised a hand.
Four cutters flashed from overlooks, hit Lissorn in midstride.
For an instant the Dyslaeror was a black core in the furnace where the beams met, then they winked out and there was nothing left, not even dust.
When his son died, Rohant screamed with grief and rage, his great voice filling the room. . . .

*Rintirry. He was a human being, just barely, but he was and someone should grieve at his passing and the manner of it. Someone. Not me.*

Loujary and Wayak came silently from the flitter and went off toward the men's quarters.

Arring Pirs dropped onto one knee and bowed his head, the watery sunlight that struggled through the clouds turning his long loose hair to melted gold.

Shadith couldn't see the Artwa's face, but she could smell the stink of his malice. He was beginning to enjoy this. ''I leave no blessing

on this House,'' he intoned, his voice blaring out through
the whine of the wind. ''There is kin blood on this House.
Until it is cleansed, I curse it and you. Kin Blood,'' he
repeated, liking the taste of the words.

Pirs said nothing. He didn't move.

Shadith shivered. It was all too apparent that he revered
his father, that he needed his approval. That he was suffering under the old man's spite, that he didn't see it as spite,
would never see it as anything but a father's justified distress
over the needless death of a son, however worthless that son
might be. The blindness startled her. He was an intelligent
man, even a good man, given how he'd been brought up.
And yet he let this . . . this vain, stupid old . . . warthog!
rule him.

Aghilo was right. Pirs would never rebel against his father. He would hunt ways around the old man's more irre-
sponsible acts and edicts, but in the end he'd do what his
father told him.

> *The Matja knows that, too, that's why. . . . Gods, the Matja
> means well, but what she's promising . . . it probably won't
> happen. The old man will see to that. And Pirs will do as
> he is told.*
> *So I do for myself or it doesn't get done.*

The Artwa went stalking down the steps.

The skimmer door closed behind him, the motors whined.

A moment later the court was empty and the flier a black
speck vanishing into the clouds.

### 3

They threw Tamburra's body into the river for the fish to
eat. The locals didn't want l'borrghas to get a taste for flesh
that walked on two legs.

At the same time, the smoke from the pyre they built for
Kulyari on Amur Hill rose black and solid into the clouds.
She was Irrkuyon and couldn't be discarded like offal; there
was only the briefest of ceremonies with Polyapo there to
represent the family and the Amur-speaker to say the Rest-
rites, then the fire was lit and a cadre of charcoalmen left
to keep it burning until even the bones were ash.

Ghanar Rinta settled into peace.

There were no more attacks from bands of tumaks. No one said anything, but they all knew what that meant—the supply of gold was cut off when the supplier died.

Allina continued healthy.

Tinoopa ran the House with unobtrusive efficiency, making points, as she'd say, with every easy day.

Pirs lost his strained look. With a facility that amounted to a Talent, he forgot old terrors and went back to his books and the business of running the Kuyyot.

Shadith's restlessness increased. She got Pirs to let her look over his histories and the atlas he kept on his desk. Whenever the Matja gave her some free time, she was in the study, making notes, trying to work out a way of reaching Nirtajai without getting herself killed.

And she began looking about for allies.

The chal wouldn't run with her, she knew that. She didn't bother thinking about them.

Vuodee and Vassika had settled in and started courting almost immediately; now they were promised, with weddings due before the month was out. They were full of plans and elated because their contracts were to be voided as soon as they took the chal-oath to the Arring and the Matja.

Tictoc, Evalee, and Dorrit had been having a grand time flirting and generally making mischief among the men, but they too were beginning to settle down. According to Tinoopa, the betting was Evalee would be promised before Summerhighday and the other two soon after.

Lyousa va Vogl was blissful with the opportunities offered by the weaving shed. Nunnikura Weavemistress had recognized her gifts and left her free to improvise. It would take a planet wrecker to blast her loose.

Jassy and Eeda had a widening circle of friends; they were hard workers, cheerful and outgoing. Contract levies were all they knew and they were content to have it so. Jassy was a practiced storyteller and she had an endless supply of strange, wonderful tales to liven meals and sit over brushtea with; in a world where books were scarce and most entertainment homemade, she was a treasure.

Beba Mahl had settled into embroidery. She'd bargained for night work and gotten it. She had a room of her own and almost no contact with the rest of the Kuysstead. She could complete her contract and move on. No one would miss her and she would forget them as soon as she joined a new levy.

Ekkurekeh and Yerryayin were hard workers and unambitious. For reasons they never spoke of, they'd adopted the Levy system as home, did what they were told and dropped into Kuysstead life without making a ripple.

The cousin convicts Bertem, Luacha, and Sabato were bored and unhappy here, they loathed the work in the weaving sheds and wriggled out of it whenever they could. The problem was, like Tinoopa, they were city-bred; the Brush scared them, they couldn't ride and didn't want to learn. They liked their comforts, baths and beer and warm beds with friendly company. Shadith considered them, shook her head. No. Better go alone than chance the miseries that trio of sybarites would bring with them.

The Jinasu (Ommla, Jhapuki, Fraji and Rafiki) spent their days with the beasts and their nights with the herders and were as likely as the young ones to take the chal-oath when their term was up, though not because they wed any of the locals. They'd branched far enough from the other Cousin races to make children unlikely and any that appeared sterile. They were candid about that early on and it made life much easier for them since they'd ceased to be a threat to local women. They liked this world and would do nothing to injure their status here.

Zhya Arru spent long lazy days tending the livestock of the Kuysstead; she liked beasts and loathed unexpected changes. Though she didn't work at it, she too had her admirers and would probably wed one of them and take the chal-oath before the end of summer—as long as it was clearly understood she wasn't about to do any housework or other boring tasks.

Anitra vanished the third night after their arrival. It was assumed she'd gone to the Brush. Pirs sent out trackers, but they found no trace of her.

Tsipor pa Prool stayed a month longer than Anitra, then she vanished, too. She was a silent women, secretive and strange. No one bothered going after her. In fact, there was a collective sigh of relief when she was gone.

## ##

In her room at night Shadith paced from window to door to wall and back again, raging at her helplessness. It seemed absurd that she couldn't get away from here. There were no bars to hold her, no walls she couldn't climb. Only that two thousand kays of wilderness.

That was enough right now . . . more than enough.

# PRISONER 3:
# Ginny slips his shackles and goes hunting a shadow

1

The minute Ginbiryol Seyirshi woke, he knew he'd been moved. They'd drugged him and shifted him from his cell on the planet to a cell on a ship.

He sat up slowly, looked around. Four walls and a floor, empty. Toeup furnishings unsprung except for the cot he'd waked on. Wallslot for food delivery. He placed his hands on his knees, dropped his gaze to the floor, and brooded.

The cell was a twin of the holding cells on his own ship and for a moment he wondered if Omphalos was playing games with his head, sending him out on a vessel they said was destroyed.

No. The reasons he'd conjured for believing them were valid; this was a case of form following function. He suppressed his surge of hope, got laboriously to his feet, and began exploring the resources of the cell.

2

Betalli smoothed gloved fingers over the back of a gloved hand, watched the monitor a moment longer, then touched it off and got to his feet. Ignoring the side glances of crewmen in dull gray shipsuits and mirror visors, he left the bridge and dropped to the living quarters. He touched the announcer on the Savant Quatorze's cabin and waited.

And waited.

He folded his arms and prepared to outlast the Savant's annoyance. This was his nominal superior, but the man had to be aware of the web of support Betalli had throughout the Powers of Omphalos. He'd listen. He wouldn't do anything, but at least he'd listen.

The announcer chimed, the door slid back, Betalli went in.

His mouth tightened when he saw the Savant was wearing

his robe, cowl, and gloves. This was supposed to be a *SE-CURE* mission, all ties to the Source carefully erased. This fool. . . . He bowed, waited to be offered a seat.

It was another lengthy wait. The Savant was making sure Betalli knew who ordered whom. Finally a gloved hand lifted, pointed at a chair.

Betalli sat, waited.

"You wanted?"

"Seyirshi is awake."

"So. It's time, isn't it?"

"You don't understand him. I do. He's a dangerous man, most dangerous when he looks most helpless."

"That again."

"I cannot guarantee to control him if you let him out of the holding cell. Leave him in there until we reach Bol Mutiar."

"You made that argument to the Mimishay Council. They didn't buy it, why do you expect me to? I was instructed to start the man working once we were in the insplit. I am going to follow instructions. If you're so worried, come up with something specific you want done to tighten security. Otherwise stop carping and do your job."

Betalli got to his feet, bowed, and left.

He was *for* Omphalos. It was the center of his life, his reason for existing. He believed passionately in what Omphalos stood for, in rule of the masses by a benevolent elite. He believed that ordinary people were incapable of regulating themselves and organizing their own lives. They needed direction, guidance, gentle coercion for their own good. Sometimes not so gentle, if they were resolutely wrongheaded.

He was honored by the Powers of Omphalos and honored them, but at times it seemed to him the lesser brethren had so little grasp of the Soul of Omphalos that they were scarcely better than the sheep they were being bred to rule. He'd met types like Quatorze before, all too often he'd brushed against them in his labors outside the comfortable ambiance of the Home Foci. He worked alone, a Focus in himself, no Brothers for him. The more conventional Brothers resented his self-sufficiency because it stood as a measure of their own limits.

Quatorze was a fool. Betalli walked into his quarters, sealed the door behind him, and sat at his console. He called up his plans and sat frowning at the schematics. Fool. Yes. The man had a small mind and a big grudge. Back on the Council with his armgraft still itching, Tierce had set this crawler over him. Tierce was an enemy. He betrayed Omphalos with every breath he took. Betalli marked that down. Quatorze was too small to bother with, but Tierce, yes. When this is over, I've got to do something about him.

Betalli leaned closer to the screen, began going minutely through his surveillance arrangements, trying to discover any place where Seyirshi might find the leverage to subvert the system. Seyirshi would find something, he was sure of it. He knew the man too well, he'd seen him poke and pry at systems until they collapsed in ruins, all the while flaking the destruction he'd set going.

Nothing. Betalli ran the system over and over, poking at it, trying everything he could think of, simple or complex. He found no entry for manipulation, but no comfort either. He recognized his limitations; he was a plodder, no way he could follow the eccentric leaps of Ginny's brain.

He tapped into the monitor, watched Ginny sit slumped on the cot, his face inscrutable, waiting with an iron patience for whatever was going to be done with him.

For nearly an hour he sat watching that stolid motionless figure. Then he called up record flakes of Ginny in his cell; he'd been over them before, over and over them, trying to discover what was happening in the man's mind, seeing nothing he could put a finger on.

Finally he sighed, shook his head. Quatorze is a fool, he repeated to himself. Passionless words, worn-out litany. Most men were fools, that was the point of Omphalos.

He got to his feet, took off the impermasuit, the gloves, stripped to his skin, and walked into the cleansing chamber he'd had installed beside his workroom.

He sat a long time in the dry sterile heat, disciplining his mind as he disciplined his body. He had to be ready when Ginny went to the workshop, he had to watch the man's every movement, hope he could spot trouble before it fruited.

Finally he retreated to his secure sleep chamber, lay under the flickering killights and slept, clean inside and out and weary beyond description.

3

Seyirshi felt the faint tingle as the ship dropped into the insplit. He tensed briefly, then forced himself to relax.

Security androids came for him, took his wrists, and led him to the workroom he'd requested. They stood in the middle of it, holding him until the release code was sent in from outside, then they separated and went to stand one at each end of the room, their scanners following every move he made.

He ignored them and walked about the workshop, checking supplies against a list on a handheld notepad, ticking off each item with meticulous care.

It took a day to finish the inventory and he logged five complaints about missing materiel, then let the androids take him back to his cell.


4

Betalli watched as Ginny checked his stock. It was a tedious process. Again and again he found his mind drifting off, again and again he jerked his attention back, acid in his mouth, wondering if he'd missed something. The process was being flaked, he could replay what was happening down there, examine it in detail—but that might be too late.

The day ended. He watched Ginny a while longer as he ate his supper from the tray delivered through the slot, watched while he washed, put on a nightshirt, stretched out on the cot, and slept.

Betalli left the screen lit, stripped, and went into his scrub room.

When he came out again, Ginny was breathing slowly, steadily, the readings said he was in the first stages of sleep. Betalli thinned his mouth, pulled on another impermasuit, sat at the screen and began replaying randomly chosen moments from the stock taking, slowing the action down, focusing in on Ginny's hands. Nothing. Nothing. Nothing.

He tapped the screen black and brooded. The bland innocence of Ginny's every move was not reassuring, it only meant he was getting ready for something—or he'd already done something and Betalli had missed it.

Missed it. Missed it. If he had, he had and would continue to miss it, his eyes sliding over and over the place.

He sighed and went shuffling into his sleeproom, stretched naked under the killights, and litanyed himself to sleep.

## 5

Ginbiryol Seyirshi adjusted the magnifier to a comfortable height, took a standard Eye from its pod and began peeling back its rough black skin.

He didn't like exposing his secrets this way—the extensive modifications he'd devised for the EYEs that made them as undetectable as dreams, that enabled them to collect emotions as well as full sensory data from his targets. When the Omphalites wanted him to do this work onplanet, under the recorders of the Foundation, he wouldn't. He hadn't argued with the Council or the Chom, he simply said no and refused to amplify his refusal.

He began preparing the EYEs exactly according to the plan he had worked out for the subversion of Bol Mutiar, humming contentedly as he constructed then tucked in new elements. What was effective for Bol Mutiar was even more so when applied within the closed system of the ship. The Omphalites had overlooked that—or if they hadn't overlooked it, they expected to be able to control the EYEs and him. He smiled. They'd lost control the minute they'd transferred him here with his prosthetic arm intact. If he'd been in charge, he'd have removed that arm, replaced it with one he could be sure of. They'd scanned it, of course, and found nothing except the minute forces that controlled its movements. And they'd left him with it. Fools.

He attached a notepad to the EYE, ran the program and input additional instructions, using his own intensely compressed prog-langue. When he was finished, he zipped up the EYE, set it in a vault tray, and took another EYE from its pack.

He worked steadily until his midday meal, lay down on a cot he toed out of the floor, and took a long nap.

When he woke, he went back to work on the EYEs.

## 6

Betalli bent over the screen, running over and over the sections where Ginny was altering the EYE programs, trying to work out just what he was doing, calling up the inputs

and studying them until he was forced to admit he didn't
understand what he was seeing; he loathed the kephali that
ran most ships and many cities, he didn't trust them, thought
of them as whores giving out to anyone who tickled their
pads, hostile whores who took a perverse delight in tempting men into destructive situations. He had no choice now,
he had to turn the program analysis over to the kephalos and
try to prevent the results from going to anyone but him.

He set the analysis going, then replayed the dayend records. He watched Ginny put the EYE he was working on
into its slot in the vault tray, pack up his tools, watched him
hold out his arm for the android escort and go placidly off
to his cell.

The second android lifted the tray of EYEs and, carrying
them delicately, took them to the heavy vault that Betalli
had installed in the workroom. The android set the tray on
its insulated shelf, tugged the door shut and set the time-
lock, then settled in front of the vault, keyed into guard
mode, ready to burn anything that moved in the 180 curve
of his watch area.

Smooth. Not a glitch anywhere he could see, nothing he
could smell, taste, nothing but a cold certainty that Ginny
was plotting something. What? That scratched at him, an
irritant that wouldn't go away. . . .

He touched the screen black, stripped and went into
his cleanroom, sat in the heat until his brain was baked,
then lay brooding under the killlights until he finally managed to shut down his mind and sink into a dream-ridden
sleep.


7


Three hours into shipnight Ginny twitched, opened his
eyes. He got to his feet, crossed to the fresher, drank a glass
of water, then returned to the cot. He bent down, took hold
of the cot edge with his prosthetic hand, twisted the hand
slightly and pushed down. A moment later he lowered himself heavily to the mattress, swung his feet up, and went
placidly back to sleep.

8

In the vault two of the EYEs stirred, began to throb.

The tiny spherical nodes slipped through slits in their
skins, rose a hand-width above the tray and hovered above
the discarded husks, minute lasers sealing the escape holes.
The naked EYEs slid down behind the tray, clung to the
plastic; they hummed briefly, spun a chameleon field about
themselves and effectively vanished.

9

Betalli sat, watched Ginny work on the EYEs.

The report from the kephalos lay at his elbow; he hadn't
read it in detail, but on the surface its conclusions were
reassuring. The additions were a series of commands to internal elements whose capacities were not fully apparent.
That might have been worrying, but the report went on to
state that the additions were entirely passive, that they
needed an outside trigger to begin operating. And there was
no way Ginny had access to such a trigger.

He began a slow search of the workroom, then probed at
Seyirshi.

Nothing.

Other than the toolfields, the only forces operant in that
room were the minute motors and fields woven though Ginny's prosthesis.

He scowled at the arm, at the lacy schema of struts and
wires. No connection with the outside. No apparent connection. He considered removing that arm. There was no
way to get it off without damaging some very sensitive link-
ages, crippling the man and canceling his usefulness. Yes,
he thought. I can't have it off, but I can put a read on that
arm. If it does anything at all beyond its ordinary output,
I'll have it off, I don't care what the Savant says.

10

Ginny looked up as a third android touched his arm. "A
moment," he said. "I cannot stop right now."

The android stepped back and waited until Ginny set the
EYE on the tray. It took hold of his prosthetic arm, swung
him around, straightened the arm out. It slit Ginny's sleeve,

glued a sensor strip to the pseudoskin, released the arm, and walked out.

Ginny touched the dangling sleeve, sighed. "Dear me," he said aloud. "How annoying." He used a small laser to cut it away, then went back to work.

### 11

Three hours into the shipnight, the free EYEs clinging under the table woke and pulsed.

Inside the vault two more EYEs woke, slid out of the skins and went to ground behind camouflage fields, waiting for the vault to be opened.

### 12

Ginny slept the six hours he allotted himself without moving. He woke, exercised, ate, went back to work.

### 13

Betalli watched and fretted, went over and over the records of the previous nights, over and over the report from the kephalos. He'd missed something. He knew it. Ginny would never submit this docilely to control. But there was nothing. Nothing at all.

Betalli wasn't sleeping well, even under the killlights in the sterile security of the saferoom. In his worst nightmare he woke and found himself staring up into Ginny's smiling face, watching Ginny's hands pour filth on him.

He doubled the watch androids, left three in the workroom every shipnight, sent one into Ginny's sleepcell with instructions to burn him if he did anything at all out of the ordinary.

And all this time Ginny plodded stolidly along, never deviating from the path he'd laid down back on Arumda'm.

### 14

On the tenth day there were only five EYEs left. Ginbiryol Seyirshi did some special work on these, more modifications to the circuitry, more complex instructions added to the standard program.

Betalli didn't wait until night to seize those EYEs. One of the androids took the tray as soon as Ginny set the fifth EYE in it, placed it in the vault, and locked the door.

Ginny smiled sadly, began filling firing tube inserts with drugs and tiny, blood-soluble darts.

## 15

On the tenth day in the insplit, in the third hour of the shipnight, one of the five big EYEs woke and hid.

On the eleventh day in the insplit, in the third hour of the shipnight, the big EYE raided the supply bins and vanished into the ventilation system to join the smaller EYES already hiding there.

On the twelfth day in the insplit, during the third hour of the shipnight, the EYEs acted. By the fifth hour Betalli and the Savant were the only individuals aboard the ship (other than the engine crew) alive and in possession of their faculties.

At the sixth hour, Ginbiryol Seyirshi rose from his bed. Ignoring the android deactivated in the corner of the cell, he dressed and went out.

By the eleventh hour, he held complete control of the kephalos and the Savant Quatorze was dead. He contemplated what he'd accomplished, smiled with satisfaction, and sent for Betalli.

## 16

Betalli stared at him from red-rimmed eyes, then he nodded. "Fools," he said. "All of us."

Ginny tapped the readouts. "Not you," he said. "They should have listened to you."

"You knew they wouldn't."

"Oh, yes. They have given me data enough to know them. You worked for me long enough that I knew you."

"How?"

"How escape your surveillance?" Ginny chuckled. "I did not. Of course I did not."

Betalli waggled the fingers of the hand imprisoned in the android's fist. "Why am I standing like this if you did nothing?"

"I did not say that. Surely it must have occurred to you

that materiel meant to subvert a world would be exceedingly effective at subverting a much smaller community?''

''I warned them and I watched you. I had the kephalos analyze your additions. It said every addition was passive, needed a triggering from outside. Had you gotten to the kephalos already?''

''Oh, no. Merely trusted my Luck and implanted a latency in one EYE.'' Ginny smiled and lied; much as he was enjoying this, he knew better than to broadcast secrets promiscuously. ''In the night, in the vault, the EYE woke and primed others. A pyramid, Betalli. Once the first triggering was done, the rest was mere reduplication.''

''The crew is dead?''

''Oh, yes. At least, all but those crucial to running the ship. You were greatly overmanned, you know. Waste of resources. I control completely everyone still alive. Everyone but you, of course.''

''I see.''

''Yes. I am sure you do. You betrayed me, Betalli. You were in my employ and used my trust to destroy me. It will take many years to repair the damage you have done to me. You and Omphalos. Your death will serve me two ways. It will discourage others from following your example and it will entertain my customers. Oh, yes. I have a new project, Betalli, a new Limited Edition. Something I haven't attempted before. It has a simple title, no need for fuss. The Fall of Omphalos. Nice play of sounds, don't you think?''

17

Betalli struggled.

Ginny flaked his struggles.

He had Betalli stripped and thrust naked into a disabled rescue pod, an EYE there to watch him as air ran out on him.

##

When the air was thick and stale, Ginny touched a sensor and a sac opened, releasing spiders and other many-legged wigglers to crawl over the prisoner.

Three hours after the pod was ejected from the ship, Betalli died, filthy and raving.

Ginny smiled and exploded the pod.

He didn't want the little lives to suffer more than they had to.

He deployed Betalli's android force to dump the dead out the lock, then took samples from the unconscious crewmen and brewed up a comealong that would turn them into permanent zombies. It cut their efficiency way down, but he wouldn't need them long, just long enough to get him to the nearest clandestine Pit where he could hire some temporary efficiency and ersatz loyalty. He thought a moment about Ajeri and the Paems, sighed, and gave orders to his clutch of Zombies.

Crew first. Then Weersyll and Bolodo Neyuregg. Then Shadith. Then Mimishay. Then—

# TROLLING IN THE TAVERN:
# Autumn Rose begins to play a big fish

1

Jacket hung round her shoulders like a cape, Autumn Rose sat on a lichen-crusted bitt and watched the surging bay water as the sun set gaudily behind her, turning the clouds into salmon chunks and touching the foam tips on the waves with a fugitive vermilion. There was a narrow alley past her left shoulder, a strip of weedy ground between two blocky warehouses, beyond that the street and across the street the Rumach where she was staying.

On the next wharf over a handful of ladesmen and night-watchers were sitting with their backs against a brick incinerator, chugging down dalbir from two-handled stoneware jugs and eating meatrolls they'd heated on wire skewers spread over the sluggish fire burning inside the brick enclosure. Even this far off with the wind blowing in off the sea, whipping her hair about her face, she could smell the grease and the gahwang.

Maybe she only imagined the gahwang. Everything she'd eaten during the last two weeks had been laced with the herb. Probably her own sweat stunk of it. She lifted an arm, sniffed at the inside crease of her elbow, straightened up, and smiled at the memory this evoked.

On the first morning Kikun slid out of bed, stretched and padded over to the basin; he opened the cold tap wide, cupped his hands to catch the stream of water, splashed his face and delicate leafform ears.

The light streaming through the window beside the basin turned them into jade, pale green and translucent. He soaped a washcloth, washed with care all the folds of skin on his face and body, then round his sheath and testicles. He extruded his bone-white penis, washed that with the same care, let it slip neatly back and lifted his foot onto the basin's edge and began to wash it.

When he'd finished soaping himself, he rinsed out the cloth and went over his body again with the same meticulous thoroughness, cleaning away every trace of soap. Autumn Rose lay with her fingers laced behind her head, watching all this with bemused amusement.

He padded to one of the chairs, shook out his trousers and tunic and pulled them on, then slipped his feet into his sandals and turned to look at Rose, a challenge in his shining orange eyes, or so she read what she saw there, but all he said was: "Don't forget to get a key made."

She frowned. "It's going to be a problem, isn't it. You go out, I forget about you, so I forget everything to do with you. How do I remember the key thing? Or anything else I'm supposed to do for you?"

"Yes." He scratched the folds beneath his chin. "I've been thinking about this." He crossed to the bed, rested his fingertips on her wrist. "May I?"

For an instant she hesitated, but curiosity and need were more powerful than her faint revulsion. "Whatever. Unless you start biting off chunks of me."

He grinned, then bent and nuzzled the inside of her elbow, rubbing his nostrils against her, moving back and forth, back and forth, his skin soft as old leather, warm. . . .

She kicked her heels against the bitt. It sent shivers of heat along her body when he did that. *You'll remember now,* he said, then went quickly to the door and was out and gone before she'd recovered enough to answer him. He was right—oh, yes. She wriggled on the smooth worn top of the bit. Every morning after that, he did the same and left. She understood what he was doing after she'd thought about it. He must have scent glands at the base of his nostrils. He was marking her. She couldn't actually smell anything, but she certainly didn't forget him again.

She rubbed her thumb across the place where he nuzzled her and wondered if there were pheromones in the exudate; she was getting so hot it was a wonder she didn't burn his nose . . . long, hectic time since she'd laid down in lust. . . . She licked her thumb, grinned, mocking herself. That was her grandda talking through her, she wouldn't exist if he hadn't done a lot of laying about in lust himself, engendering her mama in his scattershot sowing, but he was a hypocrite without peer. . . . She giggled again. Well, in

the end he was mostly peering, if what mama said was right.
Hypocrite about women, yes, the few times he'd actually
beaten her were when he'd heard her cursing one or another
of the Chateau boys. Tied up my tongue . . . when it comes
to sex, anyway. Digby would say he didn't do much for my
working vocab.

The wind was getting stronger and most of the color had
died out of the clouds. A raindrop splattered in her hair.
She swore, hugged her arms across her breasts. Where the
hell is that little worm. . . ? She freed one arm, brought
her hand close to her eyes so she could see the ringchron.
Supposed to be here a good twenty minutes ago. If I have
to winkle him out of some hole, I'll twist that rat into his
boots, there won't be a grease spot left.

There weren't any ships right where she was sitting,
through there were a number on both sides of her, sailing
ships, the wind and the swell making them rock and rub
against the fenders, their wood sides creaking, their ropes
slap-slatting with monotonous regularity. The men down by
the incinerator had stopped talking. They were watching
her. She pushed her arms into the jacket sleeves, pulled it
closer around her. It was getting cold. And dangerous.
Vaarlords didn't waste good money on useless lights. They
had guards and torchmen if they wanted to go out after dark.
Five minutes, worm. . . .

Bungkuk slid out of the alley and squatted in the shadows
on the side of the bitt away from the incinerator. "Fife
pera," he muttered. "I am haffing got all you are asking."

"Nothing till I hear. Then we'll see."

He fished in his vest, brought out a packet wrapped in
leaves. With finicking small gestures he peeled back the
outer layer of leaves and bit off a section of the plug inside.
Kunja root. Chewing busily, a strong musky, oversweet odor
rising from him, he refolded the leaves and put the packet
away. He dropped his arms onto his knees and contemplated
the heavy, heaving water. After a moment he spat, wiped
his mouth. "You are giffing me fife names, ia? So. Syous
Uppato. He is being hilang-iceer. You are understanding
hilang?"

"Gone, vanished."

"More than that, estralluar. It is meaning put down a
hole. Not something he was doing hisself. Vaarmanta are

getting 'im, is being what they say.'' He chewed some more, spat.

"There's a hole where he was," Kikun said when he came in the second day, Syous Uppato, he meant. "I looked around his place," he said, "and did some listening. There's a couple thugs sitting there waiting to jump anyone who's fool enough to ask questions. Uppato had his name on his door. Someone painted over the name and cleaned the place out. Not a smell of him left.''

"Ia," she said. "And?"

"Ghia Granzadoman is being a tjispoht . . . what you would be calling a dirty sneak who is sticking his nose here and there and selling what he snoff in. Got it? Ia, sure. Y' are not wishing to deal with 'im. Not if you are wanting to keep y' bizness prifaat.''

"Why's he alive, then, not vanished like Syous?"

"Better the tjispoht you know, ia so? B'sides he is working for the Beza Preszao, what y' are calling Bigman Policer. He is specializing most in tax 'n tariff.'' He shrugged and spat. "Maybe one day he is going down a hole hisself, screw old Beza, 'cause Gratz the Tjis is liking to squeeze anabody gif 'im the chance, for the fun a it.'' He set his fists together and turned them in opposite directions while he chattered his teeth.

On the sixth day, Kikun said: "I followed Granzadoman the past three days; he runs errands sometimes, but mostly just hangs about. I saw him meet people, get money from them, decided I should see what I could see about them, trailed more than one of them back to the Troc Istana, that's the High Vaar's little shack. Looks to me like he's an informer.''

"I'll pay for those two," she said, "go on."

Bungkuk excavated the wad from his mouth, pitched it into the water, wiped his lips with the back of his hand. "Hary Prechar is doing drugs. Y' name it, he is going to be hafing it. I am not knowing what you are needing from this lot, but Hary is being no good for anathing but pops. It is being a very bad idea to hit 'im for cash, is being even worse to get names or like that. He is having so many blocks, is taking him half hour to be getting into his own head. He is letting effabody know this, he is not liking pain, ia so.''

On the ninth day Kikun came dragging in. When she asked him what he'd got, he shook his head. ''Was looking into Prechar,'' he said. ''Can't get close to him, not even me. He's busy, all right, got people going in his place all hours, in and out, never staying long. He's paying off the local Vaarmanta, got the city guards keeping order, shooing people on if they hang about too long.'' Kikun shuddered. ''What I saw of him, he's crazy. Smells like he's going to implode any minute. Just as well we keep as far away from that one as from Granzadoman. And there's this, if I make too much of a point of my being in a place, the thing doesn't work, Rose, so I can't fool around there without getting pinned. Be easier to get at the High Vaar.'' He sighed, flung himself onto the windowseat. ''What about you, Rose, you come up with anything?''
She rolled over, pushed up on her elbow. ''I found a skambler, a hustler,'' she said, ''a mangy little dried-up mouse who knows things, name of Bungkuk. We had a conversation in the park where I met those Angatines and the blind one laid the curse on me. They weren't there, thank whatever. He's going to meet me round sundown, the wharf across the street from here.''
''You be careful, Rose.''
She grinned lazily at him. ''It's not like I haven't done this before, Kuna. I'll have a stunner in my pocket and eyes in my backhair.''

''Right,'' she said. ''That's three. I'll buy it. Go on.''
''Sai Jinksay. He is knowing effabody, is doing a bit of effathing. Is having no himkontact, but if you are wanting to put together a small deal not too complicated, is the man you are wanting to see. Or if you maybe are wanting to find someone, he can do that.''
''Downside?'' She pushed her hands into her jacket pockets, shivered as another stray raindrop splattered across her face. ''Tjis?''
''No. He is not selling it. He is getting his throat cut if he is selling it, but Beza Preszao is having him picked up effa so offen and is squeezing him dry. The squeeze is being

due any day now, it is being only to wait a week or so if
you are wanting to use him.''

"Hmm. Right. Go on.''

"Jao juhFeyn. Huh. He is being different from the others.
He is being offworlder, but he is being connect, you knowing what I mean. Is being married to High Varmantianne.
Mostly he is being taffernaman. The Kipuny Shimmery is
being his place. Where people are coming for meeting without guarda ofer effa shoulder. Or where they are coming for
playing Ffagnag without taxman or tjis are sniffing about
their winnings and losings. Jao is knowing more things and
more people than Jinksay, but efen High Faar is not putting
squeeze on him. Is being too useful for wasting. He don't
be talking, he don't be bothering anabody, they don't be
bothering him.'' He snapped his fingers at her, the sharp,
breaking sounds almost lost in the whine of the wind. "Is
being payday, estralluar.''

She sat hunched over, the cold beginning to strike to the
bone. A lot of what he'd told her she'd already found out
for herself, either her or Kikun, but there was enough new
there to justify the price, plus the fact she was fertilizing a
source. Besides, it wasn't her money she was spending, not
coming from an expense account she'd have to fight Digby
on, blood out of a stone any old day. "Right,'' she said
finally. "Worth five.'' She took her right hand from her
pocket, dropped the pouch into his twitching fingers.

As he counted and felt each coin, she could almost smell
him speculating about her possible vulnerability and how
much cash she might be carrying and she knew the moment
he decided it was better to go with what he had.

"Be you wanting more,'' he muttered, "you are knowing
how to find me.'' The sounds of his movements covered by
the wind, he went scurrying off.

She ran her hands through her hair, it felt stiff and wet,
beaded with sweat and condensation from the chilling air.
Best have a bath tonight, she thought, wash the mop. Or
I'll be scratching everywhere. Hmm. Wonder if I've got
pale roots showing. Better fix that.

She glanced down the wharf. The men at the incinerator
were still watching her. She got to her feet, shook her hands
and arms, then went strolling off, her senses alert, her hand
on the stunner in the pocket of her jacket. It was only a step
to the rooming house, but one of the first things Digby had

ground into her was closest to your base is your biggest danger.

In the narrow way between the warehouses, the wind mugged her as she walked, snatching at her, blowing gravel against her hard enough to bruise her even through the heavy cloth of her trousers.

There was a cluster of sounds behind her. A scrape. Another. Several small crackles.

She didn't bother looking back, just moved as quickly as she could without actually running.

The street was dark and empty and getting damp as the rain started falling steadily; there were a few lights from windows in her Rumach's facade and from other Rumachs along the street, pale amber squares with dark lines of bars crossing them, not much illumination on a night without moon or stars. She slowed once she was out of the alley, strolled across the street. The short hairs on the back of her neck were standing up and itching like crazy. In her right-hand pocket, she slid back the sensor cover on the stunner, felt the handle vibrate minutely against her palm. In her lefthand pocket, she separated out the front door key and held it ready.

When she was about to step from the street onto the short wooden walkway leading to the stairs and the front door, she heard another a flurry of scuffs. Coming on his toes, the oof'narc. . . .

She whipped round, triggered the stunner and dropped him, a heavy dark figure, a blob in the slanting rain, bulky, without grace in his standing or falling. Then she was back around, sprinting up the walk, thrusting the key into the lock.

## ##

She made sure the door was locked and started for the stairs. The concierge looked out her wicket, saw that Rose was alone and going quietly about her business, went back to what she'd been doing.

Rose unclamped her hand from around the stunner, blessing whoever it was who'd invented the thing. The cretin out there who tried his chances, he'd wake in a couple hours with a sore head and maybe a touch of pneumonia to give him an incentive to stay the hell away from her. No body for her to explain to the authorities.

She climbed the stairs, groaning silently each time she had to lift her weary legs another step. Old, she decided, that's what it is, I'm old and crazy. She sighed, switched keys and unlocked her door.

Kikun was waiting for her, a shadow in the windowseat. She felt a jolt in her groin, felt herself flushing bright red. She cursed her thin skin and blessed the dimness in the room, only one candle lit and that one the width of the room away, on the table by the bed. He probably felt none of this churning and would be horribly embarrassed if he noticed. So would she. She liked to have things very clear and limited between her and the occasional lovers she acquired; ambiguity and uncertainty were threatening.

She tossed her jacket on the bed, crossed to the basin and washed her hands, splashed water on her face, then sat on the bed and tugged her boots off. Still without saying anything, she swung around with enough violence to make the bed squeak under her and stretched out, the pillow folded under her head, her fingers laced over her stomach.

Kikun coughed, a failure at covering a chuckle. "Hard day?"

She wrinkled her nose, thumped her thumbs on her stomach. Cool down, she told herself. Come on, Rose, don't be a fool, it's not his fault you're hot to trot. Shayss, what a phrase, Digby would never let me forget it if he heard me. . . . "Hard night," she said. "Nearly got jumped. Not a problem, I think, just some shisskop after spare change." She gave him a quick summary of what she'd learned from Bungkuk. "You get anything more?"

"I took a look at the Kipuny Shimmery. Didn't try to go in. Busy place, even early, I went over before noon. Then I went to the auctionhouse where Sai has a grungy office—two rooms, third floor, bayside. Got a hulk guarding the place, he sits in a corner with his feet up, chewing a cud of Kunja, a ottoshot on his lap big as he is. That thing ever goes off, it'll knock out the whole front wall. Two overage whores answer com for him and take messages. When there's nothing doing, which seems to be most of the time, they chatter away, one of them does tapestry, the other works on lace, I suppose they're doing it for money, he can't be paying them much. From what the women were complaining about, he's almost never there, he stays out massaging his contacts and keeping his links clear with the different kevars.

"Two calls came in while I was sitting in a corner watching. One was a merchant looking for a shipper willing to go south, he didn't say much, but apparently there's some problem involved so he can't go through the hiring hall. The other was a shipmaster looking for cargo, specific cargo which he seemed to think Sai knew all about."

"Hmm. Sounds like he has possibilities. You'd better see if you can get a look at him, find out his patterns so we can lift him out, say we have to. I'll take the Kipuny Shimmery. . . ." She let her eyes droop closed, then forced them open; she was very, very tired. She wanted a bath before she slept, but if she didn't shift herself soon, she'd be waking up come morning with her clothes on and a mouth like something died in it. "Kipuny Shimmery. . . ." She sighed and started watching the candle shadows dance across the high ceiling. "Bungkuk says they play Vagnag there," she said, her voice dreamy. "They tell you about my grandda? No? Hnh. He was an important man, you know. Almost as important as he thought he was. When I was born, he was CEO Botanicals Division, Cazar Company. We were living in the Chateau in Juoda City, K'tali Kar-ra. He never acknowledged my mama was his daughter, but he kept her close and ran her like she was his slave, didn't quite kill the life in her, but he turned her sour, I remember . . . well, never mind. . . . The man who was supposed to be my father, he ran off, Mama said he got killed somewhere, she thought, or maybe just dived down a deep hole. Grandda raged for days when she got pregnant, wouldn't see me for almost a year after I was born. Don't know why he didn't make her abort me, or boot her out or something, well, yes, I do, it wasn't that we were family, we were property and anyone who laid a hand on us was robbing him. My sire, that oof'narc, he scuttled like a rat, he knew he was a dead man if he stayed, it wasn't that that made Mama so mad, it was because he didn't even ask her if she wanted to get out with him, she was still furious about that the day she died. Wouldn't 've gone, she said, but at least he could 've asked, anyway, what got me on this was Vagnag, when I got old enough to talk, Grandda used to keep me around like his dogs, long as I had sense enough to stay quiet, said I was his mascot, brought him luck. He had this thing about gambling games, Vagnag especially, he wanted to work out a way to win consistently without the down-and-dirty cheating which could get you killed in the company he liked to play with. I got SO bored. There was nothing to do but watch him and his sharks going at it, so I learned the games they played.'' She sighed, yawned. ''Big mistake. One day he caught me playing my own version of Vagnag with the Chateau boys, taking money off them, because I used to win most of the time, and it wasn't because they were letting me win, I was just the Chateau bastard, even the sweep was more respectable than me, at least he had real family, family to claim him. Anyway, I was about six, regular little prodigy. A natural mimic with a trick memory. Impressed the hell out of Grandda, which surprised me, scared me, actually. He wasn't an easy man with kids, and I'd heard nasty stories all my life about the kind of things he did to people when he was mad at them, so I didn't like it much when he started paying real attention to me. Besides, life went sour on me after that. He brought in men, women, had them teach me everything they knew about playing all kinds of games, especially Vagnag. Fifteen years of hell, that's what it was, Kuna, hour after hour, day after day, manipulation, math and aerobics and weightlifting, took all that and more. I ran away a couple times. He jerked me back. Third time was the winner, he was just settling in at a new place, moving up, using me to get where he wanted, I ran when I got a smell of a chance and this time, I got clear. Had a pretty good life for a while, yeh, walking the knife-blade, you can understand maybe what I felt, finally free of Grandda and his strings. Well, after a wild ride, I fell off the blade. I ran into this oof'narc who thought he was hot stuff, papa was a local bigass with a lot of pull. The oof'narc lost, accused me of cheating and tried to jump me, real loser, I didn't mean to kill him, I was trying to keep him off, clumsy cretin, it was like he threw himself on the knife, the other players disappeared, I only knew their handles and gambling was illegal anyway on that world, so they were outta there. I hadn't a hope in hell of getting off, it was the Strangler's Cord for me, I was so damn scared, I was almost ready to yell for Grandda, not that he would 've come. . . .'' She stopped talking and lay gazing dreamily at the shadow-play on the ceiling.

Kikun shifted on the cushions. "What happened?"

"Huh?" Jolted out of her drowse, she turned her head to look toward the shadow in the chair.

"How did you get out of that?"

"Oh." She pushed up, swung her legs over the edge and sat with her head in her hands. "It was Digby, he sent one of his Ops to make a deal. Hah!" She straightened up. "The Op would spring me if I either paid Digby's fee or went to work for him. Digby I mean." She pushed onto her feet, grabbed a robe off the foot of the bed. "I'm for a bath. If I'm going to get into a game at the Shimmery I can't be so ripe no one will sit next me."

2

The door was three massive planks with a dalbir jug carved in low relief head high in the center plank. She pushed the door open and stepped into a long room with bare roof beams and smoky lubrinjah-oil lanterns hanging from those beams. It was a warm and rosy room, the amber lamplight waking amber and crimson lights in the smoky oily wood and the crimson leather on the stools.

Funny, she thought, all the worlds I've been on, a bar is a bar is a bar. . . .

There were groups of men sitting at tables, others on stools at a long solid counter by the inner wall. It was built atop a knee-high platform that was just wide enough for the scatter of stools. They must lose a lot of drunks on that, she thought, fall off and break their necks. Oh well, that's their problem.

The low mutter of talk died away as she moved into the room, picked up again as she strolled to the bar, relaxed and easy. For the first time on this world she was in really familiar territory. She was the only woman here, but she'd met that before, it just meant she had to be quiet and quick to establish her credentials.

There was a brass grab rail under the counter's edge. She ignored it, stepped up and settled herself on one of the ladder legged stools. The other patrons made their hostility felt. The weight of their stares tried to push her out of the place. She ignored that, knocked on the wood to summon the barman sitting on his own stool, leaning against the cabinets behind him.

He took his time about coming but he did come, and
something in the way he moved tickled at Rose's memory.
She kept her face calm, tried to trace the tickle. Who. . . .

He set his hands on the bar, played a small impatient tune
with his thumbs.

There was a tiny white scar below his left thumbnail,
three lobed, like a classic flurdelli. Yes. Well and well and
well. . . .

Abruptly she was back in an ivory and gilt room and he was
seated across from her at the Vagnag table. . . .

She blinked. "Something in a local wine. White and
dry," she said, "No gahwang in it, I hope. It's a tasty herb,
but rather overused, don't you think?" She spoke in interlingue, not the local patter, the first step in settling what
she was. "Rather too much of a good thing, yes?"

He nodded without speaking and went off, returning with
a glass bottle stoppered with waxed leather rolled into a
tight bundle. He showed it to her, removed the stopper with
an odd misshapen gripping tool, poured a little in a glass,
and passed the glass to her.

She checked the scar again. Yes. It's him. She tasted the
wine, concealed a grimace as it bit back. "It'll do," she
said.

She wore a simple black dress back then, avrishum from
Jaydugar, outrageously expensive, a gift from her last lover
but one. He probably stole it but she wasn't fussy about
provenance those days and appreciated the thought, though
she didn't appreciate the occasion that induced the gift. A
black dress doesn't erase a black eye. He'd vanished one
day. Killed, she thought, and moved on taking the dress
with her, lost it that time she got in trouble on Tyurm,
mourned the gift a lot more than the giver. That night her
hair was braided and pomaded and set with jade and pearls,
with a necklace of jade beads and pearls dipping into the
deep vee of the dress. Three of the men in the game weren't
professionals or obsessive gamblers, they had eyes for more
than their cards; she'd dressed for them. He was the fourth
man, quiet, thin and almost too handsome. When he sat
down and brushed at his sleeve, fingers signaling a *pro*, she
was annoyed. She'd gone to a lot of trouble setting up this

game and was irritated to find another of her guild intruding onto her pasture. She drew her right forefinger along her jawline, flicked it from under her chin. Sign for back off, these are mine.

He smiled and tapped thumb against thumb, the first time she'd seen the scar. Challenge. She didn't hesitate, tugged at her left earlobe. Agreed.

They fought their war under the noses of the other players, stripping the marks almost as an afterthought; the last Chapter was between them, all for all. The dice and the cards had gone for her, and she was just enough cleverer in her play to clean Table, Pen, and Holse.

He bowed and walked off smiling, a flicker of his fingers congratulating her and acknowledging her victory. He had reason for the smile, he'd cleaned Table in at least half the Chapters and won Holse twice. The last Chapter had put a hole in those winnings, but he'd doubled his stake and that was enough to satisfy all but the pickiest. She left that night on a free trader going elsewhere at a leisurely pace and before she slept, she wriggled with a pleasure she hadn't felt in years. It was a good hard fight and she'd enjoyed it enormously.

She sipped at the wine and watched the man move off to stow the bottle in the cabinet he'd got it from, driving the stopper in with the palm of his hand and laying the bottle flat. This was a long way down from that. She sighed. For both of them. In some ways.

He should have gotten that scar removed, why he'd kept it she hadn't a clue unless it was a mascot of some kind. Ah well, ah well, that's the way it goes. He was good, but he wasn't first rank even at his peak and he'd been sliding from second the last time she'd seen him. Where was that? Cazarit? Lumilly? No, I can't remember. Long time ago. . . .

She sipped at the wine and thought pleasant thoughts. Those days she'd lived hard and fast, everything was sunbright and coalblack, the ups were shining soaring joy and the downs were misery condensed. She'd lived a calmer life since she'd hired on with Digby; there were satisfactions in that, but sometimes she yearned for the old times. . . . She downed the last of the wine, knocked her knuckles on the

wood and straightened her shoulders as he got the bottle out
again and brought it to her.

There was still some of his bone beauty left, but he was
wrinkled now, like old parchment left in the rain and put
away wet. And there was something odd about the left side
of his face. Stroke or wound. Maybe. Bad dye job on the
hair. A dead black that left him looking older than god.
"Traggan 2," she said as he filled the glass again. "The
Silver Circus. Forty some years ago. Remember?" She
brushed at her sleeve, flickered her fingers through the pro-
sign.

He set the glass down, pushed the stopper home. "They
call me Hadluk here. Been some changes. How'd you
know?"

"I'm Rose. Was blonde then. In black avrishum." She
nodded as she saw recognition flare in his eyes. Finally, she
thought. "The coloring is camouflage." She reached out,
ran the tip of her forefinger over the tiny scar. "You don't
want folk to know you, you should get rid of that."

He shrugged. "Here? Who cares. The wine's twenty kuries a pop."

She set a silver pera on the bar, watched him sweep it
away, count out her change in the copper kuries. "Ah well,
way it goes. Word is you run Vagnag here."

"Not me." He drew his thumb down the subtly distorted
left side of his face. "Past it, Rose, long past it. Gray market ananiles. Bad batch. Burnt gaps in the old brain. Can't
do the calcs any more."

"Too bad. I would have enjoyed another pass." She didn't
mean it, but it was the polite thing to say. "Buy yourself a
drink on me. Old times." She pushed the coppers back at
him to pay for her second drink and his, signed to him to
keep the change and watched, amused, as he chose a different bottle to pour for himself.

He swallowed, shuddered. One eyelid drooping, he leaned
against the wall cabinets, hip hitched on the flat top. "Heard
you hit a slippery patch a while back."

"Wheel turns, Hadluk. Just let me make the right connections and it's all back again."

He nodded, but she could see pity and a flare of malice
in his dark eyes. He'd lost his *face*, no wonder he quit, he
must have started growing tells like weeds. "Need a stake?"
he said, wariness replacing pity.

"No." She didn't elaborate and he asked no more questions.

Humming under his breath, he began playing finger games on the bar, short nails adding an edge to the thumping of his fingertips.

Rose tapped a counter rhythm. These were pleasant little sounds, innocuous, but by the time they broke off their game, they'd bargained out his commission for introducing her to a game, his percentage of the take, and set a time for her to show back here.

She took a swallow of the wine. "I don't want to come on as a whore," she said, "give me the local protocols."

"Hmm. Long skirt, arms covered in the evening. That's important. Bare arms after dark are an advert of intent."

"I'll dig something up." She drank the last of the wine, pushed the glass away. "Before I show, see the others know I don't play on my back, huh?"

"That hasn't changed, huh?" He grinned at her, a tinge of red in the whites of his eyes; whatever he was drinking, it was powerful stuff. "Don't worry, I'll pass the word on."

"Thanks." She slid off the stool. "See you when."

3

Autumn Rose hurried along the jagged semi-street, heading for the market. She needed to pick up something she could wear without binding herself into so much material she'd be hampered if she had to fight and something she wouldn't be embarrassed to be seen in. And something that was neither so expensive it was a temptation, nor so cheap and flimsy she lost "face" with the players.

She plunged across a dark sideway, flinched as a group of Angatines came out of the shadows and began to wail at her. Cursing, she turned down the next opening, turned again and yet again, losing them finally, almost losing herself before she stopped her flight and began working her way back to the market. This was what . . . the tenth, eleventh time they'd ambushed her? They were getting to be more than a nuisance, jumping out at her everywhere with the same accusing plaint, she was a demon come to do harm to the people. No one seemed to pay much attention to them, but you could never tell what spark would set the locals off.

4

When she followed Hadluk into one of the back rooms, there were already half a dozen men seated at the Vagnag table.

She settled into the empty chair. "Rose," she said, nodded at Hadluk. He went out.

The man at her right gathered up the eight-sided dice, handed them to her. He was an offworlder, probably a free-trader, big, burly, blue-black with a noble nose like a hawk's beak jutting from the gray fur on his face. He wore a long robe, earth colors in a violent design. Heavy gold earrings dangled from long lobes, brushing against his massive neck. "Tayteknas," he rumbled at her. "He tell you?"

She took the dice, remembering with pleasure the feel of the crisp points against her palm, the cool facets. She hefted them, judging the weight, the feel, the sound as they clicked together. Yes, she thought. "Yes," she said aloud; she dropped the dice on the table and watched them dance then settle. She reached into one of the large pockets the skirt came equipped with, took out the sack and laid out three gold emas on the ledge in front of her. Next to these she lined up five piles of four silver peras each. She took one ema and flipped it into the Holse, the circle drawn in the center of the dark blue felt. "Who's marker?"

Tayteknas tapped a blue black finger against the front of his robe. "Me."

"What's high so far?"

"Double eight plus three."

"Hmp. Vakkar. All gone?"

"You're the last."

"I see." She gathered the three dice, held them a moment warming in her hand, feeling for the rhythm—the beginnings of the rhythm. It wasn't there yet, but it would come. The smell of the table came up around her, a subtle aroma rising from the felt, the paint on it, the coins, the blend of odors drifting from the men—a smell that brought memories rushing back. Some places, the game rules wouldn't let you handle the dice, you had to use a cup to throw them and a scoop to pick them up; this wasn't that big a game. Just as well.

She rattled the dice, rolled them out, watched them dance across the felt. There was tumult in her then, a vigor she'd lost for years, a joy she'd made herself forget. The yellow dice flickered over the dark blue felt, then slowed and rocked to rest. "Skotsker," she said with satisfaction. Six and eight and five.

Tayteknas grunted. "Vakkar rules Skotsker," he said. "Pulleet first. Rose second. Barangkaly third. Tayteknas fourth. Kahtik fifth. Uj sixth. Nikeldy seventh." He broke the seal on a deck of Vagnag cards, peeled off the wrappings. "All entries in the Holse." He reached down, brought the rake from where it was hanging on the table, cleared the seven gold coins from the painted circle to a painted half-circle nuzzling against the side of the table. "Entries in the Sump. Open, one pera. Raise limit, fifty ema." He took a silver coin, tossed it into the Holse, set the deck on the felt, and used the rake to push it across to Pulleet.

Pulleet was a small dark man with pale splotches on his face, irregular pink, yellow, tan areas breaking up the chocolate brown over the rest of him, pigment deficit, the result of disease or birth defect. Offworlder, probably freetrader. He had small hands, the skin on them blotchy like his face. He handled the cards with a deftness and dedication she could appreciate and dealt them out in packets of three to each of the players in the order given, matching names to faces for Rose.

Nikeldy was another offworlder. Freetrader most likely. Quiet little man. Forgettable.

Kahtik wore a University ring, engineer's compass laid into the jewel. Freetech, no Companies on this world. Some freetechs were erratic but brilliant, some were merely adequate. Kahtik looked middlish, reasonably prosperous, but not flying the highwire. Vagnag was a game of combinations and probabilities; as a University-trained engineer, he'd be high on math skills; if his game sense was as good, he'd be a formidable player.

Barangkaly was a Rummer, a local merchant, she'd seen him in the market; he had several booths selling cloth and herbs.

Uj was a local, too. The paint on his face said he was one of the Vaarmanta; whatever else he was was not immediately apparent, though she had her suspicions and wasn't happy about them.

Second seat. She didn't like being second. In the first seat

she could influence the flow of play, in the last seat she'd
have the advantage of seeing the styles of all the other players. Here she had neither advantage; she had to give before
she got. She picked up her first set. Hanged man, Runner
and four diamond. Two picture cards. Not bad. Not great
either. She folded the set together and laid it down, waiting
until the dealing was finished.

The sets landed neatly in front of each the players, three
more small piles face down on the felt. Pulleet placed the
remaining cards in the Sump by his Pen (a rectangle painted
on the felt), tossed the opener into the Holse. He looked at
his first set, folded them and placed them face down on the
ledge before him, all his moves quick and neat and precise.
He scooped up the dice, clacked them vigorously, and threw
them out.

Three twos. A triple Blakkro. Without visible reaction,
he swept up his cards, chose two, and set the third face
down on the ledge. He laid the two cards face up in the Pen,
seven triangle, three diamond, contemplated the backs of
the other three sets and chose another card from the middle
pile. He looked at it a moment, still without expression,
laid it face up in the Pen, a three spot beside the three
diamond.

It was a strong opening. The Lady had kissed both cards
and dice. He looked thoughtfully at the coins on the ledge,
took a gold ema and added it to the silver already in the
Holse, took another ema, set it in the Pen, challenging table
in a second level stake, moved an ema and two peras onto
the number grid—table wager on the probable gap between
his count and any other, high/low.

Tayteknas raked the dice over to Rose. She scooped them
up, rattled and threw them and swore under her breath. One,
six and seven. A Koetta. Bust. She couldn't turn a card or
put one down. Tick-tock, what to do? Shayss damn, think I
have to count this Chapter a loser, still, let's see what we
can finesse. Get the rhythm back and not go down too bad.
There's still the Claiming round. More Vags have been
pulled from the Sump than won straight out. Besides, I'm
here for information, not prizes. She smiled with sweet confidence, took a pera and an ema and tossed them to the
Holse. ''Stay as,'' she said and laid the set on the ledge.

Barangkaly scooped up the dice, flung them out with an

expansive curl of his arm. Three Three nine. Bijjet. One of the highest throws possible.

Z'Toyff, she thought, this how it's going to go, everybody but me?

He beamed at the dice, flipped his cards over with an extravagant exuberance, dropped them into the Pen without bothering to look at them, danced his fingers over the other three sets, chose a card, flipped it over, shifted it to the Pen, chose another, started a second line in the Pen. Two Dancers, a clown, a Lancer and a seven sword. Takabul. Only a step from a sudden win. If his luck held through the Claiming round, he had this Chapter sewn. He tossed the ante pera and a push Ema in the Holse, lay down another two emas in the Pen, and spread a scatter of Peras about the Grid.

## ##

The play went on, Pass round, Claiming round, Pass and Claim for the four doubles of each Chapter. Rose went down badly on the first chapter, the dice were all right after the first round, but the combinations were miserable and nothing she could do during the Claimings was enough to make up for the weak Sets.

Barangkaly continued his expansive style and rode his luck to a win in the first Chapter, but went down and down on those that followed.

Second Chapter Rose still had bad cards, but finessed a tie with Pulleet who she judged the second best player at the table.

Tayteknas was a steady though not brilliant player, Kahtik was tight, overly cautious, wasting opportunities. Rose relaxed. He was no threat. Uj was mostly cautious, but he had a propensity for wild chances that sometimes paid off and sometimes didn't; he was unexpected, difficult to read— and she got a strong feeling from the others that it wasn't a good idea to challenge him when his calls were questionable. Lice, she thought. One of the Papa Policer's boys. Nikeldy was a plodding player. Negligible. He sweat a lot and lost consistently even with fair hands.

She won the third Chapter outright and after that could have won them all, she had the measure of the players and the rhythm of the game, but thought it wasn't wise to clean them out, especially Uj. The fourth Chapter she split with Uj, the fifth she dropped out early.

They took a Nosh break between the fifth and sixth Chapters, the usual time. This was the time she'd come for, when the relaxation of the tension from the game also relaxed internal censors and a lot of good gossip got going.

The Shimmery had set up a Nosh table along the wall with local wines, teas, and a version of kaff which smelled to her like burnt toast. Rose filled a plate with fingerfood and a glass with the white varnish she was developing a taste for. It went well with the nibbles the Shimmery provided, cutting the force of the ghawang that the Rummer cooks seemed to put in everything. She sipped, chewed, circulated, mostly listening, contributing a nod of her head here, a murmur of agreement there, her ears stretched to catch anything remotely relevant to her search.

Kahtik signed a query, wondering if she might be freetech also.

Effortlessly she returned an assent (aware of Uj watching both of them), stayed where she was as the freetech drifted over to her.

"Hunting?" His voice was high, flat; there was a scar on his throat from a wound that had almost decapitated him. With meatfarms available to anyone with an income like his had to be, she didn't understand why he hadn't had that scar fixed. Some kind of perverse pride in the narrowness of his escape?

"No, I just came off a job. Scratching an itchy foot. Anything around bigger than local?"

He grinned at her. "What's the need if you're not looking?"

She rubbed her thumb back and forth across her fingertips. "Never turn down a chance at cash."

"I'm industrial design. What're you?"

"Programs and systems."

"Just as well you're not in the market. Ain't any, not here, not for that. Unless the Mimishay Foundation." He ran his eyes over her, shook his head. "And they wouldn't hire you."

"Why not? I'm damn good, though it's me who says it."

"You're female. They don't hire women."

"Their loss."

"You play a helluva game."

She winked at him. "Programs and systems. 'Tall helps."

He glanced past her, flickered his fingers at her (in the twitter of the digits a take-care sign) and drifted off.

Uj moved around in front of her, sipping at a hot fruity drink. "New round here," he said. He had a commonplace voice, under the paint an ordinary face; he was neither tall nor short, dark nor light, shadowman, his edges shifting with the shifts of the wind.

"Hmm," she said. "Your ordinary tourist." She inspected her plate, selected a small roll of meat wrapped round a piece of fruit and took a bite of it. "Um," she chewed, swallowed. "This is good. What is it?"

Uj smiled, a grimace that bared his teeth and got nowhere near his eyes. "Babi slin," he said. "Why our world?"

"No reason, just general wanderfoot." She popped the rest of the babi slin into her mouth, chewed, and washed it down with a gulp of wine. "I finished a job here in the Callidara and decided to take a look round."

"Not a trader, then."

"No. Freetech. Programs and systems."

"Looking for work?"

"Not really, this is playtime. Of course, if I got a good offer. . . ." She matched his tooth-end smile.

"Visiting friends?"

"No. I don't know anyone here. Footloose and fancy free. Mostly looking for games. I have a thing for Vagnag; it's not that often one can get a really good game if one isn't in the megagelder range." She found another babi slin, bit into it.

"And this is a good game?"

She raised a brow. "Fair."

"If you should happen to get an offer. . . ."

"Yes?"

"There are certain formalities."

"There always are."

"Yes. I see you're experienced in this." He put a peculiar twist on the word *experienced* that gave her a chill at the bottom of her stomach. "Come see me, I would be delighted to facilitate matters for you."

"How kind," she said. Sipping at the wine, she drifted off. Complications. Rather do without complications.

## ##

The play went on, Pass round, Claiming round, Pass and
Claim for the four doubles of each Chapter. She played
carefully, winning more than she lost, deliberately letting
chances go by when Uj looked like winning. She wanted
him to go away happy. Yes, and without too much interest
in her. Again and again as the hours wore on, she felt his
eyes on her, read speculation that was an uneasy combination of sexual and professional. By the time they reached
the twelfth and traditionally last Chapter in a game like this,
though she didn't let it show, she was beginning to be very
worried about how she was going to shuck Uj when it came
time to leave. Might have to try outsitting him. Call on
Hadluk's tenuous goodwill or something.

As they moved into the last Chapter, Barangkaly dealing,
the air was stale, the lubrinjah oil was low in the lamps and
her eyes were stinging with the effluvium coming through
the chimneys and the strain of trying to see by the dim
flickering light. She inspected her first set, sighed. The cards
were too good, a Vagnateka triad; it'd take a really foul
chance at the dice to negate this, the highest combine available. It hurt her to think of breaking up a V-Tek, but there
was no way she was going to win this Chapter.

Barangkaly threw and went bust. Koetta. He spread his
hands. Out.

Shayss, she thought, that narrows the focus. And I'm last
up this time. If Uj busts out. . . .

Tayteknas tossed the ante pera into the Holse, threw a
one three six, Siettran. He dropped a ten heart into the Pen,
set a pera beside it for the table, but stayed out of the Holse
and off the Grid, passed the dice on.

Kahtik threw Siettran, inspected his cards, shook his
head. "Out," he said. He collected his cards, blended them
into a single pile and set them on the ledge in front of him.
Then he took out a square white cloth, wiped each of the
coins in the piles beside the cards, tucked them neatly away
into an inside pocket or perhaps a money safe sewn into his
vest.

Uj scooped up the dice, sat holding them loosely in his
hand, his eyes closed.

Autumn Rose tensed. If he busted. . . .

He tossed the dice, smiled. Three fours. Triple Telvi. He examined his set, lay them down, and squared them. "Option," he said, took up each of the three other sets and examined them, shifted several cards about, placed the sets face down on the felt. "Done," he said.

Rose started breathing again. She looked around, saw Pulleet watching her. His mouth hitched up in a brief smile, matching his relief with hers. He touched the left top corner of his set, moved a pile of coins onto the left bottom corner, scratched at his chin.

She tapped her chin, lifted one coin, set it back without letting it clink. Well, well. Not a freetrader after all. Like me, a ringer. Good old Hadluk, hasn't lost it as much as I thought, finessing himself a double cut. Pulleet had been playing the Table more than the Holse and had done comfortably well so far, though she thought none of the others realized just how well since he had a habit of stowing his wins away after each Chapter. He'd done better than her despite her Holse wins, done it on tiptoe as it were. Clever little man. She bubbled inside with laughter and relief, though she was careful not to let it show. They could be better slotted. Being 1-2 like they were they lost leverage. Still, the Claiming round was coming up, and with a little bit of luck they could make Uj think he was Fingers Harry himself. If he didn't do something terminally stupid. Which he was quite capable of, he'd already done several moronic plays. Like this wasting a play just looking at his cards.

Nikeldy threw another Siettram, looked at his cards and the single pera remaining in front of him. He squared the set, dropped it on the felt. "Out."

Pulleet threw seven six two. Marstori. A middle level pass. He dropped two cards in the Pen, a Dancer-Lancer combine. She smiled when she saw them. Good. With the clown and a hanged man she held, that was almost Vagnag. If somewhere in his sets Uj had a seer, a witch or a magician—or a wilder of necessary degree to depute for them, he could do a Major Claim, with the possibility of making a small, large, or double Vag.

## 

Uj pulled out a small Vag and play went on.

He was exultant—but he didn't forget her; he looked at her with a proprietary gleam in his eyes that sent cold chills down her spine.

He flew from triumph to triumph, face flushed, getting wilder and wilder, infuriating Rose and Pulleet who had a real struggle to win only the small secondary stakes and leave the Holse gelt for him.

Tayteknas suspected what they were doing, but he kept his hunches to himself, dropping out early or playing Table when he got the chance. The others plunged or teetered according to their natures.


                              5

Final Pass round.

Before the dealing began, the door opened and a cloud of Dasuttras came in with kaff and tea and small cloths dampened with scented water. Their palms were dyed pink; more dye was burnished into their nails. Dye-flowers were stamped on their bodies, a graceful spray spread across the swell of their breasts, single blooms in the center of the brow and on each cheek. They fluttered about the players, their filmy draperies whisper whispering, caressing whatever they touched. Three Dasuttras filled delicate porcelain cups with steaming local teas and set them on the ledge beside the players. Rose leaned back and let one of them have her hand while the other massaged her neck and shoulders. She closed her eyes, sighed with pleasure, the tension going out of her, drawn away by the warm wet cloths, the skillful fingers of the masseuse.

She cracked an eye and sneaked a look at Uj, suppressed a grin. Lord of all he sees, she thought. Shayss damn, that's a pretty child playing with his neck. She opened her eyes wider.

Hadluk was standing in the doorway looking amused. He met her eyes, tapped his temple in a two finger salute, and stepped out of sight.

He was a snake, but an honest snake, give him that. The way Uj was snorting at his attendants, he was going to have

little interest in fooling about after her. Probably. Well,
well. . . .

## 6

She slid unnoticed from the room as Uj preened himself
before the Dasuttras, enjoying the minor triumph of sweeping Last Chapter. Nikeldy was chewing his large bottom lip
as he tapped notes into a cardfile. Barangkaly, gone morose,
stared at a wall, now and then stroking his thumbnail down
one or the other of his rattail mustaches. Kahtik stood withdrawn, concentrating on his coins, wiping them carefully
with the white cloth before restowing them about his person. Tayteknas tossed down a cup of lukewarm kaff, wiped
at his mouth, and checked his clothing to make sure he left
with what he had when he came in. None of them noticed
her departure.

The taproom was noisy now, filled with men and Dasuttras, three servers behind the bar, none of them Hadluk.

"This way." Pulleet cupped his hand around her elbow,
turned her back into the hall and nudged her along it to a
door in the end wall. He knocked once, said, "Payday."

The door swung open.

Hadluk was sitting behind a table that doubled duty as a
desk, loading penciled notes into an interface. He looked
up, the distorted side of his face emphasized by his smile
and his tiredness. "Sorry about that," he said. He was
speaking to Autumn Rose. "I didn't know Uj was coming
till he showed. Thought you'd pick up on him, but if you
didn't. . . ." He shrugged. "Just in case," he nodded at
Pulleet, "I called in a favor."

She dropped onto a backless chair. "Lice?"

"Big lice. Collector."

"Taking a double skim."

"Way it goes."

"He's busy now."

"Not for all that long. He's short-time in the sack, a
wham-bam and good-bye." He turned to Pulleet. "How is
she? Still got it?"

"Yup."

He pulled his hand across his mouth, frowned down at
it. "Been thinking," he said. "You cleaned?"

"Pretty much. Not flat, but limping. I have passage off-world, if that's what you're on at."

"Nope. Wanta meet. Neutral ground. Angatine chapel?"

"No." She didn't explain. "You get watersick?"

"No." He looked down at his hands, ran the edge of a thumbnail down the paper he'd been reading. "Not a bad idea, that."

"Right. We can have ourselves a picnic on one of those rocks out in the bay. When?"

"Tomorrow. I'll do the food, you just be there. Gaunga wharf."

"I'll be there—out on the water, watching. You pick your island and I'll join you."

"Better that way, yes. You really haven't lost it, have you?"

"So we all should hope." She dropped the sac on his desk, waited while he counted out his cut. "Anything I should bring?"

"Got a mute cone?"

"I do indeed, battery operated." She reclaimed the sac. "See you when."

When she turned to pull the door closed behind her, she looked back. The two men were nose to nose, Pulleet talking rapidly, his hands fluttering, Hadluk listening so intently he wasn't aware of anything but the voice murmuring into his face.


7


"Two maybes," she said.

Kikun was withdrawn, a shadow curled in the windowseat. She wasn't sure he heard her, but she went on. She was mostly talking to herself anyway, trying to get things straight.

"There's something called the Mimishay Foundation. I think it's on one of the other islands. They hire techs, but they don't hire women. Could be Omphalos under camouflage. If the Institute is into ransom, they'd need a cutout in case they're traced. Could be a thousand other things."

Kikun stirred. "Mimishay. Sai has a file on them." He was silent a moment. "I only saw the directory and that by accident; one of the exwhores accessed it for something else and I was looking over her shoulder. That is not my Gift,

Rose, working akurrpa machines. Lissorn and his crew taught me to play with them, but working is something else. I smell danger on this one. Time comes, if there's need, you'll have to do the thing.''

''Time comes, we'll see. If it's all that tricky, we might have to hire the Talent. There was a man tonight at the game, a freetech. He says he's into industrial engineering, but I think he lied. He said it too easily. And he didn't like it when I claimed programs and systems. He did *friend* well enough, well as any of the techies do, but his smiles stopped at his teeth. Way he played, too, he's into systems. I think. Maybe he doesn't want competition. Second thing. I ran into an acquaintance from the time before I signed on with Digby. He doesn't seem to know about that, which is certainly plausible. It's a small world, the game circuit. You leave it and you might as well have dropped down a black hole. He's got a thing he wants me in on, something to do with a game. I go along with him, I've got some protection. I think I'm going to need it. He set me up, the snake. Pointed one of the Beza Prezao's men at me. He said he didn't know the man was going to be there. I'll believe that when it rains up. He had a ringer in the game to see if I'd lost my edge. Pulled the Lice off me when he got the signal from his ringer. I don't think this has anything to do with why we're here, but if I'm going to keep on this track, I'm going to have to go along with him.''

8

She woke sometime later; it was black outside and cold inside despite the half dozen candles burning on a plate Kikun had set in the middle of the floor. He was sitting cross-legged on the other side of the clump of candles, his eyes like orange fire, blind orange fire because it was obvious to her he was seeing nothing in the room. He was looking into elsewhere, yearning into elsewhere, swaying on his buttocks, chanting in monosyllables.

She watched for a while, but it was like watching a flake show with the sound gone and you've come in the middle of it.

She turned over, drew the covers up about her head, and went to sleep.

# DYSLAERA 10:
# Working toward escape

### 1

Rohant combed his thumbclaw through his mustache, his palm hiding a smile.

His tiny hands braced on the bottom bar of the doorgrill, Miji leaned into the room, his black eyes eager, his neck-frills extended. Reassured, he hopped through, skittered across the floor to Rohant's leg.

He sniffed at the ankle, patted at the soft bronze fur on the Dyslaeror's leg. Eeping with pleasure, he rubbed his forepaws then the side of his face over and over that fur.

Rohant waited.

Miji put a forepaw on the frayed hem of Rohant's prison trousers; he scratched at the worn canvas, caught his tiny fingernails in it, and, abruptly, scurried up the leg. He didn't stop until he was perched on Rohant's shoulder, nibbling at the Dyslaeror's mane.

### 2

Kinefray twitched in his sleep, convulsed, rolled off the cot, and hit the floor before Azram could catch him.

His claws out, his head banging repeatedly into the concrete, he thrashed wildly until he was fully awake.

Azram scrambled around, cushioned his cousin's head with his thighs and, when he quieted, helped him back on the cot. "Do you remember what it was?"

"No." Kinefray saw the fresh rips in Azram's sleeves, shuddered. "Something was after me, I think. I've got that wobbly feeling in my gut, you know."

"I know. Stretch out now. On your back first." Azram began rubbing the back of Kinefray's neck, working on his shoulders. "They've left us alone a whole week, maybe they've got what they want."

Kinefray shuddered again, began crying.

3

Nezrakan lay curled in a fetal knot. For three days he'd refused to eat. Now he was too weak to move. It didn't take a Dyslaeror long to starve himself dead.

## ##

Savant 4 (speaking to notepad):
NOTE 1: Negotiations with the Black House have slowed due to the need for a considerably greater security in handling the Dyslaera, also the difficulty in getting the value out of them since it would not be wise—or safe—to advertise their presence. Also there is a degree of uncertainty as to how many Dyslaera we will be able to provide.
NOTE 2: The cutouts have been arranged for the ransom demand. Clumsy setup, but what happened when Voallts went after Seyirshi is more than ample evidence of the need for a careful distance kept between Mimishay and Voallts. The rat with the message is on its way, we should have the answer in about forty days.

4

Rohant closed his eyes and concentrated.
He ran with Miji as the sakali scooted through the tunnels, heading for the pen and his exit into the open world. Though he couldn't see through Miji's eyes like Shadow, he felt the coolness of the concrete under Miji's feet, felt the sakali's surge of fear, felt the response of his muscles when he dived into shadow to avoid one of the warders.
He let the intensity drop and sat up. It wasn't much and at the moment he had no idea how he could use the Tie, but he had to try something. He sighed and settled to brood over what to do next.

# SHADOW WATCHING

## 1

Arring Pirs held his son over his head so chal and chapa
could see him.

The baby didn't like that. He waved his small naked arms
and legs and squawled his displeasure with a lusty enthusi-
asm that brought laughter and approving whistles from the
chal and chapa of Ghanar Rinta gathered around the Amur-
hill for the Naming Ceremony.

"Behold the son," Pirs chanted in the formal langue.
"Hear his name: Arringgarri Paji knigo Pirs ampa Cagharadad nima Procagharadad." His voice escaped the bounds
of the Rite, became a shout of pride and joy, answered by
a shout from the chal and chapa.

A restless fringe around the edges of the crowd, the children of Ghanar Rinta gasped with pleasure, shouted and
whistled as the Amur-speaker touched his torch to the conical pyre rising fifty meters from the top of the hill; satu-
rated with kerosene, the wood caught immediately and the
flames went running up the slope like an echo of Pirs' triumphant cry.

While the Amur-drums rattled in the laps of the Amur-
deacons seated around the fire and the Amur-speaker sang
the Litany of the Son, Pirs dropped on his knee and held
the baby out to his father for the Artwa to bless the child
and formally accept the boy into the family.

The drumbeat slowed, quieted; the Speaker broke off the
Litany and waited.

Chal and chapa and even the most boisterous of the children went quiet, stood hushed and grave, waiting. This was
the vital thing. This was the pledge that their lives would
be unchanged, a small red-faced surety of continuance.

The Artwa Arring Angakirs Cagharadad spread his hands
over the wriggling baby. "Behold the son," he chanted,
"Behold the Summerday child, the newest fruit on the tree

of Procagharadad. Behold the Joy, the Promise. I, Artwa
Procagharadad, declare this boy Irrkuyon of Irrkuy. I, Artwa Procagharadad, declare this boy Blessed. I, Artwa Procagharadad, call upon you, the chal and chapa of Ghanar
Rinta to declare your fealty to the Son of Ghanar Rinta.''

## ##

Standing at the back of the crowd among the children,
Shadith shifted from foot to foot, scratched at her arm. She
was here because Tinoopa turned maternal and dogmatic
and dragged her along. *Don't be an idiot,* Tinoopa said, *you
need their good will and you know it. Show your face and
behave yourself, child.*
She watched as the rite went on and on, thinking:

*Poor baby, he's going to catch pneumonia if they don't wrap
something around him. No wonder boy babies had a hard
time surviving. Jerks. Matja Allina isn't even on the Hill.
Wouldn't you know. Come on, come on. Get that poor baby
back where he belongs, let me get back where I belong. Old
bastard, I have to admit he's impressive, times like this.
Should keep him in a closet and just take him out when it's
time to chant something.*

The Amur-speaker spread scented oil over the baby's
body. Shadith wiggled her left bootheel on a dirtclod,
crushing it.

*Pirs. He's riding high right now. Daddy's spreading it thick,
almost cooing at him (old warthog, wonder what he wants?).
He's got his boy, the Brushies are friendly, and there hav-
en't been raids for the past eleven weeks. Enough to make
any amnesiac happy. Well, we get our papers out of this.
Signed and locked away. Lovely. So generous the man is,
as long as it doesn't cost him anything.*

Last night Pirs called her and Tinoopa into the study. He
showed them their contracts and the cancellation papers. As
they watched, he signed his name, stamped his seal on can-
cels. *I wanted you to see this,* he said, *in six months your
year will be completed. We will honor our promise as you
have honored yours, to the limit of our ability.* He folded

the documents together, laid his hands on them, and waited
for them to leave.

*Arring Feelgood, dispensing favors to his chosen, favors with
a call-date half a year off. Locked up somewhere in that
study. Hmmmm.*

## ##

Mingas was up there on the Hill, standing behind his
father. It was the first time Shadith had seen him, and she
didn't much like what she was seeing.

*Runt. Ugly pup.*

In a way he was very like his spectacularly handsome kin,
but his individual features were larger, their contours more
rounded; he was a head shorter and considerably bulkier. It
wasn't fat, he was rock hard, but he looked clumsy, pudgy.

*Odd what a thin line it is between beauty and ugliness.*

She *reached,* touched him, shied away almost immediately. It was like touching acid. Behind that bland, immobile face, hate and rage were bubbling, boiling. . . . Her
mouth twitched.

*Stick a pin in him and lolly save the ashes. Sar!*

Pirs took the baby down to Allina, helped her wrap him
in his blankets.

On the hill, the Speaker blew into his horn, signaling the
end of the ceremony. The chal and chapa went back inside
the walls and the party began.

### 2

Dinner with Daddy slipped by with nothing much happening.

It'd been a nothing much day, the day after the Nameday
Party, chal and chapa dragging to work, sour in breath and
spirit; Tinoopa's eyes were red as alert signals and she didn't

want to talk about anything, just got grimly on with her business. Shadith took the hint the fifth time Tinoopa moved her aside so she could get something; she went to her room and played at escape for a while. The rest of the time she slept. Which was why her head was hammering right now and her own temper on a short leash.

Paynto was playing some kind of shepherd song on his flute, too many high notes; they were digging holes in her brain. She let her fingers find an accompaniment and tried to shut down her hearing.

Ghineeli chal slipped from the kitchen door, knelt beside Shadith, touched her arm. "When this is over," she whispered, "Matja Allina says you don't need to come to her tonight, feel free to do what you want." She patted Shadith's arm, slipped away.

*Lovely. More hours looking at walls.*

She glanced at the screen, sighed. The three Cagharadad were talking about shearing and problems with getting their goods offworld, getting the money back, wandering desultorily from topic to topic, none of it meaning anything, all of it embroidery on a tension growing between them, a tension that had nothing to do with what they were saying. She didn't understand it and that put a cold shiver in her belly; she didn't trust them, even Pirs, they could explode in any direction, any time.

They were drinking the bottle of brandy the Artwa had brought to celebrate the Name Day. Pirs was trying to enjoy himself, rapidly getting drunk; as usual, he was ignoring anything he didn't want to know about. The Artwa was waiting to spring, spider in his hole; he wanted something and was sure he knew how to get it. Mingas simmered. She didn't know him well enough to know how much of that was standard and how much aroused by whatever it was that waited for Pirs. His glass was still half full; he'd taken a sip at each toast, no more.

*If Tinoopa was here, she'd say: Never trust a man who won't get drunk with his own family.*

The Artwa cleared his throat, looked at Mingas.

Mingas hurried around the table, pulled his father's chair out as the Artwa stood.

"Help your brother," Angakirs said, waited until Mingas was standing behind the Arring. "Pirs, I want to talk to you. Let's go into your study."

Pirs blinked. His eyes were clear, the blue as brilliant as ever. His face was slightly flushed, but he showed no other sign of how much brandy he'd consumed. "Study," he said amiably. He didn't move.

"Stand up," the Artwa snapped at his son, annoyed because he'd misjudged Pirs' capacity. "Take his arm, Mingas. Don't just stand there, help him."

Shadith kept playing because Paynto kept playing, same song over and over. He didn't stop until the study door boomed shut, then he sighed, shook out his flute. "Another night killed," he said. "Wonder when he's going home?"

Impajin grunted. He stretched, shook himself. "Let's get."

They nodded at Shadith, left.

She stood, slipped her arm through the arranga's carry strap, went out through the kitchen.

3

She sat on the bed, pulled her boots off. Balancing the left boot on her thighs, she slid her fingers into the slit and drew out the braincrystal knife. It was still there in spite of everything, overlooked in its incarnation as a stay stiffening the soft leather sides of the boot.

Since the Main Court had to be kept for the Name day party, the Artwa's skimmer was parked outside the walls. Guarded, of course, but the guards were probably as drunk as Pirs by now, most of them anyway.

*Might have a designated Drynose, might not. When the Cagharadads get out of the study. . . .*

She held the knife up, the candlelight shivering along the blade, then she sighed and eased it back into the boot and dropped that boot beside the other.

*I could do it. They're used to seeing me in there, I could get the papers, grab the skimmer, and run for Nirtajai.*

But she knew she wouldn't. A runaway chapa was one thing, a skimmer thief was something else. The Artwaes would stop a war to go after someone stupid enough to steal a skimmer, that'd be an attack where it hurt, an attack on their power. Even if she managed to reach Nirtajai and found a skipcom and got the call out, she'd still have to hang around until whoever was picking her up could get here.

*Travel time, you can't get around travel time.*

She'd have to hide, to survive without allies and with a price on her head that would tempt an anchorite.

*No. Too much downside. Well, you know what it is, Shadow, you just don't want to face that long lone ride.*

She thought about Rohant and the Dyslaera, winced quickly away from that. Omphalos had them. She had to do something about that. She couldn't while she was still a prisoner here. . . .

She flung herself around, face down on the bed.

She didn't want to think.

She *reached* and found a rodent burrowed into one of the walls of the study, teased it out, and sent it running from shadow to shadow until it was under a bookcase near where the three men were sitting.

She made it curl up there, nose on its forepaws, and listened through its ears.

## ##

". . . . hot Kirtaa," Angakirs was saying. "You know about Probrantarradad, 's been going on forever. We nibble at them, they nibble at us."

She heard creaks and cushion whispers as Pirs shifted in his chair. "I know. We get Kurn's tumaks out here when he comes up with the cash to hire them."

"Well, he picked up a backer two weeks ago. Kamaachadad. Old Mulyas and Kurn had a secret meeting round then. Kamaachadad found out who carried his daughter off a couple years ago. Bitch. She went willing, eager even. Rintirry swore it. Trouble is she ran off, tried to abort the cub and bled to death. That chal—what was his name? Don't remember. It's not important. The one Rintirry made so much of. Once Tirry was dead, he got to feeling Utilas wasn't treating him right and he ran off to the Brush, but before he did, he sold us. Mulyas sent me the Warblade a week ago, along with the kind of letter a sane man would have burned. He hit us at Caghar Rinta the next day. It was a close thing, Pirs.''

"Kamaachadad. Amur bless. He's got more sons than he has chals.''

"Five less now.''

"Rintirry, damn his soul to hell, why. . . .''

Mingas stirred, cleared his throat. ''Rintirry's dead.''

Angakirs' hand splatted against chair leather. ''Keep your mouth from Rintirry, both of you. I don't want to hear that. Pirs, I want you and fifty of your men at Caghar Rinta. You've got a son now, your Matja can keep busy with him, she doesn't need you.''

"Fifty men, we can't spare fifty men. You know we're coming on Shearing Days.''

"I know you owe me. I'm your father and this Rinta is still mine till you pay the last payment. Your chals are sworn to me, I could take them all if I called in my rights.''

Mingas spoke again, very softly. ''Our father has lost one son, Pirs. Our best fighter. Lost him because you were careless. You have a moral duty to replace that son.''

Angakirs said nothing, but Shadith, listening, had no doubt of his agreement with that.

Pirs drew a long shuddery breath, let it out again, the hiss loud in continuing silence. ''All right,'' he said finally. ''I'll come and I'll bring the men. If you arm them. I will not strip this Rinta for you, not even for you.''

"What good are men without arms?''

"I will not strip this Rinta.''

"Well, get them to me and I'll arm them.''

"No, Father. Send the guns here, good guns and ammunition for them. As soon as the weapons are here, my trucks will roll.''

"We need drugs and cloth and other supplies, I'll give you a list. Bring a truckload of those with the men.''

"All right.'' The chair creaked again.

Shadith made the rodent creep forward until she could see what was happening.

Pirs was on his feet. "Father," he said. "Mingas." He turned and walked out.

## 

Shadith knew she should stay and listen to Mingas and the Artwa, but she was tired of these men and their problems. She loosed the rodent and let him go scooting back to his nest. She stretched out on the bed and stared at the candle shadow shivering on the ceiling.

*One damn thing after another . . . well, maybe it'll be over soon.*

## 

The Artwa and Mingas left next morning, going without ceremony.

Shadith leaned on her windowsill and watched the skimmer disappear into the clouds. One opportunity gone. How many more would she see before she managed to kick loose?

## 

Five days later the weapons came. Mingas brought them in the skimmer, offloaded them, and left immediately.

## 4

Arring Pirs came into Allina's sitting room. He stood behind her, watching her work on her tapestry, then crossed the room to look into his son's cradle. He bent, touched the sleeping baby's cheek, then came back to her.

She looked up, managed a smile. "Are the guns what you wanted?"

"Wanted." He poured heavy irony into the word, rested the tips of his fingers on her shoulder. "Not new," he said, "but they work. P'murr's finishing the inspection."

"When will you be leaving, you and P'murr?"

"I'm not taking P'murr."

She stabbed the needle into the canvas, left it hanging there, caught hold of his hand and held it against her face. "You will," she said. "You must."

"No."

"Amurra. Amurra. Amurra," she whispered. "Please, please, kiya-mi, kaltji-mi. If you're worried about us here, what happens to us if you die?"

"You have Paji now. Father will take care of you."

She was silent. She couldn't agree and he wouldn't hear her if she tried to argue.

In her corner Shadith continued to play softly, shivering at the anger and helplessness in the Matja. She knew what Allina was thinking. It wasn't just the war that was waiting for Pirs; it was Mingas' spite, Utilas' jealousy, Angakirs' stupidity. Allina was sick with fear that Pirs wasn't going to come home from this, especially if he left P'murr behind.

"I have Tinoopa and Kizra, Wuraj for the men, the chal and chapa," Allina said after several moments of silence. "Don't you trust them, mi-Arring? Take P'murr, please? For my peace of mind, if nothing else."

"No." He pulled away, angry. "I have said, Matja."

"I hear, Arring."

## 5

Two days later, Pirs left with fifty chal in three trucks, a fourth truck loaded with supplies.

Matja Allina stood on the steps for the Ceremony of Leavetaking, calm, smiling, pride stiffening her spine. When the last truck vanished through the gate, she signaled the young Amur-drummer.

He played a quick roll, then blew into the convoluted shell of a land snail.

Matja Allina looked down into the faces of her people. "You know what this means," she said. She spoke slowly, her voice carrying to the fartherest corners of the court. "Chal, explain to chapa. Chal and chapa, take great care of your lives, you are dear to us and you are needed. There will be tumaks come to burn and kill. Don't go beyond the walls alone, don't go without a guard. I will see you have them when you need them. P'murr, bring the herders to the Great Hall in one hour. I will have arms for them. And ammunition." One by one she named the leaders of the men, those left at the Kuysstead after Pirs' winnowing, setting a time for each to bring his men to the Hall. "We must go on," she finished. "Shearing waits for no man's war to end, planting has its seasons." She signaled the drummer, turned, and went inside to the rattle of his sticks.

## ##

For three days she worked to tighten down the Kuysstead, then she took Aghilo and her baby into her suite, pulled the shades down, and grieved. She was in agony.

That agony filled the house and Shadith was sick with it; she struggled to shut it out, but could not.

Everyone but her was hard at work. P'murr and Tinoopa were running the Kuysstead; the place was busy as a termite mound with the top kicked out, but she had nothing to do but brood.

She was tired of that, so she took the arranga and went to play for whoever would have her.

## 6

Aghilo came into the kitchen, stood shaking her head, her hands on her hips.

Housemaids were clustered around Shadith, trading turns singing verses of the joke song she was playing.

Gilli chal looked up, saw Aghilo, hissed a warning. The rest of the maids stopped their giggling, scattered guiltily, ashamed of being caught enjoying themselves in a house of grief.

The Cook stilled the hand that had been slapping vigorously at the table, composed her face into dignified sobriety. "Yes?"

"Chapa Tinoopa, is she around?"

"She went across to the dye shed. Should be back in about ten minutes."

"Oh." Aghilo went out again.

Cook got heavily to her feet. "Looks like you'll be back on the job, Kiz. Scamper."

## ##

Matja Allina emerged from her grieftime.

She was pale and gaunt, but composed.

She carried Baby Paji in a sling that kept him nestled warm against her hip, an innovation she'd gotten from Ti-

noopa. Irrkuyon custom said the baby was given to a wet
nurse after Name Day, but Allina refused to be separated
from him. Polyapo protested, the chal stared, but the Matja
ignored them.

She summoned the chal leaders to the Great Hall, informed them she was going to the Brushies to get replace-
ments for the men Pirs took with him.

They protested.

She shouted them down. The cool controlled Matja they'd
known was gone. What was left was a wild creature who
filled the hall with her passion, seemed to suck up all the
air until the rest were about to smother.

She lowered her voice and went back to telling how things
were going to be.


7


Left behind, Shadith wandered through the House. She
got into the study, found her papers, sat looking at them for
a long time.

*I ought to go now. They wouldn't miss me.*

Her hands shook.

*Come on, Shadow. It's just a long hard ride, that's all.*

A bead of sweat dropped on the parchment. She blotted
it up with her sleeve, careful not to smudge the writing.

*This is freedom, Shadow. All you have to do is go.*
*I can't go. I'm not ready. I don't know which horses I can
take without being chased for them. Polyapo's in charge
while the Matja's away, she'd send men after me, Tinoopa
couldn't stop her. I can't go until Allina gets back.*

She stared at the papers a moment longer, then locked
them away again; they were safest here until she was ready
to go.

##

The days slid away; she used the braincrystal knife to cut
lines in the wall. Each mark was another day in prison; she
was building her own locks and walls, building them higher
every day. Each morning when she rolled out of bed, she
thought:

*I should go today. The chance might not come again. I should
go today.*

Each night she lay down in fury at herself, at the lethargy
she couldn't seem to throw off.


##

On the tenth day of the Matja's absence, Shadith slipped
into the Family Garden, climbed into one of the wall towers
and leaned on a window sill, looking west across the heat
hammered plain.

*What's happening out there? Could I get to Nirtajai without
getting killed? Where the HELL is Caghar Rinta? All right,
all right, let's get ourselves together, Shadow. This is a volcano about to pop. You get caught in it, you're going to get
the shit kicked out of you.*

She dropped to her knees, folded her arms on the sill,
rested her chin on her forearms. Sweat gathered in her hair
and dripped down her face, her neck. She was in the shade
up here, there was a strong wind blowing down off the
mountains behind her, but the heat was punishing.

*I can't ride in this. I can't. There's no use even dreaming I
could. What's that?*

The blotch out in the brush came gradually closer,
spreading into a ragged line of vans pulled by large creatures rather like stub-tailed lizards. Their daughters beside
them holding any infants in the family, women in bright
dresses—reds and blues and greens with patches of yellow
and orange, and yellow kerchiefs knotted into turbans—
drove the vans. Men in patchwork smocks rode horses,

spread in a wide arc enclosing the vans. Boys brought up the rear with extra horses.

Another blotch to the right of the first and several kays behind. Another and another.

Brushies, coming in for the Shearing.

She got to her feet. All around the Kuysstead the herds were coming in, woollies pouring through the brush, heading for the Shearing Ground.

She sighed with despair and relief.

The decision was taken from her; the Matja was back and the Shearing was about to begin.

## 8

Noise. Dust. Heat.

The cutters whirred with scarcely a stop. Two men threw a woolly blatting on the shed floor, while a third ran the cutter along the beast's sides in half a dozen long smooth sweeps that cut away the matted fleece intact. The throwers swung the woolly on its other flank and held it while the shearer took off the rest of the fleece. As another woolly came wide eyed and blatting from the chute, floorboys grabbed the fleece and ran to the bins with it, the beastmistress and the women drove the denuded beast into the hold pen where they went over it for pests and disease, then chased it into one of the grazing paddocks. Or into the butcheryard. Later it would be slaughtered and the meat sun-cured or smoked or ground into sausage or stowed away in barrels of brine against the winter need.

The throwers threw and shifted, the shearers sheared, the boys ran, the women inspected. Twenty sheds, twenty teams, twenty paddocks waiting; in an ordinary year it would have been thirty-five or forty, but even with the Brushies' help Ghanar Rinta was short-handed this year.

Short in everything but food, drink, and exuberance.

The Matja provided generously.

There were Shear Dances each night, bonfires and torches lighting the shearfloors where the dancing was, barrels of skatbeer hauled up from the cellars, woolly carcasses barbequed over vast beds of coals, Brushie singers and musicians taking turns with Ghanar players and singers. Round dances and slow dances, kick up your heels, rub against your partners, generating a heat greater than the fires. More

than one set of dancers left the floor for the prickly pleasures of the brush. Ingva was out there dancing with Brushie
and chal, enjoying herself enormously, running wild, ignoring all she'd been taught about the proper manners of
Irrkuyon daughters. Shadith saw her, but said nothing. She
was too busy, playing till her fingers bled, drinking skatbeer
until she was sodden. Each night she went to bed exhausted.

Day melted into day, distinctions lost in a haze of heat,
dust and exhaustion.

The paddock herds grew and grew, the bins were full of
fleeces, ready for winter's combing and spinning, the culls
were finished and butchering done. The Brushies collected
their pay in woollies, meat, cloth and sugar and prepared
to leave.

It was over.

## ##

Matja Allina stood on an upended fleece bin and spread
her hands as if she blessed the wrung-out workers looking
up at her.

"It is done," she said. "Well done."

A patter of hand against hand.

"You have worked hard and played hard." She smiled at
them, letting her eyes wander across the faces of chal and
chapa and the harder, darker faces of the Brushies. "I have
no doubt there's a crop been planted that will come to light
nine months from now, a lusty squalling crop of sons and
daughters."

Laughter and some long smoldering looks exchanged between Brushies and certain of the chal and chapa.

"This is a happy day for all of us." She spread her hands
again. "It is a great sadness for me to blacken these good
feelings, but I need to warn you all, especially those of you
going back to the Brush. Procagharadad is in Kirtaa with
two Families. You know that. Know this. The Arring Pirs
called me last night to warn me. Kamaachadad has hired a
hundred tumaks to hit at Ghanar Rinta. I said a while ago
that Shearing waits for no man's war to end, but, Amurra
bless, the war has waited for the end of Shearing. It won't
wait much longer. The tumaks will be here before the month
is out. You know them, you know what they'll do. If they
catch you in the Brush, they'll play with you until you wish

for death and send you home to be a warning. They'll fire
the Brush; yes, they're fools enough to do that. They'll kill
whatever they can't catch. We've had tumaks before, but
never so well armed and supplied. So take care, people of
the Brush. If the time comes when you want shelter behind
Ghanar walls, if I still have the say . . ." she broke off, her
composure momentarily shattered.

A sigh passed through the crowd. They knew what she
was not saying; if Pirs was killed, someone else would be
ruling on who was let inside Ghanar walls.

"If I have the say still," she went on, her voice hoarse
but determined, "you will be welcome here. Go, then, our
friends, and take care, take very good care of yourselves."

## 9

"You let her run wild, Matja. Wild. Out all times of the
night, by herself, no one watching her. The Jili should be
whipped for neglect, hasn't the girl learned anything? What
if she's not virgin? What if your own daughter has got herself a Brush bastard? Who's going to marry her then?"

Matja Allina was nursing Paji and staring out the window, her shoulder turned to Polyapo. She twitched like a
horse trying to shoo off a troublesome fly. But this fly
wouldn't be twitched away and wouldn't stop its buzzing.
She sighed, shifted around so she was facing Polyapo, moving carefully so she wouldn't disturb her baby. "Ingva's no
fool."

"Any girl's a fool when her blood is up."

"No. You don't understand her. She's got a cool head,
my girl has. She knows what she wants and she'll get it."

"Not if word of how she behaves gets out. Even if she is
still virgin, who'll believe it?"

"What's so wonderful about being wed to some grizzler
three times her age? That's what she's got to look forward
to and you know it, Polyapo Ulyinik. With my history of
stillborn sons and daughters, a second wife or a third is all
she can hope to be. Hope!"

"What else is there? Poor relation in some other woman's
house? No, running to the Brush. That's it, isn't it. That's
what you want for her. Running to the Brush. You didn't
have the nerve to do it yourself, so you want her to."

"I want her to have what she wants."

"She's a child. She doesn't know what she wants."

"You've said your say, Polyapo Ulyinik. I don't want to hear any more on this subject."

"If the Arring knew what you're doing, he'd be furious."

"Arring Pirs and I know each other's thinking quite well. And if I find you bothering him with this when he needs all his mind set on staying alive, you'll see such anger you've never seen before, Polyapo Ulyinik. Must I remind you, it's only by my forbearance you are not-chal. Hear me, Polyapo, continue to annoy me and you'll find yourself swearing the oath. Now, get out of here and consider your future carefully."

Polyapo pinched her lips together and left the room.

Paji whimpered, his milk supply interrupted by the knotting tension in his mother. "That woman, AH! that woman. . . ." Allina rubbed the baby's back. "Oooh, baby, ooo aaah, lovey yum yum. She drives me wild sometimes. Yes, baba-lirri, Paji-ji, yes my lovey. Kizra, come play me that funny little song, um, that stepchild song, I need something to wash that bitch from my blood."

Shadith brought the arranga and a cushion across the room, settled herself and began picking out the song. "Step easy, Stepchild," she sang. . . .

*Step easy, Stepchild*
*Watch where you walkin'*
*It's wolfdays, Stepchild*
*Bourghies in your garden*


## 10

As the days grew longer and hotter, Matja Allina napped through the middle of the afternoon, leaving Shadith on her own.

The Grays closed around her.

*What is this?*

She threw the question at the grayness and got no answer, but she didn't really need one. Her memories were back, the good and the bad. The Grays were closing round her. When she allowed herself to think, she told herself:

*I will die here, still dithering.*

It wasn't as bad as the time in Ginny's ship when she saw no way out and just started to die.

She knew the way out. She just couldn't scrape up the energy to take it. She couldn't plan, she couldn't go on preparing for the run to Nirtajai, the escape she kept putting off and putting off—all the reasons she found for not leaving were good reasons, logical reasons, but fake.

She slept as much as she could, spent what waking energy she had not-thinking, waiting for the Grays to pass. They would, she knew that, with interference or without, the Grays would go away. Until then, all she could do was stay alive and wait.

Then the tumaks hit them.

## ##

The Herbmistress had Eeda and Jassy and the rest of the garden chals out before dawn, working in the home gardens, harvesting the first planting of tubers. After the Shearing and the departure of the herds, Matja Allina had set chal and chapa to getting in all produce mature enough for preserving; she wanted the storage bins and shelves filled as much as possible before the tumaks made working outside the walls too dangerous.

They were digging up the roots, brushing them off and tossing them into baskets, laughing, chattering, Jassy teasing the girls about lovers in the Brush, Eeda throwing tubers at her sister when she got too graphic. A cheerful lot, working hard, trying to get the field clean before the sun got too high.

There was a shot. Another.

Jassy's head exploded, she fell sprawling across a row of tuber plants. Eeda screamed, crumpled across her sister as another pellet punched through her heart.

The watchchals in the towers began shooting.

The Herbmistress and the workers were on their stomachs crawling for the walls.

A few more shots tore through the rustling plants, a girl grunted and lay still, another screamed as a pellet tore off her braided topknot.

The top of one tower exploded. A ministinger from a dart tube. Another mini blew out part of the House's roof.

Then the fire from the towers drove off the tumaks.

The Herbmistress and the chal and chapa still alive got to their feet, grabbed the tuber baskets, and ran for the Gate.

The attack was over.

## ##

As the days passed, tumaks set fire to the grainfields and the garden plots, destroying much of the food the Kuysstead needed for the winter.

They set fire to the Brush.

They blew apart more towers, killing the watchchals and those the towers fell on.

P'murr organized roving teams who managed to ambush many of the tumak bands; the chals had the advantage of knowing the land and the brushcraft of the tumaks was sketchy at best.

When the tumaks fired the Brush, the Brushies joined the fight. They slipped round the tumak bands and slaughtered them, armed themselves with the tumaks' weapons, and searched out the base up in the mountains. It was defended and well supplied, but the Brushies knew the ground in ways even chal and chapa did not and they got in and out like ghosts, stealing whatever they could get their hands on, destroying what they couldn't carry off.

And still the tumaks hit and hit again.

## 11

In the middle of the night a ministinger crashed into the side of the House, blew out a large chunk of wall and floor, just missing Shadith's bed. The bed tilted, creaked and fell through the gap before Shadith woke enough to understand what was happening.

It landed on the roof of the women's quarters, slid down the pantiles and shattered on the paving stones.

Shadith was jolted by the sudden stop, bruised and more than a little terrified, but nothing was broken. She crawled out of the mess and knelt on the still-warm paving stones, gaping up at the hole in the wall. "Tsoukbaraim!"

More of the wall fell away and her boots came flying down, hit the tiles, and slid off to land close by the bed. She got shakily to her feet, stood looking at the boots and laughing.

"Kiz, you all right?"

She looked up. Tinoopa was leaning out her window, her dark braid dangling past her shoulders. "Bruised but intact," Shadith yelled back. "Better than the bed."

"Hang on, I'll be down and let you in."

"Th-thanks." She was suddenly shaking all over her body, shaking so hard her knees gave under her and she dropped to the mattress; she grabbed the boots, hugged them to her breasts, and started crying. She was alive. But it'd been so close. So CLOSE.

She was still shaking, still crying, still clutching the boots, when Tinoopa came down and led her inside.

## ##

She woke to afternoon heat and the realization that the Grays had gone away as if they'd never been. She was ALIVE!

# THE HOOK IS BAITED:
## Autumn Rose goes fishing in a pond of sharks

1

Autumn Rose poured more of the resinated wine into the stemmed glass and looked out across blue blue water to the lichenous city that spread gray and olive and dull brown along the curve of the shore. "I drink enough of this and I might even get to like it."

They were sitting in a nest of pillows and reed mats on one of the many small barren islets spattered across the bay; the catboat he'd come in was moored to a rock, her outrigger snugged next to it. The maneuver had gone as planned, with Hadluk providing the meal and the comforts. He liked his food and he'd used the Shimmery's cooks to good purpose. He'd also avoided even a hint at the proposition she was out here to hear from him, steering her away from it when impatience got too much for her.

A flock of birds rose from the next island over, a sudden swirl of orange and blue; they circled around twice and settled back. *Seeing ghosts,* she thought. She sipped at the wine, enjoying the harsh roughness against her palate. The birds swirled again, went screaming away, came fluttering back.

She flicked on the mute cone and turned to Hadluk. "Wasn't very nice of you, aiming Uj at me like that."

For a moment she thought he was going to turn away even that oblique attempt to focus on the reason for this picnic, then he said. "Found out what I wanted to know, didn't I."

"Did you?"

"Found out you're hungry but not desperate."

"I told you I wasn't hurting."

"So you did."

"Hunh." She refilled her glass, held it up so the sun shone through the straw-colored liquid. "So what's this about?"

"Hungry, yes."

"Belaboring the obvious, Hadluk. I'm assembling a stake. If you want a piece of that, think again."

"No gain without pain, Rose."

"I choose my pains, Hadluk. This isn't one."

"All right."

"So," she stared down into the glass, tilted it side to side to make the light wine swirl, looked up suddenly, challenging him, "do we say thanks for lunch, pack up, and go home?"

He wrinkled his nose, refilled his glass from the amber bottle he kept close to his side. The wind blew the smell of the soursweet ouiskag across to her, it was a smell that hung around him like a halo, stronger today than yesterday. Good thing she wasn't depending on him for much. He sipped from the glass, cleared his throat. "JuhFeyn opens up the Mewa Room three, four times a year for Topenga Vagnag. Same rules as always, table stakes only, no markers, truce ground, and everyone with masks. Last few years, it's been more or less the same players, same sort, anyway, some of the Southern Vaarlords . . . um, might be one, two, three, um slummers, you know the types, and probably someone from Mimishay, there's usually at least one. He'll come by flit from their place on Haed Nunn. Maybe the manager of the Black House, if he's not too busy to get away. And sometimes the High Vaar. Though juhFeyn's the only one knows for sure who's coming.

"He does the inviting; he handles the security, no bodyguards allowed; he supplies food, drink, and Dasuttras. Word is the High Vaar wanted a good game and a safe ground, got juhFeyn to handle it because ol' Jao's married to one of his cousin's daughters. Jao uses me to keep things honest; you'd be surprised what some of these types get up to. . . ." He glanced at her, shook his head. "Or maybe you wouldn't. Player gets one warning, then he's out." He coughed, squeezed his hands into fists. "Big," he whispered. "Piles of gold—there—begging someone to take it. I want some of that, Rose. I have one chance. One and run."

"Masks. Hmm. You wouldn't have to worry about tells. Or Pulleet, what about him?"

"You played him."

"I get the point."

"Even if I could do the calcs, Rose, juhFeyn would slit my throat if I tried slipping in."

Autumn Rose let her head fall back against the boulder behind her, stroked her fingers under her chin and down the curve of her throat. "I've got this perverse fondness for breathing through my nose, Hadluk."

"You're an outsider, Rose. He doesn't know you. With your help and a little luck, I can work it. If you want it."

"Oh, yeh, I want it. How good are they?"

"Better than average but nowhere as good as they think they are. I've watched those games the past twelve years, Rose. Watched and sweated. And waited for my chance. You're it."

"I like the setup, but I'm still not risking my stake. Financing's up to you. And it has to be big, Hadluk, or they'll freeze me out of every hot one."

"Pulleet and me, we've had some things going for us. We'll bank you. We'll cut the take four ways, three to us, one to you."

"Seems to me, I'm the one doing the work. Down the middle. Half to me, half to you, you can split your half however you want."

"I'll go three ways, it may be your labor, Rose, but it's also the past twenty years I've spent scraping together that stake. I'll throw in passage offworld with me and Pulleet. You do realize you'd better be somewhere else when the sun comes up?"

"Hadluk, my Luck went soft for a while, not my head."

He grinned at her and lifted his glass. He shouldn't grin, she thought, he looks deformed when he grins. "The Lady bless," he said, then gulped down the ouiskal without waiting for her to join him. He coughed and wiped the back of his hand across his mouth; his eyes glittered at her over the soft white curve of his pampered palm. "We start building you tonight. I want you in dresses like the one you wore first time we played, I want you to clean the marks down to their toenails. They love a winner on this world. A winner's as good as a saint, maybe better. Every night after that, as long as we can pull in marks who want to beat you, I want you winning, I want rumors breeding like maggots in meat. You hear?"

"Fine with me. One thing, Hadluk, and you better believe it. I start getting official pressure, you know what I mean, I fade. My nerves are a tad touchier than they were back when.''

"I'll talk juhFeyn into putting the word out. Shouldn't be hard to do since he gets ten percent of the net from everyone who plays. Even Uj pays him. Once the rumors start, you'll be hauling them in and he's a man with an eye for profit.''

She frowned. "I didn't. . . .''

"I took it out when I culled my cut, thought you'd call me on it. Slipping, Rose.''

She shrugged. "I was waiting for the deal. If I was interested, fine, if not, it could come out of your hide. Ten per, hmm? You take that out of the gross, Hadluk, not out of my third. I mean it.''

He blinked at her, let it go. "So, you don't need to worry about the lice.''

"When's this Game going to happen?''

"Don't know yet. Jao never announces the date ahead of time, but there's things he does to get ready and he's started them, he's got feelers out for prime Dasuttras, getting in a special cook, went to see the High Vaar yesterday. I'd say sometime soon, no earlier than ten days from today, not more than thirty. Plenty of time for you to get known.''

"I hear. Does juhFeyn do any banking for his players?''

"What?''

"My winnings. I'm not walking back and forth with that kind of cash stuffed down my front. I want that made very clear.''

"Good idea. You might as well start that tonight. He'll be at the Shimmery going over the books. He'll see you, he's a man with an itch, curiosity, you know. Um. Yes. He'll be in to watch you play after a few nights, just to make sure it's Luck not fingers. You understand that?''

"Luck. And what I've got in my head, Hadluk. Never my fingers, it doesn't pay.''

"That was before.''

"That's now and always. I can't help what jorkheads think, if you can call what they do thinking, I play straight.''

"I never said you didn't, Rose. I'm just saying Jao will want to make sure.''

"Fine. Long as he knows what he's seeing. You said he keeps you around for that.''

"I'm the sump, Rose. The goat. The finger. I get the bad vibes and he stays clean. Believe me, he'll know.''

She got to her feet. "Well, it's time I was busy getting ready. I take it we don't meet again until after the Game. Not to talk, I mean."

"Right. Keep it clean."

"I'm off, then." She scooped up the mute cone, dropping it in her bag, and strolled toward the boats, picking her footing with care among the weathered stones.

## 

When she was out on the water, she looked back. He was still sitting in his nest; she saw a glint of amber as he tilted the bottle one more time. She clicked her tongue. *Not good, that. Ah well, doesn't matter, I don't need this, not like I used to.*

## 2

Kikun shifted on the window seat, knocking one of the pillows onto the floor, his eye a brief orange flash. "You trust him?"

Autumn Rose snorted. "About half as far as I could throw him." She rubbed fingertips along her jaw. Kikun was tired tonight. Withdrawn. She got the feeling he was desperately unhappy, but there was nothing she could do to help; he wasn't going to talk about it. "I'm all right until the Game," she said. "He'll keep things sweet until that's over. It's worth the trouble."

Another flash of orange eye. "And you're itching for it."

"I don't know. Maybe. It's been a long time. I like working for Digby. . . ."

"Hmm."

She fidgeted as the silence developed. "I don't know, Kuna. This whole business is weird. I don't know why Digby got involved in it. He's been paid, yeh, but I doubt he's close to breaking even. He never tells us anything except what we need to know to do our part of the job. That's all right, there's no confusion that way. When I was working the team, you know, advising the Dyslaerins, when we were tracking down leads to Ginny's auction, it was business, that's all. I liked them, but that was beside the point. It was a clear, clean job. Even when it went wrong, it had . . . um . . . shape! Do you see what I'm saying? I like to do a quick, neat job. It's a good feeling, Kuna. You slide in, do the thing, slide out. No fuss. Neat. Surgical almost. Well, doesn't happen like that all the time, even most of the time . . . most of the time it gets messy one way or another . . . when it does, though . . . AH! when it does . . . when . . . things . . . click, you're wired, you're walking the edge . . . I like that, Kuna . . . but . . . I don't know . . . this business . . . it's like a fog . . . I can't get hold of it . . . makes me crazy when I think about it . . . mostly I try not to . . . think about it, I mean. The Game now . . . that's clean. Do you blame me for wanting that? Why didn't Digby call me back? I'm not . . . I'm a sprinter, Kuna, I run out of *go* on a long trail. Goerta b'rite, I'll be glad to get off this world. . . . '' She sat up abruptly. ''This is no use. Look. Have you got anything more from Sai?''

''No.'' After a minute he amplified this. ''He hasn't been in to the office once. He runs the place through the com. I don't know how to find him. Likely he's trying to duck the Squeeze, if we believe your source.'' He swung around and sat up, shaking himself as if to throw off the lassitude eating at him. ''I can't get a smell of him, Rose. I'm cut off. . . .'' He shivered, his eyes flickered restlessly. ''I don't think we can pin him, not in the time we have . . . with the Game being the limit. You want what he's got on Mimishay, you'll have to ask the kephalos.''

She grimaced. ''I hear, Kuna. You don't mind, I want you in that office in the morning, picking up everything you can get about keying in.''

''When will you go for it?''

''Sometime around the Game. Probably the night before. I don't know. Depends on how things are, what you can get, how much time I'm going to need, how much *noise* it's going to involve.'' She sighed. ''How desperate we are. Um. Had-luk says someone from Mimishay might be there, a Player. You can pin him as Omphalos?''

''Oh, yes.''

''Then we'll see, won't we.''

3

The dance began.
She won.
And won again.

She found a dressmaker and got clothes made, started the woman on a black dress like the one Hadluk remembered after so many years. Long hard years for her, harder for him, he was sculling round bottom. At first she'd been annoyed at him, telling her what to wear when she hadn't asked, hadn't intended to ask, then she changed her mind.

That was a good night, she'd been sure of herself. More than sure. It was magical how—from the time she rose in the morning until she went to sleep on the ship out—magical how everything she touched went right. She knew the value of talismans, for herself and for him. They gave that extra THING WITHOUT A NAME to people they touched. That night she'd tapped the flow and ridden it higher than she'd gone before or after. It was good to recapitulate, recapture, revivify that woman who was, that woman who KNEW. The local fibers didn't have the special sheen of avrishum, but they had their own beauties and when she drew the heavy, rich, black material across her arm, the hairs on her spine stood up. Yes, this was going to be another magical dress, she felt it wake the power in her. She gave the woman the sketch and her measurements and paid the price for the cloth without a murmur of protest.

## ##

The Angatines set up a tent as close to the Kipuny Shimmery as Jao juhFeyn would permit and held a mourning service every night she played, starting their keening the moment she came round the corner. Whitened faces and bodies moved in a somber, slow dance to the steady slow thump of the drums. The Blind Woman chanted her exorcisms in a wild rough contralto.

No one paid attention to them, they were just part of the show. She'd been afraid they'd wake hostility among the locals, but apparently the Rummers were used to the Angatines taking against somebody and calling the wrath of heaven on them. Apparently the wrath of heaven struck or didn't strike according to the whims of God and the Rummers didn't consider that any business of theirs.

##

By the seventh day there were crowds of child beggars, street singers, magicians, acrobats, cutpurses, food venders; Hadluk's rumor-mill was working industriously and producing the desired effect. He knew his Rummers.

##

The crowd grew every playday, shouting the number of the win when she came out. Seven, eight, nine. . . .

They opened and let her pass without hindrance when she arrived, there was a hush, hot and tense, like the hush before a storm. The question was there in their faces: *Would she win again? Would the Lady kiss her once more?*

They had the answer before she came out.

Yes. She won, the whisper came. She won. Ten. Eleven. Twelve. She won. She won.

##

Dasuttras ran at her, elbowed past the guards she was forced to hire; they touched her, just touched her—as if they hoped her Luck would rub off on them.

Sick people came at her on hands and knees to outmaneuver the guards, or paid child beggars to tear pieces of cloth from her dress.

She moved quickly into the maze of semi-streets, dismissed the guards as soon as the worst of the crush was left behind, depended on Kikun's *Not-There* to screen her from the more persistent followers and—somehow—kept her homeground in the Rumach secret from friend and enemy alike.

##

On the thirteenth day, as Hadluk counted out her winnings, he murmured. ''The High Vaar called Jao this afternoon, wanted to know about you, if the Luck was real or you were pulling something.''

''That's good?''

''Yup. You're in.''

''Got the date?''

''Not yet. Can you keep this up?''

''Long as the play's straight.''

''It will be.''


## ##

On the fifteenth playnight, there were only three marks waiting for her. By the second Chapter she knew what she faced. They were combined against her. She almost giggled with relief. She'd been expecting this for days.

Jao came in looking grim. She caught his eye, shook her head. He thought it over a moment, then left.

She cleaned them.

They yelled foul.

The Beza Prezao came himself and took them away.


## ##

Jao waited while Hadluk counted the coins and locked them away, then he took her arm and escorted her to the quartet of guards waiting by the door. He turned her to face him. ''That won't happen again. After Prezao gets done with them, they'll walk small and stay away.''

''Thanks.''

He smiled. ''You know what's really going to discourage repeats of this night? You cleaned them. They pulled a sneak on you and went down tails on fire. Why haven't I heard of you?''

''I play privately. Go on binges, then quit. So there's nothing to hear.''

''Some nothing. Come see me tomorrow.''

''What time?''

''Have lunch with me.''

''With pleasure. Noon?''

''One.''

''I'll be there.''


## 4

She stripped the dress off, threw it on the bed. ''We're in, Kuna. I'm having lunch with Jao tomorrow. I have a feeling he's going to offer the invitation then.''

Kikun was curled into a tight ball. His skin fell looser by

the day, his bones were starting to show. "Soon enough,"
he said. His voice was dull, dragging.

"You all right, Kuna?"

"No, I'm not all right. I'm tired, Rose. I can't sleep, I
can't eat. I need things I can't get here."

The words came to her as sighs puffing through the flicker
of the candlelight; she had to strain to hear them. She pulled
the woolly robe around her, irritated by his limpness. She'd
come home high and happy and he'd gloomed her down till
she was low as the rug. She couldn't do this thing without
him, not the way it was set up, but more than ever she
regretted not being on her own. She sat on the bed and
began taking down her hair. "It's almost over, Kuna. Tell
me what you got from the office."

He muttered words she couldn't hear, uncoiled and sat
with his legs dangling, his hands clutching the edge of the
seat. "I picked up two more passkeys. Wrote them down,
they're on the table. I don't see any pattern in his keys, I
think he's using private symbols translated through the local
ideograms. Not numbers. Gestalt of some kind. Probably
interlocking gestalts. Ideograms lend themselves to that sort
of thing. You'd probably find it simple-minded. It works for
him, lets his women get what they need to run the business
for him, keeps the rest private. Gaagi. . . ." he blinked and
looked unhappy, a small gray-green manlizard sinking into
wrinkles. "Gaagi decided to show, he says the machine is
trapped, push it wrong and the whole building goes boom."

"Lovely. Hmm. If I can get in, pull the data without
bringing the house on my head, I'll have the Shimmery for
refuge, three days, that's how long Topenga Vagnag takes.
I'll be sleeping there, won't go out till the Game's over.
That'll give you a chance to rest, if you can hang on till
then. After you get a look at the Players." She pulled the
dozens of fine plaits apart, dropped the pins and clasps on
the quilt beside her, working quickly, impatiently, ignoring
the sharp little pains when she pulled too hard. "I need you
hot and ready to go when it's time to get away. This is going
to be tricky, Kuna. Hadluk and Pulleet will do their best to
put me down, types like that always get greedy, want it all,
and the other Players will be . . . hmm . . . shall we say
MOST unhappy. And one of them's going to be the High
Vaar. They say they want a good game, what they mean is
they want to win. Mmm, we can't come back here, not after

the Game. We should have everything we don't want to
abandon packed and ready to shift before I go. When you
have a moment, Kuna, see if you can locate us a tractor,
that's about the fastest way out of town, we need to get close
to where the miniskips are before anyone wakes up to the
fact that we're gone. About milking that kephalos the night
before the Game . . . hmm . . . impossible to do it without
traces . . . you think you could get me something that would
make Sai think it was lice nosing into his business? Insignia
or something I could leave lying in some inconspicuous
spot? I should have the timeline set after my lunch with Jao.
Then we'll know where we are.'' She thrust her fingers
through her hair, combing out the worst of the kinks. ''Bath.
Goerta b'rite, I NEED a bath.''

''How much did you get tonight?''

''I don't know. All they had. I didn't bother counting it.''

''You are odd, Rose. I've never met anyone like you.''

''Why? Because I don't give a damn about money?'' She
shrugged, got to her feet. ''I can always get money. It's
other things that don't come when you whistle.'' She made
a face, collected the towel and facecloth and coins for the
heater slot. ''You want me to run water for you when I'm
finished?''

''Please.''

### 5

Jao tilted the bottle and poured a pale liquid that wasn't
even a kissing cousin to the turpentine she'd been drinking.
''Home wine,'' he said. ''From my cousin's vineyard on
Shimmaroh. I think you will like this.'' He filled his own
glass and smiled as she sipped, then sighed with pleasure.
''Forgive me in advance for intruding on your private af-
fairs?''

''After such a meal, I would forgive almost anything.''

''You have a considerable sum banked with me. Could
you perhaps have access to . . . mmm . . . say triple that
amount?''

''Possibly.''

''Yes. Good. Have you heard, perhaps, of our sessions of
Topenga Vagnag?''

''You might say it's among the things that brought me
here.''

"Ahhh. Yes. It is the custom for offworlders to deposit a certain sum with me before they play. This smooths out possible difficulties and makes life more pleasant for everyone."

"Let's have things clear, Jao juhFeyn. You are inviting me to play Topenga Vagnag?"

"Yes. If you can present the necessary deposit. I have a credit link tied to Helvetia which you may use if you wish."

"That won't be necessary. How soon must I have the deposit?"

"Three days on. By the first hour after noon."

"And when is the Game?"

"The Players will arrive four days on."

"I see. You have secure rooms for them?"

"For you also, if you wish. The room is part of the service I provide in return for my fee which is ten percent of your net wins; if you are a net loser, consider it a gift."

"Most kind. I'd really rather avoid the . . . um . . . distractions of coming and going."

"You've played Topenga before?"

"Yes."

"What name will you be using?"

"My name is my talisman, juhFeyn. I never change it. I will go by Autumn Rose."

He smiled, settled back in his chair. "So you're a tech, a systems specialist."

"Freetech. I can't talk about it. Company privilege, you understand. Silence is part of what they buy from me."

"I see. Have you ever been to Shimmaroh?"

"No. What's it like?"

"You know Spotchals?"

"Who doesn't."

"True. Something like Spotchals in a smaller system. . . ."

## 6

Kikun slid along the alley, stopped by a narrow recess. "Easiest to get in here," he murmured.

Autumn Rose fished the keypac from her toolbag, got the door open and slipped inside, a shadow in shadows. She had a black scarf wrapped around her head, and as she moved, there was a springy power in her thin body that reminded Kikun of the sohdihlo dancers back home who trained for the Holy Days at Plibajatsi Toh, the Sacred Lake. He grimaced. It seemed like everything was reminding him of home these days. Grandmother Ghost getting her pinches in.

There was a hiss from the darkness—Autumn Rose wondering why he was dallying out in the street. That was another thing about these days, Rose was impatient all the time, scratchy as the thorns on her namesake.

The building was dark and smelled of urine and dust; it had the hollow echoing feel that told Kikun it was empty. He didn't say anything, he didn't think it was necessary. Gaagi was hovering somewhere in the background; he wasn't showing his face, but Kikun could hear the whisper of his feathers now and then, just often enough to know he was there. Might or might not be a help.

Kikun slipped in past Rose, went scurrying up the gritty, sagging stairs, staying close to the wall so they wouldn't squeal on him. Or under him, as the case might be.

## ##

The door to Sai's office had a dirty mirror in the upper half, a mirror that turned into one-way glass once they were inside.

Rose looked over her shoulder, snorted. "Elegant."

Kikun shrugged. "Whatever works."

She wrinkled her nose, set her hands on her hips and looked around.

A grayish light filtered through the ancient dust on the windows, enough to show them the sagging benches lined up against a side wall, the broad armchair in an inner corner where the guard sat with his ottoshot across his knees; its seat cushion was worn and shabby, molded to the shape of his broad butt. Beside the door into the inner office, a bulky deskset pouched through the wall with a grill across a hatch. During the day the woman sat behind that grill, readouts at their elbows, and did their needlework while they waited for someone to comcall or walk in.

Rose inspected the door to the inner office, fished a readout from her toolbag and ran it along the jamb; when she was finished, she looked at the result, sniffed with satisfaction. Over her shoulder she said, "Watch my back. I don't know how long this's going to take." She keyed the door, went through it, and settled at one of the readouts.

Kikun watched her start work, then went to squat in a corner by the outer door, humming hymns that were so old even the gods had forgotten who made them.

## ##

*Jadii-Gevas the antelope spirit ran clicka-clack through the empty stinking corridors, his black eyes wild, his breath wet before him.*

Kikun quivered with him, shuddered with his fear, looked through his eyes, searching, searching for motion, the thing that Jadii-gevas was created to find, find and flee. The antelope spirit shuddered and fled as wind rattled a window, his hooves clacked on the bare wood floors like hail as he fled again when a rat came trundling from a pile of anonymous litter.

*Spash'ats the Bear sat in a corner of the room, big and dark, shining amber eyes. He yawned, opened his mouth wide enough to swallow Kikun, snapped it closed, tooth sliding against tooth. He was shadow without substance but his power was like perfume, it lingered even when the wearer was mostly absent. He was warning, he was reproach, he was the summoner.*

Kikun shuddered whenever he looked into that corner; he tried not to look, but he couldn't keep his head from turning, he couldn't keep his eyes away.

He was supposed to be watching for intruders, he was supposed to be guarding Autumn Rose, not harrowing his soul for the edification of his gods, gods he couldn't believe in even when he was looking at them. He kept looking at them. He let Jadii-Gevas do the watching.

The soft sound of Rose's fingertips came to him along with a faint flickering greenish glow from the screen. She was concentrating so hard it was like a skin of glass was pulled around her, glass tough as ship steel.

He sighed. He missed Shadith; she understood things that Rose never would because Rose didn't want to understand

them. He spent a moment wondering where Shadow was
and what she was doing right now—then was jerked from
his reverie by the challenge roar of Jadii-Gevas. . . .

*Antelope Spirit reared, huge and dark, antlers like naked trees,
eyes red, Jadii-Gevas reared, obsidian hooves hanging over
the head of the man coming unconcerned down the corridor,
coming toward the office. . . .*

Kikun whistled a brief warning to Rose, dropped flat
against the wall, the stunner ready.

There was a form on the far side of the glass, the rattle
of a key in the lock. The door opened.

Kikun fired.

The man jerked, shuddered, dropped.

*Xumady the Otter clashed his teeth and giggled, a high
whinny that scratched at Kikun's ears and called a lump
into his throat. Down among the dead men, Xumady said to
him. You've a corpse to play with, Nai.*

Kikun cursed the trickster in the reduplications of his na-
tal langue, the agglutinations. He didn't want to believe it,
but he'd felt the spirit go out of the man and he saw cold
and empty flesh lying on the shabby rug. With a last flicker
of hope, he dropped to a squat beside the body, caught hold
of the nearest wrist, tried to find a pulse.

Nothing.

He scowled at the stunner, held it close to his eyes so he
could see the setting. Minimum stun. The lowest notch.
"Rose," he whispered.

No answer. She was so tied into what she was doing she
didn't know what was happening out here.

"Rose!"

She made an impatient sound, looked up. "What? I'm
just getting somewhere, Kuna. Hold on a minute, will you?"

"No. There's a problem. I need you."

She swore, worked a moment over the pad, then came
through the door. "So? You stunned him, I hope."

"Yes. I did. But he's dead."

"What?" She strode across to him, stirred the body with
her toe. "Did you change the setting?"

"No. Look." He tossed the stunner to her.

She examined it, scowled down at the man. "All right. So why's he dead? Or is he?" She dropped to her knees, held out the stunner. "Here, take this thing." She pressed her fingers up under his jaw. "Z' Toyff. They don't come deader. Miserable luck, he must've been one of those extra sensitives. You don't happen on them often, goerta b'rite." She checked her ringchron, passing her hand across her eyes. "Yes. Who is he?"

"Don't know. I suspect he's Sai. He's got keys. What are we going to do with him?"

She pressed the heels of her hands hard against her eyes. For a moment she didn't say anything, just knelt there as if she were praying, though he suspected what was going through her head had nothing to do with prayer.

She straightened, got to her feet. "Another half hour and I'll have the Mimishay file. I was going to go for Black House, too, but might as well forget that. He can stay where he is until I'm finished. We're not likely to have more visitors. Or are we?"

"No. I don't know. Probably not."

"Mm. This building's right on the bay, there must be windows looking out over the water?"

"Yes. Just drop him out? Like he was garbage?"

"He's beyond feeling it, Kuna."

"It's not respectful."

"I don't know him, why should I respect his corpse? It's our skins, Kuna. And not just ours. What about your friend Shadith? If we get topped, what happens to her?"

He moved uneasily. "I hear."

"Right, then." She transferred her scowl from him to the body. "Jorkhead. Middle of the night. . . ." She swung round and stalked into the inner office.

Kikun heard the squeak of the chair as she sat, the patter of her fingertips, saw the unsteady light from the screen chasing shadows across the wall beside him. He sighed, caught hold of Sai's shoulders and tugged him out of the doorway, laid him against the wall.

*Xumady giggled and danced a triumph about and around the dead man.*
*Spash'ats gloomed in his corner and piled his silent demands on Naiyol Hanee called Kikun: Honor the dead. Honor YOUR dead.*

*Jadii-Gevas the antelope spirit ran clicka-clack through the empty stinking corridors, his black eyes wild, his breath wet before him.*

Watch for me, Kikun told Antelope the Bear. Watch for me.

Dance for me, Kikun told Otter. Guide, he told 'Gemla Mask, suddenly there.

He knelt beside the dead man and sang a Going-home for him.

*We drink from different rivers now.*
*O stranger, O enemy*
*We always have.*
*Surprised from life*
*Your heartsoul dances on a dry plateau*
*Cries out to me: Why?*
*O stranger, O enemy*
*I do not know.*
*Loudly your voice calls:*
*You sent me*
*Show me the way.*
*You leap past the moon*
*You run among the stars*
*You rush to me crying out*
*Bring me rest*
*I hear you*
*O stranger, O enemy*
*My hands draw the double spiral*
*Draw it in the air*
*Remember the spiral*
*O stranger, O enemy*
*Let your feet remember and run it*
*Look neither to the right nor to the left*
*Hoz'zha-dayaka lies before you*
*Garden of the Blessed*
*Run, then rest*
*O stranger, O enemy*
*Do not let anger snare your feet*
*Hold you from the blessed*
*Go quickly and do not remember your death*
*Or he who gave it unasked*
*May Shizhehoyu Father of all Bless you*

*And give you rest.*

'Gemla Mask hovered over the dead man, drawing the spirit from his body, then danced ahead of the wild-eyed ghost, teasing him on and on until the ghost ran without prodding, ran and forgot what was, drew ahead of 'Gemla and vanished.

## 

Kikun stirred, blinked, got creakily to his feet.

With the Going-home closed out, the weight of the dead man was off his shoulders. The thing before him was only rapidly spoiling meat; the sooner they got rid of it, the better.

Rose looked up as he wandered into the inner office. The minicorder was sucking up data. It didn't need her, her hands were limp on her thighs, a sheen of sweat was drying on her face. "You're supposed to be watching."

"Jadii-Gevas watches."

"What?"

"Watch is being kept. Don't worry."

"One of your gods?"

Kikun blinked at her. "Say, one of my ghost brothers."

She looked wary, tapped restlessly at her thighs. "If it works."

"Want me to start cleaning away our traces?"

"Don't bother. You'd have to burn the place down to thwart the forensic machines the lice are bound to use. Even then. . . . " She flipped a hand, dropped it back. "With luck, they won't find him before we're gone. After that, who cares?"

## 

Fighting grime accumulated over the life of the building, they wrestled a window open on the third floor, flung him out.

It was like throwing a log, he was that stiff; he fell like a log, landed on the edge of the wharf, teetered there for a long moment. A gust of wind caught in his rucked-up jacket, swayed him just enough to tumble him into the bay. The

splash he made was swallowed by the other night noises and
he sank quickly out of sight.

Rose shivered, jerked the window down, ignoring the
squeal it made in its slides. "Let's get out of here. I need
sleep and a bath before I start getting ready for the Game.

## 7

Autumn Rose lifted the mask, dropped it over her head,
and adjusted the eyeholes so she could see without difficulty. It wasn't actually a mask, but a headsman's cowl in
soft thick velvet, long enough to fall in graceful folds over
her shoulders. She leaned closer to the mirror, adjusting the
folds to leave the deep vee of her dress uncovered and the
necklace of rough crystal and knotted silver wire.

Kikun moved into the mirror field.

Rose gasped, twitched, then had to rearrange the hood
folds. "Z' Toyff, Kuna!"

He grinned at her. "You look marvelous, Rose."

"Sss!" She smoothed her hands down her sides, the black
sychoura clinging softly to her palms. "Magical. Yesss."

After a last inspection, she straightened her shoulders and
went out.

## 8

The Mewa Room had eight sides and seven doors. Six
were doors to secure-suites for the Players. The High Vaar
went home for bed.

The seventh was the exit.

The room was rich with dark woods and green velvet, a
green-on-beige rug, rich red-brown wood paneling. There
was a deep glow from crystal lamps on the walls and the
massive chandelier hanging above the Vagnag table.

Low benches set against the walls between the doors were
piled with green and gold cushions.

Dasuttras were arranged like flowers among the cushions,
faces, bosoms, and arms printed with flowerforms in the
pink dyes of ancient custom, long hair down and gleaming
under chainmetal caps set with moonstones and jasper, ci-
trine and turquoise, peridot and aquamarine, semiprecious
gems catching the light like drops of colored oil. In one

corner two Dasuttras were playing flute and lute, unobtrusive wallpaper sounds.

Autumn Rose walked in and felt her soul expand. This was her realm, hers again. She belonged here. If she'd needed that little extra bit of confidence, the room gave it to her.

Three men stood beside the table talking in low voices, two hooded, the third, Jao juhFeyn.

He crossed to her, held out a silver brooch, a full-blown rose on a circle. "Autumn Rose."

As she pinned it on, Jao stepped back, gestured. "Sunhawk."

A tall paunchy man nodded. His brooch was a raptor on a rayed circle.

"Hiu-shark."

The second man inclined his head. His brooch was a leaping shark on a plain circle.

One by one the others came, each by his separate door, received his brooch and was introduced by his use-name. *Snowcat. Tanduk-viper. Direwolf.*

The last man was tall and solid, a crackle to him when he moved. His brooch was a barracuda arching openmouthed across a silver circle. When he saw Rose, he jerked his head up, turned to juhFeyn. "A woman?"

"You object?"

"If I did?"

"You're free to leave."

"I see." He shrugged, pinned the brooch on, and stood waiting for juhFeyn to seat them.

### 9

Kikun squatted in the corner and watched the Players roll for order. He smiled when he saw that Rose got the lead; it's where she wanted to be.

*Grandmother Ghost pinched his ear.* Get your mind on why you're here, lazy boy.

He forgot about the game and looked at each of the men.

*Oozing out of the wall, feathers rustling, brushing against him, small distracting tickles, Gaagi bent over him, whispered in his ear:*

This is catalog of men.

**Sunhawk: the High Vaar Tidak Beruba**

**Hiushark: Overleader of the Metug Pirates**

**Tanduk: Vaarlord of Haemunda Pamina**

**Snowcat: Zly Zlostin, the Vamcac of Dama'tvedd**

**Direwolf: Attata Marteau, exec of Cazar Company**

**Barracuda: Enfilik Abrusso, Grand Chom of the Mimishay Foundation, a Power in Omphalos**

Gaagi came whirling out of the wall, leaping high into the air, landed on the table, shook his behind in Barracuda's face. Xumady giggled, dived from the dark, and joined Raven on the table, doing a Mock-Shock Dance, a satiric curse on the target. They finished with a howl and a swirl and dissolved into the dark.

Kikun ignored them and watched Barracuda.

The Omphalite was angry. Every time he looked at Rose he clenched his gut. He was going to go after her any way he could. Kikun smiled. Good. That was stupid and it was likely to break him fast. Yes. The sooner the better.

## ##

The game started. The fine blonde hairs on Rose's forearms shimmered in the light from the chandelier as she dealt the cards.

## ##

At the end of the first Chapter, she was a net winner, having avoided the Grid for the moment, lost two Pen wagers but won the Holse.

Despite his irritation, Barracuda played cautiously; he won one table wager, lost the other, came close to breaking even.

Sunhawk played a meticulous game, had fair cards but bad combinations. That didn't seem to bother him. He was deeply content, his mind humming with the calcs that let him finesse a small win.

Hiushark was a plunger though he kept the lid on until he had the measure of the other players.

Tanduk was a fusser, but either his intuition snapped to with every card or he could beat a kephalos at calcs. He spread his bets over the number grid in carefully plotted patterns and ignored the Holse during the first Chapters.

Snowcat was slow, refused to be pushed; he played his cards with heavy slaps, threw the dice with a force that nearly took them off the table. He played the Holse and the Pen, ignored the Grid until the last Chapter before Break.

Direwolf played quickly, spread his bets on Grid, Pen and Holse, depended on instinct for the proportions.

## ##

The play was slow at first, the Players feeling each other out, setting down their personal minimums.

Black feathers brushed around Autumn Rose, black scales glittered over her head. Her cards were good, her throws brought fine combinations. Gaagi was her Luck, though she didn't know it. Kikun could feel her confidence growing, but she kept her caution until she knew the other Players and had a feel for the flow of the game, then held back still until the Break.

Kikun squatted in his corner, bored to stupor. He didn't play gambling games, he liked watching them even less. There was no talking, no witty or even unwitty exchanges to distract him from the soporific slap-click of the play.

His NO-SEE-ME ratchetted as high as it would go, he dozed, confident no one could discover him. He knew the man now, the target. Now all they had to do was take him. All I have to do, he dreamed, yes, Rose is out of it. I will take him. When the time comes.

He shifted from the squat until he was sitting with his back against the wall, let his eyes droop, and slept.

## 10

The stirring for the first Break woke Kikun.

The Players moved to the tables, filled plates with finger-food, handing these to the nearest Dasuttra to hold for them, pointing out what they chose to drink and waiting while Dasuttras poured these liquids into the special glasses juhFeyn provided, delicate flutes with angled glass straws so they could drink through the mouth slits of their cowls.

Kikun got to his feet, slid around to the eighth wall and collected a glass of wine, retreated to his corner where he sat sipping and watching the Players circle round each other trying to find some way to pry information out of the others without revealing anything about themselves. The idea of that snoopdance was mildly amusing, the actuality was boring.

## ##

Direwolf wandered over to Rose. "Autumn Rose," he said, sucking on his straw. "It's a name that resonates."

"Oh?"

"There was a game on Cazarit some decades ago. A woman who was also Autumn Rose played in the Prime seat. Blonde woman. Attractive. Very. Good player. Very good. Stylish."

"Oh?"

"Yes. Stylish. Had a way with the cards. Never forgot it."

"Ah."

"Going to be an interesting game, once it gets started."

"Ah."

He raised his glass to her, the straw tinkling against the sides, then went strolling off.

## ##

Barracuda stood close to his door, his eyes fixed on Rose. Kikun winced at the malice steaming off the man.

Grandmother Ghost pinched his arm and muttered in his ear: *Black bile man, he stinks, baby. You watch him, you hear? He's up to something and it's nothing good, you hear? Listen to your ol' gramma. You get over there. Stand in his shadow, baby. You let him get away he'll wreck everything, you hear me?*

Gaagi danced behind Barracuda, great black beak threatening the man, black scales glittering, wing feathers shuddering around him.

Abruptly, Gaagi froze.

Then he beckoned urgently to Kikun.

Kikun set his glass down, slipped around to stand behind the man.

Barracuda took a babi slin from the plate the Dasuttra held, ate it, held out his hand to the other attendant; she cleaned it with a lightly scented cloth. "That woman," he murmured. "Who is she? Why was she invited to this game?"

"You haven't heard?" The kneeling Dasuttra (a very young, very lovely girl) looked up at him, her eyes wide, glowing. "Ah, Senhuan, she is accursed of god and blessed by the Lady. She has won thirteen days running."

"That seems . . . unusual."

"No, Senhuan." The Dasuttra at his side had a deeper voice. She was older, surer in her beauty, sure enough to venture a small contradiction. "Jao juhFeyn certifies her, she is blessed by Luck, not by her fingers."

"Yes, Senhuan," the kneeling Dasuttra said, words coming out in a rush, "I have heard a woman was cured of muteness by the touch of her dress and the ringing in a man's ears went away and another dug in his garden and found a treasure someone had buried there." She looked over her shoulder at the other Players, leaned closer until she was nearly touching his long black robe. "It is said High Ones required her presence. The highest of the High."

Barracuda made a slicing gesture and the girl shut her mouth. He tapped her cheek, fished in his sleeve and set a gold emu between her lips. He dropped another emu in the plate. "Leave me," he said and waited till they moved off, then he swung round and pushed his door open.

Kikun followed him.

There was a short foyer, then a small but luxurious room, identical to the one Rose had. Barracuda crossed to a table with a black case on it, punched a code into the case's lock, and opened it.

A com. Shielded.

Kikun dropped to his hands and knees, scooted under the table.

He could hear the soft patter of a keypad as Barracuda entered another code, then waited, fingers tapping an irregular impatient rhythm on the tabletop.

"Black House." A man's voice, a light musical tenor.

Barracuda tapped a second code.

"Tinggal here." Another voice. Deeper, rougher.

"I need a team to pick up a woman."

"When and where?"

"Day or so. Tos Tous. Kipuny Shimmery."

"That's Truceground. We could be dispossessed if we break truce."

"She's offworld."

Silence from the com.

More tapping from Barracuda's fingers, speeding up as the silence stretched out. After another few breaths, he swore softly, said, "You know who I am."

"Yes. But you're only one. I answer to the whole Council."

"I see. There're crowds outside this place. The woman is a Luck Piece, that's what I'm told, the Draw. Send the team. They needn't come onto the Shimmery grounds, they can merge with the crowd, no one will notice them. As soon as she's clear, they can take her."

"You'll mark her?"

"Don't need to. Crowd'll mark her for them."

"Yes. Anyone you prefer?"

"Sul Purgis is available to head them?"

"Yes."

"Let him choose. I want her untouched, with her full vigor on tap. You understand me?"

"Quite."

"I'll join you in say . . . four days. Out."

Whistling breathily, Barracuda returned the pad to its slips and shut the case. Leaving it on the table, he strolled out, hands clasped behind him.

Kikun scurried after him, vibrating with anger.

Grandmother Ghost waited for him in the corner. Her outline was sharper, her colors stronger than they'd been in months.

*Look at him, baby. Monster. You know what he wants to do to her, don't you? Look at him look at her. I curse him, head to toe. May his feet crack open and rot. May the hair on his legs grow so long and thick he trips on it and people laugh like fools saying see the beast, see the stupid hairy beast. May his knees turn to stone and crumble when he moves, may he know pain without end. May his thing wither and fall off, may the rot enter his body and grow upward till it meets the rot in his brain. . . .*

Kikun tuned her out. He was sick with anger, but curses were futile things; the only one Grandmother Ghost's curses worked on was him. He didn't know what to do. Rose had forgotten him and he couldn't remind her without bringing himself into focus for too many of the others in here. Play had already gone on three hours, the next break would come after the tenth Chapter. Yes. Another three hours. Maybe. Unless play slowed. She'd have to leave then, comfort stop. Surely her bladder would force that. Did she drink?

*Grandmother,* he mindshouted, *quiet!*

*Grandmother the Lael-Lenox subsided to mutters, pinched him for his lack of proper courtesy to his elders. What? What is it baby? What do you want?*

Did Rose drink anything during the break? I don't mean just hold the glass, I mean really drink.

*Yes yes, that's smart of you baby. Yes. Two glasses of wine. That should hit her kidneys hard not so long from now.*

He settled back in his corner, arms crossed on his knees, and watched the game go on.

Gaagi's black wings fluttered about her and the cards came well for her, the dice came through again and again.

He could feel her feeling the flow. She began to push the game, her wagers challenges to the others, she played Holse and Grid and Pen with machine speed and sureness, reading the odds, running the calcs, everything in her coalescing for this Game.

She won.

She lost some of the table stakes, but won the Holse again and again.

Her pale skin shimmered in the glow from the chandelier, the fine blonde hairs on her arms were curved streaks of light. There was a power in her that the others felt. They couldn't see Gaagi's wings and glittering scales, but they felt them.

Kikun's anger faded into boredom again as the play went on and on.

He slept.

11

Rose came from the fresher, went to the mirror. She inspected herself, leaned closer, touched a fingertip to the slight sag under her eyes.

"Rose."

She straightened, wheeled, relaxed. "Kuna."

"Right." He dug his fingers into the folds under his jaw; he'd turned his options around and over and around again, he still wasn't sure about it, but he'd decided the truth was best and this was the best time to tell it. "Ah . . . mmm. Barracuda is Omphalos all right. He made a com call the first break. Black House. He's arranged to have you picked up the moment you leave the Shimmery."

She moved her shoulders, looked irritated. "I don't NEED this."

"Thought I'd better tell you."

"Yes yes, you're right. You've got your stunner . . . of course you have. Look. The next break, it's for a sleep session. Six hours. You remember . . . ah . . . according to. . . ." She touched her lips, frowned. "I was told he'd come by flit, if he came at all. It has to be parked somewhere close. While we're sleeping, you think you could find it?"

"Oh, yes."

She didn't try telling him what to do when he found it; one good result of a touch of healthy paranoia about being overheard, it kept her from belaboring the obvious, something she had a tendency to do. Irritating to be treated like a subnormal child.

"Right." She sighed. "It's back to work." She caught up the hood, slipped it over her head, adjusted the eyeholes. "Let's go, Li'l Liz."

12

Sunhawk was waiting when she walked in, standing apart from the others. His hood was a gesture, no more; everyone in the room knew who they entertained. His eyes flickered as Kikun slipped in behind her, then he forgot, Kikun's Gift wiping the image away, abetted by the obsession growing in him, an obsession that became apparent as soon as he spoke.

He touched her arm. "Autumn Rose," he said. His voice was a caress. "I haven't seen such play in years."

"Oh," she said. "I suggest you find a mirror; you'll see a better one than I am."

"Gracefully said, but not true." His fingers stroked the bird on the rayed circle. "Is this your profession?"

"No. I play when I have the time and funds. My life is elsewhere and I prefer it that way. A diet of desserts is quickly boring."

"Hmm. There's no time at the moment, the game is about to begin again. Consider changing your mind. I offer security—no, more than that—luxury, anything you want. All I ask is a game now and then." He lifted a hand. "No. Don't give your answer now. Not till the end of this Game. Consider where you are and what I can give you."

Kikun's ears twitched. The voice was genial, the words innocuous, but the intent behind them. . . . Oh, Rose, it's almost comical, half of Tos Tous is going to be waiting out there ready to grab you.

Grandmother Ghost the Lael-Lenox pinched his arm: *Just like a male, look at him, preening like a fool, tchah! just because that bitty chile does something he wants to get his hands on, he reaches out and grabs, didn't his mamah teach him better? But what's a mamah to a man once he gets his growth? You try going on like that round me, baby, I'll snatch you skinless, you hear?*

Otter leaned over, patted Grandmother Ghost on her head with his stubby handpaw:

You doing THAT dance again, old woman? Boring, boring, we heard it all before. Heard it all, heard it all, kvetching carping, boring, boring.

*I stop carping when you get a brain, hair fool!*

Kikun turned them all out, leaned against the wall, and tried to sleep. The Lael-Lenox was the sole female in his personal clutch of gods and sometimes found it necessary to defend all females in sight.

When she was in one of those moods, she was capable of raising such a storm, he threatened more than once to exorcise them all and find his peace in absolute, unadorned reason. The ultimate atheism.

They were powerful, though, these gods he'd birthed for

himself from his flesh and soul and the collective experience
of his people. They were not, perhaps had never been—even
in their crudest form when he was a child groping toward
consciousness—merely convenient ways of dealing with
parts of himself he was incapable of understanding. He knew
on one level that the only reality they had was what he chose
to give them, but at a deeper level by far, he NEEDED
them. They had a grip on him he'd never shake loose. Most
of the time he didn't want to. Most of the time.

He slept.

## ##

Grandmother Ghost pinched him awake when the Game
broke for the third time. The Players departed by their separate doors, Hadluk collected the women and took them
out. Jao juhFeyn supervised the cleaning of the Mewa
Room, took a last look round and went out, locking the
door behind him.

Kikun slipped away with the women, then followed
juhFeyn as Jao checked the Shimmery's security.

When Jao left for bed, Kikun undid the alarms on the
back door, went out.

### 13

Morning.

He collected a fork, a spoon, a plate and a cup from the
kitchen, then followed the girl carrying breakfast into Rose's
room, waited in a corner while she laid out the meal on the
table, knocked on the bedroom, got an answer, then left.

Rose came out yawning, blinked when she saw Kikun
sitting at the table sipping at pinkish-yellow fruit juice from
a crystal pitcher. She looked over her shoulder, shrugged,
came across and sat down. "I don't know who's listening."

Kikun leaned back, watched her pour the rest of the juice
into her glass. "No one."

She pulled her mouth into an inverted smile, shook her
head. "I don't know," she said, "maybe so. Well?"

"Found it. There's a park out back, chain fence around
it. Guards. Three flits in there. Black and silver one with
some kind of sigil on it, that's probably his. Didn't try to
get to it. No point in that, not yet. It'll be locked. He's

either carrying the keys or has them in his rooms. I'll take a look there during the first break. See what I can find.'' He yawned, yawned again.

"You look like someone's sucked the air out."

"Just tired. Lot of things going on. Takes it out of you, you know."

"Kuna, nothing's going to happen today, except more of the same. Why don't you stay here and sleep?"

"It's an idea."

"Have a nice hot bath, stretch out on the bed. It's a good bed, comfortable, lovely sheets, like this . . .'' she smoothed her hand along the heavy silken stuff of her dress, "only white."

"You sold me." He got to his feet. "You're just a wall away. You need help, scream."

She giggled. "Go to bed, Kuna. Scream, huh! Not likely."

He wriggled all over, shaking his skin along his bones, then strolled out.

The bed was as comfortable as promised.

He stripped, stretched out between the sheets, started to sigh and was deep asleep before the sigh was finished.

## 14

Grandmother Ghost the Lael-Lenox pinched him awake a short time before the maid came in to make the bed and straighten the rooms.

Kikun pulled on his clothes and strolled out.

Rose was talking with the Pirate who was describing an improbable fish he'd encountered in the Southern seas. Kikun listened a moment, drifted on. Must be using him as shield against the High Vaar, he thought. Tlee! what a bore. He stopped beside her chair, raised his brows. The small table where her stake was piled was bowed under the weight of the gold on it, more rouleaux piled beneath it and around its legs. Rose could have herself cast lifesize in gold and make herself half a dozen copies. How we're supposed to cart that off, even a third of it. . . .

Grandmother Ghost leaned into him, inspecting the pile: *Yellow peril, sad stuff, poison stuff, that chile has the right idea, baby.*

Otter giggled, faded when Grandmother turned to glare at him. He'd suffered his share of pinches and scolds and wasn't looking for more.

Blackbear touched Kikun's arm.

The maids were coming from the suites. They circled the room and left.

Kikun yawned and went to search Barracuda's room.

## 15

Rose shook him awake.

He sat up, bleary-eyed and yawning.

She laughed. "Scream, hunh!"

"What?"

"Just a comment, not a summons. Supper's laid. Get yourself up, wash your dishes, come join me."

## ##

It was a light supper, half of a smallish bird, soup, several rolls and a large salad. A pot of local tea sat in a quilted nest, a curl of steam rising from its spout.

After she divided the meal meticulously in half, they ate in silence for several minutes. "Find anything?" she said at last.

"He keeps his keys on him, or they're locked in the combox. Which you'd have to handle; my training lies in other lines."

"Hmm."

He drank the last of the soup, refilled his cup with tea from the pot. "You seem to be doing well at the Game."

"Well enough."

"Not excited? There's gold enough there to gild half the roofs in the city."

"Gold, tchah! Hadluk's been in this backwater too long, he's lost his perspective. You know, Kuna, I've played single passes where more value changed hands. Couldn't get enough gold in that room to interest some types I've been in games with, you know, like Ginny's clients. Well, that's not why we're here, is it."

"Is it?"

"Course not." She wrinkled her nose, then grinned at

him—and he found himself liking her better than he had for
a long time. "Sure, I hate to let that idiot Hadluk cheat me,
but no way I'm going to go running off with half a tonne of
gold stuffed down my front. My fun's in the playing. Riding
the high. I told you, I can always get money." She sobered.
"Just as well we're not planning to hang around after this
is over."

"High Vaar getting possessive?"

"You got it. He's bidding for a permanent partner. Got
so far as to say I'd make someone a fine wife, someone who
liked Vagnag, him for instance. Z' Toyff!"

"Well, it'd be an easy life."

"Wash your mouth out, saaaa, easy, that plasticman paw-
ing over me, make me sick just thinking about it. Besides,
I like my work. I'd kill myself if I had to sit around doing
nothing." She looked at her ringchron. "Time in. Where'd
I put that hood?"


## 16

The Game went on and on.

At the close of Chapter 30, the end of the second day of
playing, Autumn Rose sat like an icon of the Lady inside of
walls of gold, piles of gold, a black, white and golden image
with the fugitive glimmers of the crystal in her necklace.

While the attendant Dasuttras brought the gold she'd won
in the last Chapter, she got to her feet and walked out sur-
rounded by a tense and angry silence.


## ##

"Not taking it well, are they?" Kikun bit a piece out of
a chunk of green from the salad bowl.

Autumn Rose snorted, jerked off the hood, threw it at the
nearest chair. "They say they want a good game, doesn't
matter win or lose. Hah! What they mean is I'm gonna break
you to your last copper." She backed up to him. "Unbutton
me, will you? I want to get out of this."

He wiped his fingers on a napkin, began unhooking the
thread loops. "Sounds like you're not enjoying it any
more."

She shrugged out of the dress, draped it over her arm.

"I'd forgot how boring Forty Chapter gets," she said and went out.

"When you're winning," he murmured.

"I heard that," she called from the bedroom. "Win, lose, after a while it's all the same. Booooring."

He ate more salad and waited.

She came out pushing her arms into the woolly robe, tieing it tight around her. "Goerta b'rite, I'll be glad when this is over. One more day, Kuna." She dropped into her chair, poured herself a cup of tea and reclaimed the salad from Kikun. "One. More. Day."

"Hmm." He broke open a roll, spread butter on it. "What happens when it *is* over?"

She snorted. "What do you think? Hadluk and Pulleet will try to kill me if they see a way of keeping all the gold. Sunhawk, our esteemed High Vaar, will give his best shot at disappearing me into his little place on the hill there. Barracuda will be torn between knocking me on the head and hauling me off or waiting till I walk out and letting his thugs do the job."

He chuckled. "A piece to each, maybe?"

"Hunh."

"So?"

"So, I think Jao is likely to squash Hadluk's ambitions, I'm not going to bother my head about him. . . . hmmmm, you're stronger than you look, Kuna. Could you carry Barracuda any distance, like out back to his flit?"

"Why bother? I'll liberate a rolling tray from the kitchen, fold him up on it and wheel him out."

"Good enough." She emptied her cup, refilled it. "One more day, Kuna."

## 17

Restless after his long sleep, Kikun followed the cleaning maids from the Mewa room, went out and wandered the semi-streets about the Shimmery.

The crowds had left, gone home for the night.

That was usual. Once the sun went down, Tos Tous was dead. No lights and crazies in the shadows.

He wandered to the wharves near the Auction House. There was no sign Sai's body had been found. No new ships in port. Quiet. Dull. Ropes slapping, wood creaking. Not even a strong wind.

The Harbor Watch as usual hung about the incinerators spread along the bayfront, standing in clusters of two or three, talking, drinking, taking a leak over the edge of the wharf, strolling out to look up and down for stragglers trying to sneak onto the ships or steal the rescue ropes hanging in coils from mooring posts at intervals of half a kilometer.

Kikun drifted near one of those groups, listened to the men talking.

Nothing about Sai. One man was cursing his wife who'd walked out on him, going on and on about what he was going to do with her when he found her. After a while the others got bored with this and shut him up.

At the next incinerator a man had a pair of lottery tickets and the others were hooting at him, telling him the things were always rigged, he wasn't anyone's nephew, he hadn't a hope of winning.

"Better than that," he said. "I got a bit of cloth from her dress, slept over it, and dreamed those numbers. I'm gonna win, you'll see. . . ."

"Who'd you buy it from, Djikki the Snot? He stole my wife's sister's skirt off the wash line, tore it up, been selling it to any fool who'd bite."

"Naaa, I snatched it off a Angatine and she got it from some crip who tore it loose hisself. I saw the whole thing. I'm gonna win, I know it."

"You seen the woman?"

"Yah. Tall, skinny thing, bet you'd do yourself a misery on those bones you tried to djink her. Not bad looking. . . ."

Kikun moved on as the men traded comments on Rose's attributes, not especially flattering ones. It was their way of rebelling against circumstances that set them down at the bottom of their world, discards, straw to be walked on and used by the powerful. He understood it, didn't like it, was glad he didn't have to deal with the anger disguised by those mocking debunking words.

He met more of that anger as he walked along. The men by the bricks admired and hated Rose, used her as a way of talking about tabu things, complaining about her supposed excesses as a way of getting at the powerful they didn't dare speak against. The Players in that game of Topenga Vagnag could lose more than a hundred men could make in a year, a thousand men. Ten thousand like them. And who'd pay? They would, people like them. The Vaarmanta would squeeze their losses out of their people's hides. It was a story he knew only too well. It was happening on his world, the conquerors acting like conquerors everywhere, the sweat of his people paid for Daivigili excesses, kept the eternal queen in luxury. It was why he'd come away with Lissorn, to find help, weapons maybe, knowledge mostly, someway, somehow to throw the Daivavig out of Keyazee, send them back to their hot, dry southlands.

He twitched his ears, scratched at the skin folds under his jaw. Soon. Like Rose said. One more day.

He went to the Rumach, used the spare key, and went up to the attic where he'd hidden their gear after Rose left.

He roped the travelsacs to his back, went shuffling through the streets, his NOT-THERE blasting out to keep the predators off him. When he reached the Shimmery, he went round to the woodshed beside the fenced-in flit park and stowed his burden up in the rafters where only the spiders went.

Back inside the Shimmery, he found an empty room and curled up to wait for morning when juhFeyn would open the Mewa again and he could get to Rose.

## 18

Autumn Rose stalked in, tore the hood from her head and flung it on the floor, plucked the pins from the knot she'd twisted her hair into and tossed them on the hood. She shook her head, scratched her fingers vigorously through her hair, turning it into a fright wig. She flung her arms out. "Aaaaghhhh!"

Kikun chuckled, tilted his head. "Well?"

"Well!"

"Clean 'em?"

"Near enough." She scowled at a knock on the door, combed her hands through her hair, trying to smooth it down. "It's not locked."

Jao juhFeyn came in, Hadluk a shadow behind him. Jao bowed, straightened. "Autumn Rose, you are the sole net winner. Do you understand that you'll be paying my full fee?"

"You made that quite clear."

"Will you trust me with the count, or would you prefer to do it yourself?"

"Do it. I couldn't keep my eyes open. What do you charge for using your credit-link?"

His eyes laughed at her, his teeth were very white between the black beard and mustache. "Be my guest," he said. "My fee is large enough to embarrass even me."

"I doubt that, but I'll take your offer."

"No no, this is a win that will make legends, Autumn Rose. There'll be stories about it after we're both dead." He sobered. "You have your credit bracelet with you?"

"Naturally. When the count is finished, wake me. I want to transfer a third of the net to Helvetia, the rest I'll bank here. I have to pay my backers."

"Ah. I see. It will be several hours. Sleep well, you've earned it." He left.

Hadluk winked at her, followed him out.

## 

Kikun wiggled his ears.

Rose snorted. "All right, so I was exaggerating a little. It's nice to have and I don't like being cheated. And I knew about the credit-link when I said all that—so what? I meant it. In essence. If the credit-link weren't available, I'd walk away without a quiver."

"All right."

She yawned. "Let's get some sleep. We've got a few hours while they finish the count."

"I think we ought to talk about. . . ."

"Later, Kuna, later. Plenty of time."


19

Autumn Rose pulled the door shut, came in sliding the credit bracelet back on her wrist. "That's done." She flung herself into a chair. "Clearing up out there. Getting ready to put all that metal away." She checked her ringchron. "Two hours till dawn." She held out her arm. "Mark me, Kuna. I need to know where you are."

"Why?"

"Just do it, hmm? I'll explain in a minute. Hurry, we haven't got much time."

He widened his eyes, flicked his ears. If she wasn't going to talk, nothing he could do to make her. He looked past her.

Grandmother Ghost the Lael-Lenox was in the corner sitting on Otter's back, giggling in a way she had when something was about to hit him in the face. She wasn't going to talk either.

Sighing with exasperation, he nuzzled Rose's arm, felt her heat up and tremble. That wasn't something he wanted to think about so he didn't.

"All right, that's done. What now?"

"Hadluk and juhFeyn should still be out there. Take a look and see, hmm?"

He looked at Grandmother Ghost. She nodded. "I don't have to look," he said. "They are."

"Good. Kuna, stun them and tuck them away under one of those benches. We can't let juhFeyn button up this place, we need to leave without a major fuss. I have to get ready for Barracuda, so I can't do it."

"Barracuda?"

"Uh-huh. Second break, he made his move. Came on to me, strong." She grinned. "Annoyed Sunhawk which I wasn't unhappy about, you better believe. I made like I was fluttered and flattered by his . . . um . . . masculine force. Made an assignation with him for after the count. He wouldn't come here, the jerk, so I'm supposed to go across and knock at his door. Twenty minutes on. See?"

"Nice when they do it to themselves."

"Uh-huh. Got your stunner?"

"Rose."

"Sorry. So go, will you?"

## ##

Hadluk was stacking the last of the gold coins on the second cart when Kikun stepped into the Gameroom; juhFeyn was moving around the room, straightening a pillow or two, checking to make sure the maids had swept

properly and all the glass straws, spoons, forks, napkins and
other paraphernalia had been cleared away.

Kikun stood in the shallow recess of the doorway, waited
until both had their backs to him, lifted the stunner. For a
moment he couldn't touch the sensor, all he could see was
Sai falling and falling, hitting the floor, hitting the wharf,
falling into the water. His hand shook. Grandmother Ghost
slid a hand through the door, pinched him hard. He moved
his thumb, hit juhFeyn first, then Hadluk. Then scooted
across to them to make sure they were still alive, Grandmother Ghost clucking after him.

The pulse was strong under his fingers. He closed his
eyes.

Grandmother Ghost patted him gently, he could feel her soft
hands touching him:
*All right, baby, all right. Cum-ya, cum-ya, Gramma's chile.*

He got to his feet, began moving the bodies under the
nearest bench.

## 19

Rose turned slowly. "How do I look?"

She'd washed the coloring agent from her hair; it was
blonde and shining, hanging loose about her shoulders like
a spill of liquid gold. Her face was fair and flushed with
excitement, her eyes were blue again, sparkling with glee
and malice. The shining black dress clung to her torso,
swirled about her ankles.

"Barracuda will be enchanted."

She laughed, it was a wild sound, rather like the cough
of a cat on the hunt, big cat, lion lady, golden and ready.
Kikun's ears twitched and he was very glad he was dinhast
and too alien to be her prey.

She looked at her ringchron. "Time. Let's go."

## ##

Barracuda opened the door. "Lovely," he said. "You
surprise me."

"I hope so," she said and moved toward him, forcing
him to step aside.

Kikun tapped the trigger sensor, caught the man as he fell.

"Right." Rose straightened. "Get that tray, Kuna, faster we move, the better."

## ##

By the time he got back from the kitchen, Rose had stripped out of the dress, changed into tunic and trousers. She'd gone through Barracuda's suite, cleaned the place, including the case with the shielded com. "I thought I'd leave most of my stuff and clear him out. Might confuse folks about who did what to whom. For a while anyway. Anything moving out there?"

"No. Nothing till we hit the pad out back."

"Good. Let's go."

## 20

Thirty hours later, tired and grimy, but with everything they'd gone in for, they were in their ship on the isthmus and Autumn Rose was talking with Digby.

"We've got some strong leads and a prisoner. He's Omphalos, Kikun says, though his papers say Mimishay Foundation. Kikun thinks the oof'narc knows where Shadith is and the Dyslaera. We're going to talk to him in a little bit."

"Wait. If he's really Omphalos, you won't be able to touch him with what you've got on that ship. Bring him here."

"Now?"

"Fast as you can kick it. You can do stasis?"

"There's a box on board."

"Good, Keep him under, you don't want him suiciding."

"That oof'narc? He wouldn't. . . ."

"Listen, Rose. I don't care what kind of jerk he is or how much he loves himself, if he's pushed to the wall, he'll be dead before you know what's happening."

"Right. I didn't go to all this trouble to waste him. See you soon."

# UNPRISONER 1:
# First leg on the Shadow hunt

1

Weersyll 2 was a small rocky world inhabited by lichen and worms.

Weersyll the star was a hot greenish-yellow dwarf out in the middle of nowhere like a spark that popped from a fire into the middle of a black rug.

After the slavetrading debacle, when Omphalos acquired Bolodo Neyuregg Ltd. through heavily insulated surrogates, the reconstituted Company set up headquarters at the Bolodo substation on Weersyll—there wasn't a populated world in Known Space that would have them and they couldn't operate out of a Clandestine Hole.

The new set of Execs made the best of what they had; it wasn't bad. Weersyll might be in the middle of nowhere, but it was also equidistant from three clusters thick with planetbearing stars, clusters undergoing an explosion of development and lusting for cheap labor they could kick out once the job was done. Ships buzzed in and out every hour of the day and night, customers looking for specific types of laborers, transports bringing in cadres who'd finished their stints, taking other cadres from the domes to the worlds who'd bought their services, still more bringing in new contractees—surplus men and women who preferred the security of the cadres to starving, convicts dumped into bondservice by one world or another, people on the run from some danger or other, seeking safety in the anonymity of a labor cadre. Names didn't count here. There weren't even numbers. They were listed by cell prints and vended that way.

Omphalos hadn't bothered themselves about what happened to Shadith once they stripped what they thought were her memories and handed her over to the Contract market. All his annoying them got Ginny no farther than that. It did get him her cell print—and sneers behind their privacy shields, he didn't have to see their ugly faces to know that.

After he'd collected a Pilot, a pair of mercs, and a Sikkul Paem for drive crew at Ilkabahar Pit, Ginny headed for Weersyll and the Records of Bolodo Neyuregg Ltd. He spent the insplit time laboring in the workshop, retooling a number of the EYEs, constructing and programming specialized ticks and borers. He had everything he needed for the work, all the tools and materiel. The Omphalites at Mimishay had spread themselves on this ship; they drooled when they thought of Bol Mutiar.

On the fifteenth day the ship surfaced at Teegah's Limit and began moving sublight toward Weersyll 2.

## 2

A gnat among the swarming transports, the ship slid into one of the outermost slots of the orbitpark and settled to wait.

Three hours later there was a tentative flicker on his screen, then a harried face appeared in the center cell. "You haven't logged in."

Ginny waved the Pilot to silence and answered himself. "This is the *Caprisi Kumat* out of Blagn. I claim emergency status, glitch in the splitter. My engine crew are working on it at the moment. The chief is sure the matter can be rectified without outside help, so I have no reason at the moment to bother you down there. I just want a place to perch until the repairs are effected. You may have noticed there aren't that many systems about." He rambled on for several minutes longer repeating in other words and a dull monotone what he'd just said, watching the Controller's eyes glaze over.

Pushed to desperation, the man interrupted him. "Right. Emergency. Be sure you let us know if you're going to move again." The screen went gray.

Ginny smiled.

The Pilot raised her blonde brows. "That was easy."

He slid out of the Captain's Chair, stood with his hands on the arm. "It is all Traffic Control can do to keep the incoming and outgoing ships apart and at the same time juggle the shuttle slots. They are not about to challenge anyone who provides a reasonable excuse. I will be busy the next few hours, Mertoyl, same story for anyone who gets bothered by our presence.''

### 3

He transferred to the workstation, watched the shuttle traffic carefully, chose a moment when the confusion gave even him a headache and dropped a shell to the surface, its tiny fields lost in the soup. It curved through the thin cold air, went to ground over the horizon from the headquarters complex and the clustered mud-colored domes of the Levy Pens.

He shut it down and waited. One hour. Three. No reaction.

He cracked the shell, sent the EYEs flitting toward the Complex, ticks and borers piggy-backed on them.

The EYEs were tiny and relatively slow. It was nine days before they reached their target.

He spent a day exploring the outside of the massive headquarters building and another day insinuating the EYEs through outvents.

Down and down he sent them until they reached the memory banks of the Company kephalos.

For four more days he explored the hardware until he was sure he knew the configuration, then he flew the EYEs where he wanted them and offloaded the ticks and the borers.

And waited.

Nine hours later data began flowing into his kephalos, keyed by Shadith's cell print. A few clucks and a click and the flow stopped.

He triggered the secondary programs in his tiny vermin army, shifted to the Captain's Chair and called the Pilot to the bridge. "Be ready," he said. "Say nothing, just take us out on the route I planned."

He called Control. "Glitch repaired. Departing now."

The screen lit again. "Wait. What sector?"

"Take grid?"

"Send."

He tapped the sensor that sent his proposed exit route. He'd worked it out with great care, keeping to the least busy sector. It meant he headed nearly straight up, hitting the Limit at a wide angle from the orbital plane. Made navigation difficult once he was in the 'split, but it was more likely to be approved without argument.

"Path approved. Do not deviate, three transport convoys will be surfacing within the next five hours; approach the ecliptic and you will be warned then blown away."

"Information received. Will not deviate."

## 4

Ginbiryol Seyirshi sat in the Captain's Chair and smiled at the image of the world dropping away behind him.

In about thirty hours Bolodo Neyuregg Ltd would be out of business again. And Helvetia would be most annoyed if Weersyll accessed it at any time during that thirty hours— which was more than likely considering how busy the place was.

*There is a disease about,* he thought as he watched the sphere shrink, *warn your sexpartners, you poxy whore.*

# MIRALYS/DIGBY 2

1

Miralys stormed into the room, threw the flake on a table that appeared at her side, politely provided by the naked man lolling in the bubble hanging under the dome.

Digby stretched out on his stomach among flurries of bright cushions, propped his chin on his palms, and contemplated the Dyslaerin. "That's a major snit, Miralee, me-luv."

"Read that!" She slapped the table hard enough to make the flake bounce.

As a concession to public form, Digby closed his eyes a moment and pretended to scan what he already knew, then opened them wide. "So? Isn't it about what we expected? Except, perhaps, their rather excessive optimism as to the sum they're prepared to accept."

Miralys snorted, looked round for a place to sit. "I'm in no mood for your games, Digby."

"All right." His exaggerated sigh blew like a gale through the veils undulating about the room. "A good host honors his guest's grouches, even when said guest is self-invited."

Miralys gave the chair that appeared a hefty nudge with her thigh, then sat, lowering herself with undiminished wariness. "Better adjust your acid levels, Dig, you're beginning to sound bitchy. What do I do? That lot threw in so many cutouts, it'd take a century to trace them back."

He acquired clothing and sat up. "I assume you don't intend to pay the ransom."

"No. Only to eat the bastards raw." She curled her lips up and back, baring her tearing teeth in the Dyslaera threat-grin.

"Would you be willing to stall for a while, go through the motions of getting the cash together?"

"Why?"

"Late last night I got a call from Autumn Rose. No no, she doesn't know where your Ciocan is, but she's got her hands on someone who may."

"I thought she was. . . ."

"No, Kikun got them both clear. Seems they overlooked him."

She scowled at him. "How long have you know this?"

"A while."

"And you didn't bother telling me."

"No."

Her ears flattened against her skull, she started to get up, then, with visible effort she controlled her anger and resettled herself in the chair. "Why?"

"Kikun identified the enemy. Omphalos."

"And?"

"Omphalos has ties in places even I can't reach. Until this moment no one here knew but me."

"I see. And?"

"One. Don't talk about this. Two. Rose is bringing a package for me; when it's unraveled, I should know a lot more. A good possibility; I should have the location of Rohant and the others. Travel time's around four weeks, so you'll need to stall. Five million Helvetian gelders, could you raise that if you wanted to?"

"Not from Voallts Korlach. If I went to the Family. . . ." She extruded her claws, sheathed them. "We don't pay ransom." Her ears flattened against her head, she brought her claws out again, sank them into the simul-sides of the chair. "If I were serious about this, I'd have to take the Korlach public, bring outsiders in. No!"

"Tss, Mira-lili, you could start negotiations. Make it look right, but they don't have to go anywhere. Send off your reply, say you're going to need time, then start looking for buyers."

"Don't have to look."

"What?" Digby snapped his eyes wide. "Someone has approached you. I hadn't heard. . . ."

Her ears came up, twitched. "I am shocked, Digby all-knowing. Sssah!"

"Don't tease, Miree me-luv." He brooded a moment, then smiled. "Omphalos. It has to be."

"I couldn't say. The approach was through brokers, Vidloeg Gavinda of Helvetia."

"Hmm. Using Rohant as a lever into Voallts Korlach. Right. That gives the answer to how you're going to stall. Start talking with Vidloeg Gavinda."

Miralys' ears flattened again, her lips curled back, baring her tearing teeth. She hissed with rage.

"Restrain your instincts, Toerfeles. Go home and get ready to ride and make sure none of your people so much as sneezes beyond your compound walls. You don't want outsiders noticing, hmm?"

She stared at him, gold eyes blind with fury, then she bounded to her feet, scooped up the flake, and stalked out.

Digby clicked tongue against teeth, then faded from the bubble, sinking into the circuits of his kephalos as he began to ready his House for the Peeling of the Chom.

# SHADOW RUNNING

## 1

Matja Allina bent over the sleeping chal, touched his face. "His fever's down. What's the stump look like?"

The Herbmistress consulted her list. "It was checked two hours ago, cool, no infection. Um. Appetite good, wanted solid food, turned cranky when he saw the broth, but drank it down, ate his biscuits. We can send him home by the end of the week."

"Good." Matja Allina moved to the next cot and looked down at the form swathed in bandages. "Burns?"

"Yes. He's still alive, but we don't have much hope unless we can get him to the ottodoc in the Center at Nirtajai. Is there any chance of that?"

"I'll ask the Arring when he calls." She sighed, shook her head. "The Artwa isn't likely to spend fuel on a chal. Do what you can. Brushie healwomen have some herbal pastes they use on burns, summer Brush being what it is and summer storms. I'll send to see if they have something we can use." She bent over the motionless form, curved her palm over the bandaged face, not quite touching the cloth. "Amurra bless and give you peace." She moved on.

## ##

Aghilo looked through the door.

Shadith touched her arm. "The Matja says the world could burn down, but she's going to finish this first. What is it? The Arring?"

"P'murr's on the com, he wants the Matja."

"Tell him she's in the infirmary, it'll be at least another half hour before she's finished. Is it urgent?"

"I don't think so. He said they've taken the base."

"Good. We can do without more of this."

Aghilo mimed wing-flutters with her hands, her sudden

293

brief grin lighting her face. "And you won't be flying your bed again."

Shadith grinned back. "Right, it's a dead loss as a glider."


2


P'murr had a bandage on one arm and a new scar on his face; he looked exhausted, but he was smiling. "Flat," he said. "Razed to bedrock. Tumaks are dead or scattered with Brushie hunters after them. It was the fires did it, Matja. Bad enough when lightning starts the SummerBrush burning. They tell me this lot had the habit of riding out and tossing incendiaries for the fun of it. With the winds they have out here, nothing could outrun those fires and there were families caught. I wouldn't want to be a tumak in those hunters' hands. The result for us is good. We won't be bothered by tumaks. Not any more. When news gets back about what happened, danger pay won't do it."

"What did it cost us?"

"Five dead. The wounded? Every man's got a nick here or there, most of them not serious. Ten bad, but they'll live. Brushie healwomen are tending them. I suggest we leave them at the Mirp until they're fit to ride. We made a pyre for the dead and spread their ashes over the base site."

"Brushie dead?"

"I'm not sure, about twenty, I think. Most of their wounded are in good shape. If they didn't get killed, they just got a few scrapes, a broken bone or two. We owe this to the Brushies, Matja. They raided the base arsenal before the tumaks tightened security, they got grenades and guns and cussives. When we hit the base, they blew out the gunposts before the tumaks knew what was happening. We'd have had a lot more dead, if it weren't for that."

"Good work, P'murr. One thing. Before you come home, would you see the healwomen and ask what they do for burns? And see about the Bloodprice for their dead. I want that cleared as quickly as possible. We've a lot of rebuilding to do."

"Right. Don't relax the watch yet, Matja Allina. The bands that were outbase when we attacked are still around. Either the Brushies will get them or we will, but it'll take a while."

"I hear. Amurra bless, P'murr."

"Amur bless, Matja Allina."

Matja Allina touched the com off, slumped down in the chair. One hand absently patting Paji in his sling, she stared for a long time at the study wall. "Kizra," she said finally, "get the chapa Tinoopa, please."

## ##

"Chapa Tinoopa, send maids to the chalmistresses and chalmasters, I want a meeting in the West Reception Room; set the table up with pads and pencils, I want an urn of tea and those cheese straws Cook's got packed away. Tell the maids to pass the word that the tumak base is taken and burnt to bedrock. People should still be careful, but the worst is over. I'll need you here, too. We have to replant and rebuild or winter's going to be murderous. Go now. The sooner we start on this, the sooner it will be done."

When Tinoopa had bustled out, Matja Allina swung round to face Shadith. "Kizra Shaman, I'd like you to go back to the infirmary, the convalescent ward. Play your songs for them for an hour or so, brighten the day a little. It's a dreary place, such a dreary place. The rest of the afternoon is yours to do what you want."

### 3

By the time Shadith left the infirmary, the worst of the afternoon heat was over. The air smelled of dust and smoke, but the wind sweeping in off the mountains was damp and almost cool in comparison to the swelter of high heat. She found a hat, pulled it down to shade her eyes and wandered out to the paddocks east of the Kuysstead.

The Jinasu had the Kuyyot horses out for the first time in weeks; they were playing with them, riding bareback, racing them, joying with them in the return of their freedom to run.

Shadith climbed the fence, sat on the top rail with her feet hooked behind the rail below. She spent a while enjoying their enjoyment, it was a splendid antidote to the pain and boredom in the infirmary; then she swung the arranga off her back, began improvising to the beat of the horses' hooves, the high fluting laughter of the Jinasu.

They danced the horses to the music, black and gray and roan, pinto and bay, a mosaic of color and shape, necks arching, manes and tails swinging in the wind.

## ##

Jhapuki rode over to her, sat on the big black smoothing her hand along his neck, scratching through his mane. "Wanna ride?"

"Uh-huh."

"Done it before?"

"Yeh. Was years ago, though."

"Any good?"

"Not bad."

Jhapuki twisted her body around. "Ommla, get the bay gelding, the rocking chair, huh?"

## ##

Shadith slipped the strap of the arranga over her head, hung the instrument from the nearest upright, swung onto the bay's back—grabbed a handful of mane as he quick-stepped away. She'd forgotten how wide a horse was when you had to straddle the creature—and how quickly you felt his backbone in your tenderer parts.

With the Jinasu giggling with glee at her clumsy efforts, but patiently helping her to recover her form, she walked the bay around in circles. The girl whose body she wore now had ridden almost from the day she was born, so the body knew in muscle and bone what she had to relearn.

It didn't take long.

By dusk she had her balance back and her feel for the horse's rhythm; she couldn't come near the skill of the Jinasu, but she was racing with them, laughing with them, enjoying the play of muscles in the beasts, the sting of the mane against her face, the thunder of their hooves.

## ##

When she slid off the bay's back, her legs had no strength left, she crumpled to the ground, sitting splat in a pile of droppings.

The Jinasu held their sides and laughed so hard they nearly fell off their mounts.

She shook her head, laughing with them as she slid sideways onto a clean tuft of grass, wriggled back and forth to wipe her bottom off, then rolled onto her knees and staggered up. "Oh, god," she groaned. "Oh, god, I hurt."

She waddled bowlegged to the fence, crawled over it, collected the arranga and tottered back to the House.

## ##

Slowly, laboriously the Kuysstead recovered from the terror. New gardens were planted, ditches dug, and a waterwheel erected by the river to bring water to the plants. It was dry season, high summer, it wouldn't rain again until fall.

Matja Allina nursed her son and worked tirelessly to restore the Kuysstead, alive only when Pirs called.

Shadith continued her riding lessons and began gathering supplies for her flight to Nirtajai.

### 4

Aghilo came into the Matja's sitting room, stood quietly beside the door, waiting for Allina to look up from the account books.

The minute she saw the chal, Shadith knew what was coming; she set the arranga aside, crossed the room to Matja Allina. She touched the Matja's arm.

Allina yawned, stretched. "What is it, Kizra?"

"Aghilo."

"Oh." She set the stylus down, flattened her hands on the table. "Aghilo chal, come."

Aghilo walked slowly across the room, stopped beside the table. "I. . . ."

"Tell me quickly. Don't make me wait."

"My half sister, you know, Tribbi. She called to warn us. Mingas is . . . is bringing the Arring's body home."

Allina closed her eyes, moved her tongue over her lips. "Amurra. . . ." she said finally. "And the chals?"

"No. The Artwa must be keeping them. Tribbi says the only men with Mingas are his own guards."

"Aaaaah. . . ." Allina's hands twitched on the pages of

the account books. "Mingas. The Artwa isn't bothering to
come."

"So it seems. Um, Matja Allina, there's something else
Tribbi said."

"About Mingas?"

"Yes. He got drunk with his men and started boasting.
He's turned off his wife, sent her back to her parents. He
says he's going to get him a new one, a young one. Un-
spoiled. Ingva."

"I see."

"And . . . um. . . ."

"You don't have to tell me what he plans for me."

"Tribbi says he went into lots of detail what he was going
to get out of you. She didn't repeat any of it, just said it
was enough to make a goat sick. She called soon as she
could, he's still drinking, him and his men. They won't leave
the aynti until tomorrow sunhigh at the earliest which means
it'll be round sunset tomorrow before he's here."

"Yes." The word was hardly more than a whisper. Allina
shook herself, scrubbed her hands across her face. "Find
Ingva, will you, dear? Send her to me."


                              5

"That is what waits, daughter." Matja Allina leaned back
into Shadith's hands, closed her eyes a moment, sinking into
the calm Shadith was feeding her.

Ingva was more angry than afraid. She ran her hands
through her hair, caught up a china ornament, flung it
against the wall, hissed through her teeth as it crashed to
the rug, shouted curses she'd learned from the Brushies.
"H'Ra! Nguntik! No!"

The Matja straightened. "Listen to me. I want you to
think carefully, Ingvalirri. You have three choices. You can
wed Mingas. No. Listen to me. You'll have rights as a wife
you don't have as an unmarried girl and if you're clever
enough, you'll learn to manage him. You are clever enough,
you know. He's full of spite and anger and he's apt to take
out his frustrations on you, but he's stupid, stupider than
the Artwa without any of the Artwa's charm; you understand what that means."

Quieter now, Ingva twisted her face into a grimace of
distaste. "Gah!"

"You'd be comfortable, you'd have a place to be, plenty of food, clothes."

"No."

"I was hoping you'd say that. The thought of him. . . ." Matja Allina sighed and let Shadith once more soothe away her tensions. "I can send you to foster with one of my mother's brothers. They'll take you, find a husband for you when the time comes for that. And I'll see you have a proper dowry."

"H'ra! No." She snatched up another ornament, caught her mother's eye and set it gently down. "My uncles are. . . . No!"

Allina smiled. "They are, aren't they. You'll be safe there, but you'll have to be what they want. Are you sure?"

"Amurra! yes."

"You know what the third choice is, luv. Go Brushie. It'll be a hard life and a brutal one. You've seen enough of it to understand that, I think. I'll tell you this, Ingvalirri, if I hadn't met your father at just the right time, I'd be out there myself."

"Come with me now." Ingva rushed to her mother, dropped to her knees, caught hold of Allina's hands. "We can both go, take Yla with us. Just leave."

"I can't, luv. There's Paji. This is his Kuyyot, I have to hold it for him. Yla? She'd be miserable out there, she's not like you. And I'm too old to bend, daughter, I'd be a drag on you and the Brushies. And a danger. You'll be neither."

Ingva dropped her head, rested her cheek a moment against her mother's hands. "I'll come back and see you when he's gone."

"If you go, luv, don't yearn for what you've left behind. That's a chart for disaster. Believe me."

"I don't yearn for things." Ingva gave her mother's hand a last squeeze, got to her feet. "Only for people. Still," she rubbed at her forehead, frowned at the wall without seeing it, "I'm going to need things. What can I take with me?"

"Well." Matja Allina got to her feet, resettled the sleeping Paji. "Kizra, would you spend the next hour, please, with the convalescents? After that, do what you want for until an hour before supper, then I want to see you and Tinoopa in the Arring's study." She crossed to Ingva who was waiting by the door. "You'll want horses and gear,

Ingvalli. I'm going to give you your father's Blacks. I can't stand the thought of Mingas getting his hands on them. I'll tell him they were killed in the Terror. Sugar and cloth, guns. . . .'' Her voice faded as she went out and up the stairs with her daughter.

## ##

Shadith wrinkled her nose, got the arranga and went out. Singing for the maimed and the sick depressed her, but it was only an hour, then she could go riding for the rest of the afternoon. She was sore and stiff yet, but it was wearing off.

It was time to go. No more lingering or dithering. Leave or live under Mingas' rule.

Whistling under her breath, she strolled from the room.

# 6

Matja Allina walked beside the black horse her daughter rode. She walked with head high, her hand on her daughter's knee, signifying to all who watched her approval of this thing.

P'murr waited for them on the ferry landing. He stood beside Matja Allina watching Ingva nervously following the instructions of the ferryman as she led the two Blacks onto the ferry.

"I told you to go with her. You should have gone," Allina said.

"No. My fealty is with the Arring Pirs, not with his daughters."

"Pirs is dead."

"His son isn't."

"I see. Then you'd better move your things into the House and sleep each night in the nursery."

It was irony in her mouth but not in his ears; he bowed. "I will do so at once."

Startled, she watched him walk off; she hadn't realized how much he disliked her. He blames me for Pirs' death, she thought. I'm the reason he wasn't with Pirs and couldn't save him or die for him.

The sound of the winch motor changed. She closed her

eyes a moment, then turned slowly and watched Ingva lead
the horses up the far bank of the river.

She watched her daughter mount one of the Blacks and
ride off leading the other.

Ingva neither turned nor waved.

Matja Allina stood silent on the landing until the Brush
had swallowed Ingva, then she turned and walked back to
the House. Her head was high, her eyes blind with the tears
she wouldn't shed.

7

Matja Allina's face was drawn, weary beyond description. She waved the two women to chairs across the table
from her and began talking without bothering with any of
the usual courtesies. "Pirs was determined to keep you here
the full year of the bargain." She curled her hand under the
weight of her baby, not so much holding him as taking comfort from him. "He thought we'd need you even more while
Paji was getting through these first months, the hard months.
Things . . ." she swallowed, "things have changed." She
eased forward, careful not to wake the baby. "I want you
to have these." She lifted the rolled-up documents from the
table, held them out. "The papers Pirs signed on Paji's
Nameday."

Shadith leaned over, took both scrolls, looked down at
them. The names were written on the outside. She handed
Tinoopa her papers and sat holding her own.

Allina flattened her hands on the table. "Kizra Shaman,
you've been working up to leaving us."

Shadith gaped at her.

Allina shook her head, "My dear, you have forgotten
how small a place this is. Everything is known. You might
as well have shouted it from the roof."

"Oh."

"Yes." Matja Allina touched her tongue to her lips. She
started to speak, changed her mind. For several minutes
there was no sound in the room but the whine of the wind
outside and their own breathing. "Mingas . . ." she said
finally.

Shadith nodded. "You told Ingva," she said. "Stupid,
malicious, a weak man, a bad man." She thought a minute.
"And ugly."

"Yes. Utilas has been the heir, Pirs . . . was the . . . the beautiful one . . . the one everyone liked. . . ." Allina closed her eyes, pressed her lips together. She shook off the weakness, went on, "Rintirry was the baby, spoiled, you saw him. Mingas was the accident. He was a son so he was adopted into the family, but the Artwa never bothered to marry his mother. I remember her . . . she was still alive when I married Pirs. . . ." A long shuddering sigh. "Now he's got his chance. I know he's talked Angakirs into appointing him Paji's guardian. Otherwise it would be Utilas coming with the . . . with the body."

"When he finds out you let Ingva go. . . ." Tinoopa tapped the papers on the curve of her knee. "What can he do to you?"

"Whatever he wants. Oh, not legally, but who's to see out here? And he has his guards with him, like the pair he brought with him to the Nameday."

"Thugs."

"Yes."

"What about Yla?"

"As soon as I can, I'll send her to fostering. He can't stop that. She's too young for marrying. While they're still children, girls are the mother's responsibility."

"Will he marry you?"

"Not during my year of mourning. Not marriage."

Shadith stirred. "Look, Matja, you don't have to take this. You should get out of here. With Yla and Paji. You could come with me, or go to the Brush."

Allina tapped her fingers on the table top, a curiously restrained expression of the passion Shadith felt seething in her. She shook her head. "No. This House, the land, they're Paji's birthright. I will not let that viper steal them from him."

"A pillow over Paji's face, that's all it would take to clear title, isn't that right?"

"Oh, yes."

"You want us to guard him? If you can't stop Mingas, how could we?"

"You couldn't, Kizra Shaman." She twisted her fingers together, stared past Shadith at the wall. "I will. I will do anything I have to."

"Oh."

Allina shivered, flattened her hands again. "I'm still the

Matja here. Until tomorrow night. I can give the two of you what I choose to give. Kizra Shaman has chosen her way, what is yours, chapa Tinoopa?"

"I'll wait here, thank you. I'm too old and fat. And citybred besides. I know from jits, not horses. Fall off and kill myself two kays out." She looked thoughtfully at Matja Allina. "You want to be very careful or you'll bring down the roof on you and the children."

"What?"

"Something happens to Mingas, hmm, the Artwa doesn't like you, thinks you're uppity. I've run into that myself. Way things are here . . . how old's Utilas' son, or is he the next heir?"

"You have it. The oldest inherits unless he's totally unfit and Rulas isn't. He's . . . a lot like Pirs. Reelyn is the second son; he's a little younger than Rintirry was. I don't know much about him . . . which is . . . good."

"Right. Then Utilas won't be wholly hostile to . . . um . . . say Fate for giving young . . . what was it? . . . Reelyn a break. That's a plus. What's he think of Mingas?"

"Detests him."

"Another plus." Tinoopa frowned at the roll of papers. She made a circle of thumb and forefinger, began sliding the roll back and forth through the round. She looked up. "Mind some blunt speaking?"

Matja Allina smiled wearily. "I haven't so far, have I?"

"Do you want more children?"

Allina touched her fingers to her lips. A sudden wave of grief and pain and loss rolled out of her, filling the room like fog. Tinoopa didn't see it, but Shadith was almost drowning in it. "No," Allina whispered. "Pirs is dead. I'm an old, old woman. No."

"Right. I got to talking with a circle of Brushie healwomen. During the Shearing, it was. You've some interesting herbs on this world, hmm, when you're feeling more like talking business, I know a drug prospector who'd be interested, we could work out connections with the Pharmaceuticals, improve your credit line. We started out, the healwomen and me, talking about contraceptives and abortifacients. Subject of rape came up. Told me sometimes tumaks come looking for Brushie girls, drunk enough they'll jump anything with a hole in it and it's safer to meddle with Brushies, no blood feuds or private wars brewed up that way. If the Brushie girl's family catches him, well, they find themselves a s'met colony, bury him up to his neck next to a mound, and smear his face with sugar syrup.'' She smiled. Not a nice smile. ''My youngest daughter, I lost her to a diaper salesman. That's not what you think, he sells children to pedophiles. I never found him. I ever do, I'll bring him back here. Well, that's beside the point. Sometimes, the tumak gets away. Keeps getting away. Comes back time after time. The healwomen go round the Mirps and choose someone, a woman, maybe even a girl, someone who doesn't want children and is willing to take a chance on being killed. They prepare her, stake her out for the Sekerak, that's what they call him, though I suppose you know that. Sooner or later he takes the bait, does the deed. Before the month is out, he's dead. The girl's sick for a while, the ointment dries her up inside and the antidote turns her eyes yellow, but they say she doesn't mind and afterward she's fine. Sterile, but fine.''

Matja Allina contemplated the older woman for several moments. ''If I were wise, I would say interesting but nothing to do with me. I'm sorry about your daughter, that's true.''

Tinoopa shrugged. ''It was a long time ago.''

''In some things, time has no meaning.''

''No.'' Tinoopa drew her thumb along her jawline. ''You're wrong there, Matja. It does have meaning, what I'm saying is this: grief heals and rage cools.'' She dropped her hands onto her thigh. ''But you're also right, hate doesn't die, it just gets old and cold and harder than stones.''

''Yes.'' Matja Allina got to her feet. ''Kizra, you'll have to leave by dawn tomorrow so you'll be far enough away by the time Mingas arrives that it won't be worth the danger going after you. I can supply you tonight. Afterward. . . .'' She shrugged. ''It's short notice, I'm afraid, but you were going anyway. So. Make a list, let me know what you'll need.'' She didn't wait for an answer but turned to Tinoopa immediately. ''I will take supper in my room. When Kizra's list is ready, bring it to me. I'll mark what I approve and authorize you to dispense the materials. Be careful around P'murr. He isn't liking me much these days so he'll do what he can to make problems for anything I try.''

A knocking. "Kizra?"

Shadith rolled out of bed, pulled the robe around her and crossed to the door. Yawning, she let Tinoopa in. "That time already?"

"Not quite. Cook's got breakfast ready for you, some sandwiches for later, she's waiting to give you a sendoff."

Shadith ran her hands through her hair, scrubbed at her eyes. "Gods, does everybody know? Some sneak."

"Sit down a minute. Want to ask you something."

Shadith dropped on the end of the bed. "Huh?"

"The Mindwipe didn't take, did it?"

"There were um complications the operator didn't know about. Things came back to me."

"And you know where you're going, what you're going to do, who you're going to call?"

"Yeh."

"I thought so. Catch."

The sac landed in Shadith's lap with a series of dull clunks. It was heavy. She loosened the drawstrings, pulled the neck open. Coins inside. She raised her brows.

"Incentive," Tinoopa said. "I'm a thief, remember? What I'd like you to do, get word to my son where I am. Jao juhFeyn. He runs a tavern called Kipuny Shimmery on a world called Arumda'm. Iskalgun 9. Let him know where I am. All right?"

"Consider it done."

"Thanks. The Matja authorized hot water. At least you can ride out feeling clean."

"Tinoopa, this Mingas . . . he's mean, maybe a bit crazy."

Tinoopa waggled a hand. "He's not going to live long enough to be much trouble. If the Matja doesn't get him, I will."

"All I can say is, I'm glad I'm going to be somewhere else."

"Interesting times." Tinoopa straightened. "The Lady bless, young Kiz." She left.

Shadith cupped her hand under the sac, hefted it. "Well."

*The weight of it makes all this real. No more dreams, no more dithering. In a few hours I'm going. I'm really going.*

She felt like throwing up.

*Terror, that's what it is. Sheer sick-making terror.*

Swearing under her breath, her legs shaking, she stood, tossed the money sac into the knot of quilts, and went out.

9

Shadith rode out from Ghanar Rinta an hour before dawn.

She had a packer on a lead rope, one of the rough-coated ponies that the shepherds used; she rode a small sturdy bay pony with a black mane. The Matja had offered horses, but the Jinasu Jhapuki insisted on the ponies. *It's a long way,* she said, *horses will die on you, get a notion in their silly heads and go down and they won't get up. The ponies won't go fast, but they'll get you there. Walk as much as you ride and give them plenty of time to browse.*

The Matja had provided a map, with roads and ayntis marked on it, notes Pirs made about water and campsites, estimates of time between trailmarks, notes about ambushes, the map he usually carried around in his gear. He'd left it behind when he took the chal and the supplies to Caghar Rinta.

The pony's head bobbed rhythmically before her, his hooves beat out a slow syncopation on the hardpan underfoot, his tail switched, now and then stinging against one leg or the other. Mesmerizing. Put her into slowmotion, into a drifting inconsequent reverie. She thought about memory.

Memory was everything.

Its fragile, dead-leaf lace was threaded through her present and in a way controlled her future.

When her memories were temporarily displaced, she turned passive, fearful, every step she took threatened to drop her off the brink of the known; in a way her brain and body began reverting to the dead meat she'd revivified such a short while ago. Only her underlying toughness and the prodding of those nightmares she'd resented so much had kept her alive in those pre-lizard days. The nightmares and Tinoopa providing a stable pole she could revolve about.

After this business was over, if she survived it, she'd move with measurably less assurance through her days. That was one thing she'd learned. Another thing—maybe more important—was how desperately she needed other people in her life. She'd known people quietly content with living alone, preferring a filled solitude to empty company, but these were always settled into stable societies where tradition and the ambient culture were sufficient surrogates for family and friends.

*It's what Aleytys was hunting for all those years. A context. That and a family to replace the one that drove her out. She's got it now, family and friends and work. I want that. Not the details. Gods, I'd be petrified on Wolff, I don't even like Grey that much. Family and friends and work. . . .*

She thought about Mingas, the Artwa, Matja Allina in the prison of her culture, wasted and unwanted, distorted by what was demanded of her and by what was forbidden.

*You'd better be careful what kind of context you pick, Shadow. Very careful. There're downsides to everything, you want to be sure what they are before you commit. Ay-yah. That's the third thing you've learned here and likely the most important.*

## 

She pushed hard at first, letting the ponies alternate between a fast walk and a canter; riding the little bay was like sitting a jit on a corduroy road, but she spared neither herself nor her mounts.

The day heated up as the morning winds dropped and finally she knew she couldn't go much longer. She let the pony slow to a tired shuffle and fished out the map. The brush on both sides of the rutted dirt road was a meter higher than her head. There was nothing else to see but the tan road and a sky yellow with a punishing heat. She checked the angle of the sun. Almost directly overhead, around a half-hour past sunhigh. She pulled the map into the shade of her hat brim to cut the dazzle of the parchment, squinted at the tiny black writing. There was a bridge some way ahead, built over a wide swooping bend of the river that ran past the Rinta. Water and browse. A good place to stop and wait out the worst of the heat.

She folded the map again, tucked it into the saddlebag, and slumped into the sway of the pony's walk.

## 10

She reached the bridge at the beginning of the fourth hour past sunhigh.

The river was silt-laden and sluggish, but under the pohn trees there was a tentative small breeze that hugged the water and barely stirred the stiff leaf lozenges and the shade was balm for her burning eyes.

She watered the ponies, stripped their gear off, gave them some grain on a square of canvas, and left them to eat and browse as they wished. She hung the saddleblankets over a low limb to dry out, laid down her groundsheet and stretched out on it, using the saddle as a pillow. She was asleep in seconds.

## 11

It was two hours later when she woke, she was sticky and sore, she had a crick in her neck and a hollow feeling in her stomach. The shadows were longer, thicker, the sun low in the east. She sat up, rubbed at her neck and *felt* around for the ponies.

They'd stayed close by; they were nosing among the dried grasses under the trees, nipping at choice bits and chewing patiently once they had a mouthful.

She dug her fingers into her hair, scratched extravagantly. "Half a day . . . Sar!"

She dug the map out of the saddlebag and sat studying it. "Well, Shadow, I might as well spend the night here, can't reach the next water before dark. Hmm. Looks like I'd better do some planning, isn't going to work riding straight through, that sun's a killer." She scowled at the map, dismayed by the tiny distance she'd covered in those hours of riding. At this rate, it'd take forever to reach Nirtajai.

A high whining broke through the whisper of the leaves, the mutter of the river.

Off to her left a black dot arced by, cutting in and out of sulfur-colored clouds, gone before she could get to her feet.

"Mingas. Ahead of schedule. Hunh." She yawned,

rubbed at her eyes. "Since I'm going to spend the night here. . . ."

## 12

She sat watching the fire die. The wind was rising; the clouds had blown away, taking the heat with them; the blanket round her shoulders actually felt good.

Alone. She was starting to feel comfortable with that. As long as there was an end to it. Comfortable. Even happy.

*I know what it is. I'm not drifting any more. I'm doing something.*

She wrapped the blanket around her, stretched out on the groundsheet, her head on the saddle.

*Even if I had to get booted into it.*

She sighed with pleasure and gazed up at the sky; the moon hadn't risen yet, the stars were thick and brilliant. It was like the sky she'd seen as a child when she was so young she still had the skin on her eggsac slinging.

## 13

A spark popped from the circle of stones, landed on her hand, startling her awake.

The Raska Tsipor pa Prool was sitting across the fire from her, watching her.

"You built it up," Shadith said.

"Yesss."

"Why?"

Tsipor shrugged her narrow shoulders.

"You want something?"

"Omphalos."

"What?"

"You going to make them hurt."

Shadith wriggled free of the blankets and sat up. "That good or bad?"

"I felt your purpose. I came."

"Huh?"

"To ss-see them hurt."

"At the moment, I'm not too capable of hurting anyone."

"You will. I feel it." Her black eyes reflected the flames; she undulated her torso; her mouth was open a little and her thin black tongue flickered in and out of the gap. There was a force in the woman, something unleashed in her that she'd kept hidden all the time she was in the truck and at the Rinta.

"How? I mean, what're you talking about?"

Tsipor did an odd, twisting movement of her hands. Talking seemed difficult for her. "I know. I come with you."

Shadith frowned. Oh, hell with it, she thought. "Why not."

Tsipor nodded. She came round the fire, reached out, held her hand above Shadith's arm, not quite touching the skin. She waited.

"All right," Shadith said.

The hand touched her, soft, warm, dry. Power flowed into her, jolting her, as if she'd stuck her finger in a light socket. After her first startle-reflex, she *reached*.

There was a horse a short distance off, tied to a tree with a tether long enough to let him graze on a patch of grass.

There were l'bourghhas sniffing round the ponies. She twitched a nerve in the predators and sent them running off. The ponies kept on grazing and didn't know what had just passed by them.

Her *reach* leaped beyond the horizon, all the way back to the Kuysstead. She felt Allina's anguish, Mingas—she wrenched herself away from him, sickened.

She touched the back of Tsipor's hand.

The Raska moved away, the powerflow was gone and Shadith felt deeply diminished, as if she'd suddenly gone deaf or blind. It took minutes for her sense of herself to settle.

She contemplated Tsipor. "I look through beast eyes, do you look through mine?"

Tsipor nodded.

"Telepath?"

Tsipor shook her head. "Not thinking, feeling." She held up her narrow hand. "Only touching."

Shadith relaxed. "Why don't you go untie your horse, let him graze. I'll bring him in when it's time to start on. Unless you. . . ."

"No. Is feeling, is not riding. Is not like yours. Is other
things, but. . . ." Once again she did that painful twist of
her hands, it seemed to be her equivalent of a shrug.
"You had something to eat?"
"Yess. You sleep. I watch."

## 14

On the second night, Shadith gazed across the fire at Tsipor. "Tell me," she said.
The Raska nodded. Her story was a performance, part
body (a dance of torso and arms and face), part words (single words, short phrases), part ghost images that appeared
and dissolved between them.
Despite her resemblance to the Cousin baseform, Tsipor
pa Prool was not a Cousin; her way of seeing and saying
was skewed at an odd angle to Shadith's so Shadith was
never quite sure she understood what Tsipoor was saying to
her in her multilevel langue.

*IMAGE: Sipayor siRasaka, Tsipor's homeworld. Sense of
dryness, of complexity—crystalline? Scoutship finds it, the
sigil on the ship is the circled spiral of Omphalos. Something happens. Omphalos controls the world now. Omphalos
is doing things to the Raskas, making them different? Sur-
gery? Forced breeding? Terror, anger, grief.*
*IMAGE: Raska males, conical mounds of flesh, can move
some, slowly, sloooowly, prefer stillness, contemplation.
Makers of songs and joy. Receivers of life, taking, fertilizing, incubating the eggs of the Raska females.*
*IMAGE: Mating rite, wonder, power, pleasure. Raska fe-
males dancing in the light of seven moons, rubbing themselves against the male, mindflow as music. (Shadith heard
it as a grand symphony played by an orchestra of hundreds).*
*IMAGE: Time has passed. The Raska females return to the
male, deposit eggs in the prepared cavities of his spongy
flesh. Explosion of tenderness. Love. Joy. And then, Omphalos came.*

Tsipor wept, not tears, but with her hands and her pain.

*IMAGE: The eggs cut from the male. He keens his agony
and his loss. The females tied to him come racing to him.*

*Are captured or killed. Tsipor is one captured. The male
dies. He cries out his grief, his pain, and dies. She feels
him die. Her sister/mates die. She feels them die.
Omphalos keeps her alive. Alive and alone.*

Tsipor cut off the story at that place. What happened after
that did not matter; she would not speak of it. "Why?" she
said finally, her hands and body repeating her confusion,
her anguish. "Why make such pain?"

"Don't ask me," Shadith said. "I didn't understand
Ginny, I don't understand Omphalos. Tell you true, I don't
want to. I'd be afraid it'd rub off on me."

### 15

They rose before dawn, rode and walked, walked and
rode to the next water on the map, slept through the worst
of the heat, rode and walked, walked and rode for several
hours after sundown.

Day faded into day.

They saw no one, no traveling chals, no wandering Brushies or tumaks, no trucks on the road or skimmers overhead.

After the second night they didn't say much to each other;
there was no need.

### 16

On the fifteenth day, shortly after dawn, four silver
spheres flared into sudden visibility, before, behind and on
each side of them. Tsipor and Shadith shot at the same time,
each hit their mark, but the pellets rebounded from the
spheres without damaging them.

"I permitted that as an exercise in futility."

"I know that voice," Shadith said. "Ginny?"

"Singer."

"What do you want?"

"Not your death."

"That's obvious. You don't waste words on targets."

"Yes. I will be joining you in one moment. I prefer not
to have to wait for you to recover from a stunning, so stay
where you are."

"All right."

## ##

A small flit dropped to the ground ahead of them, opened
up its side. Ginbiryol Seyirshi stepped onto the ramp, beckoned to them.

Shadith kicked her heels into her pony's sides, dropped
the lead rope, and rode forward.

Tsipor pa Prool stayed back, watching, rifle held loosely
under her arm.

Ginny held up a hand. "Truce," he called out. "Do you
agree?"

Shadith stopped the pony five meters off, sat frowning at
him. "Last time you didn't bother asking, just grabbed.
Why all this?"

"I need your active cooperation."

"Why should I have anything to do with you?"

"Omphalos."

"The enemy of my enemy is my friend? I never much
believed that."

"Does it matter? No matter what you think of me, you
do have friends and Omphalos has them. Not for long. Ex-
perimental material has a short life line in their hands."

"Why should I believe you?"

"*Read* me."

"Tell me."

"Destruction breeds round you, Singer. I need you."

"I don't trust you. I can't."

"Your own words, Singer. Last time I didn't bother asking, just grabbed. We both remember how wrong that
went."

"True. How did you get away? You were a prisoner, wer-
en't you?"

"They meant to use me to take a world for them, so they
sent me out on a ship with a workshop built to my specifi-
cations."

"Fools."

"Yes. As big a fool as I was, trying to contain you."

"Truce till when?"

"One year, during which time neither attempts to kill the
other."

"Good enough. One last thing. My companion. She has
reason to loathe Omphalos. She comes."

"Necessary?"

"Yes."

"Agreed, provided she swears truce also."

Shadith twisted around, waved Tsipor to them.

The Raska came slowly, her dark red eyes fixed on Seyirshi.

"He offers truce," Shadith said. "While we go after Omphalos."

"Iss true ssaying?"

"At the moment."

Tsipor flipped the rifle around, handed it to Shadith. She slid from the saddle with a boneless ease and walked up the ramp. She stopped in front of Seyirshi, reached toward him.

"Let her touch you, Ginny. There's no harm in it. Tsipor, the right arm, not the left."

Tsipor pa Prool dropped her hand lightly on Seyirshi's true arm, jerked it away, hissing as she did so. She stepped back, turned to face Shadith. "Bad," she said. "To trust, now iss yess."

"All right," Shadith said. "We're in."

# DYSLAERA 11:
# Rohant edges toward escape

## 1

Rohant lay on his back, his hands resting one below the other under his ribs. It was dark in the cell, as dark as it ever got, the lights in the corridor outside dimmed to a grayish twilight.

## ##

As he had night after night for weeks now, Miji the sakali trotted along an unlit corridor, frill erect, senses alert for insomniac wanderers. It was about an hour before dawn on a night as uneventful as last night and the night before and the night before that, and so on, but he was never at ease inside the prison wing.

## ##

For weeks now Rohant had been using the sakali like a blind man's cane, probing the corridors around his cell and throughout the prison wing.

It was a frustrating process. He could not see through Miji's eyes, or hear what he heard, he could only read the sakali's reactions, feel the play of his muscles. Despite this he was acquiring considerable information about his surroundings. Dyslaera had unusually accurate perceptions of distance, direction, and duration. Each pitpat of Miji's tiny feet told him more about the maze around him.

The Omphalites took him out of his cell nearly every day, sometimes twice. Every five days they took him to the exercise court so he could wash, get some sun and work the kinks out of his body, running round and round inside those slippery walls. The other times he went to the saferoom where the techs made lifeflakes of him. In the first one they made him shave off half his mustache, then read out a message to Miralys. The degree to which his half-mustache grew back was a timing device for subsequent flakes, evidence that an extended period was being recorded.

And they took him to dine with the Grand Chom who discarded his mask and robes for these encounters.

The serviteurs were androids, not flesh to be shocked by the Chom's departure from the rules of behavior before outsiders. There were no guards inside the room, but he wasn't being foolish; there was a stunfence down the center of the table, ceiling to floor, between Omphalite and Dyslaeror.

"Come here," he said, the first night they dined.

Warily Rohant came toward him. He touched the screen and went down.

He was out for twenty minutes.

When he woke, he found that the serviteurs had lifted him away from the screen, settled him in his chair, crossed his arms on the table, laid his head on them.

"A lesson," the Grand Chom said. "It's a stunfield. It won't kill you, you're much too valuable to waste."

The third night they dined, the Chom showed Rohant the flake they'd made for Miralys. Rohant shaving half his mustache, then reading the statement. Then six successive views with related physical data, then the final message detailing how the payment was to be made. "We have you," he said. "If your Toerfeles wants you back she has to sell us a piece of Voallts Korlach, she won't be able to raise the ransom elsewhere, we've seen to that. And once we have the piece, we have the whole." He held his hands up, closed them into fists. "Before the year's out, your Toerfeles will be working for us."

Rohant said nothing. Let the Chom think he was chagrined by this development. He wasn't. It wasn't going to happen. He'd learn his mistake when Miralys was standing in front of him tearing his throat out.

They kept flaking Rohant every two or three days after the first demand was sent out. They've done this before, he thought, they're almost as slick as they think they are.

He hadn't been called to dinner for over two months. The Chom was away somewhere, or so the gossip went. He didn't know if he missed it or not. The food was better than he got in his cell, but the company took his appetite away.

## ##

Miji pattered through the corridors, growing more restless as the minutes passed; dawn was approaching and he needed to be out of this place and in his burrow before the sun was up.

Rohant brought him back through the maze of corridors, took him out to the exercise court; he gave the sakali a mindrub, felt him wriggle with pleasure, then let him go.

Miji dived into the murky water of the sump, swam vigorously through the outflow pipe and went scurrying off, hurrying to get home before the sun brought the tjejunga birds out hunting for stray sakalis and other small-lives.

## ##

He was ready to go.

He had his escape route planned. Into the Novice living quarters, out into the Novice garden, through the Pleasure House to the Postern Gate that stood open night and day (far as he could tell), propped open by something cold and heavy that Miji didn't like touching. Once he was outside the Compound, he'd head for the nearest cover and keep running, hoping he could stay clear long enough to get outside the range of their seekers. It wasn't much of a plan, but it was better than sitting around on his tail-bone waiting to be skinned for the amusement of these stupid sheep.

There were three conditions that had to be met before he could make his try.

He had to be out of his cell; only the kephalos could open that grill for him.

He had to have a means of overcoming his flesh guards, always two of them, one going before him, the other following.

He had to have a way of distracting the android guard, one android always, always the same one.

Leaving the cell was no problem. For one reason or another he was out nearly every day.

The guards weren't a problem either. Thanks to Miji.

##

Miji pattered along an offshoot of the main corridor. There were cells on both sides. In a cubicle in the middle of that cellrank, a man.

Miji's startle response alerted Rohant to the presence of the man; the speed with which curiosity replaced wariness suggested he posed no threat.

Miji pattered into the cubicle and began nosing at the man, poking and tugging at him with his agile, six-fingered hands, gaining confidence every moment as the man showed no response.

In his cell Rohant was sweating with the effort to stay calm. He could feel what Miji's fingers felt, he got the textures of the cloth and the skin, the prickle of the fine hairs, the looseness of the muscle under the skin. He knew when Miji had worked his way up the man's body to his arm.

There was something under the sleeve. A sheath. Leather, probably—because Miji nibbled at it. A metal rod in the sheath. Short, about the length of Rohant's thumb, but thinner. It could be a stunrod. Rohant squeezed down his surge of excitement; it was disturbing Miji who backed off and was about to scuttle away.

Sweating, his face twisted with concentration, he coaxed the sakali back to the arm, got him to pop the snaps, take the rod from the sheath, and bring it away.

Again and again he had to convince Miji to bring him the rod; he caressed and cajoled the little sakali, kept him trotting along on his hind legs, the rod clutched to his chest.

##

After what seemed an eternity, Miji was crouching outside the grill, his bright black eyes sparkling with satisfaction.

Rohant knelt by the grill, reached between the bars and brought him into the cell, palming the rod at the same time, getting it into the front of his prison shirt. He sat with the

sakali on his knee, scratching gently about the frill with the
tip of his foreclaw. Miji closed his eyes and went limp, his
tongue hanging out; he trilled with pleasure, a tiny bubbling
whistle that was pure joy.

## 

Later, when Miji was out and sleeping in his burrow, Rohant manage a brief look at his prize. It was indeed a stunrod—small, short range, but all he needed to take out the
flesh guards. He opened a half-inch of the hem of his shirt,
slid the rod into the opening, and went to work on figuring
a way of distracting or disabling the android.

## 

"I went," she told Rohant when he came back. "I didn't
know what o expect. What I saw was odder than I expected,
still . . . I don't know.

"Digby was sitting in a pulochair inside an image bubble;
he was a square brown man with black eyes, wide cheekbones, and a smile that could light up all of Spotch-Helspar.
I liked him the minute I saw him. He had a good smell,
well, you know what I mean. It was the same thing with
that odd creature Frittagga Addams. Anyway, I let him take
the language extract, then we talked. And he told me he
already knew what part of the problem was. The Watchman
program.

" 'You're running it on full cycle, aren't you.'

" 'Yes, that's the way I was told to do it when I bought
the androids.'

'Everyone is. The jacals love it that way.'

'What?'

'I suspect that's what you've got raiding your stocks.
Someone hired a jacal, probably to get the jinnkitt, I hear
you've refused three separate offers for it.'

" 'Yes. We won't deal with brokers and we won't sell
where we don't trust.'

" 'Right. You know the reason why Watchman androids
are sold in threes?'

MEMORY:
It was early days for Voallts Korlach. They'd just opened the
compound in Spotch-Helspar, Miralys was pregnant with Lissorn and they had a single Capture ship out bringing in stock
for their cages. Rohant was their sole Capture Chief and his
cousin Napos ran the ship. In addition to the Dyslaerors they
had four Grydeggin trackers in their capture team, a
University-trained Katsitoi triad acting as a communal xeno-
biologist and two Trumpet Viner Cousins as ecologists, setting the pattern for mixed crews that Voallts Korlach
continued till the present day.

A series of thefts had been giving Miralys fits. Despite sen-
tries and a triad of watchman androids, someone had been
getting to the stock, carrying off small but valuable birds,
beasts, reptiles. The thief had twice got close to their most
valuable beast, a pure white Mersallan jinnkitt with a base
worth of fifty thousand Helvetian gelders, its actual price
probably double that. Miralys had already turned down two
bidders, because she didn't like the way they smelled. A third
had used a broker; she sent the broker away without bothering to listen to his offer. It was something she and Rohant
had agreed on from the beginning. They would not sell so
much as a feather through brokers, the buyers had to represent themselves. They wanted to know where their stock was
going and what was going to happen to it.

"I was wondering what to do next," she told Rohant when he
got back, "when Zimaryn brought in this card, it made me
laugh, there was this mini-holoa up in the left corner, a
shovel dancing. Silly thing. Of course I'd heard of Digby and
Excavations Ltd. Is there anyone on Spotchals who hasn't? I
wasn't sure what to think of him and his business and most of
all his prices.

"The . . . well . . . the exceedingly ambiguous being who
sent the card in, I'll say she for convenience's sake, was a
blonde beauty, I'm not that good at judging the attractions of
outsiders, but it seemed to me she was rather past her prime.
She sat in the pulochair, crossed her legs and smiled at me,
and said her name was Frittagga Addams.

"I tapped my claw on the card and gave her the hoteye.
'Why?' I said.

‘‘ ‘Five thefts in the past three months. Police nowhere,
though they’re trying. Here on Spotchals the P-T-B like to
encourage young, healthy, expanding enterprises.’

‘‘ ‘Young. So right,’ I said. ‘We can’t possibly afford Digby’s
fees, even if they’re only half what they’re rumored to be.’

‘‘ ‘Digby is willing to take his fee in services rather than
gelders.’

‘‘ ‘Specify.’

‘‘ ‘Digby is a man with a voracious hunger for knowledge.
Dyslaera are very little known outside of Dysstrael. He
wishes to learn the language and history of your people.
Nothing sacred or private, just whatever is public knowledge,
what you teach your children. If you will provide a language
extract and would agree to come and talk with him once a
week for the next year, he’ll consider that sufficient fee for
his services.’

‘‘ ‘Which are?’

‘‘ ‘He will discover the thief, the means by which the thefts
are accomplished and, if possible, recover the stolen stock.
He can’t guarantee this last, because he doesn’t know the
purpose of the thefts.’

‘‘ ‘I understand,’ I said. ‘I’ll have to consult the Family
first.’

‘‘ ‘Do that, then come and speak with him. You’ll see.’

‘‘ ‘Wouldn’t it be better for him to come here so he can see
the place?’

‘‘ ‘Not possible. Come. You’ll see.’

‘‘And then she left.’’

‘‘I quoted the brochure to him,’’ she told Rohant. ‘‘I was
irritated; he was belaboring the obvious so I might as well
respond in kind: ‘To insure flexibility of response and reaction speed in a casing of reasonable size, memory capacity is limited. The intake must be sorted and downloaded
every three hours; the three androids must download in
staggered series so that at least one is at full efficiency at
the moment when one is taken out of circuit. What’s wrong
with that?’ I said, ‘It only takes a minute.’

‘‘ ‘It means that the jacal has an opportunity to raid every
hour of the night. He had already acquired plans for your

pens, he knows when the full-response droid is as far away as it's going to get, he *chaffs* the half-loaded droid, overwhelming its intake, flips in his scoop and gets the target out before the full-response can locate the trouble and cross the intervening space. He can do it over and over again, whenever he wants. If you add flesh guards, he'll kill them. I take it you've moved the jinnkitt once or twice?'

" 'Yes. First night, it was off its feed, we had it in the infirmary. The second time was just before a client was coming to look at it. We were grooming it and playing with it so it would be in good spirits.'

" 'Right. That's the only reason you still have it. The first part of the answer is simple. Change the routine. New pattern of patrol every night, for one thing. For another, download after one hour, not three. You keep your droids livelier, time down is much shorter, and the change in pattern will annoy the jacal no end.'

## 

"I hadn't thought of that, Ro, it was such a simple change and so obvious, once he said it. It was worth whatever trouble this chatting business put me to. Besides, I liked the man, I already liked talking to him. I did what he said, we caught the jacal, Digby got enough on the one who hired him, a turd named Tambaedee, to scare him off, and the rest you know."

## 

Omphalos was using the same android every time they came for him; it had a scratch underneath its right visionlens which gave it a rakish look, almost like a dueling scar. He was sure they were keeping it on full-cycle, twice he'd seen signs it was near saturation, a faint hesitation in its movements, a sluggishness in its responses. The first time was before he had the stunrod, the second time they made him strip in the cell before they took him out, they were taking him to a special session in the lab, so he had to leave the rod behind.

Now he was cultivating a hunter's patience, waiting quietly till all three factors clicked in.

It would happen soon. Had to be soon. Before they gave up on Miralys and moved him to Black House.

The Grand Chom was away, they said. How true that was Rohant didn't know. Or where. Or what had happened to him.

There was a restiveness in the place that was connected with the Chom's absence. Something has gone wrong for them; they can't figure what, but they feel things aren't right. He knew that nervousness, it was the kind that passed through a herd when a predator was eying them.

He had to get out of here.

Soon.

## 2

Savant 4 (speaking to notepad):

Subject 7R (native name: Rohant) has emerged from the fugue state, but continues in a curious passivity. Tech 1 insists this has nothing to do with passivity but is rather the typical huntmode of a predator, the time of waiting before the strike. NOTE: Tech 1 is showing further signs of deviation, I recommend removal from Mimishay and rehabilitation at the Institute; if his attitude does not improve subsequent to such actions, I must advance a suggestion of termination with prejudice; his skills as a tech are without question; however, his growing insubordination is a corrupting force among his juniors.

FURTHER NOTE: Negotiations with Voallts Korlach are proceeding slowly, but there is no real problem. Another rat is being prepared to increase pressure on the Toerfeles so she will expedite the bargaining and reach the point of decision. Despite the losses, this has been a markedly successful ploy. Congratulations to the planners. May their fertility increase.

# WORMS IN THE WALLS, WASPS IN THE RAFTERS:
## Wherein Mimishay learns the folly of messing with Dyslaera and distorting the creations of dedicated artists like Ginbiryol Seyirshi
## SHADITH / GINBIRYOL SEYIRSHI / TSIPOR

Shadith followed the android onto the bridge.

She stopped in the doorway, shuddered. It was the ugliest place she'd seen since Stavver stole the diadem from the RMoahl towers: what wasn't starkly utilitarian was heavily, disastrously ornamented. The cabin Ginny gave her was stripped to the bones, nothing there but toeup furniture and gray walls. As she looked around, she decided he had redeeming qualities she hadn't noticed before since he hadn't put her in a suite with this sort of decor.

Ginny was seated off to one side, working at the comspec's station, a habit she remembered from the first time he'd hauled her off somewhere.

He braced his prosthetic hand against the sensor board and pushed the chair around. "You slept a long time."

"I was tired."

"Apparently. Tell me something, Singer; was Ajeri Kilavez among the prisoners in the hold? You do remember her?"

"She was there, in the pod beside yours."

"Ah. I thought so. The Omphalite told me she died at the Hole." He brooded for a moment, staring down at the unflesh hand, watching the fingers and thumb twitch; then he looked up. "I had to replace my crew. The pilot is one Mertoyl. There are two mercs in crew quarters, they will

324

handle beams and missiles, and I have acquired a Sikkul Paem in bud to tend the drives. I prefer Sikkul Paems as engine crew; they do not interfere in what is not their business. It is an attitude I recommend you adopt.''

"Tui-tui, where's all this cooperation you flourished when you roped us in?''

He contemplated her a moment, produced a small tight smile. "Cooperation? I do not think I mentioned the word. My recollection is that we have agreed not to kill each other for the moment.''

"Right.'' She settled herself in the co-seat, crossed her legs, and rested her hands on her knees. "So. What now?''

"We will talk in a moment. I must finish what I am doing here.'' He pulled himself around, bent over the slantboard and went back to tapping the sensor plates, watching the hexa cells in front of him as the half-dozen he was working with flickered through image after image.

Shadith rubbed at her eyes, let her head fall back as she considered the new pilot.

Mertoyl was a thin, fair woman with wispy ash blonde hair and gray eyes so pale they were nearly colorless. Her trousers were gray leather, its shadow diamond texture identifying the leather as murraskin which meant it was contraband and almost as expensive as her tunic. That tunic had the deep subtle sheen of avrishum, probably cost more than many people earned in a year. A single earring dangled from her left ear, a teardrop of silver with a gray shimmerpearl in the cut-out center. She was a ghostimage of a woman, but a ghost with very expensive tastes.

*Where does he get them, these etiolate blondes? These peculiar pilots with their penchant for absolute loyalty? Because she has it, too, bad as Ajeri. Has it already, though she can't have been with him more than a few months. Is it catching? Gods, I hope not.*

Tsipor was squatting by the back wall, her arms crossed on her knees, her dark red eyes empty of expression. Though she was hard to read, her rhythms so alien they only rarely approached Cousin norms, she seemed powered-down, almost dormant.

Shadith glanced at her, shivered, looked away. During the nights and days of the ride across the Brushland she'd felt close to the Raska; their shared needs and the solitude they were locked into had overcome instinctive dislike. Mutual dislike—Tsipor found the monkey Cousins as repellent as they found her and had no difficulty making that revulsion apparent. That closeness . . . pseudo-closeness . . . whatever . . . it was gone now. Probably because Tsipor had transferred her loyalty, such as it was, to Ginny as the one most likely to see Omphalos rolled in the dust.

A hexa cell pulsed, widened until it touched top and bottom of the forescreen. A world image swam in the center of the cell. "Arumda'm," Ginny said. "That is where we are going."

Shadith blinked.

*Coincidence? That's the world where Tinoopa's son is. Hope he's not in this, if he gets killed, what am I going to tell her?*

Ginny tapped in a code, took the POV in a rapid slant downward until it hovered above an island shaped like a tadpole trying to bite its own tail, a curving ridge of mountains the bony protrusions of the tadpole's spine. "Haed Nunn," he said. "The Mimishay Foundation is there." He tapped a sensor and a small red light began flashing at the back of the circle of water the tadpole's head on one side and tail on the other. "There is some manual capacity, but its defenses are mostly controlled by the kephalos. I intend to infiltrate EYEs into that kephalos; once I have control of it, I can turn their defenses against them and slag the place."

"Sounds simple enough. What about Rohant and the Dyslaera? They're in there, aren't they. How do we get them out?"

"Even before I left, half of them were dead and the others in such misery they would welcome death. Why complicate things?"

"Complicate! One tooth and a fingernail left, they're coming out. . . ."

## 

As the ship swam through the insplit, the argument went on and on, taken up and dropped, taken up again.

##

Shadith stalked restlessly about the bridge; she stopped beside Ginny, fists on hips. "Why'd you bother coming for me? You don't need what I do. You don't listen to me. Why?"

"You are the one who will not listen. I have told you again and again, I do not know why I need you. That will only become apparent when you do something."

"Do what?"

"You see? You do not listen. Is it too simple for you? I have no idea what. I will not know until you do it. I do know this. You will destroy either Mimishay or me. Because I am no threat to you at present, I can hope it will be Mimishay that will receive the force of your . . . aah . . . presence."

"So I'm some goddam primal force?"

"Precisely."

"You're crazy. I suspected that and now I know. Primal force? Gah!"

He smiled at her, that characteristic small tight twitch of his pale lips; he was undisturbed by her skepticism and felt no need to defend himself.

Shadith went stomping off the bridge before she drowned in her own futility.

##

"Look, getting Rohant and the others out, that comes first. Then you can do what you want with Mimishay."

*If I'm a Primal Force, I might as well make it mean something. Ginny, you worm, I won't let you fool with me. Sar! you want to see primal force, just keep this up.*

"You cannot even know that any of them are alive."

"If they aren't, then there's no problem, is there? If you go on with this the way you've planned it, you better call off the truce and shove me out a lock, because I'm going to use everything I've got to stop you."

He stared at her a long moment, as if he considered that option, then, abruptly, he gave in. "Very well. How close must you be to control large beasts?"

"It depends on the beast and the circumstances, but say a circle of radius . . . um . . . twenty kilometers."

"Then you can't work from a synchronous orbit."

"No. Certainly not."

Tsipor stood up, came across the bridge with the short-legged sinuous walk that was like no other. "She lies."

Ginny opened his eyes wider. "Really?"

"Linked to me her range is extended a hundredfold."

"Well, Singer?"

Shadith scowled at Tsipor. "All right, she's right, it's certainly extended, I don't know how far. Hundredfold? I doubt it. And in any case I don't intend to try the limits. I mean to be on the ground when I work."

"Very well." He recalled the image of Haed Nunn. "Most of the . . . aah . . . pirate swarms are in the south, but there are several that make forays into northern waters. Mimishay has set up a rather primitive defense against attacks from these infested flotillas. It is primitive but effective since the ships are wood hulls and the weapons on them pitiful. Mimishay has strung a cable net across the mouth of the bay. There." A red line leaped across the open section of the circle of water. "It can be charged with enough current to electrolyze the seawater and char any hull that slams against it. It usually is not. However, Mimishay does keep a certain number of sensors alert for intrusion."

He shifted the POV down the curve of the world until Haed Nunn vanished and a string of rocky islets occupied the center of the cell. "Haedsa . . . that's island chain . . . Chavada. Barren, not much fresh water, a few fishing families. I will take the ship down, land her there." Yellow light flashing on one of the midsized rocks. "This is a free-trader world, ships come in all the time, many use the Field at Tos Tous, but others land wherever they take a notion. Mimishay notes but ignores them.

"It is my intention to approach Haed Nunn on miniskips and come through the mountains rather than take the easier approach on the bay side. Mimishay has been undisturbed on that Haed for at least two centuries, so the Brothers and the Powers are careless about security; they depend on those kephalos-driven defenses. Because these neither sleep nor lose their edge, they forget that such things have their limits and if focused in one direction will ignore a small, non-threatening intrusion coming at their backs, as it were. We will need a distraction. If you are able to locate and mind-ride a number of large sea beasts, drive them against the net at the mouth of the bay, that should be sufficient to cover us. Can you do this? Remember, you will be straddling a miniskip while you work.''

"Can you put my emskip on a lead? I can't boot whales and navigate at the same time.''

"Yes. We can do that.''

"Then you've got your distraction.''

## ##

The storm wind beating at their backs, they rode the heavily-laden miniskips across the water, flying so low the spume whipped from the wavetops slapped into their legs. Clouds boiled low overhead and phosphorescence ran in crooked green lines through the troubled swell.

Shadith felt the storm as a distant discomfort; the greater part of her consciousness was in the calm deeps, split between three megaforms, great black creatures half a kilometer long from blunt nose to the tips of the massive tentacles whose slow steady beats drove them through the water. They were solitary beasts, uneasy so close together. Again and again, she had to herd them back as they struggled to turn aside, to put a more comfortable space between them. She was troubled by what she was doing, *riding* them to their deaths, but Rohant was her friend and he needed her help. Her eyes were squeezed shut and tears leaked from under her lids, yet each time the beasts tried to peel off, she tightened her grip and drove them on.

The beasts hit the net as the miniskips passed from water to land and began the steep winding climb through the jagged cliffs on the stormside of the mountains.

Shadith shivered and groaned as a massive jolt of electricity fried one of the beasts before she could free herself from his brain; she heard the hooming roars of pain and fury as the other two exploded with killing rage and flung themselves against the lethal net.

The winds snatched and shoved at the emskips, tried to drive them into the walls of the ravine they were sweeping along. The tether joining her emskip to Tsipor's whipped her about, threatened to wheel both of them into a down-spiral that would turn them into bloody meat.

Shadith struggled back into herself, fought with the clip connecting the tether to the emskip shaft, finally managed to trip it.

The minute she was loose, the emskip swerved wildly, her left leg scraped along the stone; part of her trousers tore away, a flap of skin ripped loose, then off; the skipfender squealed and threw up a fan of sparks, the noise hammered at her, the winds hammered at her, the skip bucked under her.

Grimly she fought for control.

After what seemed an eternity of confusion and noise, the drive bit, the emskip straightened out; she pushed the speedlever down and hurried after Tsipor and Ginny who were both nearly out of sight.

## ##

The place Ginny had chosen for their base was a moraine flat with a tumble of huge boulders and a litter of stones from the size of eggs to sofa pillows; the flat was halfway up the tallest mountain west of the Mimishay compound.

They labored to clear a space for the domes, a figure eight with one lobe twice the size of the other. Though the wind had abated once they reached the eastern slopes of the mountains, the rain lashed at them, coming down hard and cold as they bent and lifted the stones, carried them to the ragged wall they were building about the site. Bent and lifted and carried. Jammed fingers in the dark against stones they couldn't see and scraped off skin and worked their backs until even their bones ached.

In the bay below, the tumult was calming as the last two black beasts died and their bodies heaved against the net, lifting and dropping with the storm swell, nearly invisible in the dark water. After one look, Shadith bent to the stones and labored with a desperate intensity, using pain and fatigue to shut out the things she didn't want to see or think about.

Ginny inflated the shelters into mottled gray domes that shed light even more efficiently than they shed the rain, then he exploded anchors deep into the mountain to hold them steady despite the snatching of the wind.

## ##

Shadith crouched in the backcurve of the larger dome using a small handpump to blow up an air mattress. Her head was wrapped in a towel and now and then she stopped her pumping to shiver; the thin silken undersuit she'd put on was dry, but no barrier to the drafts the air machine was blowing through the domes.

Tsipor crouched silently across from her, holding herself as far from the others as she could in the cramped space.

Ginny sat on an air cushion before a low table, working quickly, neatly, clipping components together, sliding accumulators from their cases and snapping them into the receptors of the shield generator, the EYE controls, the viewscreen, and the rest of the equipment that ran the domes.

## ##

Half an hour later he grunted and sat on his heels. "That is done." Over his shoulder, he said, "I must wait for the storm to abate further before I launch the EYEs. Singer, are you able to reach into the Compound?"

Shadith moved onto the air mattress, sat with her legs drawn up, her arms draped over her knees. "I wouldn't mind a cup of tea first. I'm still cold to the bone."

Ginny smiled, startling her with the sly amusement she felt in him. "I live only to serve you, Singer."

"Yeh, yeh, sure you do." She spread a blanket over her knees, pulled the towel off, and began to rub at her hair.

## ##

Shadith set the mug on the floor and stretched out on her stomach, her head resting on crossed forearms. Tsipor knelt beside her, narrow hand cold on the back of her neck.

She *reached*.

## ##

Rohant lay awake and tense on something hard and uncomfortable enough to keep him shifting position frequently. He was waiting—she didn't, couldn't, know for what.

She left him at it and felt about for the other Dyslaera. Ginny said half of them were dead. She didn't believe him. He'd say anything to get what he wanted.

Nothing, nothing, nothing.

One Omphalite, probably a guard on watch.

Nothing. Nothing. Nothing.

Out and out she spiraled the point presence of her *reach*, a sick cold hollow growing beneath her ribs.

Nothing but Omphalites—except for a few local women clustered in a small tight area near the northern end of the Compound.

It didn't have to mean the other Dyslaerors were dead; they could have been mindwiped like her, dumped in a Contract labor levy. Could have been. It was only a thread of a hope and it shriveled as she tried to cling to it. Ginny's report about Omphalos' intentions was too convincing. They were dead, disposed of, all but Rohant.

She sprang back to Rohant, scanned his body. No real damage. Relief flooded her and she sobbed before she could stop herself.

Tsipor's hand tightened on her neck.

She steadied and went back to *searching* the Compound, locating and counting the Omphalites so Ginny could better avoid them when he sent in his EYEs. And she could begin planning to break Rohant free.

## ##

Shadith opened her eyes, groaned, pushed herself up till she was sitting cross-legged on the mattress, the blanket draped loosely about her. "Stylus," she said.

Tsipor crawled across the dome to the place where she'd been squatting before, sat there, crimson eyes narrowed to slits, face blank.

Ginny tossed Shadith a clipboard, a stylus held to it with a small magnet.

"Five hundred and nine," she said. "Five hundred and ten if you count Rohant. No Dyslaera there except him. . . ." She began marking clusters of circles. "These are sleepers, not to scale, though I'm keeping angles and organization as accurate as I can. I didn't find any of the other prisoners. I suppose they've been processed and sent . . . wherever. . . ." She finished the circles and began laying down x's, some of them with dotted lines and arrows indicating direction. "This lot are the wakers. The ones without pointers aren't moving, probably sitting at terminals or watchposts, the others are going here and there, either insomniacs or guards on patrol." She added a rectangle. "Rohant. He's not far from the outer wall; it shouldn't be too hard to pry him loose."

"The EYEs go in first."

"Yes. But once you've got them in place, I'm going to blow that cage and pull him out."

"That argument is finished, Singer; you annoy me when you bring it up again and again."

"All right. I just want things clear." She stretched out again on the mattress, flipped the blanket over her. "Wake me when you're ready to go."

## MIRALYS AND VOALLTS ON THE HUNT— BLACK HOUSE

The three Dyslaer transports plunged into the atmosphere and sped across the night sky sheathed in halos of superheated gases. They dipped low over Haed Ke, released a swarm of Capture Landers and went flaring up and out, settling into synchronous orbit above Tos Tang, a small unimportant seaside town, and Black House, a rambling structure growing like lichen on the stony mountains above Tos Tang.

## ##

Aboard Anyagyn's *Cillasheg*, Miralys prowled restlessly about the bridge, maintaining a precarious control on her temper and her needs.

Huddled in one of the observer seats by the offside wall, Kikun watched her with admiration and apprehension; it was rather like hanging around a volcano about to erupt.

Beside him, Autumn Rose was busy with the totacorder tapped into the ship's kephalos, recording for Digby the attack and everything that happened aboard the *Cillasheg;* this was his price for the data he provided, and the contacts.

## ##

Agile as stingships and almost as lethal (courtesy of Digby's sources), the Capture Landers swept down on the Black House, blew out the nodes where the defense centers were located, then retreated into a ragged disk hovering over the House.

## ##

Her face filling the center cell, Tasylyn twitched her scarred ear. "Got 'em all, they couldn't light a match."

Anyagan the Szajes showed her teeth. "Good work, cousin."

"You want us to go in? Wouldn't take us ten minutes to fetch ours out."

"Down, kit. We want ours alive, not dead. We'll take the long road first. Ta." She blanked the hexa, swung to face Miralys. "You ready, Toerfeles?"

Miralys settled into the co-seat. "Get them."

## ##

The sweaty, furious face of a man filled the central hexa. His thick gold hair straggled about his ears; his eye paint was smudged and his lip rouge rolled into crumbs at the corner of his mouth, a mouth working in a futile frenzy, futile because the sound was off.

Anyagyn sniffed, the small sound heavy with distaste. "You want to hear that, Toerfeles?"

"No. Can that hear me?"

"When you want."

"Do it."

"Done."

The man blinked and started yelling more furiously, waving his arms, hands appearing and vanishing as they swung in and out of the viewcone.

Miralys dug her claws into the padding on the chairarms. "Shut your mouth, fool, listen to me." Her ears twitched, her lips curled up and back in the Dyslaera threat grin.

There was a flicker of fear in the man's eyes, understanding immediately suppressed. His face smoothed out, acquired a sudden patina of grooming. He smiled, bowed his head, spoke briefly, then waited.

"I am Miralys vey Voallts tol Daravazhalts, Toerfeles of Voallts Korlach. You have blood kin of mine prisoner in that abomination of yours. I want them, without delay and intact." She turned to Anyagyn. "Let me hear that."

The man smoothed nervous fingers over his hair, pressing it into a semblance of order. "What are you talking about, Toerfeles?" His voice was pleasantly rough, more interesting and attractive than his surgically enhanced face. "There are no Dyslaera here. Someone's been lying to you."

"Who are you? Would you know?"

"I am Pinjaro da Tinggal." He was almost purring now that he knew what he dealt with, sure of his ability to defuse the situation. "I am Pengurra of this House. I know what happens here."

Miralys' ears went back against her skull. "Anyagyn Szajes, do it."

"Hannys, Sugnarn, Tasylyn. Go."

## 

Three Capture Landers left the disk, swooped down and blew away a section of Black House, went spiraling back to their places. A breath and a half and the attack was over.

## 

Tinggal yelped and vanished from the screen.

He reappeared a moment later. "There were people in those suites. Important people. You killed them."

Miralys snorted. "Turn about, worm. How many dead. . . . " She broke off. "That doesn't matter. You have ten minutes. After that we will remove another sector and another, one every ten minutes."

He started to speak, then snapped his mouth shut and vanished once again.

Miralys turned to Anyagyn, ears up and quivering.

Anyagyn wiggled her nose. "They can't hear for the moment."

"Any chance the worm can come up with a defense?"

"If Digby's right, no."

"Hmm. Get Hannys."

"You sure? Her Mum raised crazy kits."

"We need craziness right now."

A side hexa pulsed awake. Hannys was a red Dyslaerin with bright yellow eyes and a round face. Her eyes sparkled and her lips were curled in a friendly grin, teeth carefully covered. "Toerfeles," she said. "Can we bite 'em? Hey-hey, can we do it?"

"Maybe, cousin. I want you ready go in and snatch ours if the worm down there starts trying to argue with me."

"Forget him. Let's do it."

"Cool your blood, cousin, you don't move till I give the word, you hear?"

"Aaah."

"Not a whisker, or I'll snatch you naked and feed you to the nearest Ri-tors."

## ##

Tinggal slid back into view. "I must apologize, Toerfeles," he said easily, with a quick charming smile to underline what he intended to be a rueful sincerity. "We have two young guests who appear to be Dyslaera. It seems one of my subordinates was overzealous in his attempts to please our clients and acted without authorization. Be sure he will be dealt with. This will not occur again."

"Only two?"

"If you doubt my word, Toerfeles, ask them yourself." He stepped aside.

Azram and Kinefray moved into the viewcone; they were thin and strained, but seemed otherwise unharmed.

Miralys sucked in a breath, then said quietly, "Azoe, Azram, Kinefray."

Kinefray stared down at his feet; Azram answered her. "Azoisha, Toerfeles." There was a touch of mischief in his reddened eyes.

"Worm says there's only the two of you."

Azram's ears crinkled forward, his eyes glazed over, spilled tears despite his effort to stay calm. "True," he managed. He rubbed at his nose with the back of his fist. "Rest 're dead. 'Cept the Ciocan," he added hastily. "That other lot kept him." He looked to one side, nodded, then he and Kinefray shifted out of sight and Tinggal was back.

"As you hear, Toerfeles."

"As I do see, slime. You're not thinking nonsense like hostages, are you?"

"Certainly not, Toerfeles. Purely as a matter of curiosity though, say we were?"

"We take our own by force, then Black House and everything in it will be slagged to bedrock."

"And if there is no further fuss?"

"We collect ours and leave. My word on it."

"And what is your word worth?"

"More than anything you've got within your walls."

"Very well. We will send the young Dyslaera out immediately. The main entrance. There is sufficient room in the garden there for one of your landers to alight."

## ##

Miralys watched tensely as the Hannys' lander touched down, collected Azram and Kinefray, zipped up, and leapt off for the circling disk of landers.

As soon as Hannys was in place, the landers swirled up in a grand helix, reached the transports, and were swallowed by them.

The transports went arcing onward, going deeper into the dark.

### MIMISHAY

Savant 4: (Answering the com) The Grand Chom is elsewhere at the moment. I speak for the Council. What is the problem?

Tinggal: Problem? I'll tell you the problem. We've got a fleet of Dyslaera hanging over us. Someone talked. They know about the subjects you passed to us.

Savant 4: Fleet?

Tinggal: (speaking with a growing impatience) Three armed transports and I didn't bother to count the landers. Armed! Better than a lot of governments. Took out our defenses before they bothered to say a word. Knew just where to hit, too. Someone talked. Yes, someone talked. Burned down four suites, killed everyone inside and what we're going to tell their families I don't know.

Savant 4: And?

Tinggal: (with obvious satisfaction) Better look to your
own defenses. The Toerfeles has given us ten minutes to
produce her kin and turn them over. We'll do that, we've
got no choice. Which means less than half an hour from
now she's on her way to you.


                              **##**


Savant 4: Ward Master, I want that Dyslaera brought to
the Question Chamber. (His voice took on a shrill note
despite the distorter he was wearing.) I want him there
so fast the air smokes around him. You hear?
Ward Master: Yes, Savant. Anything special you want,
tools, personnel, whatever?
Savant 4: Prepare for full hostile Probe.
Ward Master: The Chom. . . .
Savant 4: The Chom isn't here, he's not going to be here
any time soon. This is an emergency, fool, the Dyslaera
are on their way here now.
Ward Master: Should I order a full alert? You have to
authorize it.
Savant 4: Do it. Don't just stand around asking stupid
questions. Do it.


### ROHANT

"On your feet!" The wardbrother was rattling the doorgrill, shrieking the order; he sounded terrified, as if he
were apt to do something terminal if given half an excuse.
And he was alone.
Rohant rolled off the cot and stood beside it, hands
clasped behind him, head down. They hadn't come for
him before like this, in the middle of the night, or sent a
singleton guard after him; he stared at the floor and wondered what was going on.
After a delay that drove the young ward twitchy, the grill
slid open and the watchandroid came in.
Rohant snatched a look at it. Yes . . . good . . . not just
hesitations, the warning light by its left sound receptor
was pulsing red. This wasn't his usual escort, no scratch;
it was older, too. They were scraping bottom with this
one. Why? No matter. He pressed his arm against his
body, felt the stunrod in the hem of his shirt. Yes. If they

took him past the Novice quarters, this was it, good-bye Mimishay.

When the watchandroid was in position behind Rohant, the guard yelped, "Out, blitsor. You know the drill. Move it. Hup hup."

## 

Rohant trotted through the corridors, the meat in a loose sandwich between guard and android, the android lagging farther and farther behind. One more turn . . . if we go to the right . . . past the Novice quarter. *Go right,* he thought at the youth ahead of him. *Right, not left.* He reached under his tunic, began sliding the stunrod from the hem.

The wardbrother turned right, turned again, the watchandroid clattered along far behind . . . out of sight. . . .

Rohant stunned the guard, kicked the door open to the Novice area, and plunged inside. His bare feet padding silently on the thick matting, he ran full out past the closed doors of the sleeping cells, first block, not a sound, not even a snore, second block. . . .

The Novice Master backed from a cell, pulled the door shut, turned. . . .

Claws out, Rohant slammed his hand into the Omphalite's throat, jerked away before the gush of blood could saturate his fur. He caught the man as he started to fall, threw him across the narrow hallway like a fleshy speed bump, and ran on.

Just before he reached the door at the end of the corridor, he heard a metallic clatter and curled his lips back, baring his long, yellow tearing teeth. Android tripping over the dead man. Good. He slapped his palm on the sensor and pushed out before the door was halfway open.

It was dark out, wind howling round corners, clouds covering the moons. Blinking at the rain that stung his face, he raced along the walkway to the small Pleasure House built into the wall. He kicked the door open, ran inside.

A woman came from one of the bedrooms, bleary eyed and still half asleep. "Wha. . . ."

He ignored her and ran for the back of the House, jerking doors open, cursing the barriers that kept slowing his flight. The android was coming after him, gaining on him. . . .

He reached the postern door, ran through it. It was open

as it always was, day and night. The Omphalites hadn't yet got round to closing the holes in their defenses, God be blessed. And Ossoran and Feyvorn be blessed for killing off half the Council, apparently the smarter half. And a triple blessing for whoever took the Chom out.

Something slammed into his back, sent him tumbling into grass and gravel, rolling toward the stream that slipped past the compound walls and danced into the sea.

He sprang onto his feet, swung round.

The wind-driven rain was hissing and sliding off a dome-shaped shimmer over the Compound—the defense shield. With the android trapped inside. He laughed aloud, a full-throated laugh, his offering to the gods of absurdity.

Deafening squeals, a crash that shook the rock under his feet. What. . . . He squinted through the rain at a swarm of small ships like dots of light moving in and out of the clouds above the dome. Others were swinging back from their first attack.

He saluted them. "The Lady kiss you, whoever you are," he shouted, then turned and began trotting toward the mountains a few kilometers away.

## MIRALYS

The man in the screen wore a coarse brown robe with the cowl pulled so far forward his face was lost in shadow, all but the point of a long narrow chin. He sat at a rustic desk, his hands hidden inside his voluminous sleeves. "Who are you and why do you threaten us?" he said, his voice mild and faintly metallic, passing through a distorter, something that undercut the image he was trying to project. "We are peaceful students here, acquiring merit through works of the mind. If you want gold, we have none. Why do you come with intent to attack?"

Miralys' ears snapped down and back; her lips came open showing her teeth; anger-musk rolled off her. She waited for several seconds before she spoke, waited until she had control. "You have ours," she said. "We want ours and payment for our dead. You have stolen my mate, my Cio-can. Give back what you have taken from me."

"I do not understand what you are saying, Dyslaera. We are simple Brothers here. Whoever told you . . ."

Kikun squeaked as Grandmother Ghost nipped him hard. "Now," he shouted.

". . . we were holding . . ."

Anyagyn tapped the sensor under her thumb.

Down below, the Capture Landers shifted position in a preset repatterning that left no lander occupying the original space of another.

". . . any of your people . . ."

A double dozen cutter beams drove through the suddenly empty places where the landers had been. They wavered a moment in futility, then swung about, hunting the targets that had moved too fast for them, slippery sliding dots of light flipped about by Dyslaera muscle and Dyslaera reflexes, sliding too fast, too fast. . . .

The screen went blank, the transmission interrupted as the defensive shield flashed into place around the Compound.

The landers struck back. Some played cutter beams of their own, probing at the shield, getting nowhere while others used more specialized weapons Digby had dug up for them. . . .

## DYSLAERA FIGHTERS

Sugnarn pulled his lander in a tight circle about a cutter beam, dusted it with rot grains that went skittering and glittering down the beam edges, crawled inside the projector, and began eating everything they touched. Twenty seconds later the beam withered and died, but Sugnarn didn't bother looking back, he was already dusting his third beam.

## 

Once she was sure there was a flesh operator behind it, that it had been clipped loose from the kephalos, Hannys flirted with a cutter beam, letting it come close enough to graze the side of her lander but never NEVER close enough to do serious damage, teasing it down and down until it was straining in its gimbals, jammed so hard the operator could barely move it, then she dropped into the hole created in the defenses, skimmed along the shield and laid down a line of thermix eggs that hit the ground and began to melt down into bedrock, following the shield down and down, stone bubbling and seething until that section of the Compound was resting uneasily in a thin layer of lava while steam generated by rain hitting the melt rose in agitated clouds about the dome.

Hannys went screaming up and out, dancing, elusive as a thought, hunting for another beam to tease.

## ##

Tatakarn was a hair slow on one of his turns; a missile caught the edge of his drive projector, blew the lander into dust.

## ##

When Jarnys saw her brother die, her concentration went—only momentarily, but it was enough; The cutter-beam sliced into her lander, carved away a third of it, took most of the rightside of her body with it. Dying she went nincs-othran and shut the pain away; the drives were partially intact, she had some power; she fought the machine around, sent it screaming at one of flickering cuttergates in the defense shield, got her timing perfect, and took a large chunk of the Compound with her as she crashed.

## MIRALYS
On the bridge of the *Cillasheg* Miralys watched the battle below her, her claws shredding the padding of the co-seat. Rohant was dead, his body might still be alive down there, somewhere, but that didn't matter, he was dead and gone, beyond her reach. She wasn't grieving yet, she wasn't even angry now, just grimly determined to take that island down to bedrock, not even a microbe left alive.

## KIKUN AND HIS GODS
Kikun watched the deathdance on the great forward screen and mourned the lives he'd known and not known. This was what his grandfolks had seen when the daivavig landed their guns on Keyazee's shores, when they'd flown their hot air balloons overhead and dropped incendiaries around the eas-terness forces. This is what they'd seen and he could feel the terror of it.

His gods came to him.

Suddenly they were there, watching, demanding. . . .

Jadii-Gevas stood behind Miralys, wild black eyes fixed

on the screen. He was snorting and jerking his head, the antlertree swaying up and down, forward and back.

Spash'ats stood at the back of the bridge, bigger and darker than before, his darkness pressing against the glow from the screen.

*LIFE NOT DEATH, Spash'ats rumbled at Kikun. What must be done, see that it is done without excess, that it is finished quickly and cleanly as such things go. You can do this, Nayol Hanee, you must do this.*

Xumady snorted and danced across the control panels and sensorboards beneath the great forescreen, his nimble black paws flickering over and around the nimble clawed hands of the Dyslaera working there, his long limber body humping and flattening. He sang a wordless song of fierce triumph, a hot joyous song of rage and hate as the Mimishay compound began to crumble under the blows from the landers. And when a lander burned to ash or went tumbling in a black arc to the boiling stone, he sat up on his haunches, his long back straight and stiff, his short forelegs stretched wide, and he keened his grief and the Dyslaera grief. He was all passion and heat, his fire beating at the cool restraint of Spash'ats' dark reason.

'Gemla Mask hung before Kikun, white stripes across the black base flushing red with Xumady's song, going ice-white and pure when Spash'ats was stronger . . . change and change again, a rhythm as steady as the splash of waves against the island's shore. Kikun was Mask, was caught in the ebb and flow. . . .

Then Grandmother Ghost was back, pinching him, her strong ancient fingers as punishing now as they were when she was still alive and he was a small naughty tokon playing in the mud.

*Your girl's down there, chile. You want her alive, you'd best go get her. Her and that Rohant. What I can see, they going to get themselves roasted any minute now. Gaagi, you gormless shade, haul your tail out here and show him. . . .*

She pinched at Kikun till he swung his chair about and stared at the emptiness where Spash'ats had drawn back into himself.

Gaagi bloomed from a speck of darkness and stood, a shining black figure against the matte black cloud of Spash'ats. He spread his arms, stood with his head turned so Kikun saw only one glittering eye and the powerful jut of the Raven's beak. Gaagi did not dance this time, his feet were not defined this time; this time he spread his wings and swayed his torso to make the black scales shimmer. Light came from those shimmers, gathered in a cloudy sphere floating before his chest.

The clouds cleared to crystal and in the crystal Kikun saw two bodies lying facedown on the earth, Shadith and Rohant lying facedown and very still, dangerously close to the creeping melt around the periphery of the Compound.

## SHADITH/GINNY

Tsipor shook Shadith awake; with an awkward undulant flip of a hand, she pointed at the small screen.

It was divided into several cells, all but one dedicated to the EYEs worming their tortuous ways down toward the Compound kephalos buried deep in bedrock. The singleton cell was tied to the EYE Ginny had grudgingly sent to over-look Rohant; at the moment it was expanded by a factor of three and dominated the screen.

*Rohant stood beside his cot, staring at the floor. An android was moving around him with ponderous weightiness and outside the open grill, a robed, cowled ward jigged from foot to foot, rapped the back of his metalled glove against the edge of the heavy steel grill, physical expressions of his agitation.*

Shadith knelt beside Ginny, frowning at the image. "What's going on? Middle of the night, isn't it?"

"You see what I see."

She heard the guard scream at Rohant, then watched the trio go trotting off. The EYE followed them. She glanced at the other cells on the screen, but there was nothing in any of them to explain the guard's nervous distress or this sudden summons. "Well, what do you think is happening?"

"I do not know. It has been very quiet down there since the sea beasts died." Ginny hesitated, reached for the control pad, drew his hand back. "If I were where I should be . . ." he glanced at her, annoyance in his face and voice, "I would have the resources to explore this properly."

Shadith snorted. "You can play that tune for someone else, Ginbiryol Seyirshi. If you'd meant to run this from orbit, we'd be there right now. Take too long, wouldn't it. And you'd be too vulnerable a target. What do you want me to do?"

He gazed at her without expression for a long moment. "I could start another EYE for the Compound, but it would not arrive for an hour and that would most likely be too late. I want you to *reach* into the Director's Chamber and tell me what is happening. . . ." He swore shrilly as Rohant stunned the guard and took off running. "That could ruin . . . I have to know what the Omphalites are doing. Go *search*, Singer. That fool could bring the whole island down on us."

"Good ol' Lion. All right, all right." She glanced at Tsipor, but the Raska wasn't offering this time; she was focused intently on the cells of the screen.

Shadith swallowed a giggle, crawled back to the mattress. Rohant was out and running. Free. Running free. He'd done it for himself, he hadn't been waiting for anyone to come and cut him loose. She felt like whooping, giggling, running out to meet him. She didn't feel like stretching out and hunting eyes-and-ears inside that Compound, so she took her time getting there.

Ginny swore again as the images in most of the cells began breaking up; he bent over the pad, working frantically to reestablish full contact with his infiltrating EYEs.

"What is it?" she called to him. "What happened?"

"Defense shield came on," he muttered. "Do what you are supposed to do, leave me alone."

Shadith wiggled her brows. "Touch-ee," she murmured, then sighed and crawled onto the mattress. Before she stretched out, she looked again at Rohant's image. He was running easily, heading toward the mountains, now and again squinting up through the slackening rain at something she couldn't see because the EYE was focused downward, centered on the Dyslaeror.

Tsipor hissed, scooted for the dome's lock, was through it before either of the others had time to react.

## ##

She was back a few moments later. "A-ship-ess," she said, worked her hands and did the other things she did better than words, creating corner-of-the-eye images of small ships darting restlessly about. "Attacking that." One hand shot out, undulated toward the Compound.

"Miralys," Shadith said.

Ginny twisted round, stared at her. "You *looked*?"

"No. A guess. But I'd bet my skin on it. Which is all I have at the moment. Kikun and Miralys, come for Rohant, maybe me. Rohant for sure. Who else is going to attack Omphalos?"

"Mimishay."

"Whatever."

Ginny danced his fingers over the pad, changing the direction and focus of the Rohant EYE, turning it upward so he could see and evaluate the attackers.

Shadith watched the conflict develop, saw one of the landers get hit and go down, taking out part of the Compound as it crashed, saw others teasing the cutter beams into a deadly sword-dance, saw sparkles sliding down beam edges, then the beams withering, winking out. . . .

Ginny twisted his mouth in his small tight smile. "The way those landers are being handled, I suspect you are correct in your assumption, Singer. I am much reminded of the skirmishes at Koulsnakko's Hole." He tapped his thumb on the pad, the Rohant EYE shifted focus once more.

*Rohant flung himself to one side, went rolling into brush, came onto his feet and fled deeper into the scattered clumps of trees, breaking line again and again until the beam hunting him winked out and left him with singed fur and a laboring wheeze.*

"Hmm." Ginny tapped a code into the pad, slid off the cushion and got to his feet. "We had better go collect him before he is killed by his kin or by accident. Singer, you will ride back with me, since our combined weights will be less than his. The skip would be dangerously sluggish trying to haul the two of you."

\* \* \*

## SHADITH/ROHANT

"Ro!" Shadith shouted. "Old lionface, look up." She brought the emskip swooping around him, leaned over, tugged at his hair, swept away again, landed the skip a short distance up the mountain, wriggled free of it, and ran for him.

"Shadow girl!" He scooped her up, hugged her so exuberantly she couldn't speak or breath. Still laughing, he swung her round and round, then set her on her feet and held her away from him so he could look at her. "I thought you were dead."

"Not quite. I'm hard to kill, Old Lion."

"That yours up there?"

"More yours. Miralys and Voallts."

"But you brought them."

"No. I suspect it was Kikun. You'd never in your wildest dreams guess who. . . ."

## GINNY/TSIPOR

Ginny slid the stunner back in its loops, tapped the caller. "Tsipor, come."

The Raska rode her skip around a bulge in the mountain, landed beside him; she dismounted, walked across to the bodies. "Dead?"

"No. Merely stunned. Help me load them on the spare skip."

"Why?" Tsipor lifted Rohant with an ease that startled Ginny, laid him along the bar of the miniskip, went back for Shadith, then began fastening them down, pulling the narrow woven straps tight and slapping the velcro patches together. "Why not dead?"

"I said I would not kill her for one year, Tsipor." Ginny freed a clump of Shadith's hair from a patch, pressed the closure tight. "Besides," he straightened, "she could very likely still be an important force against Omphalos. You have not seen destruction swirling in a vortex about her, leaving her untouched. I have. You have the tether?"

Her eyes so dark a crimson they were almost black, the Raska tossed him the plastic cable. "Canna take cross t' water ssso."

"I have no intention of trying. We will leave them down by the Compound." He looked at the clumsy bundle on the shaft, his mouth tightening into a shallow curve. "If she

dies from friendly fire, that is the Lady's Throw, not mine.
I would like that. I do not expect it. Come.''

## 

They slipped downslope following the stream that curved
past the northern corner of the Compound, sheltered from
observation by the trees that grew thickly along its banks.

As they reached the edge of the attack zone, chance took
the hotspots of the fight to the south, away from them. Ginny
nodded his head, signed his thanks to the Lady, and brought
both the skips to land. He dismounted and began ripping
loose the straps. Without comment, Tsipor joined him and
helped him free the bodies.

''You take him, I will take her. You will not place him
in the melt, but on the grass that is left.''

''Iss better dead.''

''Perhaps so, but not by your hand or mine.''

## 

They laid Shadith and Rohant facedown in the brittle dead
grass at the edge of the trees, retreated to their skips, and
started back along the stream.

## 

Ginny shifted his arm, read his wristchron. ''One hour,''
he said aloud, enjoying the sound of the words. ''In one
hour the EYES will reach the kephalos and trigger the self-
destruct. There will not be a microbe left alive.'' He entered a code into the pad, got to his feet. ''In Mimishay or
in that swarm of landers.''

Tsipor was crouched against the back wall of the dome,
brooding. Her eyes flickered as she saw him stand. She followed him out, bent to the nearest of the miniskips,
straightened it up, and straddled the saddle.

Ginny laughed aloud. ''No no, Tsipor, you will not need
that. Ah. Yes. Mertoyl is admirably prompt.''

The small spherical lander came arcing down, hovered a
hand-width above the ground, the lock irising open.

Unhurried despite the Capture Lander breaking from the
melee over the Compound and racing toward them and a

second ship, a skimmer, dropping down at them, Ginny stepped into the lock, passed through it into the small compact cabin. Tsipor came diving after him, gasping in her urgency. Before she had time to settle herself, the lander sealed up and darted away, fire from the chasing ship splashing after it—too late, much too late as Ginny's transport came rushing down in a halo of overheated air, sucked the Lander into itself and went racing off, flaring from the atmosphere, heading for Teegah's Limit and the Insplit.

## SHADITH/ROHANT

Shadith groaned and sat up, brushing fragments of sodden grass from her nose and mouth, pushing soaked hair from her eyes. "Ro?"

Rohant lay beside her; he was still out, but beginning to twitch. There was an odd little creature rather like a miniature Kikun crouching in his dreadlocks, holding onto the hair with tiny six-fingered hands. It was eeping pitifully, blinking bright black eyes at her, shivering with terror but unwilling or unable to run.

A cutter beam came slicing past them, took the top off the tree behind them.

"Tsoukbaraim!" Shadith threw herself onto hands and knees, grabbed at Rohant's tunic, and tried to haul him farther into the trees, away from the attack zone.

He was too heavy, she couldn't budge him.

A missile exploded fifty meters off, sprayed them with earth and half-molten stone. The noise punched at her, the pressure slammed her onto her back, her mouth popping open. Steam from the rain drifted around her, the heat from it reddened her skin, burned her nose and throat.

The Dyslaeror snorted, then groaned, lifted his head and sneezed. "Sar! What. . . ."

Shadith scrambled back to him, pinched his earlobe hard. "Move, we're in the middle of a war."

A section of the Compound shuddered then fell in on itself, the debris melting into stone liquified by the heat seeping through from that seething boiling ring outside the shield.

Rohant got unsteadily to his feet. "My head. . . ."

Shadith caught hold of his arm. "Move it, Ro. Lean on me. Come on."

A lander turned too late, exploded; the pieces pattered

down among the trees, starting small fires that died when
sap gushed forth from the injured branches and cup-shaped
leaves flipped over, dumping the rain they'd collected.

They staggered through the tree clumps and brush thick-
ets until they reached the stream. The water was hot, steaming, but they got across at the cost of some minor burns and
sank onto the relatively cool earth on the far side.

## ##

Rohant leaned against the trunk of a tree, winced as his
weight shook a spatter of drops from the leaves overhead.
The rain was almost finished, but there was still a steady
drip here under the trees as their leaves released what they'd
captured.

The creature in his hair shifted position hastily to avoid
being drowned, burrowing deeper into his tangled mane.

"What. . . ." He reached up, touched it. "What happened? Who. . . ."

"I was about to tell you . . . be careful. . . ."

Rohant sneezed again, held his hand still so the creature
could crawl onto it. He grinned as he set it on his knee.
"Miji," he said. "He's a sakali. Friend of mine. You were
about to tell me?"

"Right. About to introduce my rescuer and sometime
partner. Ginny Seyirshi."

"What!"

Miji eeped with fright, went running down Rohant's leg.
He sat on the Dyslaeror's ankle, tiny hands pressed to his
ribs, black eyes shifting from Rohant to Shadith and back
again.

"Long story how that came about, tell you later. Looks
like he decided to dissolve the relationship."

Rohant ch'ch'ed at the sakali; without looking at her, he
stopped his coaxing a moment, said, "So why are we
alive?"

"He gave his word, said he wouldn't kill me for at least
a year. It was Omphalos he was after."

"You trusted him?"

"Didn't have much choice right then." She ran her hands
through her hair, shivered as a vagrant draft hit her soaked
undersuit. "Besides, he keeps his word. You just have to
be careful you know what he means by it. Like, he'd be

clam-happy if Miralys ashed us both, but he wouldn't do it himself. Um, not too long from now, this place isn't going to be very healthy.''

Deflected by the defense shield, a missile hit the ground, blew a hole in it, and sent fragments of stone scything through the trees a short distance downstream.

Rohant coaxed Miji onto his arm, drew his thumbclaw down his mustache, raised a brow at her. "Don't know why you say that. Consider our gently salubrious surroundings.''

"Hah!'' Shadith pulled herself onto her feet. "Discounting little things like . . .'' she waved a hand at the shattered trees and steaming water, "this is going to be ground zero of a humongous meltdown.''

Rohant stood, scowled at her. "Meltdown?''

"Yeah.'' Shadith shivered as another explosion shook earth and air. "Ginny's sent his special EYEs at the kephalos. They're going to trigger Mimishay's self-destruct. Good-bye island, good-bye all of us, them included.'' She jerked her thumb upward, waved her hand in a circle to include the attacking landers.

"How much time?''

"God knows, not me.''

Rohant scratched absently behind the neckfrill of the sakali. "Shadow, could you reach Miralys?''

"Not Miralys. Kikun maybe and that's only if his gods have him looking.''

"Well, try it.''

"Not here. Hunh.'' She began walking upstream.

Cuddling the sakali, Rohant shook himself all over, spat, and started after her. "This doesn't work, we can always climb on a rock and dance. Hope they see us and don't shoot us.''

## AUTUMN ROSE/KIKUN

Autumn Rose booted the skimmer away from the *Cillasheg*, started descending in a wide spiral, keeping her distance from the attack zone. Without taking her eyes from the board, she said, "Just where is it you want me to put down?''

Kikun scratched at the skin folds under his chin. "North side, close as you can get.''

"Big place. Mountainside north or seaside?''

He frowned. "Tlee! I don't know.''

"Then we better go loo . . . Z'toyff!"

An immense elongated form went rushing past the skimmer, sending it into a wild tumble, falling end over end toward the ground.

Autumn Rose's crashweb snapped tight and the emergency pad popped up under her hand. With the argrav spurting out streamers of blue smoke while the skimmer flipped over and over and Kikun lying unconscious in the co-chair, twisted under his crash web, half strangled by it, Rose rode the wild oscillations, praying for time, widening and flattening the curves, holding the skimmer longer and longer in the flat mode until she had control over the drives again and took a look round to see where she was. . . .

And found herself in a descending slide across the top of the Compound with cutter beams dancing around her and the swarm of Dyslaera Landers swinging in and out of view and she was heading straight for a broad beam that was also sweeping toward her, seconds away. . . .

*A black Bear fifty meters high reached out a smoky paw and the beam was deflected, turned downward, the blade-end slicing through the already tortured earth.*

*AND*

*A black Raven flew before her, feathers glinting like shards of jet.*

She followed it out of the turmoil. Nothing touched her, cutter nor missile, rot grains nor melt fields. Nothing touched her.

She got the skimmer to ground on a grassy meadow some distance up one of the smaller mountains west of the Compound.

For several moments after the web loosened, then slid into its receptacle, Rose lay in the chair shaking all over, teeth chattering as she cursed Kikun, Digby, Seyirshi, the Dyslaera, and everything and everyone in her life that had brought her to this point. She'd never been this close to death, even when she was sitting in that condemned cell waiting for the Strangler's cord. Never this close, never this helpless, never. . . .

When she calmed enough to reason, she remembered the Bear and the Raven. Kikun's gods? She laughed, stopped laughing when the sound went crazy on her. "Never imag-

ined I'd be the subject for miracles," she said aloud.
"Kikun, you all right?"

No answer.

Shakily she pushed herself upright, groaning as every
muscle protested; she was bruised all over, battered,
scraped, bonesore. She twisted around and frowned toward
the co-seat.

Kikun lay limp in the seat, one arm tangled in the semi-
retracted web, a trickle of blood drying at the corner of his
mouth. Blood bubbles formed and burst in his nostrils as
he labored to breathe.

"Goerta b'rite!"

A tiny ancient crone of a dinhast came dashing at her like
a puppet on strings, a glass puppet brightly colored but so
translucent it was hard to see, yammering soundless words
from a mouth snapping open and closed like a puppet's jaws.
Soundless words—yet Rose knew the ancient was crying at
her to get on her feet and do something for Kikun. Something, anything. Get on her feet. Get moving. Help him. Comic
and terrible, the crone swept at her, through her. Her skin
prickled all over as if from a thousand tiny pinches.

Rose struggled from her chair, stood with her hand on
the arm, gathering herself so she wouldn't fall on her face.
The knee she'd injured at Koulsnakko's was sore again, she'd
bumped it or something. She was still shaking, nauseated
by her brush with dissolution and her brush with the inex-
plicable. . . .

A dark, musky smell spread through the cabin from a
great, deerlike creature looming over Kikun, shaking his
antlers, roaring soundlessly, his dark eyes ringed with white.
His head was clearly visible though translucent like the
crone, colored glass lit from within, but the rest of him was
vague, shapeless.

Rose stood clutching at the chair arm, swallowing, hair
standing stiff along her spine. What she saw was ancient
beyond counting, immensely powerful and essentially un-
controllable, a demiurge in beast form. Terrifying. . . .

She forced herself to cross the short distance between the
chairs; it was hard, walking into the ambience of that beast.

The Bear was there, too; she couldn't see him, but he was
present in the darkness that boiled in the corners of her
eyes. . . .

As she bent over Kikun's trapped arm and began working

the web free, she couldn't see THEM anymore, but she
knew THEY were still there, she could feel them, feel the
pressure of their demands, their fears.

There was no sound in the cabin and the musky aroma
had vanished with the deer form. With that gone, she could
smell the acrid stench of burning insulation and the more
elusive odor of hot metal.

The web came loose finally, slid home. She examined
Kikun's arm, wrinkling her nose as she felt bones grating
under her fingers.

The crone came back, tiny hands, long for their size,
curling round Rose's wrists, pulling at them. Rose yielded
to the pull that wasn't there and let Grandmother Ghost
guide her as she straightened Kikun and eased him as much
as she could without injuring him more than he was already.

Freed by his coma, Kikun's gods swirled round her, at
times merging into an amorphous shimmer, at times hard-
ening briefly into Raven, Otter, Bear, Antelope-deer.
Grandmother Ghost stayed beside her, seen sometimes,
sometimes unseen, as Rose plundered the emergency med-
kit, gave Kikun painkillers, splinted his arm, stabilized his
chest so the broken ribs wouldn't do more damage to his
lungs.

Time passed.

She finished all she could do down here, locked the crashweb properly in place over him so it would support him,
keep him motionless. Everything was set for liftoff. . . .

The pressure faded; Kikun's gods folded back down into
him.

Autumn Rose straightened her aching back, wiped at the
sweat, pushed the hair off her face and spent a moment
staring blankly at her hands, not at all sure what had just
happened.

"All right," she said aloud. "So. You want me to get
him back to the ship and the ottodoc? Well, then, show me
where they are, Rohant and the Singer. I can't leave till I
have them." She felt like a fool talking to herself or worse,
to figments of hysteric imagination.

The screen turned itself on. In the darkness outside, glinting in the uncertain glow from the beams that still walked
round the Compound, a large black bird flew in tight circles, squawking.

"Well." Rose limped back to the pilot's chair, lifted off

a few meters, then followed Raven through the clearing storm until he began flying in circles again, this time over a line of thickly set trees growing along the creek that ran past the Compound.

Grandmother Ghost pinched her.

Gaagi faded.

Feeling a fool again, Autumn Rose settled the skimmer onto a patch of grass and gravel, activated the external speakers:

**SHADOW. ROHANT. IF YOU'RE OUT THERE, SHIFT ASS OVER HERE. THIS IS AUTUMN ROSE. KIKUN'S WITH ME. MIRALYS SENT US TO COLLECT YOU.**

After a tense eternity when all she could see were trees and all she could hear was silence, two small figures broke from the shadows and ran for the skimmer.

## AUTUMN ROSE/ROHANT/SHADITH

"Get me through to Miralys. Fast. Then get the hell out of here."

Autumn Rose raised her brows. "Well, hello, the two of you."

Rohant growled.

Subdued, weary, Shadith ignored both of them and went to inspect Kikun in his support cocoon of foam and bandage.

"All right, all right, keep your hair on." Autumn Rose got through to the *Cillasheg*. "Anyagyn, Rose here. Give me Miralys. Quick, huh? Got something to show her."

Miralys bloomed in the mid-cell of the screen; when she saw Rohant, her ears snapped up, her eyes shone, she sang without being aware of it a wordless croon of joy and yearning.

Rohant leaned toward the image, his ache matching hers; he reached toward her—then he shook himself all over, wrenched himself back to more pressing needs. "Toerfeles, get ours out of there. That thing's going to blow any minute and it'll take them with it."

Light shimmers fled about the cabin, power thrummed through it, a deep subsonic CH'M that poured into Shadith.

"Go, go, go," she cried, her singer's voice driven by the immediacy of the threat, filling the space. "Go."

Autumn Rose felt the gods come back, Grandmother Ghost was pinching her and pinching her and the antelope/deer was belling terror in her ear. She booted the skimmer up and went racing along the mountainside, rising at a steep angle, going for distance rather than altitude; she crossed the mountains, dropped again, putting those tonnes of stone and earth between her and the Compound, then she fled out out over the sea. . . .

## MIRALYS/CILLASHEG

"Get out now, get out, get out, going to blow, get out," Anyagyn sang into the speaker, her voice rising and falling in Dyslaer Warn.

Miralys watched the skimmer dart away, her Ciocan inside; as it vanished below the mountaintops, she brushed the back of her hand across her mouth, turned her attention to the Compound.

It rested on the ground like a gray clenched fist.

The fist cracked—leaked a blinding blue-white light—opened wide—spilled light like molten milkglass—filled the bay and flats—rolled up the mountainsides—boiled up and up into the clouds. . . .

Specks of light lost in the great glow, the landers fled from the expanding explosion.

## ##

"How many?"

Anyagyn smiled wearily. "Hannys got her tail singed, that's all. Everyone's tucked in and hitting the freshers." She scratched at the fur between her ears. "Autumn Rose is on her way back, passengers intact, except Kikun who needs the ottodoc rather badly, she says. Once she's docked, any reason we should hang around here?"

"No. Let's go home. We've a business to whip into shape."

# EPILOG

1

Digby wore a white linen suit imported out of the mists of memory and sat in an elaborate wicker chair with a soft white hat on his knee and the shimmer-glimmer of his bubble around him.

Rohant and Miralys came in; she was quieter than usual and dressed in mourning white, a long robe, cream colored velvet that complimented the fading bronze of her fur and moved elegantly with the vigorous shifts of her lean body. She looked around. Her ears twitched. "This is . . . different."

He'd changed the decor of his meeting room to a deliberately exotic simplicity, recreating a room in a house where a family had lived for generations, perhaps a farm house, comfortable, but far from rich. The furniture had the feel of age and hard use, the fabrics were faded and frayed, the colors muted. There was a fireplace with logs burning in it and oil lamps spread their flickering amber glow in patches that left the corners dim where paintings and shelves of trinkets sprang into jewel clarity one moment and sank into shadows the next.

Digby smiled. "Nostalgia lives," he said. "Hello, Rohant. It's been a long time."

"Digby." Rohant bowed his head, then settled himself in a chair close to the fire and sat gazing into the flames. His robe was crisp and starched, snow white, cold white. He was withdrawn, physically present, mentally absent. The Dyslaer way of grieving was to sink into the minutia of mundane life as Miralys had, to grow excessively busy, exhausting themselves with work and planning. The Dyslaeror way was to create stillness within and without, to withdraw from the world and contemplate meanings—the meaning of particular deaths and generic DEATH, of particular lives and generic LIFE. Voallts Korlach had an estate in the Sar-

357

inim, a patch of gentle wilderness they kept to soothe their spirits when urban life became unbearably abrasive; Rohant was leaving tomorrow to spend his Mourning Year in a shrine Miralys had built there. His mind was already in retreat.

Miralys wandered restlessly about the room Digby had created for her, lifting objects, setting them down again. Over her shoulder, she said, "Who all's coming?"

"Shadith, Kikun, Autumn Rose. They'll be here any minute now."

"Ah."

## ##

Shadith came in, moving with a crackling energy and impatience, even her hair seemed about to explode from her head. She wore traveling gear and her harpcase was slung across her back. She dumped it on the floor beside a chair, flung herself down. "Well?"

Kikun unfaded, kicked a hassock over and sat beside her; he shared her impatience, sat with his orange eyes fixed on Digby as if by will alone he could bring this final conference to its end and be off about the matter that was troubling him now, the freeing of his homeland from its invaders.

Autumn Rose walked in a moment later, glanced quickly around and dropped into a chair beside the door, sat gazing at her hands. They had a newly pampered look, manicured, the skin creamed to a moist delicacy; her tunic was avri-shum, a glowing dark blue-green with fine white piping, her trousers wide and flowing, more like a long skirt; she wore silver and takka-azul earrings, matching silver and takka-azul bracelets. Like Shadith, she was ready to go; she'd booked passage on a Gancha Worldship leaving the Transfer Station later today. *Back on the Gamer Circuit. This is the last I'll see of her for a while. Until she gets bored and is ready for a reality connection.*

Digby contemplated his guests and thought they looked like the seeds on a ripe and ready pfeffri plant, primed to explode at a touch and scatter to the corners of the universe.

He crossed his legs, tented his hands. "This, my friends, is the denouement, where we tie off dangling ends and get on with our lives. Questions?"

Shadith scratched at her wrist. "Tinoopa. You said you'd take care of her."

"Right. Tinoopa has been picked up and is on her way to her son, one Jao juhFeyn on Arumda'm."

Rose leaned forward. "He's all right, nothing went wrong for him, the Chom you know and Mimishay?"

"Rumors and tall tales, that's all. He's as prosperous as before. No trouble, Rose."

She relaxed. "I liked him. Was a good Game we played there."

Shadith moved her shoulders. "Did Tinoopa give you any messages for me?"

"Yes. She says: Greetings to Kizra. That's you? Right. She says: They've settled into peace at Ghanar Rinta after the last funeral. A very sad thing to see a man in the full flower of his vigor wither and die in less than three months. She says: Utilas sent his second son as guardian to the child; he seems a mild, intelligent youth with the wisdom to let the Matja run things."

"Ah. Good."

"You promised me the tale if I brought her out, Singer. I don't have it yet."

Shadith unzipped a pocket, took out a flake case and tossed it onto the table beside her. "You do now."

"Thank you. Questions?"

Miralys glanced at Rohant, then stared down at her hands; she smoothed the back of a claw along the velvet of her robe. "Seyirshi got away. Have you heard anything about him?"

"Not a murmur. You?"

"Nothing yet."

"Singer, you spent some weeks with him, 'splitting. What do you think, is he going after Voallts again?"

"No."

"Just no?"

"He has a new project that's going to require all his attention for a while. He calls it the *Fall of Omphalos*. He told me about it because he likes the taste of those words."

"One man?"

"I know what it sounds like. Crazy. But don't you write him off. I suspect fifty, maybe a hundred years from now. Ginbiryol Seyirshi will be peddling a new Limited Edition and scholars will be prospecting the debris of Omphalos trying to discover what brought them down.''

''Hmm.'' Digby dropped his hands on the curved arms of his chair. ''Seems to me Omphalos and Ginny deserve each other.''

''Maybe so. Here's something else to think about. Ginny never forgets an injury.'' She turned to the two Dyslaera. ''Keep watch on Omphalos, Rohant, you and Miralys. When Omphalos falls, he'll be back for you.'' She straightened. ''For all of us.''

''Depressing thought. Let's end on a high note. Sing for us, Shadow.''

''What?''

''I've been jealous of every Bogmakker and traveler who's heard you perform, Singer. You have your harp and your friend. Sing a dream for us.''

Shadith worked her fingers, looked down at Kikun who'd sat silent through all of this. ''What do you think?''

''Drum,'' he said and smiled as Digby created a small handdrum and dropped it beside him. ''Break the knots,'' he said to Shadith, ''untie the ends and let us go.''

''All right.''


2


The brush/tunk of the drum lay down in the ground and beat in the blood, while the notes of the harp were as lush as brilliant as the patches of crimson and sapphire, emerald and amber the lamps' light picked out from the paintings, the deep green-blue glows in Rose's tunic, the warm cream of Miralys' robe, the brittle white that Rohant wore.

Shadow crooned wordless sounds, her voice rich and flowing. Cool. Caressing. Magical. Like spring rain falling from clouds so high the drops seemed to come from the sun. She had doubted herself. She doubted no more.

*They came from the shadows, slender and angular, black and silver similitudes of Naya, Zayalla, Annethi, Itsays, Tallitt and Sullan, spinning threads from themselves in a weave more complex than any she'd tried before, spinning dreams for Autumn Rose, for Miralys and Rohant, even for Digby, dreams she didn't know, couldn't know, didn't want*

*to know. What she wanted was her own dream. What she got was that AND Kikun's dream blended:*
*Her sisters danced with pattering feet and busy hands—a strange dance, a dance she didn't know. And Gaagi Raven came and danced among them, black scales glittering, black wings sweeping among them, closing about each one in an oddly protecting embrace (if it could be called an embrace when neither touched the other), wings closing and spreading, closing about Naya, then Zayalla, then Annethi, then Itsays, then Tallitt, and finally Sullan.*
*The Joy came then, the Purpose. She sang laughter as she saw Itsaya wink at her, saw Naya smile and clap her slender hands, saw Zayalla shake her snaky hips, Annethi dance with Sullan around and around Kikun, and touch his shoulders and bend to touch his hands and dance away in joy, dance in circles about Spash'ats and Jadii Gevas, Xumadi and Mask while the Lael-Lenox the Grandmother Ghost pranced in a tight little circle of her own. . . .*

## ##

Shadow crooned wordless sounds, her voice rich and flowing. Cool. Caressing. Magical. Like spring rain falling from clouds so high the drops seemed to come from the sun.

AUTUMN ROSE saw:

*HERSELF in gold and diamonds and pure black avrishum, under a crystal chandelier that gilded the delicate hairs on her ivory forearms. She played Vagnag and across from her, her only mark was her grandfather. The cards came and the dice leaped to her fingers. She stripped him to his skin, laughed at him and went walking out, a man beside her, a shadowy figure without a face who sheltered her and protected her and . . . loved her.*

## ##

MIRALYS saw: ROHANT \

AND

ROHANT saw: MIRALYS /

Lissorn with baby S'ragis sitting on his shoulder—dead baby, golden baby—shining in the hot yellow sun. Jes-

gejarn, young and shining
with the vigor of the young.
In a ring around them, clan
Voallts, the living and the
dead, arms on shoulders
dancing.
In the sun on the Savannah,
Miralys and Rohant danced
with their children, the dead
children and the living,
danced the Varavany about
the carcass of a grand bull
yrz.

## ##

DIGBY saw:

*Moonlight on an ocean he knew in his cells, the ocean into
which he was born so many years ago he'd long ago lost
count.*
*Moonlight on black sands and fans of land coral. The shim-
mering blue water lifted and shaped into nine girls dancing,
nine glass girls with moonlight shining through them, dancing on black sand shores that were glass and ash now, on a
world burnt to bedrock by the folly of his kind, no water
left, no girls dancing. It was pain to watch, but sweet pain
to see his sisters dancing.*

### 3

And then it was done.
Over.
Rohant took Miralys' hand and they left.
Eyes on elsewhere, Autumn Rose came quietly to her feet
and left.
Shadith shut the harp in the case. Kikun set the drum
aside and took her hand. They left.
Digby sat for a long time in his bubble in the empty room.
Then he, too, was gone.

DAW

DAW Presents the Fantastic Realms of

# JO CLAYTON

Epic Science Fiction Adventures
# C.S. Friedman

☐ **IN CONQUEST BORN**                    (UE2198—$3.95)

Braxi and Azea, two super-races fighting an endless campaign over a long forgotten cause. The Braxaná—created to become the ultimate warriors. The Azeans, raised to master the powers of the mind, using telepathy to penetrate where mere weapons cannot. Now the final phase of their war is approaching, when whole worlds will be set ablaze by the force of ancient hatred. Now Zatar and Anzha, the master generals, who have made this battle a personal vendetta, will use every power of body and mind to claim the vengeance of total conquest.

☐ **THE MADNESS SEASON**                 (UE2444—$4.95)

He'd had many names over the centuries. Now he was Daetrin, a name given to him by the alien conquerors of humankind, the Tyr. Three hundred years ago, the Tyr conquered Earth, isolating the true individualists, the geniuses, all the people who represented the hopes and discoveries of the future, imprisoning them in dome colonies on poisonous worlds. There the Tyr, a race which itself shared a unified gestalt mind, had left these gifted individuals to work on projects which might reveal all of humankind's secrets. Yet Daetrin's secret was one no one had ever uncovered, for through the years he had buried it so well that he had even hidden his real nature from himself. But, taken into custody by the Tyr, there was no longer any place for Daetrin to hide. Now he must confront the truth about himself—and if he failed, not just Daetrin but all humans would pay the price.

**NEW AMERICAN LIBRARY**
**P.O. Box 999, Bergenfield, New Jersey 07621**

Please send me the DAW BOOKS I have checked above. I am enclosing $_____
(please add $1.00 to this order to cover postage and handling). Send check or money order—no cash or C.O.D.'s. Prices and numbers are subject to change without notice. (Prices slightly higher in Canada.)

Name_____

Address_____

City _____ State _____ Zip _____
Allow 4-6 weeks for delivery.

**DAW**

# C.J. CHERRYH
## THE ALLIANCE-UNION UNIVERSE

**The Company Wars**
☐ DOWNBELOW STATION                     (UE2431—$4.50)

**The Era of Rapprochement**
☐ SERPENT'S REACH                       (UE2088—$3.50)
☐ FORTY THOUSAND IN GEHENNA             (UE2429—$4.50)
☐ MERCHANTER'S LUCK                     (UE2139—$3.50)

**The Chanur Novels**
☐ THE PRIDE OF CHANUR                   (UE2292—$3.95)
☐ CHANUR'S VENTURE                      (UE2293—$3.95)
☐ THE KIF STRIKE BACK                   (UE2184—$3.99)
☐ CHANUR'S HOMECOMING                   (UE2177—$4.50)

**The Mri Wars**
☐ THE FADED SUN: KESRITH                (UE2449—$4.50)
☐ THE FADED SUN: SHON'JIR               (UE2448—$4.50)
☐ THE FADED SUN: KUTATH                 (UE2133—$4.50)

**Merovingen Nights (Mri Wars Period)**
☐ ANGEL WITH THE SWORD                  (UE2143—$3.50)

**Merovingen Nights—Anthologies**
☐ FESTIVAL MOON (#1)                    (UE2192—$3.50)
☐ FEVER SEASON (#2)                     (UE2224—$3.50)
☐ TROUBLED WATERS (#3)                  (UE2271—$3.50)
☐ SMUGGLER'S GOLD (#4)                  (UE2299—$3.50)
☐ DIVINE RIGHT (#5)                     (UE2380—$3.95)
☐ FLOOD TIDE (#6)                       (UE2452—$4.50)

**The Age of Exploration**
☐ CUCKOO'S EGG                          (UE2371—$4.50)
☐ VOYAGER IN NIGHT                      (UE2107—$2.95)
☐ PORT ETERNITY                         (UE2206—$2.95)

**The Hanan Rebellion**
☐ BROTHERS OF EARTH                     (UE2290—$3.95)
☐ HUNTER OF WORLDS                      (UE2217—$2.95)

**DAW**

# Charles Ingrid

## THE MARKED MAN SERIES

☐ **THE MARKED MAN** (UE2396—$3.95)
In a devastated America, can the Lord Protector of a mutating human race find a way to preserve the future of the species?

☐ **THE LAST RECALL** (UE2460—$3.95)
Returning to a radically-changed Earth, would the generational ships aid the remnants of a mutated human race—or seek their future among the stars?

## THE SAND WARS

☐ **SOLAR KILL: Book 1** (UE2391—$3.95)
He was the last Dominion Knight and he would challenge a star empire to gain his revenge!

☐ **LASERTOWN BLUES: Book 2** (UE2393—$3.95)
He'd won a place in the Emperor's Guard but could he hunt down the traitor who'd betrayed his Knights to an alien foe?

☐ **CELESTIAL HIT LIST: Book 3** (UE2394—$3.95)
Death stalked the Dominion Knight from the Emperor's Palace to a world on the brink of its prophesied age of destruction. . . .

☐ **ALIEN SALUTE: Book 4** (UE2329—$3.95)
As the Dominion and the Thrakian empires mobilize for all-out war, can Jack Storm find the means to defeat the ancient enemies of man?

☐ **RETURN FIRE: Book 5** (UE2363—$3.95)
Was someone again betraying the human worlds to the enemy—and would Jack Storm become pawn or player in these games of death?

☐ **CHALLENGE MET: Book 6** (UE2436—$3.95)
In this concluding volume of *The Sand Wars,* Jack Storm embarks on a dangerous mission which will lead to a final confrontation with the Ash-farel.

---

**DAW**

Exciting Visions of the Future!

# W. Michael Gear

☐ **STARSTRIKE** (UE2427—$4.95)
The alien Ahimsa has taken control of all Earth's defenses, and forces
humanity to do its bidding. Soon Earth's most skilled strike force,
composed of Soviet, American and Israeli experts in the art of war and
espionage find themselves aboard an alien vessel, training together for
an offensive attack against a distant space station. And as they struggle
to overcome their own prejudices and hatreds, none of them realize
that the greatest danger to humanity's future is right in their midst. . . .

☐ **THE ARTIFACT** (UE2406—$4.95)
In a galaxy on the brink of civil war, where the Brotherhood seeks to
keep the peace, news comes of the discovery of a piece of alien technology—the Artifact. It could be the greatest boon to science, or the
instrument that would destroy the entire human race.

## THE SPIDER TRILOGY

For centuries, the Directorate had ruled over countless star systems—
but now the first stirrings of rebellion were being felt. At this crucial
time, the Directorate discovered a planet known only as World, where
descendants of humans stranded long ago had survived by becoming a
race of warriors, a race led by its Prophets, men with the ability to see
the many possible pathways of the future. And as rebellion, fueled by
advanced technology and a madman's dream, spread across the galaxy, the warriors of Spider could prove the vital key to survival of
human civilization. . . .

☐ **THE WARRIORS OF SPIDER** (UE2287—$3.95)
☐ **THE WAY OF SPIDER** (UE2318—$3.95)
☐ **THE WEB OF SPIDER** (UE2396—$4.95)

---

DAW
# Kathleen M. O'Neal

Powers of Light

☐ **AN ABYSS OF LIGHT: Book 1**          (UE2418—$4.95)

Only the Gamant people dared to resist subjugation by the Galactic Magistrates. For the Gamants knew they were the Chosen Ones, blessed with the gift of an interdimensional gateway to God. But were the Beings of Light with whom the Gamants communed actually God and the angels? Or were they an advanced race to whom the Gamants were mere pawns in some universe-spanning game? Either way, the Gamant faith would soon receive its ultimate test as the Galactic Magistrates mobilized to put an end to their rebellion, even as many among them turned to a messiah who might betray them all. . . .

☐ **TREASURE OF LIGHT: Book 2**          (UE2455—4.95)

With the Gamant worlds under siege by the military starships of the alien Galactic Magistrates, Jeremiel Baruch, commander of the rebel human forces, has seized the Magisterial battle cruiser *Hoyer*, though not in time to prevent a deadly scorch attack on the planet of Horeb. Rescuing all who have escaped the attack, Baruch heads for the world of Tikkun to recruit others to his cause. But what neither Jeremiel nor the Magisterial enemy pursuing him knows is that far more powerful forces are about to take control of the future, beings capable of and prepared to destroy humans, aliens and the entire universe. . . .

---